BLACK AND WHITE

BOOK ONE OF THE FRONTIERS

Mark Wandrey

Seventh Seal Press
Virginia Beach, VA

Chris Kennedy/Seventh Seal Press
2052 Bierce Dr.
Virginia Beach, VA 23454
http://chriskennedypublishing.com/

Publisher's Note: This is a work of fiction. Names, characters, places, and incidents are a product of the author's imagination. Locales and public names are sometimes used for atmospheric purposes. Any resemblance to actual people, living or dead, or to businesses, companies, events, institutions, or locales is completely coincidental.

Ordering Information:
Quantity sales. Special discounts are available on quantity purchases by corporations, associations, and others. For details, contact the "Special Sales Department" at the address above.

Cover Design by Brenda Mihalko
Art by Ricky Ryan

Black and White/Mark Wandrey -- 1st ed.
ISBN 978-1950420230

Prologue

Pacific Cetacean Research Institute, Molokai, Hawaii, Earth
May 19th, 2035

Dr. Matthew Clark watched the ocean from his office balcony at the PCRI. There was a dense bank of clouds to the northeast, which looked like it might be over them by midday. Not uncommon in Molokai in the spring, yet still annoying.

He turned his head and looked at the computer through his out-of-date prescription glasses, scowling slightly. A budget spreadsheet was displayed, with a lot of red entries. Tourism was down, way down. Kaunakakai still got a lot of traffic from tourists trying to get off the beaten path, sure, but they weren't looking to see tanks full of stressed cetaceans in the process of being rehabilitated. Nobody was interested in whales and dolphins anymore, not with aliens coming to visit.

Hearing a high-pitched whining, he looked to the south. There was one of the multi-fanned air cars they called "flyers" coming in over the ocean, no doubt from Honolulu. The island's air traffic control was still leery of the craft and insisted on routing them over the ocean as much as possible. If what Matthew had heard was true, they needn't have worried. The alien-manufactured craft were safer than the kiddy rides in an amusement park.

"The Galactic Union," he said, shaking his head. He'd been a scientist all his adult life, dedicated to the pursuit of truth. The existence of many thousands of alien races in the galaxy was an undeniable scientific truth. He'd seen many images on TV, and had even met a couple the previous year during a scientific symposium in Washington DC held by the new world government. They'd been installing Earth's first GalNet node—the Union's version of the internet, but on steroids.

A decade ago, he'd been a relatively young researcher doing postgraduate work on deep ocean sea life in the Atlantic, when first contact was made. The aliens landed in New York City and began negotiations to bring humanity into the Galactic Union. It had seemed to be going pretty well, until some Iranian-sponsored terrorists blew up the UN.

Many of Matthew's friends considered that almost a public service. The UN was a constant pain in the marine research community's ass, after all. The problem was, the bomb also killed the alien ambassador, one of the owl-like race known as Buma. She'd perished along with several of her MinSha guards. The Buma were inclined to be forgiving; the MinSha were not. Those aliens looked like huge praying mantises and fought like demons. Iran, and many of the surrounding countries, no longer existed.

"Dr. Clark?" he heard from his intercom.

"Yes, Sheila?"

"There's a tour group due in an hour."

"Get Benjamin to take them through," Matthew said. The young grad student was both competent and passionate about cetaceans. He always managed to get some good donations.

"They've requested the director personally," Sheila said.

"Who is it?"

"Someone named Kodu'ku," she said.

"Are they kama'āina?" he asked, referring to native islanders.

"No, Doctor, they're aliens."

"Oh," he said, and quickly headed downstairs.

The institute had started life as a posh resort, but had suffered from crib death. Financing had fallen through before it was completed due to the economic downturn in 2008. In 2033, it was purchased by NOAA, the National Oceanic and Atmospheric Administration, not long after they were ported over from the USA to the world government and their responsibilities expanded to ocean life conservation. With some fresh funding, they set about rehabilitating cetaceans abandoned by ill-fated parks around the world.

Their problem had always been getting enough funding. The world government kept their doors open and paid their salaries, but had never given them quite enough money to make a difference. When Dr. Clark had come on board in 2034, just over a year ago, he'd formed a conservatory endowment—with help from some rich family friends. It allowed them to improve their outreach and bring in some tourists. People had liked whales and dolphins, at least until the aliens had become more popular.

Matthews waited impatiently for the elevator to arrive on the top floor, where the administration offices were located. While he was waiting, his son Terrence came running up.

"Did you hear?" he said, his eyes wide with the kind of excitement only a ten-year-old could manage.

"Yes, Terrence, I heard."

"Terry, Dad," he said, rolling his eyes. "Call me Terry."

Terry is the name you give a street sweeper, Matthew thought. He'd never preferred Matt; he refused to understand why his son now insisted on being called Terry. "Where's your mother?"

"She's down at the docks waiting for the fishing ship," he explained. "She heard a trawler had a large load of Hapu'upu'u they were trying to get rid of."

Matthew grunted in understanding. Hapu'upu'u, also known as Hawaiian sea bass, wasn't a particularly popular fish. More often found in sushi, it had fallen out of favor. If the boat was unable to sell it, the fish was probably getting ripe. The institute was a well-known market of last resort to many of the fishing boats. Nine orcas and nineteen Pacific bottlenose dolphins ate a lot of fish every day. If the boat captain could make fuel money, and the institute could get some still edible fish, a meeting of the minds was possible.

The elevator arrived, and Terrence—Terry—practically bowled his father out of the way. Shaking his head, Matthew followed his son in and pressed the button for the visitors' level. Terry danced from foot to foot as the elevator descended, even reaching out to push the visitors' level button again, as if it would speed their descent.

"Patience," Matthew said. "You don't want to make a poor impression on our visitors, do you?"

"No, Dad," Terry said. With a visible effort, he composed himself.

Very good, Matthew thought, but felt a barely-suppressed thrill run up his own spine. *Aliens, here, at my institute!* He realized their arrival likely explained the flyer, as well. Few but the superrich could afford those yet.

The elevator dinged, and the doors slid open. Terry possessed just enough presence of mind to allow his father to exit first. Matthew walked out into the rotunda to find a huge tour group composed of mostly typical tourists, dressed in shorts, brightly colored shirts, and a plethora of floppy hats and sunglasses. There were around 30 of them, and they'd created a crescent around two more members of their group. One looked for all the world like a two-meter-tall bear standing on its back legs, except that bears on Earth weren't bright purple. The other alien was a meter-tall bipedal gecko!

Benjamin Anderson, the assistant he'd asked to take the tour, was talking to the gecko and turned when Matthew stepped into view. He moved forward, and the lizard followed. "Dr. Matthew Clark, may I introduce you to Kodu'ku," Benjamin said and gestured to the lizard with a bow. "He's a member of the race known as elSha."

Matthew nodded, came a little closer, and gave a slight bow, a greeting he knew many aliens used. Shaking hands wasn't something most of them understood. "An honor to meet you," he said.

Kodu'ku made some hissing and clicking noises, then a clearly understood English voice said, "The honor is all mine." The voice emanated from a silver medallion hanging around Kodu'ku's neck.

A translator, Matthew realized. The incredibly powerful little computer translators were starting to turn up in places on Earth. The government had quite a few, as did some large corporations. Now programmed with most languages on Earth, they were breaking down national boundaries in a way even being bombed by aliens hadn't managed.

"I understand you research marine mammals here?" Kodu'ku asked.

"We call them cetaceans," Matthew offered. "Cetaceans are a clade, a monophyletic group of marine mammals." He added a bit of a questioning tone in his voice, uncertain if the alien would understand, then berated himself for doing it that way, realizing it was unlikely the computer would render such an inflection to his voice.

"I understand," Kodu'ku replied.

"Oh, are you a scientist?"

"Life sciences," the alien replied. "My consortium reworks starships from existing designs to suit various other species. I'm here to meet with some of your primitive space contractors and discuss a possible expanding market." He shrugged, a disconcerting gesture for a meter-tall lizard. "I think bothering with a merc race is a waste of time, but my boss doesn't agree."

"We don't all make our money killing things," Matthew replied, a little put off by the alien's back-handed swipe at his world. Though Human mercenaries were increasingly leaving to go fight off planet, he didn't approve. The so-called mercs made inconceivable amounts of money, but it was all wasted on more guns. He got angry just thinking about what he could do with a fraction of that money. Galactic Union credits were worth thousands of dollars apiece on Earth.

"You are a strange race, this is true," Kodu'ku agreed, "however you are also apparently pretty good at killing, despite your complaints. What do you call your leading merc companies? Four Ponies?"

"The Four Horsemen," Terry offered from just to Matthew's side. He'd forgotten his son was there.

"A hatchling Human?" Kodu'ku asked.

"My son," Matthew said, placing a hand on the boy's shoulder and moving him forward. "This is Terrence Clark." Terry shot his father a disapproving look for not using his *proper* name, then looked back at the elSha. He was clearly piqued by the fact Kodu'ku was maybe a couple centimeters taller than him.

"How old are you, Terrence Clark?" Kodu'ku asked.

"I'm ten," Terry answered.

"Do you also study these cetaceans?"

"I help Dad out," he said and looked up at his father. "I'm too young to get a job, though."

Matthew and Benjamin both laughed. It was well known Terry thought he should get paid for the work he did. The boy didn't entirely appreciate the tradition of working for the family business on a pro bono basis.

"He'll help on the tour." Matthew looked at the crowd of tourists, who were all curiously looking at the aliens instead of the massive 50,000-liter tank behind the 10-centimeter Lexan wall to their left. A pair of dolphins raced by, unnoticed. The big purple bear followed the animals with its tiny black eyes. "May I inquire as to your friend?" He indicated the ursine.

"Friend?" Kodu'ku turned and almost seemed startled to notice the other alien. "Oh, him? He's just an Oogar merc, a company-hired bodyguard." The Oogar regarded Matthew with cold detachment.

As Matthew suspected, the tourists were an impromptu retinue Kodu'ku and his bodyguard had picked up when their flier landed nearby. More curious about the pair of aliens than a marine biology institute, they'd simply followed the off-worlders inside and continued to tag along.

Matthew began his tour with an informative film on the different types of marine mammals and what made cetaceans unique. It eventually moved on to why they were in danger and various types of conservancy. A bit on the end of the movie thanked the guests for their interest and encouraged them to support the institute's non-profit endeavors.

The next step was the part most tourists were the least interested in—the inner workings of the institute's six huge seawater aquariums and two habitats. However, this was the part which interested Kodu'ku the most. He wanted to know all manner of details concerning heat exchangers, pump capacities, filter workings, and even what kinds of alloys went into the pipes. Matthew ended up calling his chief engineer in from his lunch to answer the questions.

Kodu'ku took little notice of his bodyguard's difficulties in maneuvering around the various tighter areas. The elSha's diminutive size made the passageways no more difficult than if Matthew were walking down a city street. The Oogar nearly got stuck twice; the second time required three technicians to undog a door from its top to free the alien.

If anything, Kodu'ku found it amusing. "They're brutish, but reliable in a fight," he told Matthew quietly at one point. "To be perfectly honest, I didn't expect much more from you Humans until I got here." He examined a huge seawater pump humming with power. "Your engineering, while lacking finesse, has potential."

"Thanks," Matthew said out of the corner of his mouth.

"Think nothing of it."

As the tour moved on to the reason for the institute, the cetaceans, Kodu'ku seemed less interested to the point of indifference. Matthew would have assumed he only stayed out of a sense of common courtesy, except the alien didn't seem to possess the trait. He didn't ask any more questions, merely watching the dolphins leaping meters out of the water to intercept thrown fish with one of his two independently-controlled eyes. The Oogar was slightly more curious— though only slightly.

When they reached the first of the three large orca tanks, Kodu'ku perked up slightly as he caught sight of one of the four new Russian Resident orcas. Kray, the dominant male, breached to get a better look at the visitors. The orca's head hovered a short distance out of the water, his eye examining the Oogar for a long moment before submerging.

"Why are they here?" Kodu'ku asked.

"All our cetaceans are rescues of one kind or another. These four are from Russia and were once on display at a park." The elSha cocked his head. "A place where they're kept for amusement. Sometimes for education, as well."

"Terry!"

Matthew looked over and saw his wife Madison coming in, with two men and a tub of fish in tow. He smiled. She'd made a deal. His son left them and went over to his mother, helping her with the fish.

"You Humans enjoy seeing and experiencing other species?"

"Yes," Matthew said.

The elSha shook his long head, both eyes going over different parts of the Human tourist group at the same time. "I think scientists will be trying to understand Humans for a long, long time."

Matthew looked over to where his son was feeding Kray. Terry had a feeding pole, three meters long and telescoping, with cotton twine holding a large Hapu'upu'u out over the tank. The familiar shape and grayish color of the Hawaiian sea bass dangled just above the surface. Kray's great shiny black head broke the surface, an eye examined the fish for a second, and he submerged again.

"Dad, Kray won't take the bass."

The orca tossed its head and Matthew felt the distinctive ultra-low frequency feeling of the orca pulsing his sonar. "I saw," Matthew said. "We'll have to do some blood tests and see if there's a problem."

"There is nothing wrong with the creature," Kodu'ku said.

Matthew turned back to look at the alien, who was observing the orca. The two seemed to be staring at each other. "My apologies, but how do you know our orca is well?"

"Because he told me." Matthew shook his head, not understanding. Kodu'ku focused both eyes on Matthew for a long moment, then placed a hand on his head. "Oh, right, you don't have ready access to these." He placed another hand on the pendant hanging around his neck. "One moment."

The elSha reached into a pouch around his waist and removed another pendant and one of the small computers they called slates. Kodu'ku touched the slate a couple of times, closed his eyes, and the slate flashed. He placed the pendant on top of the slate and both flashed red, and then he handed the pendant to Matthew.

"What do I do with this?" Matthew asked.

"Place it near your mouth," was the reply.

Matthew did as he was told, and Kodu'ku pointed at the orca, which wasn't looking at him. "Now what?" he asked.

The orca pulsed his sonar directly at Matthew, and he shook his head from the power of it. Then the pendant spoke in strangely-accented but understandable English, "*I no like funny fish.*"

Matthew's eyes were open wide in shock as he looked from Kray to Kodu'ku, and back to Kray. "Was that you speaking?" he asked. The pendant he was holding thrummed against his skin, the frequency similar to the one the orca used. In adjacent tanks, several other orca heads popped out of the water. Kray rolled slightly in the water. The move was eerily similar to the way a dog cocked its head.

"Yes, I speak. I like hear you speak me!"

Matthew almost dropped the translator in surprise as he turned to look at Kodu'ku, then he laughed out loud. "Holy shit!" he said, and Kray laughed as well, bobbing his head up and down in an unmistakable nod of his huge head. Terry watched his father, the young man's mouth hanging wide open and the fish dangling, forgotten.

Matthew knew the world had just changed for him in ways he might never fully understand. He was also more excited than he could ever remember being in his entire life. "I think I'm going to go buy Kray a tuna," he said. Kray nodded with even more vigor.

* * * * *

Part I

The Tower of Babel

Chapter One

Kaunakakai Elementary School, Molokai, Hawaii, Earth
August 10th, 2035

Terry leaned as far forward as he could without falling over and watched the pitcher. The boy glanced at the runner on first base, then back forward. Terry grinned; the pitcher had forgotten he was there. He led off several steps as the pitcher wound up. Terry glanced at the shortstop, who glanced at him. The shortstop's eyes widened, and he opened his mouth to yell. Too late.

The pitcher released the ball at the same instant Terry broke into a sprint. The shortstop barked a warning as the ball went *tink* against the batter's bat and bounced against the ground, hopping up just enough that the pitcher's frantic jump for it fell a good half-meter short.

Terry passed the shortstop, tossing a wink to the kid, who snarled a furious curse in Polynesian. He cut around 3rd, his foot just touching the base, and straightened out for home.

"Go, go, go!" the 3rd base coach yelled as he passed, and Terry *ran.*

Out of the corner of his eye, he saw the shortstop take a shot at catching the 1st base runner. The kid there had to jump a little to catch the ball, and the runner tagged before the 1st baseman came back down. Safe! He made up for missing the tag by making an in-

17

credible sideways throw. Terry took two long running steps and dove for home. The catcher reached for the ball, nabbed it, and swept his big mitt toward Terry, who slid just under it.

"Safe!" the umpire called, and the parents of his team cheered.

"Terry Clark scores!" the announcer yelled, and his team came out of the dugout to high-fives.

The game over, Terry and his team were sitting in the dugout, a humidifying fan blowing on the kids as they drank ice-cold sodas. It was the 3rd year Terry had played on the Mokoka'I summer league, and they were getting good. There were coeds in the advanced group that played all over the islands. Most of his friends played with him, and despite the mid-summer heat, it was the second-best time of the year for him.

"You suckered the pitcher big time," Yui said.

"I saw he didn't check 2nd very often, even when a runner was on," Terry said, and Yui winked at him. Yui Tanaka played 2nd base, while Terry was a shortstop. As their positions were next to each other, they'd learned to depend on each other. Last year, the two had discovered their other passion—besides baseball, of course.

"Okay, team," the coach said to get their attention. "We're undefeated, so that means we get to go to the All-Island Tournament on O'ahu next week." The kids all cheered and pumped their fists in the air. "Practice Wednesday. Make sure your uniforms are clean, and I'll call your parents to give arrangements for the shuttle to Honolulu."

Terry raced Yui out to their bikes. They tossed the empty soda cans into a recycling bin and unlocked their bikes. "You hear from Doc?" Yui asked as she took her phone and started her bike.

"Yeah," Terry said, starting his own bike. "He says to meet him at Kiowea, Pond Place."

"Oh, cool!" she said.

Terry verified his bike had enough charge. From Kaunakakai Elementary School to Kiowea Park was just over 2 miles. He'd had his bike plugged into the baseball field's common solar bank, but the weather was a hazy overcast, and thirty other kids were charging their bikes, too. His phone said the bike was good for 3 ½ miles. He made a face as he jumped on and followed her. Yui was already heading down the driveway toward Ailoa Street.

He had a 20-watt panel in his backpack, sure. While they were out with Doc, it would give him a little juice. Probably not enough to get back to the institute, which would mean pedaling up the hill. He could ask Yui to pedal part of the way with him. He shook his head. For some reason he didn't want to admit, he'd screwed up and hadn't put his bike on the charger last night. He gritted his teeth and used the electric motor to catch up to her.

The early afternoon traffic along Route 450, Mauna Loa Highway, was busy. August was tourist season, and things had picked up since the aliens moved in. A dozen of them were always coming and going from the institute, and groupies were also always coming and going. Aliens were cool and all, but who wanted to follow a big stinky purple bear around, or one of those monkey-looking Maki? Yesterday, something that looked like an anteater had been talking to his mother. Gross!

Buzzing along at 15 kph, they were soon passing Paddlers, then Molokai Burger. He was hungry after the game and hoped Yui would pull in for a snack. No such luck; she sped on by. One of the Kaunakakai police officers was standing on the opposite corner talking to an elSha about something. He waved at Terry, who waved back. The elSha focused one eye on Terry for a second before pivoting it back to the cop.

Mauna Loa slowly descended to just a few meters above sea level. Terry enjoyed the cool ocean breeze as he nursed his low battery while keeping up with Yui. At one point she looked back at him lagging and waved for him to keep up. He smiled and waved back, glancing down at the phone locked onto the handlebar. Only 10% battery remaining. *Crap.*

The last of the town fell behind them, and the ocean was just to the left as they rode. Finally a small coconut grove appeared between them and the ocean, and he heaved a sigh of relief. They turned on Kapuaiwa Road as his battery indicator started flashing at 5%. He switched to pedals for the last hundred yards.

The road turned to the right, becoming Pond Place. However, if you went a little further without turning, there was a dirt turnaround which put you on the beach. There, just off shore, floated an old red and white trawler that had seen better days. A man so suntanned most people would guess he was African-American was sitting on the fantail, messing with gear.

"Yo, Doc!" Terry yelled. The man looked up, shading his eyes from the glare, and waved.

"You want I should bring the skiff over?"

Terry looked at Yui, who stuck her tongue out and shook her head. "Naw, we'll be right there!"

They locked their bikes and sealed their backpacks, making sure the tape locked in place. The contents would stay dry for hours, maybe days, even underwater a few meters.

"Last one there's a sea turtle turd!" Yui said and sprinted for the water.

"Damn it!" Terry yelled, jamming his finger onto the *LOCK* icon for his bike. He stuffed the phone into his front pocket, zipping it as he ran, and somehow got his backpack in place, too. Despite her head start, he was a better sprinter, and by the time her feet hit the water, he was only two steps behind her. Almost in tandem, they lept into a wave just as it reached them.

In the water they were equals. Try as he might, though Terry was unable to catch her before she made it to the boat's transom one stroke before he did.

"You're a sea turtle turd!" Yui crowed as she flipped up onto diving deck.

"Shut up," Terry mumbled.

"Sorry, what? Did you say I won?"

"You kids knock it off," Doc said.

Terry looked up at Doc, who was now on the flying bridge. He didn't know how old the man who called himself Doc was. Maybe sixty? Who knew? Terry knew he'd lived in Hawaii all his life, growing up in the warm Pacific waters. He thought maybe Doc was a doctor of some kind. He'd met the man and his ship on a fishing charter their family had taken the year they'd arrived on Molokai. He was average height for most adults, with a thick body and heavily-muscled arms. Despite his age, his abdomen showed a fully-defined six-pack that made Terry hope he looked that badass when he grew up. The shaved, bald head was cool, too, but his mom wouldn't let him shave his own head.

Charters were his main source of income. Mainly fishing, but also diving. It had been Terry's introduction to diving, and probably the most exciting moment in his life. After they'd moved to Hawaii, the excitement of surf and sun quickly wore off, and it became just another place to live.

Then he dove underwater with a scuba tank, and everything changed for him. It was like being on another world, another universe. He could glide like a bird in a reality full of infinite variety. Each moment revealed another new thing—a new fish, a new coral formation—anything was possible. Since the first time, he'd spent every moment he could steal underwater. He'd even introduced Yui to it as well. Through it all, Doc had been his guide and teacher.

"Good baseball game?" Doc asked, messing with the boat's controls.

"Yeah," Terry said, "we won."

Doc nodded and hit the starter. The boat looked old and worn, yet it started with the roar of a well-maintained machine. "Let's dive."

* * * * *

Chapter Two

PCRI, Molokai, Hawaii, Earth
August 10th, 2035

"Did you hear me?"

Matthew looked up from the display and noticed his wife standing by the door to his office. He bit his lip and tried to remember; she'd been saying something? "Terry?"

"Yes, Matthew, our son?"

"I know he's our son," Matthew said, making a face.

Madison crossed her arms under her breasts and glared. Matthew's expression went away. "That's the first step, now you can tell me where he is? His game was over two hours ago."

Matthew looked back toward his office window to see the sun falling toward the horizon. He looked back at the display—an alien-manufactured, true 3D holographic display known as a Tri-V. It showed the anatomical makeup of a cetacean's brain—an orca, to be precise. The images were like the Tri-V, thousands of times better than anything that had existed on Earth prior to the aliens' arrival. The image called him with its siren call.

"Goddamn it, Matthew Davis Clark!"

Oh, shit, he thought, and his head spun around. "Uhm, I think he went scuba diving."

"And *I* thought we were going to talk about whether he should be diving with that man. Terry wants to shave his head to look like him."

"I think we're safe. I checked on Doc with Kaunakakai PD."

"What did they say?" She walked over to stand next to him, her own attention drawn to the anatomical model.

"He's fine," he said. "Vincent 'Doc' Abercrombie has lived on Molokai his whole life, except when he was in the military."

"Military?"

"Yeah, a Navy SEAL, apparently. He was injured on a dive and medically retired. The boat belonged to his brother, who was killed in a traffic accident while Doc was in the service."

"Oh, wow," she said, looking back at him.

He nodded. "Terrence is quite safe."

"He wants to be called Terry, you know."

"I know," he said, then shook his head. "I don't understand why, though."

"Because he's an independent being, *Matt*."

Matthew's head came around in annoyance. She was grinning ear to ear. "Okay, fair enough." He touched a control and the Tri-V changed to show a device hovering next to the brain. "He said he'd be back before dark."

"What about dinner?"

"I admit, I didn't think about that," he said.

"Well, I did. I saved him some." She put a covered plate on the desk. "Saved you some, too."

"You're awesome," he said. The cover popped off the plate and the delightful smell of roasted fish and vegetables filled his nose. "Oh, yummy." He grabbed the fork and took a greedy bite. "I forgot."

"Of course you did," she scolded. Again, her face didn't show any anger. She pulled a chair out and sat next to him. While he devoured the food, she slid the alien computer over to herself. The device was no bigger than a normal tablet computer, though it was anything but normal. Less than five millimeters thick and completely transparent, the aliens called it a slate. The Tri-V was projected from it, and it didn't move a millimeter as she slid it over. The slate instantly compensated, keeping the image frozen in space.

"Such amazing casual technology," she said, shaking her head.

"Casual, sure," he said between bites. "That 'casual' tech cost 200 credits."

Madison whistled. "Two *million* dollars for what the aliens consider a ubiquitous toy."

Matthew shrugged. "Translators are 150 credits each." He looked at the translator sitting on his desk. The institute now possessed three of them—all on loan from the Logoo Syndicate, the alien organization Kodu'ku worked for—in exchange for engineering assistance developing aquatic life-support systems.

"Looks like you have it worked out," Madison said and pointed at the display.

"I think so," he said. "The file we got from the Science Guild helped. The race known as Selroth have brains amazingly like cetaceans. I looked on the Aethernet and found these." He reached over and clicked the slate. The orca brain was replaced with a tiny technological device. Popup explanations of various components appeared. "They're designed for the Selroth, but were apparently rejected for use."

"Rejected?" she asked. "Why?"

"The customer didn't like the size. These are apparently large for a Selroth." He clicked again, and the device was rendered next to an orca. It was almost invisible. "Obviously it won't be a problem with our orca." He glanced at her. "Probably not the bottlenose, either."

"Then you're thinking about both?"

"Why not?"

"The question is, how much?"

"They're listed as scrap. Fifty of them for 15 credits each."

"Seven and a half million, Matthew," she said, doing the math. "Where are we going to get that kind of money?"

"What would someone pay to talk to a dolphin?" he asked.

"Matthew!" she exclaimed. "You're talking about an amusement park! That goes against everything we've worked for." She pointed back toward the tanks. "All our cetaceans are rescues, for God's sake!"

"You don't think I know that?" he snapped. She shot him a sharp look, and he calmed himself. "Look, don't think of it as a side show, think of it as education."

"I'm not feeling it," she said.

"You don't think Joe Sixpack would leave here with a better understanding of why we should take care of the oceans after talking to someone who lives in them?"

"You think Joe Sixpack will sit and be lectured by a *fish?*" She said the last with a decidedly sloppy but recognizable southern accent to emphasize her scorn.

"No, of course not. We'd have to have some fun with it. I bet the dolphins will have a blast. It's a small price to pay to advance cetacean sciences a hundred years in just months! Think of how much we can learn."

"I know as well as you," she said. "If you recall, our PhDs are the same."

"Of course," he said.

"But still, how do we earn over seven million dollars without first having our talking dolphins or whales?"

"I talked to the Bank of Hawaii," he said. "They're willing to see a demonstration."

"We can't demonstrate anything without the machines first."

Matthew reached into a drawer and removed a metallic box smaller than a pack of cigarettes. She gasped when she saw the alien writing on it. He pressed a release and it popped open, showing the exact device displayed on the Tri-V.

"Where did you get that?" she asked.

"I dug into our bank account," he admitted.

"Matthew," she hissed, "even one is $150,000!"

"I got it half price, as a sample." He swallowed. The $75,000 was almost the entirety of their savings, including Terrence's college fund. "We've always been committed to the institute, right?"

"Of course, but our savings?"

"It was the only way," he admitted. "We can't go to NOAA or the Trustees with this and risk losing control." She nodded slowly. The Trustees were heavily risk averse.

"When are we doing the surgery?" she asked.

"As soon as I talk to one of the orcas."

"Who do we use?"

"Who do you think we should?"

"Kray," she said.

He nodded in agreement; that was his choice as well.

"Let's have a chat," he said, and picked up the translator.

They rode together down the elevator to the tank holding the Residents. All four of the Resident breed were together in one of the two biggest tanks. As soon as Matthew and Madison came out the door, a huge shiny black head popped out of the water, and an eye looked to see who was there. Matthew held the translator between them.

A whistle and thrum came from the orca they recognized as Kray. "*Wardens,*" he said, using the word the orcas had chosen to refer to anyone who took care of them. "*Who these Wardens?*"

"Matthew and Madison," he said, and they both knelt at the edge of the pool. Madison scooped some water into her hand and rubbed Kray under his mouth.

The big male gave several deep clicks. "*Rub good, Warden mates Matthew/Madison.*" He submerged for a second, and the other three surfaced a few feet away, clicking and whistling their own greetings. "*Not food time?*" Kray asked. The others tossed their heads in agreement.

"No, not meal time," Madison agreed. The orcas' sense of time was extremely hit or miss. They knew night from day and could usually tell meal time. However, even mounting a clock in the tank room big enough for them to see hadn't produced any progress. It was part of the reason they wanted to do the implant.

"We wanted to ask you something."

"*Ask,*" Kray said. "*Pod like ask things, like answer things, like Wardens!*"

"We like you, too," Matthew answered. "You know the translator?" He held up the device, and Kray's big eye locked on it.

"*Talk box,*" Kray said.

"*Talk box!*" all the others echoed.

"Yes," Madison agreed. The orcas splashed water with their pectorals and shook their heads, happy to get it right.

"We want to put a talk box inside you," Matthew said, hoping they'd understand.

"*How do?*" Kray asked. "*Eat talk box? Eat like fish?*"

"No," Madison said, shaking her head in an over-emphasized motion so they could see it better. "We would need to cut."

"*Cut Kray? Make Kray gone?*" The translator conveyed alarm.

"Not gone," Matthew said quickly. "It's called surgery. Ulybka, do you remember when we helped fix your tail?"

The female named Ulybka had come in with an injury to her fluke which hadn't received proper medical attention in Russia; the result was a persistent wound that didn't want to heal. They'd put her under general anesthesia and debrided the wound, applying a waterproof bandage, and it had healed up just fine.

"*Yes, yes!*" Ulybka said. "*Fix tail, tail good now!*" She dove and flipped over, her tail popping out of the water to flip back and forth. The notch was clearly visible, but the bandage was long gone.

"Like that," Madison said, "but we'd have to put a talk box into your head." She reached out and touched Kray just behind his eye. "Right here."

"*Hurt Kray?*" Kray asked.

"A little afterward," Matthew admitted.

"*Why?*" Kray asked.

"You'll be able to talk to everyone," Matthew explained.

"*Not only Wardens?*" Kray asked. "*Talk Warden calf?*"

"Terry, our son?" Madison wondered to her husband.

"Yeah, I think that's what he means," Matthew agreed. The translators were so expensive, Terry had never been allowed to use one, or even hold it. Call it adult paranoia, but Matthew had forbidden it. Kids were kids, and the risk of losing or damaging a multi-million-dollar piece of equipment wasn't worth taking.

"Yes, you could talk to Terrence, our calf. Anyone else, too."

Kray and the other three dove underwater and moved around each other. From experience, Matthew knew they were talking to each other. The orcas had adapted soon after understanding the Humans could talk to them. It had caught all the scientists completely by surprise.

Dr. Patel had suggested they record their conversations on the hydrophone and run it through the translator later, but both Matthew and Madison had vetoed it. They'd agreed the orcas deserved at least some basic dignity and some privacy. For the same reason, they were now *asking* the orcas if they wanted the translators installed.

Kray and the others surfaced, and Kray again spoke, "*Why you ask?*"

"We think we can learn a lot from you," Matthew said.

"*No. Why ask? Why not do?*"

"Do you mean, why didn't we do it without asking?" Madison asked. Kray's head bobbed in an orca nod. "Because you're a person and deserve to decide for yourself."

"*We not Wardens,*" Kray insisted, and they all nodded.

"No," Matthew agreed. "We take care of you, but you have rights."

"*Rights,*" Kray said, trying the word. "*What rights?*"

"It means you can say yes or no," Madison explained.

Matthew pressed the mute button on the translator. "A little oversimplified," he said.

Madison shrugged. "Close enough?"

He nodded, agreeing.

"*I say no, or I say yes?*" Kray asked. "*I say no, you no do?*"

Both Madison and Matthew nodded their heads.

All four orcas floated for a long time; several took breaths, their respiration blowing mist over the pool. *They're thinking about it*, Matthew realized. The orcas just kept surprising them.

"*Can pod all do talk box?*"

Madison looked at Matthew, who looked back at her; both of their eyes were wide with surprise. "Do you all want them?" she asked.

"*Yes,*" Kray responded.

"We would need to have one for now," Matthew explained, hoping they would understand. "Kray would be first. If everything's good with Kray, the rest of the pod, then, later. Other pod, then, also," he said, referring to the pod of five Pacific Transient orcas in the next tank. "If Kray's talk box works good, we'll also give them to the bottlenose dolphins."

"*Little brothers get talk box?*" Ulybka spoke up. "Little brothers" was what the orcas called dolphins. The dolphins struggled more with the translators. Their language seemed to be more contextual, often speaking in metaphors. Ironically, the dolphins called the orcas, "Dark Killers."

"Yes," Matthew confirmed.

"*Good, good, good,*" the orca pod all agreed.

There was no discrimination between the cetaceans the researchers had seen. Matthew was quite keen to see one day how well the device would work with other cetaceans. There were rough-toothed dolphins in captivity, and beluga as well. The other scientists at the institute had also talked to several other research establishments about trying to talk with a pod of blue whales to see if they could strike up a conversation.

"One more thing," Matthew said. Kray focused on him. "There is risk."

"You could die," Madison said.

Matthew looked at her, his eyes narrow. She stared him down, and he shrugged. It was true, there was risk.

"*I not fear,*" Kray said without hesitation. "*I want talk box.*"

"Okay," Matthew said, "let's do it."

* * * * *

Chapter Three

Kapukahehu Beach, Molokai, Hawaii, Earth

August 10th, 2035

Doc set the autopilot on his boat, the *Krispin*, and swung down from the flying bridge to greet the kids. He tussled Yui's hair, and put Terry in a headlock. The young boy escaped with the nimbleness of a martial artist in a move Doc had taught him the previous month.

"Where we going?" Yui asked, looking over the diving gear arrayed on the rear deck.

"Kapukahehu Beach," Doc said.

"The *Dixie Maru*?" Terry asked, excited.

"Yup," Doc confirmed.

"You said we can't go down below 40 meters," Yui said.

"You can for a few minutes without decompression," he explained. "However, we have a game changer." He picked up a strange clamshell-style case.

Terry immediately became more interested. The aliens who'd been visiting the institute over the last few months often carried cases just like it. They called them, "Union Standard" equipment cases, though they came in a dizzying variety of designs. He tried to imagine some factory floating in space, cranking out these cases for whatever you wanted to store. Everything from crazy alien toothbrushes to laser blasters!

"You got some alien stuff," Terry said.

Doc looked at him with the appraising look he gave them sometimes when they surprised him. "Yeah," he said. "How do you know that?" Terry explained. "I had heard there were a lot of aliens coming and going at Kaunakakai lately. You guys and your fish research?"

"Cetaceans, yup," Terry replied.

"Fish," Yui said, poking Terry in the ribs with a particularly sharp elbow.

"They're not fish," Terry said, and gave her a push. Anyone else might have gone right over the transom. Yui just caught herself and stuck her tongue out at him. "They're mammals, like us."

"I wish I had fins," Yui said. "That would make diving even cooler!"

"Or be able to hold your breath for 10 minutes, like dolphins," Doc said.

"Fifteen minutes for orcas," Terry said. He got the appraising look from Doc while Yui's mouth became an O. Terry enjoyed knowing something Doc didn't. "So what's that?"

"This," Doc said and popped the case, "is badass." Inside were four metallic cylinders and several sets of plastic grids.

"Looks like waffles," Yui said.

Doc winked and took one of the cylinders out. Terry reached for another, and the man gently stopped him. "Hold up until I show you," he said. "Remember what I taught you?"

"Learn, then do," Terry and Yui chorused.

"Bingo," he said. Doc took the cylinder and closed the case, much to Terry's disappointment. Holding the cylinder in his lap, he opened a regular dive case and began removing equipment. Over the next few minutes, as *Krispin* motored along the Molokai coast, he used tools to attach other items. A rubber head strap, a wireless monitor, and a mouthpiece.

"It's some kind of rebreather?" Yui guessed, about a second before Terry was about to say the same thing.

"Yes, it is," Doc said and gave her a thumbs-up. Terry scowled. Doc attached a standard dive mask and slipped the unit over his head. The silver cylinder was maybe five centimeters long, and one centimeter thick. It wasn't much wider than the mouthpiece when Doc slipped it between his teeth. It looked kind of comical compared to the long rubber tubes linking a standard regulator to dive tanks.

"That's it?" Terry asked.

Doc removed the mouthpiece so he could talk. "For a low dive, yes," he said. "It's self-contained and has one of those crazy alien batteries, so you're good for two hours."

"How big is the battery?" Terry asked.

Doc took the equipment off his head and popped a compartment open with a twist. The battery was a centimeter long and half the diameter of the cylinder. He showed them the intakes, which brought in seawater and extracted oxygen to breathe.

"Wow," Terry and Yui said.

"It's like something from '60s James Bond," Doc said. Yui and Terry gave him an uncomprehending look, and Doc shook his head.

"What about the plastic waffles?" Yui asked.

"Ah, yes," Doc said and grinned as he opened the case again. "Remember that 40-meter limit?" They both nodded as he took out the plastic pieces. "These attach with a couple little hoses, and they're extended gas extractors. They can pull anything from the water you want them to."

"I don't understand," Terry said.

"They can suck nitrogen or helium from the water," Doc said.

"Oh," Terry said. "So you can go deeper because you can add helium?"

"Bingo," Doc said.

"How deep?" Yui asked.

"As deep as you want," Doc said, and winked. "At least as long as the battery lasts, and you can hot-swap batteries."

Terry looked at the units, and then at Doc, thinking about the dive breathers. "Where did you get them?"

"Friends in the service," he said.

Terry knew Doc had been in the military, and that was where he'd learned to dive. It was also where he'd been hurt, though what the injury was, he'd never explained. "Are we going to use them?"

Doc checked his phone and glanced around the cabin to verify the boat's progress. "That's the plan," he said. "We're going to use them to dive down to the *Dixie Maru.*"

"We get to use them the first time?" Yui said in disbelief.

"No," Doc replied and laughed. "I've been using them for a month now. I love you guys, but do you really think I'd test alien stuff on a couple of ten-year-old kids?"

Terry didn't answer, because that would have been just fine with him. Doc briefed them on the basic operation of the apparatus.

"I've already programmed them," he explained. "There are only a couple controls you need to worry about."

As the boat neared their destination, Doc shepherded Yui into the cabin so she could change into her diving gear, and Terry changed out on deck. Doc was already wearing shorts and a vest. Yui came back out just as the boat throttled back, and Doc's phone beeped. They'd arrived over the wreck of the *Dixie Maru*.

Doc set a sea anchor and programmed the boat to hold position. Terry ran up the red flag with its white slash, a universal dive flag to warn passing boats that people were in the water. Doc set dive lines over the side, then helped the kids get their weight belts in place.

"Now, since we have the alien breathers, rate of rise isn't an issue. If something goes wrong, pull the release on your weight belts and come straight up. Always keep me in sight down there, and let's go slow on the descent. Got it?"

"Yes, sir," Yui said.

"Yes, sir," Terry echoed. That was part of the deal; they were no-nonsense while diving, and had been from the first time Doc took them snorkeling.

Doc helped attach the plastic filters, which would allow them to go deeper. They were lightweight and attached to the back of their vests, where tanks would have been before. Once in place, Terry couldn't even feel it. Then it was time to get in the water, and both kids hesitated.

"What's wrong?" Doc asked.

"It feels weird," Terry said. They were both standing on the diving platform, *Krispin* bobbing gently in the offshore swells, dunking their feet in and out of the water.

"Yeah, wrong without the tanks," Yui agreed.

"Maybe this is a bad idea," Doc said, rubbing his stubble-covered chin.

"No, I'm good," Terry said and jumped in the water feet first. He quickly surfaced, put the breather in, and stuck his head back underwater. He breathed in and felt cool, delicious air. Other than a tiny lag between drawing in the breath and the pressure catching up, it was no different than a scuba regulator.

"Okay?" Doc asked.

Terry gave him a thumbs-up. Not to be outdone, Yui jumped in, too. A few seconds later, she was using the breather as well. Doc nodded and slipped over the side, entering the water as smoothly as any dolphin Terry had ever seen.

Doc gestured to the kids to take hold of the dive rope. Once he was sure they had a good grip, he pulled the release and grabbed it himself. The weight fell, and they went with it into the dark.

As they descended slowly into the deep, Terry experienced a feeling of excitement mixed with fear, and he tried hard to control his breathing. Then he checked the monitor strapped to his wrist and saw the battery level at 99% and not changing. He'd become used to a tank with a fixed amount of oxygen. Doc preached constantly to carefully control your breathing to maximize dive time, and to give you a safety margin in order to escape problems. He relaxed and breathed normally.

Every few meters he forced himself to swallow, equalizing pressure in his inner ear. The earplugs he wore kept any pressure damage from getting through to his eardrums. His mask pressed ever harder against his face. He drew some of the pressure away by letting it out through his nose and exhaling.

The surface light fell off to only a dim hint of illumination. It reminded Terry of being under a sheet with only his room's light on. Merely a hint of light, without being able to see its point of origin. He'd never been down a fraction of the distance. It was amazing, and spooky.

The descent stopped suddenly, and Terry realized they were on the ocean floor. Bright light stabbed out, and he could see Yui in stark relief. Doc had turned his mask light on. Terry did the same, and Yui did so a second later. Their beams played around as they looked at the dark volcanic sand below them. Occasional plant life sprouted where there were rocky outcroppings, and a couple of light-dazzled fish swam past. Compared to the sea life he'd seen closer to the shore at shallower depths, it was almost dead where they were.

As he played his light around, a shape came out of the darkness. It had to be the ship, but it only looked like a jumble of broken wood. He got Doc's attention by flashing his light at him, then pointed at the boards. Doc nodded; that was it.

He'd told them about the *Dixie Maru* more than a year ago, shortly after they'd begun diving with him. He'd been down to it a few times before. He had the equipment to do it, but had absolutely refused to take the kids down.

The boat, a fishing junk which had sunk in 1916, still had some stuff Doc called "wreck trash." They poked around for a while, digging in the sand. Terry found an old spoon, which still showed a little engraving. Yui found an amber bottle with the decayed remnants of a cork in it.

The water temperature was in the high 70s, and they were getting cold. Terry spotted Yui shivering. Doc must have seen it, too, as he pointed toward the surface and made a thumbs-up motion. As per the rules, neither of them disagreed, and they repeated the gesture. He led them back to the dive rope, and they ascended into the light.

It was only as they were ascending that Terry noticed he'd felt different at the bottom. He guessed it was the mixture of gasses extracted by the breather now in his blood. Doc had taught him about nitrogen narcosis and the dangers of it. Breathing helium kept the nitrogen from building up and forming bubbles in their blood. Also known as the bends, it could be horrible. Doc had shown them pictures, and he kept seeing them in his mind all the way up.

The display on his wrist said the breather was down to 77%. All the time they'd spent on the ocean floor, and the alien battery had gone down less than a quarter. Terry was amazed. They broke the surface, and sunlight hit their faces. He felt like he'd come up from a dream.

"That was *amazing!*" Yui crowed after removing the breather.

"It sure was!" Terry agreed.

"You kids feel okay?" Doc asked, checking his own display.

"Yeah, great," Terry said. Yui nodded. Terry looked up and saw the sun was approaching the horizon. He needed to get home before too long. Besides, he was shivering now, too, despite the surface water being much warmer. He pulled himself up onto the diving platform and was soon followed by the others.

Doc went into the trawler's cabin and came back with a couple of huge, fluffy towels. Getting all the water dried off quickly warmed them up. While they did that, Doc got the boat back underway.

As they motored toward their starting point, Doc brought them hot chocolate, while Yui and Terry talked excitedly about the experience. Doc listened to them, smiling a little smile and enjoying their enthusiasm.

"Doc," Terry asked eventually, "how do you dive deep? I mean, *really* deep?"

"Well," Doc said, checking his phone for progress, "when you go below about 300 meters, you use hard suits."

"You mean like the combat armor the mercs are making to fight aliens?"

"Kinda like that, yeah," Doc said. He tapped at his phone and held up an image for Terry to see. The suit looked more like the cartoon monster at the end of *Ghostbusters* than a diving suit. The diver only had a tiny window to look out of.

"How deep can it go?" Yui asked as she looked at the picture.

"Record is 410 meters," Doc said. "Now if you wanted to go *really* deep, you could go down further if you just stayed."

"You mean forever?" Terry asked.

"You could come back up," Doc said, "but it would take you weeks to decompress."

"Even with helium?"

"Yup." Doc finished cleaning the breathers and put them back in the case. He glanced at them for a moment and nodded. "The guys are going to like my report," he said as he locked it closed.

The boat motored onward as Terry thought. He tried to imagine what it would be like to live deep down, deeper than even the cetaceans dived. No light at all reached past 200 meters. Perpetual night. What would it be like to spend your life down there? The sun fell behind Molokai as they continued on. The excitement remained, even when his bike's battery died halfway home.

* * * * *

Chapter Four

PCRI, Molokai, Hawaii, Earth
August 29th, 2035

Terry watched the TV news in the kitchen with half his attention as he ate breakfast. His tablet sat unused, his unfinished homework languishing as he ate. There'd been a brief bit about the Hawaiian junior baseball league championship on the Big Island. He was still stinging from the beating his team had taken in O'ahu two weeks ago. Yui said they'd been beaten so bad, charges should have been filed.

"In further news, it has been reported from China that the infamous Golden Horde mercenary company, one of the so-called Four Horsemen, has experienced a change in ownership."

Terry focused on the news report. Anything about Human mercs was interesting stuff. All the kids in his class were completely fascinated by the stories of the Horsemen, or any of the other myriad companies which had sprouted up in the last few years.

"When we contacted the Golden Horde's press liaison for a more in-depth interview, however, they declined to offer information beyond their basic press release. In further news, the world government has approved the Global Development Incentive Act which, among other things, establishes a 5% tax on all mercenary income…"

Terry tuned it out as his interest in the story waned. His mother came in and offered him some more toast.

"No, thanks," Terry said, so she headed back for the kitchen. "Oh, Mom?"

"Yes?"

"Is Kray going to be back in the tank today?"

"Yes, the doctor said he's clear to return."

"Do I get to find out what kind of surgery he had?"

His mother grinned slyly before she answered, "I'm sure you will. Kray says he's been missing you."

"Really? Cool!"

"Hurry back from practice after school. We need you to help with the dolphins, too, before you can see Kray."

Terry nodded, glad they hadn't had plans to dive. Doc had been too busy since the dive on the *Dixie Maru* to take them out again. Yui and he had been forced to subsist on snorkeling at the beach just down from the institute.

The day's lessons went slowly, partly because they'd just started back to school the previous week and were spending a lot of time going back over stuff, and partly because he was eager to see Kray again. They hadn't been using the translators much since Kray had had his mysterious surgery. The other orcas didn't want to talk about anything. They'd all seemed nervous about something.

Yui wanted to go snorkeling after class, but Terry told her he needed to get back and do chores. She was suspicious; he could tell. He took off the first chance he got and rode his bike back to the institute as fast as it would carry him. He forgot to plug it in, and had to go back down to attach the bike to its charger before he could do his chores.

After an hour of mopping the fish room and helping feed the bottlenoses, he went into the residence for dinner. He fairly jammed the food in his mouth, and his mother clucked with disapproval. She didn't stop him, though, because she knew why he was so excited.

"Can I be excused?" he asked, though his plate was still half full. She looked skeptically at what was left. "Please?"

"Go," she said, and he bolted.

When he got to the Resident tank, all four orcas were there. The other male and the two females floated next to Kray. As he entered, they immediately noticed him, and Kray gently floated over.

"Terry, I greet!"

Terry took a step back in surprise.

"You can talk without a translator?"

"I get talk box," Kray said. He turned sideways slightly, and there, just behind his huge eye, something was embedded in the orca's flesh.

"The surgery implanted a translator," Terry said in amazement.

"Talk box, yes! You like, Terry?"

"Yes, it's excellent." Terry considered for a second. "You know my name now, too?" Kray and the others had always called him "Warden Calf" before, a name he liked even less than Terrence.

"Talk box help me know stuff."

"What kind of stuff?"

"New stuff."

That's informative, Terry thought.

"Enjoying Kray's new side?" his father asked as he entered.

"Yeah, it's cool! Alien stuff?"

"An implant we bought to showcase their abilities. If we can get enough interest, we'll be able to get them for all the cetaceans."

"Even the bottlenoses?"

"Yup."

"Wow, Dad, that would be incredible. Who did the surgery?"

"Dr. Jaehnig. You remember, he did the surgery on Ulybka's fluke?" Terry nodded. "James has done more surgery on orcas than just about any other marine biologist."

"So it's a translator and something else?"

"Just a translator," his father replied.

"Then what does Kray mean by 'new stuff?'"

"We're not sure," he admitted. "We're still running tests."

Terry looked back at Kray, and the orca looked back. "Can I help?"

"It's better if you just do your chores and help with feeding." Terry looked down in disappointment. "I'll tell you what, maybe after we've finished our evaluation?"

"Excellent," Terry said, and went to get the fish cart.

Despite his complaints, he really enjoyed feeding the cetaceans. He'd been around a couple of times as the scientists had tried to get the hang of talking to the bottlenoses, which seemed to be going nowhere fast. He'd also talked with all the orcas. He wasn't surprised they'd chosen Kray to give a translator to. The Resident orcas were far more talkative and willing to learn. The Transients were another matter entirely.

Terry rolled the cart into communal tank #2 and saw a group of scientists working with the Transients. He looked at the orca talking. The long, thin dorsal fin meant it was Uila, the dominant female. She was also the most communicative of the mostly quiet Transients. The head of the group talking to the orcas was Dr. Orsage.

Dr. Penna Orsage had been researching cetacean language long before the aliens had brought translators to Earth and revolutionized the process. Scientists had known cetaceans communicated for many years, though they were uncertain how and to what order. Did they merely express desires and information like where food might be? Or could they convey complex meanings and theories?

Orsage had already been learning how orca society interacted and was correlating sounds and actions against those interactions. When the alien translators provided the words, Orsage put her previous knowledge toward making more sense of what the orcas were trying to say.

Terry put fish on poles and held them out for the orcas to take one at a time. These animals weren't the passive, trained ones you found in places like SeaWorld. Their actions weren't as predictable, and even SeaWorld had experienced loss of life in spite of the training. Only a few of the most skilled marine biologists could enter the water with the orcas. Terry was certainly not qualified.

While he fed the other five, he listened in on the conversation with Uila.

"…was a decision based on many things," Dr. Orsage was saying.

"*Not ask us,*" Uila said. "*Not ask Uila, not ask Ki'i.*" Ki'i was the dominant male, and her mate. The Transients took their lead from a female, unlike the Residents, who followed a male. It was some of the sociological details Dr. Orsage was studying.

"No, we didn't."

"Wardens do without ask."

"There are complex factors you would not understand."

"Wardens think we calves."

"We don't think you're children," Orsage said in a steady voice.

Uila snapped her jaws twice, rolled over with her pectoral fins, and showed her belly. She pushed away from the tank wall with her flukes and moved toward Terry, evidently to get a fish.

Dr. Orsage sighed and turned off the translator before speaking. "I guess the interview is over," she said.

"They're mad because you gave a translator to Kray?" Terry asked from across the pool. He held a big mackerel out on his pole. Uila snapped it away so viciously, she almost pulled Terry in after it. She shook the fish, tearing it apart. The other orcas moved away from her anger.

"Not that we gave it to Kray, but that we didn't give it to her," Orsage said.

"You could argue she's jealous," another scientist said.

"That's a reasonable assertion," Orsage said, picking up her tablet computer and making some notes. "The Transient and Resident pods have never been seen to interact directly."

"But orca specimens with Resident traits have been spotted with Transient pods," another marine biologist pointed out, holding up his computer stylus. "Five separate discreet occasions."

Orsage nodded. "And in each occasion the Residents were eventually gone from the Transient pods."

"Dr. Gene Meander suggested it was kidnapping for breeding purposes," still another marine biologist said.

"That's been pretty roundly criticized as apocryphal," Orsage said with a wave of her own stylus.

Terry kept feeding the orcas, keeping a careful grip on the pole after the earlier incident. He liked listening to the scientists arguing. His mother and father did the same thing sometimes. It wasn't like other grownups argued; this was science arguing. His father called it searching for consensus. He wasn't sure if he completely understood.

After a while, all the other scientists left, and only Dr. Orsage remained. She watched the five Transients eat and talk to each other. Her brows knitted together in concentration. He didn't know why they didn't just listen in; he would have. When the fish was all gone, he rolled the cart toward the door. He stopped before leaving.

"Dr. Orsage?"

"Hmm?" she replied, not looking up from the orcas.

"Do the Transients hate the Residents?"

She turned her head and focused on him, seemingly realizing who was talking. "That's a strong word," she said, "maybe too strong for the orcas. We don't know if any other species have hate in their repertoire." Terry's brows knitted, and she smiled. "I don't know if they can hate the way we do."

Terry looked at the way Uila was swimming, then back at Dr. Orsage. "Ma'am, she looks pretty pissed off to me."

* * * * *

Chapter Five

PCRI, Molokai, Hawaii, Earth
September 7th, 2035

Dr. Matthew Clark watched the bankers' reactions and smiled. The entire group, all ten of them, were staring wide-eyed as Kray spoke.

"Shool moved in deep water. Deepest water. Shool was alone. Shool made first pod. Boy, girl, so have calves. Pod grew. Alone long time. Pod lonely. Shool fill water with life. Shool fill sky with life. Life good. Pod good. All good."

Alice Kemp, president of Hawaiian Bank Corporation, turned to Matthew with her eyes wide and shining. "That is beautiful," she said. "Did you teach it that?"

"Not at all," Matthew said, shaking his head.

"Then where did it learn that?"

"Him," Madison said.

"I'm sorry?" President Kemp asked.

"You said 'it.' Kray is a male, 'him.'"

"Surely it doesn't matter," another banker said. "Him, her, it? They're just animals."

"Tell me, please, how many animals have a God?" All ten of the bankers gasped.

"That really doesn't matter," Matthew interjected, stepping forward to stop the fight he sensed was coming. "They, the orcas, told

51

us this story after the translator was installed, after a week or so for Kray to become used to it. He talked to the others in his pod, and they put this story into words we could understand. Don't you see? They *created* this!"

The bankers all nodded and looked at each other. Matthew could see an overlay of skepticism, so he pushed forward. "Think about people coming here, to Molokai, to interact with these noble…" he looked at his wife, "beings. What other stories might they have within themselves? Ladies and gentlemen, we've met aliens from the stars. They came here and told us we were not alone. Now we fly off across the galaxy and do what? Kill them? Get paid? Is that our sole destiny?"

He gestured to Kray, who was floating on his side, lazily pumping his massive fluke to slowly move around the tank. "Other intelligence was right here, among us, all along. The cetaceans are intelligent. They have language, a sort of oral history, perhaps even a mythology. People will come to hear about this."

"And pay to hear it?" Kemp asked.

"Oh, without a doubt," Matthew said.

"You have your talking fish," she said, gesturing to Kray. Madison scowled as she continued. "Why do you need millions of dollars then? We appreciate the opportunity to invest in this project, but couldn't you do it yourself with this one talking whale?"

"Sure," Matthew said, then shrugged. "Probably. But with money, we can give all the rest of our wards these translators. More of their stories will come out, and they can grow as their own people—realize their potential!"

Kemp laughed, but the humor didn't reach her eyes. "You talk as if they're people."

"Maybe they are," Matthew said. "Maybe they are valuable people who can make you and I a lot of money."

* * *

"I feel like I need a shower," Madison snarled as she waved. Matthew grunted as he waved as well. All the scientists of the institute stood at the steps by the main drive as the investment bankers climbed into their limos. In a few minutes they'd be on private helicopters flying back to Honolulu.

"Yeah, but we have this," he said and showed her the check for $10 million.

"Sure," she said. "That's part of why I feel dirty. Twenty-five percent of the institute's profits from public outreach programming and any advertising revenue," she spat, "all for filthy lucre. Sickening."

"Without this *filthy lucre*, as you so eloquently put it, we'd be dead in the water, and Kray would the only cetacean to ever have a translator. Or worse, someone else would do it, and we'd sit here and watch. Think of the papers we'll publish!"

"Is that what you're most concerned with, Matthew?" she asked, turning a baleful glance his way. "Getting famous?"

"I want to help cetaceans," he insisted. "If it takes some bankers' money and a couple of jet ski commercials? So be it."

"Still feels like exploitation to me," she insisted.

"Perhaps, but we've agreed." He looked at the check. "I'm going to turn this over to accounting and arrange to purchase the other implants. Looks like James has his work cut out for him."

"I'm sure Dr. Jaehnig will be excited." Matthew didn't notice his wife's facetious tone.

"Yes, I bet he will be!" The limos pulled away, and Matthew fairly ran inside, leaving his scowling wife behind.

* * * * *

Chapter Six

Kaunakakai Elementary School, Molokai, Hawaii, Earth
September 17th, 2035

Terry turned in his tablet computer with the completed test. His teacher, Mrs. Teel, smiled as Terry slid it into the data slot on her desk, then he went out into the busy hallway. He rather enjoyed being a 5th grader, the biggest kids in the school. Though he was right in the middle percentile for height as a 10-year-old boy, he towered over the little kids, and he loved it.

After math, they usually had social studies, one of his least favorite classes. However, today there was something different going on. An assembly was called for all the 5th grade kids. No description was provided; the only thing they were told was that a new program would be rolled out. Scuttlebutt was they were going to build a new middle school, but Terry doubted they'd call an assembly just to tell them about it. Besides, he'd have heard about it from his parents long before it was talked about at school.

When he got to the school's auditorium, a huge room under a plexiglass dome that allowed in Molokai's natural sunlight, he saw he was one of the first kids to arrive. Of course, Yui was there already. She'd finished her math test 10 minutes before Terry. It was her favorite subject, while history was his.

As he moved over to where his friend was sitting, Terry looked up on stage. The school principal, Ms. Kalani, was standing there talking to several teachers. A man he didn't recognize was standing toward the back, with one of the transparent computers the aliens sold on Earth, called a slate. Next to him was a woman in a US military uniform. *Now that's weird,* he thought. Yui was gesturing wildly for his attention.

"What's up?" he asked when he was close enough.

"Don't you see who's up there?"

"The military lady?" Terry asked.

"No, stupid, next to her!"

Terry looked again. The man was wearing a casual suit but didn't look comfortable in it. He chatted confidently with the military woman. He was built like a football player, with a shaved head. *Holy crap!* "Doc?!"

"Yeah," she said. "In the flesh."

They hadn't seen him in quite some time. He'd left them both messages the week after they dove on the *Dixie Maru* to explain that he'd been busy, then nothing. Now he'd suddenly shown up at some strange school assembly? And who was the military woman he seemed to know so well?

Terry waved when Doc looked their way. Doc saw Yui and him and gave them a subdued wave in return. Terry narrowed his eyes. *What's up?* he silently wondered.

The rest of their fellow 5th graders came in slowly until the period was over, then the remainder showed up in a small flood, until they were all there. The 5th grade teachers closed the auditorium doors and took seats to the side, not on the stage. Principal Kalani walked over to the podium and picked up the mic.

"Good afternoon, students."

"Good afternoon, Ms. Kalani," they chorused.

"I know you're all wondering why you're here. Well, it's to announce a new program that you'll be participating in, beginning next year in middle school. The United States' government has been working on this program for more than a year, and funding has finally been approved." She tapped the computer built into her podium, and the screen behind her came to life showing a shield-shaped logo. Along the bottom was, "United States of America District," and just above it, "Republic of Earth." In the center of the shield were the initials, "M.S.T."

"M.S.T.," Ms. Kalani said. The display showed words under the initials. "As you can see, it stands for Mercenary Service Track. Currently, Humans working as mercenaries for off-world employers are bringing in vast sums of money. As you may or may not have noticed, the government recently passed a modest tax on that income. These funds will help keep our government, and the planet, running."

"Now this isn't going to be a political discussion, and many of you wouldn't want to hear it anyway. Mercs, as mercenaries are often called for short, are soldiers. But many of them don't actually fight. Some are technicians, some are medics, and some do logistics. Being a merc is a complicated job which pays well. With the introduction of the MST, all US schools, from grade six up, are being given a budget to teach certain classes and provide knowledge which will help you decide if you want to pursue a mercenary career or not. Upon reaching junior year in high school, each of you will also be required to take a test, the Voluntary Off-World Assessment Test."

"If it's voluntary, why do we have to take it?" Yui asked, and Terry snorted. Several others in their class were wondering the same thing.

"I'm sure you are curious why it's called, 'voluntary' if it's compulsory. Apparently the test was labeled prior to the decision to make it mandatory." Ms. Kalani shrugged, then grinned. "You can all consult your social studies for a reminder in how government works, and doesn't."

She looked down at her notes, then turned to the military lady and Doc. "Behind me here is Captain LeEllen McCartney. She's been assigned by the US Military as your pre-6th grade liaison. Next to her is Lieutenant Commander Vincent Abercrombie, a US Navy SEAL, retired. He'll be the MST instructor for the Molokai General School district."

"Navy SEAL?" Terry whispered.

"Holy cow," Yui said, "I didn't know he was a SEAL! How cool is that?"

Explains why he's so good at diving and stuff, Terry thought.

Captain McCartney came forward and took the mic. "Good afternoon, boys and girls. I'm excited to be here today. The opportunities you'll be offered next year, and every year going forward, are multifold. Besides being given specialized instruction on how to maximize learning to possibly begin a *very* rewarding career as a mercenary, you'll have the chance to give future generations on our own planet an incredibly brighter future!"

Terry looked around as Captain McCartney spoke, noticing the various reactions. Some of his fellow students were listening with rapt attention, while others were indifferent. Yui was listening intently, though she seemed to be staring at Doc more than anything. The teachers' reactions were much more interesting. Most of them looked, for lack of a better word, *pissed.*

"So, I think it's time to meet your new MST instructor, Lieutenant Commander Abercrombie."

There was polite applause from the teachers; a few seemed to be pretending to applaud. Terry and Yui, like a few other of their classmates, knew Doc, and they applauded enthusiastically. He took the microphone and cleared his throat. "Some of you know me as Doc. After leaving the service, I became a charter boat captain and part time teacher at Hawaii Community College. When Principal Kalani asked me to be the MST instructor, I accepted.

"You see, I'm a former SEAL. I was injured and had to retire. Ten years ago, my former team went off on the Alpha Contracts, and none of them came back alive." He looked down for a second and shook his head. "They were cock-sure and convinced they were the best. And they might have been the best—on Earth. In the stars, they were ill-prepared. We know a lot of you might decide to be mercs someday. Who doesn't want to be rich and famous, right?"

From the looks on the faces of the teachers, nobody would. Terry didn't notice Yui grinning.

Doc went on, "We're going to teach some of the lessons learned out in those stars and, thanks to information provided by the Horsemen, we think we can help. Now, I know a lot of the teachers aren't happy with this plan." He looked at the aforementioned men and women, many of whom were openly glaring at him. "Unfortunately, this idea wasn't mine, and we don't really have a choice. You don't believe it's proper to give what amounts to military instruction in a public school." He smiled, then shrugged. "Maybe you're right. Maybe not. Either way, I'm here, so I hope we can all make the best of this. Thank you."

Terry thought a few of the teachers' applause was less grudging than before. Doc was easy to listen to, and what he said made sense. Terry wondered what it had felt like to have all your friends die a million lightyears away. Not good, he guessed.

A pair of teacher's aides began to move among the students, handing each of them a green folder with a red, white, and blue stripe around it, and the same logo that had been up on the display. Terry and Yui got theirs and opened them to find pages describing a lot of what they'd just been told, and a description of the assessment test to be administered in seven years.

"It's a lot of work to do for something nobody really wants," Terry said to Yui. She made a noncommittal noise. As they walked out of the hall, Doc was there talking with the principal and Captain McCartney. "Hey, Doc!"

"Hi, kids," Doc said.

"Or should we call you Lieutenant Commander Abercrombie?" Yui asked, a twinkle in her eye.

"Knock it off," he said. "LeEllen, I'd like you to meet a couple of the kids I teach diving." He gestured toward them. "This is Terry Clark and Yui Tanaka."

"Oh, well, nice to meet you two. Did you have any questions?"

"Not really," Terry said.

"Yui?" Doc asked, looking at her.

Terry glanced at Yui, who cast a furtive look back at him, then shook her head. "No," she said.

"Well, don't be late for your next class," Doc said.

"Will you have time to go diving soon?" Terry blurted out.

"Yeah, in about a week, I think. I'll send you a message."

"Excellent," Terry and Yui said at the same time. Terry waved goodbye, as did Yui, and they headed off.

"The whole thing is so strange," Terry said a minute later as they walked toward the science building.

"What do you mean?" Yui wondered.

"Well, mercenaries. You watch old 20th century movies and stuff, and mercenaries are the bad guys. Everyone hates them. Now, they're heroes?"

"Yeah," Yui said.

Terry glanced at her as they walked. He wasn't sure in what way she agreed with him.

* * * * *

Chapter Seven

PCRI, Molokai, Hawaii, Earth
October 27th, 2035

Terry watched the crowd. Several hundred people were crowded into the new auditorium listening to Kray talk about *Shool*, and how she created the world. In the month since he'd gotten his implant, the leader of the Shore Pod, as he'd renamed his group, had become incredibly more understandable. He'd also become somewhat of a religious character, Terry thought. A 9,000-pound televangelist, his mom called Kray.

"Shool mean us have world forever," Kray was saying. "We like have talk box to tell people about us. We all good. You all good. We all be good together!"

Terry was pretty sure a lot of the people in the auditorium had been there before, just like the last Saturday he'd worked there.

He finished his chores in the auditorium, emptied the trash cans, and moved to the educational center. Ki'i, the leader of the Wandering Pod, as her group was now known, was talking with some kids near Terry's age.

"Why haven't you talked to us before?" a girl asked her.

"We try," Uila said. "We speak not same. Talk box Wardens give us make good talk."

"What Uila is explaining is, the implants we've obtained are like the alien translation pendants," Dr. Orsage explained. She usually worked with the Wandering Pod. She wouldn't admit it, but Terry thought Kray and his talk of the orca god annoyed her. "We've been studying their vocalizations for a long time." She pressed a button on the control she had, and the ghostly clicks and thrums of wild orcas played over the auditorium's PA system. "We're still really trying to understand. The technology in the alien devices is very fast and very smart. It recognizes elements of thousands of languages and can render them into English, or another 100 Human languages."

"A hundred?" a boy said, eyes wide. "There are 100 languages on Earth?"

"Oh, no," Dr. Orsage said. The boy grinned, thinking he'd gotten her. "There are more like 6,500 that we know of. Mind you, that doesn't count dead languages or some dialects." The kids all shook their heads. Their parents nodded and commented to each other. "The translators we have from alien sources can handle 100 common Human languages. Some of the languages on Earth are just as alien as the various cetaceans'; however, we have one advantage over our marine mammal cousins. Do any of you know what it is?"

The kids began throwing out ideas. One boy said computers, another that Humans had thumbs, and one said Humans could sing.

"We sing," Uila said. "You play sing just now."

"Nobody knows?" Dr. Orsage asked.

"Common point of reference," Terry said.

Dr. Orsage turned, saw who it was, and smiled. "Meet our resident young expert on the orcas. This is Terry Clark, son of the director, Dr. Matthew Clark, and his wife, Dr. Madison Clark." The kids looked at Terry in his coveralls pushing a big bucket of garbage in confusion. He grinned like the Cheshire Cat.

"What does that mean?" a child asked.

"It means the cetaceans, in some ways, are as alien as our extra-terrestrial visitors. Uila's never lived in a town, and we've never lived under the sea. Hard to understand each other, right?"

"I understand now!" said a little girl from the back, sitting on her mom's lap.

"Good!" Dr. Orsage said and clapped. "That's why we're doing this!" One of the adults in the back raised her hand, and Dr. Orsage pointed at her.

"Do these orcas also believe in their god like the other ones?"

"That's a good question," Dr. Orsage replied. "They do share some of the same concepts, which have been translated by the devices into English. We're still trying to fully understand those beliefs. There are two pods of orcas here; these are the Wandering pod, as they call themselves, and they are made up of Pacific Transient orcas. They were caught in this ocean and are hunters, eating seals, whales, and other large animals.

"The other orcas are the Shore Pod, which is made up of Pacific Resident orcas. They live close to shore and like fish. They talk about their religion more."

"They Shool different."

Orsage turned to look at Uila, who was up close to the glass looking at her. "Sorry?" she said.

"*Shore say Shool everywhere. Shool like you say ghost.*" She tossed her head and splayed her flukes. Terry watched with curiosity. "*Shool down deep.*"

"You mean in your heart?" Uila shook her head side-to-side in an unmistakable answer. "I don't understand."

"Down deep, deep, deep."

"You mean under water? At the bottom of the ocean?"

"Yes. It why we dive deep," Uila said.

"*Meet Shool!*" Ki'i said.

"*Meet Shool!*" the other three orcas echoed.

Like a sea monster? Terry wondered. Cool!

Dr. Orsage had grabbed her tablet computer and was furiously typing. Her assistant took over the questions for the rest of the encounter. After the normal encounter time, the group moved on, and it was only Terry, Orsage, and her assistants. He decided he could ask a question.

"Dr. Orsage, do you think *Shool* is a sea monster?"

She glanced up from her typing and shook her head before going back to it. "No, it's probably nothing. Verbal histories passed down by Humans are often filled with some differences, even among the ones who share core beliefs."

"Is it maybe why the Shore Pod and the Wandering Pod don't like each other?"

"It's not that they don't like each other," Orsage said. "I think it's more like a rivalry. Because they have different lifestyles, it breeds some natural contempt sometimes."

"Are you going to put them together at some point?"

"We're still evaluating how that would work with the new translators factored in."

Terry grunted. *That's adult for 'we don't know,'* he thought. Dr. Orsage went back to her notes. Uila was looking at him through the thick glass, her massive eye watching closely. "Uila?"

"Yes?"

"You said you understood the song Dr. Orsage played?"

"Yes."

"What did it mean?"

"It song of death."

Dr. Orsage looked up and blinked.

"What kind of death?"

"Pod mate die."

"Terry, can you leave me to talk to Uila, please?"

Terry made a face, but left as he'd been asked, heading into the bottlenose habitat. He wondered why it was so important.

He thought the orcas were interesting, especially since they'd had translators implanted. Now the Pacific bottlenose dolphins? They were freaking *cool!* If they were Human, they'd fit right in with many of the hip, young surfers he met regularly on Molokai. He also had to admit, his opinion of the dolphins was at least partially biased because he *was* allowed to swim with them.

Where the orca tanks were as massive as engineers could make them to allow the huge cetaceans room, the bottlenose habitat was a series of ponds with deep areas in the center, and shallow at the edges. The habitat was staffed with four institute employees, and at least 50 people were either in the water with the dolphins or watching curiously.

Terry had seen video of people lining up 20 deep for a chance to touch a dolphin at some parks. In some of those parks, the guests would pay hundreds of dollars to get in the water with the animals. His parents hadn't shared all the details about how admission worked here, but he'd overheard the face-to-face encounter with the pod of Pacific bottlenose dolphins was $2,000 each and lasted an hour.

It seemed like a ridiculous amount of money, until you participated. The bottlenoses were an amusement park ride, a workout, and a comedy show combined. They only talked about how fun it was to be a dolphin, or about the games they often made up on the fly.

They didn't preach about *Shool*; they didn't believe in it. They said life was a gift of then and now.

"They're hedonists," Dr. Orsage had told him. Terry'd had to look up what that meant, then he'd laughed afterward.

They hadn't asked for much after getting their translators, using the same description for them as the orcas, talk box. The one thing they'd asked for, and gotten, was live fish.

"Miss chase, catch, eat!" they said.

Terry's father had balked at the extra cost, until he'd found out they didn't care what kind of fish, as long as it was fast and alive. They happily caught and ate fish they'd previously turned down before getting their translators. Just as he came in, the bottlenoses were playing a new game.

They picked a Human, who would then get a live fish from the holding tank and put it in the water. If the fish evaded the bottlenose dolphins for more than 10 seconds, the Human who'd released the fish got to ride a dolphin. Everyone was having a grand time. The Humans in the water were trying to get in the bottlenoses' way, which looked like a brand-new strategy by the Humans. The dolphins responded by performing incredible leaps over the Humans, much to the latters' delight.

The tactic worked the first time; the fish was caught 12 seconds after release, and a teenage girl with incredibly long blonde hair tied in a ponytail and in an alarmingly skimpy bikini got to ride one of the dolphins. *Skritch,* Terry thought. There were 19 of the bottlenoses, and he hadn't had enough time with them to memorize more than a few of them by sight alone.

Terry marveled at the athletic girl's body as she rode the dolphin through tight turns and a couple of jumps out of the water. The way her hair flowed behind her and the fit of her bikini made him feel…funny. Kind of like when he'd seen Yui changing into her diving clothes one time.

The ride ended, and the spell was broken. Terry finished pushing his garbage trolley into the habitat, and the bottlenose inhabitants instantly spotted him.

"*Terry! Terry! We greet you!*" the cheer went up around the pool, making the people who'd been enjoying the encounter look around for the source of their excitement.

"That's Terry Clark," Dr. Jesus Hernandez said. He was the senior scientist in charge of the bottlenose dolphins, and was an old, short, balding Hispanic man with a large tummy. Terry liked him a lot. "Terry's the son of our director here, and a favorite of our dolphin pod."

"Sunrise Pod, Sunrise Pod!" the dolphins yelled.

Dr. Hernandez smiled and bowed. "I'm sorry," he said to the guests and the bottlenoses, "Sunrise Pod. Although I think they only gave themselves a name because they were jealous of the orcas." Three bottlenoses flipped over and used their flukes to send jets of water at Dr. Hernandez, nearly knocking the portly man into the pool. The 19 dolphins laughed uproariously. Terry had never heard the translators render cetaceans' language into a laugh.

One of the bottlenoses surfaced next to Terry and spoke.

"Light fem ride me now?"

"I think she has to win again," he told the bottlenose he recognized as Hoa.

The dolphin shot water at him with his long mouth, the equivalent of a snort, and spun away. While Terry worked at cleaning out cans, another fish was tossed into the water, and the dolphins were in hot pursuit. Two of them raced to corner the fish. Then, just as they were an instant from catching it, Hoa swam into their way, stopping them from completing the catch, and letting the Human win the game.

The entire pod exploded in angry chatter; much of it was not rendered into English. Terry had noticed that happened most often with the dolphins. The researchers weren't quite sure why, either. An alien elSha technician who'd helped with the implants was working on the programming, something called a translation matrix algorithm, trying to find out what was wrong. Skritch swam over and came out of the water next to Terry.

"What he do?"

"What do you mean?"

"Hoa break game! Not play right way! What he do? Word?"

Hoa was over by the blonde girl, paddling lazily next to her.

"Oh, I guess he cheated."

"Cheat? That word?"

"Yes," Terry said, "it means he didn't play fair, or by the rules."

"Cheat, cheat, cheat!"

Meanwhile Hoa was discovering it wasn't the blonde teenager who won the ride, but a man in his early 20s who'd released the fish, and he wanted the ride.

"*No,*" Hoa said, "*give ride light fem!*" He squirted some water at the blonde teenager, who looked confused.

"I'm the one who let the fish go," the man said.

Hoa flicked his flukes and hit the man in the face with a powerful wave of water, knocking him on his hind end. "*Light fem ride!*" The girl looked confused and backed away, up out of the water into the shallower area. Hoa pursued. She gave a squeak of concern, and

Skritch plowed into Hoa's side, sending the other dolphin rolling into the deeper water.

"*No more game you play!*" Hoa said, the clicks emphasized with powerful snaps of his rostrum.

Dr. Hernandez checked his watch. "Okay, folks, that's about all the time we have for the encounter now. If you'll head for the locker rooms and change, I believe lunch is probably waiting for us! You'll have a few minutes after lunch to talk to the dolphins, after they've had time to rest."

The blonde girl looked around, confused, but an older man, her father maybe, came over and put a hand around her shoulder to lead her away. The mood was more somber and confused as the group began to leave.

"Terry?"

"Yes, Dr. Hernandez?"

The doctor had walked over to Terry, and he looked disappointed. "Did you teach Skritch the word 'cheat?'"

Terry felt his face getting hot. "Yes, Dr. Hernandez."

"Please don't do that again. You know how much trouble we're having with the bottlenoses, getting them to interact with Humans in a constructive manner."

"Yes, Dr. Hernandez."

"*Terry swim?*" a bottlenose asked. Terry recognized the female, named Ihu due to her particularly long rostrum and sleek melon, the bump on their head where a Human's forehead would be. It was the organ which let them send sonar pulses in the water.

"I think Terry still has work," Dr. Hernandez said.

"*Work,*" Ihu said, and let out a convincing raspberry sound, requiring no translation.

"I'm done," Terry said. "May I, please?"

Dr. Hernandez looked at him sternly, placed his hands on his hips, and scowled. Terry put on his most innocent smile, and the doctor laughed. He looked at the pod, and could see Hoa was off to one side with two other males. They appeared to be talking, and Hoa was slowly flexing his side. Even under a couple meters of water, Terry could see the bruise. "If it is okay with Skritch," the doctor said.

"Like Terry swim," Skritch said, "like Terry play."

"Very well," Dr. Hernandez said. "One hour."

"Thanks, sir," Terry said, and bolted for the staff locker room, his garbage trolley completely forgotten. He came out of the locker room in less than a minute, facemask already in place, still tying his swim trunks as he ran. Ihu saw him running and swam along his path, her powerful flukes moving almost too fast to see. When he was a few meters from the edge of the pool, he leaped into the water. Ihu jumped, turning her body to present a dorsal fin—which Terry caught—and they hit the water together.

In the water, Ihu rolled on her belly, swimming upside down, while Terry lay against her, one hand holding each pectoral fin, his body melding with her mighty strokes. They rocketed through the water with such powerful strokes, his mask compressed against his face hard enough to hurt. He didn't care, he felt like a Human torpedo!

"*I like swim you,*" Ihu said later. She was breathing in and out from her blowhole every few seconds, which was the equivalent of a Human gasping for breath.

"It's fun swimming with you, too."

"Yui swim more?"

"Some time, I hope." She'd come over just before the bottle-noses had undergone their surgeries for translators. None of the researchers had been there with translators, but it hadn't mattered. Ihu and several other dolphins had played in the water with Terry and Yui. The Humans threw volleyballs, which the bottlenoses either caught or bounced off their rostrums. The Humans had marveled at how accurate the dolphins could be with nothing more to strike the balls with than the tip of their noses.

"Yui you mate?"

Terry slipped off the edge he'd been holding to catch his breath. His head dipped below the surface, and he sucked in a mouthful of the tank's treated seawater. Ihu pushed him back above the surface with a pectoral fin and watched him as the Human spluttered and gasped for breath.

"No!" he said finally.

"No like Yui?"

"Yeah, I like her just fine."

"Then mate!"

"Ihu, we don't work like that." The dolphin lifted out of the water so her eye could regard Terry suspiciously. "I mean, yeah, Humans do, but we're just kids!"

"What kid?"

"You know…" He was so flustered, it took him a minute. "We're just calves."

She regarded him again, and he felt a *thrum* against his torso several times. He'd never felt anything like that in the water before, and wondered if something was wrong with the treatment system or the pumps. Then he saw Ihu had her melon pointed at him, and felt it again. "Ihu, what are you doing?"

"Kleek you."

"Could you stop? It feels funny." The thrumming stopped. "Thanks. Well, I better go. Thanks for the play, it was fun."

"Fun, yes, bye."

Terry used his arms to push out of the water and walked toward the locker room. He looked back and saw Ihu watching him go with an inquisitive eye. Two other bottlenoses were gliding up next to her, and he was sure they were talking about him. That was twice in one afternoon he'd been embarrassed. Once by an adult, and then by a damned dolphin.

He was mumbling to himself in the shower when Dr. Hernandez came in. The man stripped out of his soaked coveralls, courtesy of the spraying he'd gotten earlier, and went to the next shower over. "Did you have fun, Terry?"

"Sorta," he said.

"What happened?"

He thought about it for a minute, then decided his curiosity was worse than being further embarrassed. Besides, it seemed less embarrassing to talk to Dr. Hernandez than his mother or father. When he was done, the older man gave a half-grunting chuckle and sighed.

"So what was that all about?" Terry asked after nothing more was forthcoming.

"The cetaceans have a hard time telling adults from children. Once we're about half adult size, they just figure you're small."

"They know I'm a...calf," he said, saying the word with some distaste. He wasn't a baby, and "calf" made him think of a baby cow.

"Yes, but apparently in the cetaceans' language, there are no different words for children of a parent and grown children. Either that, or the difference is too subtle for the translators to pick it up."

"Oh, I think I get it," he said. "But what does that have to do with…Ihu saying what she said?"

"Sex, to the dolphins, isn't as big a deal as it is to us," Dr. Hernandez explained. "Sometimes it's just a bonding thing. In captive groups, it's been observed as an activity they engage in, almost out of boredom."

"Weird," Terry said.

"Maybe, maybe not. We don't have enough wild observations to know if it's abnormal and a stress response from captivity. Either way, your unwillingness to mate with your friend confuses them."

It confuses me too, Terry thought. "Do you know what 'kleek' means?"

"We only figured it out a few days ago. It's in relation to using their sonar. They've been observed pulsing sonar at the opposite sex to see if they're receptive to breeding."

Terry was immeasurably glad there was a metal wall between himself and the doctor, because he was sure he was blushing from his head to his toes. "She was sonar scanning my…my body?"

"Yes, I suppose she was. It was just curiosity. I don't believe they think in perverted ways."

"What about Hoa?" Terry suspected he knew what the dolphin's behavior meant. He might only be 10, but he knew an erection when he saw one.

"Yes, Hoa," Dr. Hernandez said. He laughed, then sighed. "Let's just say, some dolphins aren't particular about what species is the target of their desires."

Terry was glad to finish drying off and get dressed. He'd had enough of such conversations for one day. Maybe enough for the year. He went back to tend to his forgotten trolley. Luckily, the dolphins had left the encounter pools and gone on to talk with the guests.

* * * * *

Chapter Eight

Poaiwa, Shipwreck Beach, Lanai, Hawaii, Earth
November 23rd, 2035

Terry surfaced and shook the water from his hair before pulling his mask back and orienting himself toward *Krispin*. The Saturday afternoon skies were growing darker, hinting at possible rain. Doc was sitting on the diving platform, skinning one of the uku, or gray snapper, they'd caught. Yui surfaced next to him. Part of the *YOGN 42* wreck was just poking out of the water, and they'd been exploring the superstructure. Doc had caught the fish and surfaced a minute before the two kids, first making sure they were clear of the wreck.

"Find anything?" he called as they paddled toward the boat.

"Yui found a plate," Terry said. She held up the item, half barnacles, half tarnished steel. "I struck out." Terry sighed and shook water out of his eyes. He wished he'd found something interesting or that the fun had gone on longer. He didn't want it to end, because he'd have to give Yui the bad news.

"*YOGN 42* is just a junk pile," Doc admitted, flipping guts into the water. "It's got a big open superstructure, so it's fun to dive in." *YOGN 42* was the resting remains of a WWII liberty ship. When the war had ended, instead of scrapping it, the military had simply grounded the ship and left it to rust.

"Yeah, it was cool," Yui agreed. "It's like a haunted castle or something."

The two young people reached the platform as Doc finished cutting up the uku. He helped them as they handed up their tanks and flippers, then the kids got themselves up onto the platform. As Doc gathered up the fillets, Terry watched small reef fish helping themselves to the uku remains.

A few minutes later, they were sitting on *Krispin*'s transom as Doc fanned the coals to white and put the fillets on a grill. Yui and Terry sipped bottles of Coke, enjoying the cold sweetness. Doc had a beer.

"Do you believe they're talking about making it illegal?" Doc said, pointing at the bottles with a spatula.

"Coke? Why Coke?" Terry asked.

"Not Coke specifically," Doc said, flipping a fillet and checking its doneness. "The sugar in it."

"I like sugar," Yui said. Terry nodded and took a big drink, making an over-exaggerated "*Ahhh!*"

"Of course you do," Doc said. "It tastes good because Humans were programmed over a million years of evolution to crave it."

"Then why do they want to make it illegal?" Terry asked.

"Because some people abuse it. They get overweight, and then they get heart disease, which kills them."

"So, that means I don't get sugar?" Terry asked. Doc nodded. "Why?"

"Some people think if someone abuses a thing, nobody should have it."

"That's stupid," Terry replied.

"That's government," Doc said, "*and a certain political ideology,*" he said under his breath.

"What was that?" Yui asked.

"Nothing. Fish is done!"

They spent an hour eating on the small inset chairs up on the flying bridge. Doc microwaved some rice and vegetable packages to go with the uku, and Terry loved the taste. Fresh seafood was something he loved about Hawaii. He liked hamburgers more, but those were expensive on the islands.

"Doc," Terry said as he chased a last bit of fish with a plastic fork.

"Yeah, kid?"

"Why didn't you tell us you were a Navy SEAL?" Yui looked up, quietly listening. "And please don't say we never asked."

Doc laughed and shook his head. "Well, you didn't ask." Terry threw his fork at Doc, who caught it. He sighed. "Look, being a SEAL was a big part of my life. I had a grandfather who was one of the first. From the moment I was old enough to be a SEAL, I wanted to be one. Having the trident punched on my chest was the single greatest moment of my life." Terry looked confused. Doc held up a hand. "Some other time."

"Anyway," he continued after taking a sip of his beer, "we were being inserted during the attack on Iran. A 'target of opportunity,' they called it. If everything went right, we'd get a once-in-a-lifetime opportunity while the aliens were kicking the shit out of the jihadis." He shrugged. "It didn't go right."

"What happened?" Yui asked.

Doc looked at them for a long time, thinking. He seemed to come to a decision. "I knew going off to the stars to fight those alien bastards was a mistake. Only I wasn't conscious enough to tell anyone at the time. By the time I was, it was too damned late." He drained the beer and tossed the bottle into a can on deck. "You want to know why I'm teaching MST? Because I think I can help some kids make the right decision, or at least keep them from making the *wrong* decision."

The three sat in the lengthening afternoon light and watched the clouds heading in from the west. Doc looked over at the controls. Terry could see him thinking about how long it would take to get back to Molokai, and wondering if they could beat the storm. He got up to put away the grill, and the kids pitched in, securing everything. In a few minutes, *Krispin* was roaring to the north, toward Molokai.

"We diving again next week?" Yui asked.

"Sure," Doc said. "I have weekends free for quite some time."

"I can't," Terry said. Yui and Doc both looked at him in surprise.

"Work with your parents?" Doc wondered.

"No." Terry tried to think of a way to explain it that wouldn't be as hard as it felt. He couldn't think of one. "Mom, Dad, and some of the scientists are going on an expedition to contact wild humpback whales. They're hoping to validate theories about cetacean society." He looked at Yui. "I have to go to the mainland and stay with an aunt until they get back."

"How long will it be?" she asked. Her eyes were wide with surprise and hurt.

"I'll be back in time for school next fall."

"Oh," she said. Yui got up and went down below, into the trawler's cabin.

Doc looked after her, then at Terry, who was looking off into the distance toward Molokai. Rain began to fall as they motored toward home.

* * * * *

Chapter Nine

The Queen's Medical Center, Honolulu, Hawaii, Earth
August 2nd, 2036

Terry watched out of the robotic taxi's wide window as it turned off H1 and onto Ward Avenue. He was full of conflicted emotions and unable to concentrate. Twenty-four hours ago he was having lunch with his aunt at Café Du Monde in New Orleans. Warm hot chocolate and beignets. His phone had beeped a text message. His father was on the way back from the arctic, and there was a ticket waiting for him to catch the next flight to Hawaii. His mother. He couldn't think.

The cab turned onto South Beretania Street. The multiple towers of the Queen's Medical Center came into view, and the cab beeped an announcement that the destination was less than a minute away. He grabbed his bag. Most of his stuff was still in New Orleans. His aunt had packed an overnight bag and a few things, and got him to the flight just in time.

The cab turned into the hospital drop off. Dad was waiting as the door swung open. "Mom?" he asked, his voice shaking.

"She's alive," his father said.

Terry grabbed him around the waist, hugging him. He couldn't remember the last time he'd cried for any reason other than pain. Emotions overwhelmed him, and the tears came. "Dad," he bawled.

"It's okay, Terry," he said, stroking Terry's hair. The cab beeped for attention. "Just a second," he said and gently detached. "I need to pay the cab."

Terry let go and stood on the sidewalk, shaking and trying to control his emotions. He wiped snot away with his sleeve as his father used his new ID card to pay the fare. The cab closed its door and rolled away. His father turned back to him. He tried to smile, but it didn't really work. He held out a hand. "Come on, Son, let's go."

Terry took his hand, and his father picked up the daypack. They went into the massive hospital.

Inside, there were hundreds of people, all doing their own thing. Adult visitors moved about on unknown missions. Occasionally children accompanied them. A few looked at him. Sometimes they were curious, sometimes they looked afraid.

His dad took him to an elevator, and they went up to the 22nd floor. Terry noticed the floor was labeled Intensive Care. The elevator rose in what seemed like slow motion to him. When the doors opened on the 22nd floor, he felt as if he was in a dream, walking along the white halls and black floor, holding his father's hand.

"You've gotten taller," his father said almost idly.

"Aunt Wilma said over a centimeter," Terry replied robotically.

They reached the end of the hall, where a nurse's station was.

"Here to see Madison Clark," his father said.

"Family?" asked the woman, a nurse dressed in a red uniform.

"Yes, I'm Matthew Clark, her husband. This is Terrence...I mean Terry, our son." He held out the new ID card.

The nurse examined the card—his Universal Account Access Card, which everyone called a Yack—and handed it back. She reached into her desk and gave him two yellow cards with clips. He gave one to Terry and clipped the other to his shirt. The card said, "Visitor." Terry mechanically clipped his on as well.

"This way, sir." Another nurse had arrived and was holding open a door with "Authorized Personnel Only" written on it in red. His dad took his hand again, and they followed the nurse.

This hallway was lined with windows and doors. Each window showed a small room on the other side, and machines, but Terry was too short to see more than occasional people or doctors standing in the room. It was all just images to him. He was walking in a nightmare.

They turned into a room about halfway down the corridor. The door closed behind them. There was a bed inside, and on it was his mom, though it was almost impossible to see her under all the hoses, wires, and other apparatus. Machines stood on metallic stands, others were mounted to the walls, and all were hooked to her body. Rhythmic beeping was audible constantly, and bellows moved up and down, reminding him of the old film villain, Darth Vader.

His dad stopped next to the bed. A woman stood there, a tablet computer in her hand. She was examining one of the machines and making notes. "Any change, Doctor?" he asked.

"No, Dr. Clark," she said, shaking her head. "No better, but no worse, either."

Terry let go of his dad's hand and reached over to touch his mother's. There was a needle in the back of her hand, with clear fluid running through it into her body from a bag suspended on a hangar. Some kind of machine beeped there, adding to the endless cacophony of beeps, whirs, and buzzes. The hand was cool to the touch, cooler than he thought it should be.

"Momma?" he asked.

The doctor and his dad looked down at him, and he began to cry again.

* * *

The room was private, like an office, but there was just a small table with several chairs around it. The doctor he'd seen was sitting on one side of the table; Terry and his dad were on the other side.

"I'm sure you have a lot of questions," the doctor said to Terry. "However, I'll leave the details to your father for explanation. I just wanted to tell you we're doing everything we can."

"Will she wake up?" Terry asked.

"We don't know," the doctor admitted. "Her brain is injured. We're giving her the best treatment we can. It will be another week or so before we can see if she'll regain consciousness."

The doctor went on for another minute with more technical details for his dad. Terry listened with half an ear until the meeting was over. He knew a little about the accident from the conversation with his father.

On the way to the airport, his father had gotten through to Terry on the phone, and they'd talked for five minutes. There'd been an accident while they were diving in the arctic. His mother had been hurt, badly. He was with her in Honolulu, and Terry was to fly back immediately. An hour later he was getting on the plane at New Orleans International Airport.

They were back in the intensive care waiting room. It was smaller than the big ones Terry saw in hospitals. Only a few people were sitting in the chairs and couches. Nearby a woman was sleeping, a young girl using her lap as a pillow to sleep, as well.

"Okay," his dad said once they'd found a quiet place. "Let me tell you what happened."

He spoke in quiet words so nobody could hear or be disturbed by what they might overhear. "We set up operations in the arctic with a previously identified pod of humpback whales. Your mom and I were both in the water, swimming in specially-made drysuits for the arctic water. We were attached to a submersible, cruising along next to the bull male whale. We'd been trying to talk to him for weeks.

"Over and over again we dove with the pod, following along behind the manned submersible like being towed behind an airplane. We tried everything we could think of. The translator was working perfectly, communicating in the humpbacks' language of moans, clicks, and wails. Only they wouldn't respond.

"Finally, we had staff at the institute talk to the bottlenoses and ask them to send a message. Bottlenose dolphins had been seen with humpbacks, though rarely. Maybe it would work? We didn't know. The dolphins called the humpbacks "Dreamers." They did as they were asked.

"So we played the dolphins' message. First in the humpbacks' language, and then, when nothing happened, in dolphin. The bull looked directly at us for the first time. Your mom and I were surprised, of course. It was a breakthrough. Then the bull turned suddenly and sped away. When it did, the whale's flukes slammed into the submersible, shattering the hull."

His dad paused, looking down and taking a couple of breaths. Terry's eyes widened as he tried to imagine the huge whale smashing a submarine like a toy. Then he remembered his mother and father had been tethered to the sub. His father was talking again.

"It was an accident, everyone agrees. Your mom wouldn't want the blame to fall on the whale. He merely wanted to get away from us. When you're 20 meters long and weigh more than 60,000 pounds, anything as small as a Human submersible is almost too tiny to notice."

He paused again before continuing, "Two people died in the submersible, probably instantly. The crushed sub was sinking. We'd been connected to the submersible by tethers and our air supply. Mine were cut by the impact. Sheer luck. I was knocked silly, but I floated to the surface. I don't remember, but the support ship picked me up immediately."

"What about mom?" Terry asked.

"She was pulled down with the sinking sub. The rescue divers got her loose, but not until she'd been without oxygen for nine minutes."

Doc had taught Yui and him a lot about what happened when you were without oxygen for just a few minutes. Nine minutes was a *long* time. The world record was something like 20 minutes, but his mother wasn't a trained athlete. She'd been unconscious. He'd also learned as little as 6 minutes could cause brain damage.

There wasn't much more to talk about. They sat in the waiting room for a time. Terry saw a reporter on TV talking about his mother. They had a picture of her, along with the rest of the family. It was a celebration at the institute several years earlier. The caption said, "Marine Scientist Injured, Several Dead."

Eventually his dad stood and stretched. "Let's get you home," he said.

"I want to stay here," Terry insisted.

"The doctor said it could be days." Terry stared at him. "You can come back tomorrow."

Terry thought about being defiant, then despite himself, he yawned. "Okay," he said, "let's go home."

* * * * *

Chapter Ten

PCRI, Molokai, Hawaii, Earth

August 17th, 2036

Terry looked up from his cart to see Yui standing by the main door. He was excited to see her, but she seemed uncertain and looked like she'd been about to leave. "Yui?"

"Hi, Terry. I just found out you were home," she said, tears rolling down her cheeks. "Oh, my God, I'm so sorry about your mom."

"I wanted to see you, but I've been spending a lot of time at the hospital." *And I was afraid to call you after the way you were the last time I saw you.*

"Is she better?" Yui walked over to him and glanced at the cart full of fish. Since it was Sunday, the institute was essentially empty.

"The doctors say her brain activity is increasing." He shrugged. After two weeks, he wasn't feeling the same sense of loss he'd felt when he'd first arrived at the hospital. He was still worried about his mother, of course. It just felt different, and he hated himself a bit because of it. He'd been back there every day, for an hour in the morning, and another hour at night. The staff encouraged family to come and talk to her, saying it helped people in a coma to hear familiar voices. Yesterday, he'd skipped the evening visit.

They talked about nothing as Terry pushed the cart into the orca tank and got the feeding pole ready. An orca surfaced next to the edge of the pool. He immediately knew it was a female by the small, straight dorsal fin, then he saw the tiny, almost nonexistent eye patch, and knew it was Maka.

"*Hi, Terry,*" Maka said.

"Hi, Maka, hungry?"

"*Fish?*"

"Yes, sorry."

She made a snorting-burp sound from her blowhole. "*Fine.*" Terry fixed a fish to his pole and held it out for her. The orca took it in a less than enthusiastic manner.

"Why doesn't she like the fish?" Yui asked. "I thought all orcas ate fish."

"She's a Transient," he explained. "One of the Wandering Pod. They're hunters and specialize in eating seals and other whales."

"Oh, wow," Yui said.

"Yeah, the first orcas anyone saw were probably Transients, and that's the reason they were called killer whales." Maka tossed her head and opened her mouth above the surface, so Terry gave her another.

"Why don't you give them meat?" Yui asked. "Lions and tigers get meat."

"I don't know," Terry admitted.

"*Want meat, yes.*"

Another orca swam over and pushed Maka out of the way. Terry knew it was Uila, the dominant female of the Wandering Pod. "Sorry, Uila," Terry said. "Fish?"

"*Give,*" Uila said.

Terry was a little taken aback by her attitude. He'd noticed since coming home that the orcas weren't as deferential as they'd been before he went to New Orleans. Uila's attitude toward him was surprising. The female orca's attitude verged on rude.

Nobody had asked him to do the chores; his father was too busy running the institute by himself. He'd decided to do it because he was bored. Thinking about his mother all the time had kept him from realizing how differently the orcas were acting. School was scheduled to start on Monday, and he was looking forward to it. The distraction from his mother's condition was welcome.

"Let me," Yui said, and Terry let her take the pole and give Uila a fish. The dominant female took the fish and disappeared below the surface without a word.

"They're kinda weird now, aren't they?"

"Yeah," Terry said. "Something's changed."

None of the other Wandering Pod came out for food, and someone else had already fed the Shore Pod. They stopped in the prep area, and got more fish in the cart, then into the bottlenose habitat. He was greeted by the customary, "*Terry, Terry!*" cheer from the dolphins. Several leaped from the water in graceful single or even double somersaults. Despite his mother, Terry smiled.

"Hi, Sunrise Pod!" Terry yelled. They responded with more dolphin-quality applause, several riding their tails out of the water and across the habitat. Dr. Hernandez was sitting on a bench tapping away on a computer. He tossed a wave toward Terry and went back to what he was doing.

"*Terry!*"

He looked toward the voice and saw Ihu. Despite it being months ago, he immediately remembered her asking about Yui and felt his blood run cold. "Hi, Ihu," he said and swallowed.

"*That Yui?*"

"You remember me?" Yui asked, obviously delighted.

Oh, sure she does, Terry thought, here we go.

"*I remember,*" Ihu said. She rolled on her side and looked at Terry, then at Yui, then back to Terry.

Oh, crap.

"*Like Terry?*" Ihu asked.

"Me? Yeah, I like Terry a lot."

"*Terry like you.*"

"Oh, that's good to know." Yui glanced at Terry, who was looking decidedly green.

"*Terry like lot.*"

"Hi, Terry." Dr. Hernandez had walked over while he was distracted. "Ihu, please leave us alone."

Ihu threw her head twice, gave a chirp of assent, and left.

"Thanks," Terry said. "Really, thanks." Hernandez grinned and gave him a little wink.

"What was that all about?" Yui asked.

"The bottlenoses get out in left field from time to time," Dr. Hernandez explained. "They don't entirely understand Human relationships." Yui looked at Terry and blushed. Hernandez had a hint of a grin on his face as he went back to his tablet.

"Hey, is that a slate?" Terry asked. It was a chance to change the subject, and he was genuinely curious.

"Yeah, sure is," Hernandez said.

Terry and Yui crowded in closer and looked. The alien-manufactured computer was about the size of an average Human tablet, but that was where the resemblance ended. They were less than five millimeters thick, while looking like they were made of a sheet of plastic, yet still as tough as bulletproof glass. Each possessed the computing power of a modest supercomputer, operated on a power supply nobody quite understood, and could be infinitely networked. They were so expensive, currently only mercenaries, government, and rich people possessed them.

"Can I see?" Terry asked. The doctor smiled and handed it over. The two young people spent a minute examining the machine. Even though it looked transparent, the material could be opaque selectively, depending on what angle you chose to use it.

"It has a built in Tri-V, too," the doctor explained.

"No way!" Yui exclaimed. Hernandez reached over and tapped the screen, causing a three-dimensional image of a bottlenose dolphin to appear. It swam back and forth a dozen centimeters above the slate, rendered so realistically Terry thought he could touch it.

Three-dimensional images had been around for decades, sort of. The best Earth science had managed was projected into mist, or was done by fooling the eye with slightly offset images in each eye through goggles. The alien Tri-V tech was perfect in every way Terry could see.

"Those a lot more expensive than the regular ones?" Terry asked.

"I don't think so," Hernandez said.

"Hey," Terry said, "where did you get one of these? They're like a couple hundred credits, right?"

The doctor shrugged. "I think this model was 75 credits each. Your father got a deal on a case of 20."

"That's 45 million dollars!" Terry gasped. Dr. Hernandez shrugged. "Dr. Hernandez, where did Dad get the money?"

"You've been gone a long time, Terry. Your father's been doing a lot of, shall we say, publicity work, with the cetaceans?"

"What kind of publicity?"

Dr. Hernandez counted off on his fingers. "There's a half a dozen advertising campaigns being developed, a TV show, and there's the *Shool* thing."

"What's *Shool?*" Yui asked.

"The orca's god," Terry said. "Advertising? TV show? I thought Mom was against all that."

"I don't know what you mean," Hernandez said. "Dr. Clark, Matthew, has been working on this for weeks. The money started rolling in right after the accident. Terrible timing, but I bet Madison would be happy to see how well this is going. The institute's accounts are in great shape, enough to buy us out of NOAA's control. As of two days ago, the institute is privately funded."

Terry was too stunned to reply immediately, so Dr. Hernandez went back to what he'd been doing. Finally Terry remembered something. "What did you say about *Shool?*"

"Some kind of 'outreach,' is how your father describes it. I haven't had time to look into it. If you'll excuse me now, I need to get some of these notes transcribed." He didn't wait for Terry to say anything before walking off.

"Terry?" Yui asked. "What's wrong?"

"I don't know," he said, confused by what Dr. Hernandez had said. It didn't make any sense. "Can you help me feed the Sunrise Pod?"

"*Food, food, food!*" the bottlenoses were chanting.

Terry usually took his time, watching the dolphins race after the live fish. This time, with Yui's help, he rolled the cart over and flipped the dump lever. A small waterfall of fish cascaded into the habitat. The dolphins went nuts, thinking it was a new game, and attacked the panicked fish with zeal.

Terry stared into space, not paying any attention. He turned the cart around and quickly rolled it toward the storage area.

"Terry, are you okay?"

"Fine," he said, remembering she was there. "I have to do something. See you at school Monday?" He gave her a distracted hug, parked the cart, and headed for the elevator, leaving her staring after him in confusion as he went to his father's office.

"Dad?" Terry pushed the office door open, but found the office empty. He was about to leave when he noticed some of the new things there.

A big easel held a meter-tall poster. The image showed an artist's rendering of an underwater town where dolphins were swimming next to scuba-suited people. "Atlantis Reborn" was written in an exciting font across the top. Another easel held a poster of orcas in an underwater classroom, a Tri-V image of a spaceship displayed before them. "Killer School," the poster said.

"You have *got* to be kidding me," Terry said. There was a third easel, its poster covered with a black fabric cloth. He walked toward it, hand outstretched.

"Terry."

He spun around to see his dad standing at the door. Two strangers were with him, a man and a woman; both were laughing at something and wore expensive suits.

"Dad," Terry said, "what the hell is all this?"

"Son," his dad said and quickly moved to stop Terry from reaching the covered easel, "what are you doing in my office?"

"Checking out Killer School," Terry said, filling his words with scorn, "and Atlantis Reborn."

"See," the woman said and laughed. She had a drink in one hand and looked like she'd already had several. "The boy recognizes a good idea."

"Atlantis Reborn?" Terry asked, pointing at the other easel. "What does the Sunrise Pod think of the idea?"

"Who's that?" the man asked.

Terry gawked at his dad in unabashed confusion.

"Mom was okay with this?"

"Terry," his father said, "we'll talk about this later."

"Dad, I—"

His father put a hand behind his back and began leading him toward the adjoining office door. "Give me five minutes, and we'll talk."

"But, Dad…"

His father pushed the door open and none too gently moved Terry though it. "Five minutes, young man." He closed the door behind him. Terry grabbed the handle and found, to his surprise, his dad had locked him in!

The office was nothing more than a place to have a small private meeting. A few chairs, no desk, and some small tables which could be moved around. He plopped into one of the chairs and glowered. As the minutes slid by, he got angrier and angrier. How could he do this without Mom? She hated the idea of exploiting cetaceans. She'd worked with her father to create the institute the way it was. What would you call those ideas he'd seen except theme parks and stupid TV shows?

It was almost 20 minutes before the door unlocked, and his dad came in. He stopped just inside and put his hands on his hips. "What was that all about?" he demanded.

"Dad, Mom would freak out if she saw this!"

"Who do you think helped design those concepts?"

"What?"

"I said, who do you think helped design those concepts?" Terry gawked. "Terrence, your mother loves cetaceans like nobody I've ever known. She also recognizes that what we're doing is expensive and difficult. These projects are ways to obtain funding."

"It doesn't make sense she'd support them," Terry complained, now questioning his own understanding.

"Some of them were a bit much for her, but more's going on here than you understand."

"Then why don't you explain it to me?"

His dad looked at him for a moment. Terry thought he looked conflicted. Then he sighed and sat in the nearest chair. "Terrence, sorry, Terry, do you know how badly injured your mother is?"

"Pretty bad," Terry said timidly.

"Yeah, bad. But do you know how expensive her medical care is?"

"Isn't there insurance?"

"Insurance? Terry, what kind of insurance covers you when you go free diving with 30-ton whales in the arctic?" Terry shook his head. "The answer is none. So I decided to go forward with some of the plans we hadn't finalized yet." He gestured back to his office. "Those ideas are just preliminary. People are so excited by the orcas and bottlenoses, they're practically *throwing* money at us. We're going to use it to do the best we can for them."

"Including buying the institute out from the government?"

"Yeah, including that," his dad said. "They didn't want to pay for the humpback expedition, and they certainly weren't going to pay for your mom's medical bills. Two people died in the submersible, as well. We couldn't simply leave their families with nothing." He sighed. "Do you understand better now?"

"I think so," Terry said, embarrassed. "I'm sorry, Dad."

"It's okay, Son. It looks dodgy, and I should have told you about it last week when much of this went forward. I'll be sure to talk to you in the future. Okay?"

"Yeah, thanks."

"Don't you start middle school on Monday?"

"Yeah, I do," Terry said.

"I can't believe how fast you're growing up," his father said, and he stood to give Terry a hug. Terry smiled a little. "I need to get back to work. Okay now?"

"Sure. Thanks, Dad." Terry left through his father's office. As he was walking down the hall toward the elevator, one of the institute's staff passed with a cart holding buckets of ice and wine.

* * * * *

Chapter Eleven

Molokai Middle School, Molokai, Hawaii, Earth

August 18th, 2036

Terry's first day at Molokai Middle School wasn't all that different from the first day in a new grade in elementary school had been, except there were lots of orientation lectures. Unlike elementary school, now he'd have periods with different teachers on various subjects around the large campus, and those periods rotated daily. Some of the kids seemed intimidated by the variability. Terry wasn't too bothered by it. They were also issued the newest generation tablet computer, which looked sad next to an alien-made slate. Their schedule was loaded into it.

For their first year in middle school, the kids shared the same schedules. He was glad for that, because he got to see all his friends, and of course, Yui. He wasn't happy to be bombarded with questions, though, when they weren't being given lectures or instructions.

"Is it true your mom was eaten by a whale?" "Is she a cyborg now like Dale Edwards said?" "Did you really travel to another planet while you were gone?" were a few of the stupidest questions he got just in the three hours before lunch period. Yui had helped by answering many of the worst well before school, during a one-day pre-term meeting Terry hadn't attended.

"You said there were worse questions?" he asked her, walking between 2nd and 3rd period.

"Oh yeah, lots worse," she said. Terry was a little curious, though not enough to ask.

Lunch in the larger middle school was a more scattered affair. Everyone in elementary ate at the same time; now they were broken into times by grades. You only saw other age groups in the hallways between classes. The 8th graders were quite a bit bigger, in general, so Terry was fine with that. He settled on tacos from the lunch bar and found Yui.

They chatted and ate their lunches. A couple of mutual friends who also played baseball came by. Terry was afraid still more questions were coming about his mother, but instead it was all about school and baseball. Neither of the others were into diving. He'd always been surprised so few people on Molokai were. Plenty of surfers, not many divers.

After lunch was the first class he'd been excited about. Introduction to MST. When he went into the classroom, he almost didn't recognize Doc, or Mr. Abercrombie as it said on his desk plaque. He was dressed in a suit at least as nice as Terry had seen him wearing the previous year when they'd first been told about the MST classes.

The entire class took their seats and became quiet quicker than normal. This was the first ever session of the new class, and everyone was excited to find out what they would learn about being a mercenary.

"Good afternoon, Class," Doc said. "As you'll remember from last year, my name is Mr. Abercrombie. However, you can call me Doc in class, if you want." Smiles broke out around the room. "You'll recall my job is to help guide your instruction in subjects that will help you decide whether you want to become a mercenary or not.

"Institutions around the country, and elsewhere in the Earth Republic, have expressed an interest in adding the VOWs scores to their battery of test data in accepting secondary educational candidates. So even if you don't want to be a merc, and I can tell many of you may not want to be, getting a good score on those tests will be useful to your educational career. Any questions?" A couple of hands went up, and he pointed to a boy.

"Mr. Abercrombie?"

"Doc is fine."

The boy smiled. "Doc? Why wouldn't we want to be a merc?" A dozen others echoed their agreement. "You can get rich!"

"Sure," Doc agreed. "No doubt about it. Can anyone tell me how rich 96 out of the 100 Alpha Contract merc companies got?" Terry raised his hand, and Doc pointed to him. "Terry?"

"They didn't get rich. They're all dead."

"That is exactly correct. You see, it's statistically the most dangerous job in history. Thousands of men and women went offworld 10 years ago; only around 200 came back alive. Even in the four companies that returned, there were still higher than acceptable casualties.

"You all know I was a Navy SEAL?" Many nodded; all were listening. "We were the best-trained, best-equipped, hard-as-nails warriors in the US military; some would argue the whole world. A whole bunch of my fellow SEALs took an infiltration and scouting contract. None of them came back alive. None. So you see, it's not a *safe* job, regardless of the riches involved."

"So now that I've explained, do some of you still want to be mercenaries some day?" A few heads bobbed up and down, though, Terry noticed, without the enthusiasm he'd seen earlier. "Okay, good. We fully expect some of you to decide later it isn't for you, and still more to decide it is. That's your choice. Now, if you'll open the file I sent out this morning, we'll look at some classes coming up, and why they're important."

"That wasn't at all what I expected," Yui said after the class.

"Me either, actually," Terry admitted. "I thought it would be more stuff about fighting."

"Yeah, who needs to know about math to be a merc?" another kid asked on the way by.

"Hey, Terry," Doc said, coming over. "What did you think of my first class?"

"Interesting stuff, Doc," Terry said.

"Hey, Yui, can I talk to Terry for a sec?"

"Sure thing," Yui said. "Cool class."

"Sorry about your mom," Doc said as soon as they were alone. "I thought about coming by, but it didn't seem like the right thing to do."

"Thanks," Terry said. It sounded lame, but it was all he could think of.

"Is she recovering?"

"The doctors are worried about her brain," Terry explained.

"How long was she without oxygen?"

"Nine minutes."

Doc winced. "Yeah, that's bad." He looked sideways, his brows crinkling up. "You know, I have some friends in the service who are working with some stuff."

"What kind of stuff?"

"Stuff that might be able to help your mom."

"Oh! That would be amazing."

"Let me make some calls. In the meantime, why don't you and Yui come by next weekend and we can dive on the *Dixie Maru* again."

* * * * *

Chapter Twelve

Kapukahehu Beach, Molokai, Hawaii, Earth
August 25th, 2036

The afternoon sun was deliciously hot, prompting Terry to remember why he loved Hawaii so much. His tan had only faded a little from his time in New Orleans. It was hot, like Hawaii, but lacked the excellent cool ocean breezes of his home. Lake Pontchartrain gave no relief to those living on its shores in the summer, despite being just off the Gulf of Mexico. Worse, the city seemed to be a hell pit of humidity capable of melting a battleship.

He had a stomach full of fish, rice, and vegetables, and couple of Cokes had washed it all down. He was almost asleep in the perfect afternoon. He lazily watched a line of clouds moving east a few miles away, wondering if they'd get close enough to give them some cool rain. Rain in the summer had been insane in New Orleans.

"I gotta hit the head," Yui said and rolled off the deck where they'd been lying. He glanced over when she got up and noticed how nice it was to look at her. She didn't quite look like the blonde girl Hoa had been so interested in, but she also wasn't a little girl anymore. Suddenly he needed to sit up.

"Hey, Terry," Doc said, stepping through the hatch after Yui had gone down.

"Yeah?!" Terry blurted, afraid Doc had noticed his condition. Even worse, Terry's voice cracked. *Oh, for the love of...*

"I wanted to wait until Yui went below to ask you something. Did your dad mention anything about the email my friends sent?"

"The doctor with that mercenary company? Yeah, he did." Terry was just glad the question wasn't about what he'd been afraid it would be.

"What did he say?"

"He said the last thing mom would want is some mercenary nut job chopping her up."

"Did he?" Doc sat down next to Terry and scratched the stubble on his chin. One of the things Doc seemed to enjoy the most about weekends, besides diving of course, was not shaving. "You know the merc doctor used to work for Johns Hopkins? You know what that is?"

"Yeah," Terry said. "They're really good." Doc nodded. "Then why did dad say that?"

"Has he been acting weird?"

"No." Terry thought for a second. "I mean, all the stuff he's been doing at the institute has kept him busy. He's doing it to afford medical care for mom, too."

"Oh? What's he doing?" Doc listened as Terry talked about all the things he'd seen in his dad's office, including the confrontation.

"Yeah," Doc said, looking down and scratching his chin again. "I saw some of that."

"Is there something I can do? Maybe I can talk to Dad."

"No," Doc said, and made a sweeping motion with his hand. "Let it go. Don't worry about it for now. In fact, don't even mention it to your dad. Okay?"

"But, Doc."

"No, just drop it."

"Okay, sure."

Yui came back up with a couple of Cokes and stopped when she saw the looks on their faces. "What did I miss?"

"Nothing," Doc said. "I'm going to get a beer. You kids enjoy the Cokes; we'll have to head back in another hour." He climbed down to the cabin, leaving them alone.

"Did you guys have a fight?" Yui asked cautiously.

"No," Terry said, taking the offered drink. He looked to see the man was below decks and told her.

"Oh, wow," she said, "I wonder why he got so upset?"

"I'm not sure," Terry said and shook his head. "Adults are so frustrating."

* * * * *

Chapter Thirteen

Monday was a lot of fun at school, especially science. The Hawaii school district had paid to get access to the Galactic Union's version of the internet, called the GalNet, and the science class spent an entire hour wandering through it. The interface they used, something called the Aethernet, had a built in translator. However, it was slow and seemed to struggle on some things. The teacher, Mr. Finch, kept it to astrophysics, making it mainly a lesson about hyperspace.

"I know this stuff is mostly math," Mr. Finch said, pushing his old-fashioned glasses back up onto his nose, "but the basics are pretty fascinating." The class's big display showed a graphic representation of hyperspace, strange lines and calculations surrounding an almost comical- appearing ship. "Ships are shunted into another dimension via the stargates and pulled to their destination via their hyperspace navigational computer. It's apparently very old technology, and little of it is explained. Fascinating."

"Every trip, no matter how far you travel, takes exactly 170 hours. A strange coincidence."

For the last fifteen minutes of the class, students were allowed to use their tablets to access the GalNet. Terry tried looking up scuba diving and found they didn't have a direct analogue. However, he found the respirators Doc, Yui, and he had tested. They'd been developed by a race called the Selroth, who reminded him of an old movie called *Creature from the Black Lagoon*. Yuck!

Yui held up her tablet, showing an alien that looked like a squirrel with a huge pistol; a Flatar. "Cute!" she said. Terry had his doubts an alien with a huge gun would like to be called cute. He looked it up himself. Flatar—a mercenary race usually partnered with Tortantula. Looking up the latter, he gasped. A wasp crossed with a spider. *Holy crap!* He almost held it up for Yui to see, just for the shock factor, then decided against it.

The rest of the day went by without anything nearly as interesting. He said goodbye to Yui and fired his bike up, heading toward the inter-island shuttle. His dad had given him a pass just after he got back, and he regularly rode the high-speed boat to Honolulu to visit his mom. He hadn't gone that weekend because he'd gone diving, and now he felt guilty.

He was lucky; the boat was just finishing loading. He swiped the pass and walked his bike onboard. By the time he'd gotten a seat, the boat was leaving the harbor and already climbing onto its hydrofoils.

"We'll arrive in Honolulu in 15 minutes," the announcer said.

Just enough time, Terry thought, and went to the onboard snack bar. Back in his seat, he munched the obligatory hotdog and Coke as the ocean raced past at 120 kph.

Honolulu had all kinds of ridiculous rules against riding powered bicycles like his on the sidewalks, and even more rules against riding them on the roads. What they didn't have was a way of stopping him. He always grinned as he zipped along the sidewalk, ignoring the annoyed pedestrians and the occasional yell from a cop. He got to

Queen's Medical Center 10 minutes after the boat docked, less than half an hour after leaving school.

"Personal record," he said as he locked the bike into a space on the rack outside the main entrance. A woman walking past looked askance at him, and he smiled back, which didn't help. Bike secured, he swung his backpack off the bike frame onto his shoulder and headed inside.

The receptionist barely looked up when he walked past. When he got to the elevator, he swiped the pass they'd given him, giving him access to the 29th floor, where the coma-care ward was, and where his mom had been transferred after she'd been pronounced stable.

When the doors opened, he immediately noticed a commotion by the nurse's station. An orderly looked up at him and back to the tumult. Terry wasn't sure he'd seen the man before. Figuring it didn't have anything to do with him, he walked to the "Restricted Access" door and used the pass again. It slid aside with a slight buzz, and he walked in.

Terry took out his tablet and began calling up saved images. He'd kept captures of the aliens they'd seen, along with a few other things like mask-camera footage from their last dive. He planned to talk about it with his mom. He also had a book he'd been reading on the tablet as well. He was busy scrolling through pictures when he pushed the door open to her room, so he didn't see her immediately.

"Terry?"

His tablet and backpack clattered to the floor when he looked up and saw her sitting up in bed looking at him.

"Mom?!" he gasped.

"Hi, Baby."

Terry nearly launched himself into her arms, and once again found himself crying. She wrapped him in the most awesome hug he could ever remember having.

"Hey, you're not supposed to be in here!" someone snapped from the door.

"This is my son," his mom said. "He most certainly belongs in here."

"I'm sorry, Mrs. Clark," the man, a doctor, said. "I meant we're still evaluating your suddenly changed status."

Terry pulled back and looked at her. The bandages that used to cover her head were gone, and he could see a little scar just above her right eye where they'd operated a week ago. It looked completely healed. How was that even possible?

"I'm fine enough to visit my boy while you do your tests," she said.

"What happened?" Terry wondered. "The doctors were talking about surgery to maybe relieve pressure, or something?"

"Nobody knows," she said. "I woke up this morning like any other morning. I feel great!"

"Do you remember the accident?"

She squinted and made a face. "Sort of. I know we were trying to talk to that big humpback bull when Matthew played something he'd recorded, and the whale…"

"It hit the submarine," Terry said.

She put a hand to her mouth. "Are the crew okay? What about your father?"

"Dad's fine," he said. "The crew were killed."

"Oh, my God," she said. "That's horrible." She looked outside at the sunny Honolulu afternoon. "How long have I been here? What's the date?"

"You were hurt August 2nd," he said. "Today's the 23rd."

"I've been in here three weeks?" He nodded. "Where's your dad?" She looked past him at the doctor.

"We tried calling him at your work number. They said he was in Seattle. Something about a television commercial?"

His mom looked at the doctor, uncomprehending. "A commercial? For the institute?" The man shrugged. "I need to figure out what's going on. Where's my computer?"

"Your husband has all your personal goods."

"Damnit," she said.

"Here, Mom," Terry said, and handed her his tablet.

She took the computer and looked at it. "Yeah, this should work." She signed into the internet and logged into the institute's server. Two passwords later, she was into her personal account and reading emails, as well as institute messages. Over the next few minutes, her expression went from curious, to confused, then straight into anger.

Uh, oh, Terry thought.

* * * * *

Chapter Fourteen

PCRI, Molokai, Hawaii, Earth
August 29th, 2036

Terry met the cab at the curb in front of the institute. A robotic version, it rolled up and opened the door. It took his mother a few extra seconds to get out, leaning on the cane they'd given her at the hospital.

"Everyone here, Son?" she asked.

"Yes, Mom."

She stopped next to him as the cab pulled away and looked at him. "I know you can't be happy about this." He shrugged. "Your dad—"

"I know," he said. "You don't have to go into it."

She sighed and said, "It's impossible to be sure how this will play out."

"I know that, too," he said. Terry followed her up to the office floor and the main meeting room.

All the doctors of the PCRI were there. As soon as she opened the door, a round of applause greeted her. She smiled sadly and held up a hand.

"Welcome back, Madison," Dr. Patel said.

"Your recovery was amazing," Dr. Jaehnig said.

She looked at Terry before answering. "I think there was outside help, but it really doesn't matter right now." She walked slowly with the cane over to one of the easels, which had been moved from Terry's father's office. She limped over to the most spectacular, "Killer School." She lifted it off the easel, examining the art, then snorted and dropped it to the floor.

"I had nothing to do with any of this and never would," she said. "All this…" She reached out and knocked the "Atlantis Reborn" poster off its easel. "All this *exploitation*. I'm disappointed you all went along with it."

The circle of scientists gawked in horrified shock. Several looked at each other, while some wouldn't meet her gaze. Terry sat in a chair by the door and felt horrible. Horrible that his father had lied to him. Horrible that he'd told his mother about the lies. Finally, horrible that he was in the middle of what looked to be the end of his life as it was.

"Madison?"

"Yes, Sanjay?"

"Did Matthew arrange your injury?"

The room fell deathly silent, except for the sound of Terry gasping. His mother turned and seemed to remember he was sitting there. "Terry, can you go to our apartment and wait?"

He didn't want to, though at the same time, he didn't want to be there. He got up and left without saying a word. Their apartment was empty, of course, and Terry looked out a south-facing window. A rain storm was slowly moving in. On the other end of the apartment, a window overlooked the bottlenose habitat. It only took a second to realize they weren't all there.

Terry got off the elevator and entered the bottlenose habitat. For a change, he wasn't greeted by the customary calls of his name. A female swam over and looked up at him.

"Hula, is that you?"

"*I Hula,*" the bottlenose said.

"Some of the Sunrise Pod are gone."

"*Yes. Sad. Not with pod.*"

"What happened?" he asked.

"*Warden take. Go big shore.*"

Dad took them with him to Seattle, Terry realized. What the heck is he doing with several bottlenoses in Seattle? He found his answers a few minutes later.

Bored and worried about what was happening in the meeting room, Terry took his computer and opened a browser window. He'd been thinking about seeing if he could access the GalNet from home on the issued machine. The teachers said they could, though their access was limited to a certain number of users at the same time. He'd just logged on when his phone beeped for attention. It was Yui.

"Terry!" she said when he answered, obviously excited.

"Hey, what's up?"

"Have you seen the news?"

"News?" He wondered what he would have cared about on the news. "What news?"

"Terry, your dad; he was arrested in Seattle."

Terry didn't even say goodbye, he just hung up and quickly pulled up a regular browser. It only took a few seconds to find the story. "Hawaiian Marine Biologist Arrested on Charges of Animal Cruelty and Fraud."

He quickly read the article. Inset within the story was a short video from a stringer showing his father being walked out of a hotel in handcuffs. Being walked out along with him were the two people Terry had seen with him just the other day. "Dr. Matthew Clark, co-director of the PCRI in Molokai, Hawaii, was arrested and charged today on multiple charges of animal cruelty and conspiracy to defraud investors.

"Dr. Clark was in Seattle, meeting with a large group of potential investors. They were being pitched a theme park, which would operate in the open ocean and highlighted Clark's modified dolphins and killer whales." The article hypertexted to another article on what the institute had been doing with the cetaceans. "However, Dr. Clark brought four of the modified animals with him, putting on a display at the Seattle Aquarium. Dr. Maia Taumata happened to be in town and attended the presentation, which was open to the public.

"Dr. Taumata, from Auckland, is head of the Earth Republic Animal Rights Commission. One of their more recent tasks has been to ensure that alien flora and fauna isn't accidentally introduced to Earth. However, they also see to it that native life isn't exploited illegally by aliens. Upon investigating one of the dolphins in Dr. Clark's care, she determined that the animal had undergone implantation of a brain augmenting apparatus known in the Galactic Union as a *pinplant*, and not a simple translator, as Dr. Clark had professed.

"The animals were taken into protective custody, and Dr. Clark and two unnamed associates were arrested. We contacted the PCRI this morning and were surprised to talk to Dr. Madison Clark, Dr. Matthew Clark's wife. She was injured on an expedition several weeks ago and was purported to be in a coma.

"Dr. Madison Clark provided us with a prepared statement. 'The PCRI is not in the business of developing attractions of any kind. To the contrary, our mission statement is to provide rehabilitation for cetaceans who have themselves been the unfortunate victims of such misguided attempts to profit off their interesting nature. My husband's endeavors were undertaken without my knowledge, and as such, the approval of the PCRI's Board of Directors. We are severing all dealings with Dr. Matthew Clark forthwith.' Considering the statement came from his wife, it was very strongly worded.

"Dr. Taumata further stated that investigators would be arriving in Hawaii in the next week to discuss the matter with Dr. Madison Clark, and decide on a course of action going forward."

"I wonder if I'm going to jail, too," Terry wondered aloud in the empty apartment.

Hours later, his mother limped in. She took one look at her son and knew he'd found out.

"You had Dad arrested?"

"No, Terry, your dad did that to himself. We fired him."

"But why did they arrest him?" he asked.

"Well, the charges of fraud are a direct result of making deals on behalf of the institute, which he was not legally allowed to do. He made promises, signed contracts, and took money."

"To help you," Terry said, afraid he'd cry again, and furious at himself for it.

"No, Terry." She limped over and sat on the couch next to him. "I know your dad told you insurance wouldn't cover what we were doing, but that was just another lie. No, it didn't cover all my treatments, or the payouts to the dead crew of the sub, but it did cover most of it. Our backers and the government would have helped with the rest."

"Then why did he do it?"

"I'm afraid we're going to have to ask him that ourselves." She shrugged. "I want to think it's just a misguided attempt at helping the cetaceans."

"You want to, but you don't think that."

She shook her head no. "I'm afraid there's a lot of money involved. A lot of it went right into his personal account."

"How much?"

"Several million dollars. Maybe as much as $50 million."

"Oh," Terry said. "What Dr. Patel said in the meeting room?" His lip quivered a little. "Do you think dad hurt you on purpose?"

"No," she said, "it was just a horrible accident."

"An accident he took advantage of." His mother looked down. She reached out to put a hand on his arm, but Terry pulled away and walked to his room. She didn't try to follow, and he closed the door behind him. He dropped into a chair and stared at the other wall of his room. His phone rang, and he ignored it. Eventually, he lost the battle against his emotions.

* * * * *

Chapter Fifteen

PCRI, Molokai, Hawaii, Earth
September 11th, 2036

Terry got the chance to meet Dr. Maia Taumata briefly when she showed up with several Molokai police officers, a pair of Republic Marshalls, and some paperwork demanding she be allowed to inspect the cetaceans. Accompanying her were a pair of marine biologists and an alien who looked to Terry like a bipedal Pteranodon he'd read about a year before while studying dinosaurs. Only this one was a specialist in the pinplants the article talked about.

"Who are you?" Dr. Taumata asked when she saw him feeding the Wandering Pod. "A little young for an employee." She was even shorter than she'd appeared in the internet article, and she had a funny tattoo on her lower lip.

"Terry Clark."

"A relation to the doctors Clark, then?"

"Yes, ma'am, I'm their son."

She'd nodded and gone about her business. They closed the institute to the public and proceeded to question the staff and then the cetaceans themselves. A week after the incident in Seattle, the four bottlenoses his father had taken to Seattle were flown home in a government flyer. Dr. Taumata had been worried about the bottlenoses' seemingly depressed states until the four came back, at which point the Sunrise Pod instantly returned to their formerly jubilant selves.

The morning of the 11th, Terry was asked to a meeting room, where he again met with Dr. Taumata. She had the alien he'd since found out was a Sidar with her, and one of the marine biologists. Since he was a minor, his mother was there as well.

"Now, Terry, you don't have to say a thing if you don't want to."

"You don't want me to lie, do you?"

"No, we'll leave the lying to your father." Terry looked askance, and she shook her head. "I'm sorry, I didn't mean that. Just answer any questions they ask, unless it makes you feel uncomfortable. Okay?"

"Okay."

"Hi, Terry," Dr. Taumata said, rising to shake his hand. "Do you remember me?"

"Yes, of course."

"Good. This is Dr. Trudeau, a marine biologist like your parents." He shook the man's hand. "And this is Klaak; he's a member of the Sidar race, a specialist in cybernetics and the devices known as pinplants. Do you know what those are?" Terry nodded.

"Before we begin, I need to establish something," his mom said as she rose from the chair she'd been sitting in before Terry came in. "Terry is a minor and my child. He's under no obligation to testify and is doing so on his own initiative, with my approval. If either of us don't wish him to answer a question, he won't."

"Are you attempting to shield him from this inquiry, Dr. Clark?" the man named Trudeau asked. Terry had to listen carefully; his accent was fairly thick. He guessed by the sound and his name that he was French.

"I'm attempting to shield him from any culpability, because he's too young to be either responsible, or to fully understand his legal jeopardy."

"This is unsettling," Trudeau said.

"What, that I would defend my child?" Terry knew his mom was getting mad. He'd seen it more than enough times. She also seemed quicker to anger after her recovery.

"I don't think we need to turn this into a confrontation," Dr. Taumata said in a calming voice. She looked at Terry. "All the cetaceans hold a very high opinion of you, young man."

"I like them," Terry said. "I think they like me."

"They do."

"Of course they do," Trudeau said. "He feeds them."

"Not all that often," his mom said, and passed a file to the argumentative man. Terry recognized a checkout form from the food preparation area. "As you'll see, over the last two years, Terry has fed them less than 50 times out of a total of 1,533 feedings. Three percent isn't even statistically significant. They like him because of their own feelings."

"Feelings," Trudeau said, and snorted. "Just a sense of the familiar."

"Did you notice the change in the dolphins' behavior when their missing pod mates returned?" Taumata asked Trudeau. "I understand this sort of behavior is common among all cetaceans."

"What is your specialty within marine biology?" his mother asked the man.

"Mollusks are my specialty," Trudeau said. Terry's mom and Taumata exchanged looks, and Trudeau's expression darkened.

"I see," his mom said, and Terry suppressed a smile.

"Terry," Taumata said, "can you tell me your impression of the cetaceans before and after their augmentation?"

"You mean besides their ability to speak English?" She nodded. "Well, they've become much easier to work with, of course. I could only tell personalities by actions before, but now I can tell they all speak differently, as well. The Wanderer and the Shore pods of orcas are also much more different than I could tell by just watching them before."

"Can you elaborate?" Taumata asked.

"Sure," Terry said and glanced at his mom. She nodded for him to go ahead. "The two pods are different kinds of orcas. I knew this already, but now I can tell they think differently, too."

"How so?"

"Well, they both know about *Shool*, but they think about it differently."

"There is this fantastical *Shool merde*," Trudeau said.

"I'll ask you to watch your language," his mother said.

Terry had no idea what *merde* meant. Now he knew it wasn't a good word. Trudeau's face turned slightly red, but he nodded.

"Do you believe it's a religion with them?" Taumata asked.

"Yup," Terry said. "They talk about it a lot, but the Shore Pod are much bigger into it. They act more like it's God. You know, everywhere? The Wandering Pod thinks of *Shool* like it's a thing, deep down under the water."

"Klaak, can you elaborate?" Taumata said. "Is this religion possibly a side effect of the implants?"

The Sidar's elongated head turned so one eye could fix Terry in its black-on-black gaze before he spoke. "An improperly administered pinplant could have unforeseen complications. As I've previously stated, these pinplants are a simple model designed for the Selroth. I've provided basic neural details on the race, and confirmed they are remarkably like your primitive cetaceans. I've also examined the simple scans of the...*dolphins?*"

"Dolphins," Taumata corrected. "Pacific bottlenose dolphins."

"Yes, sorry, *dolphins*. The scans indicated good nanite penetration of their cerebellum and properly functioning interfaces. Coprocessing is in place, and the four I examined appear to have adapted to them remarkably well, considering they're considered non-sentient by Union index standards. I haven't examined the orcas yet, but if the implants were handled with the same skill on them as they were on the dolphins, I don't anticipate a problem. I've never observed a bad implant causing any sort of delusional behavior. Psychosis or neural failure, yes. But not making up anything as complicated as a religion."

"As I've already shown you," his mom said, "they mentioned *Shool* before any of them had the implant, just using an external translator. We'd assumed it might be a problem with the improvised matrix, but after the implants, the terminology remained and was greatly expanded."

"Mom," Terry said. She glanced at him. "I don't understand all this. What is Klaak saying about the translators?"

"They aren't translators," she explained.

"Indeed not," Klaak agreed. "In the Galactic Union, they're called pinplants. These are used to interface with computers, store data, and augment learning. They're nearly ubiquitous among many established races." He turned his head slightly, reached up with a wing which sported a vestigial wing membrane, and touched the side of his head. Terry could see a little circuit board there. It had something plugged into it and a tiny yellow light.

"Your father," his mom said and sighed. "He bought the implants without doing any research. They were old technology."

"Yes," Klaak agreed. "Those pinplants are extremely old and not used anymore. The Selroth haven't used them for 500 years."

"So they were broken?" Terry asked.

"No," Klaak said, shaking his huge head slightly from side to side. "Just old. They are medical class devices, and if the seals are properly maintained, they will be useable for thousands of years. Based on the packaging I've examined, the ones used were in perfect condition. We guess an unscrupulous free trader took advantage of your race's ignorance to get rid of some old inventory."

"That sucks," Terry said. "Isn't it against the law in the Union to do that?"

The Sidar made a coughing sound, his translator turned into a "Ha ha ha" sound. "Law? You Humans have much to learn about the Galactic Union."

"The Union takes 'caveat emptor' to an entirely new level," his mom said. Terry looked at her in confusion. "That's Latin for 'buyer beware.'"

"Oh," Terry said.

They asked a few more questions about care for the cetaceans and how they were looked after when guests came in. Had any of them been harmed by an interaction with a visitor? Had any of the cetaceans harmed a visitor?

"No, none of that," Terry told them.

"Do you think they're stable?" Dr. Taumata asked. Trudeau rolled his eyes dramatically.

"I'm sorry?" Terry asked.

"She means are they acting normally," his mom said.

"Like normal dolphins and orcas?" Terry asked. Dr. Taumata nodded. "No, not really."

"See," Dr. Trudeau crowed.

"Wait," Terry said. "They don't act like other dolphins and orcas because others can't talk! How *could* they be normal? They act fine, just more like people."

"Outrageous," Trudeau said. "The opinion of a child."

"Still worth listening to," Dr. Taumata said. "Thank you, Terry, for answering our questions. You can go."

"Can I ask a question?"

The two Human doctors looked at each other, but Taumata answered before Trudeau could say anything to the contrary. "I think that's the least we can do, young man." Trudeau sighed and sat back in his chair.

"What's going to happen to them? The whales and dolphins?"

"The Earth Republic High Court will have to make that decision," Dr. Taumata said. "I believe, ideally, removal of the implants would be the ethical thing to do."

"They're unlikely to survive the procedure," Klaak said, then shrugged. Terry was surprised to see a talking dinosaur shrugging. "I'm a little surprised they worked at all. Probably because they're basic pinplants."

"You mean they'll die trying to take them out?" He looked at Dr. Taumata in horror.

"That's what Klaak has explained." She looked at his mom. "I'm afraid euthanasia is not out of the question, considering what the animals have been put through."

"They're not animals," Terry said defiantly. "They're people."

Dr. Taumata looked at him with a slightly sad expression. "I'm afraid that isn't what the law says."

"Well, then the law is *wrong*," Terry said, and left. Later his mom came back into their apartment looking tired. "I'm sorry if I was rude," he said.

She smiled and limped over to give him a hug. "You have no reason to apologize, and you weren't rude. I think they were."

"Would they really kill them because of the implants?"

"I don't know," she said. "I just don't know."

"I'll do anything to keep that from happening," Terry said. "Anything."

"Thanks, Son," she said, and gave him another hug.

* * * * *

Chapter Sixteen

Terry ate slowly, watching his mother across the table. The turkey had been bought at a local deli, as was the entire meal. She looked tired—more tired than he'd seen her since she'd returned home from the hospital. Doc was sitting next to him, quietly eating, looking out of place.

"Thanks again for inviting me, Terry," he said. "And you, Mrs. Clark, for having me."

Terry glanced at his mom when Doc called her Ms. Clark. She glanced up sharply, then nodded and said he was welcome. It wasn't public knowledge that she'd both refused to put up bail money for Dr. Matthew Clark and also filed for divorce more than a month ago. All anyone in town knew was that Terry's father was still in Seattle, and still in jail.

Yui though, of course, knew it all. He'd also invited her to Thanksgiving dinner. She had to stay with her family, though she'd wanted to go with Terry. Especially after he'd told her about the divorce.

Later, after dinner, they sat in the living room overlooking the cetaceans' tanks. Doc and Terry's mom were drinking wine, and Terry had hot chocolate. Quiet music was playing, and for some reason,

Terry felt it was awkward, and he didn't know why. It turned out he wasn't the only one, because his mom suddenly said something.

"I never thanked you," she said to Doc.

"For what?"

"You've been a real friend to Terry. He's had so much fun learning to dive; it's all he talks about."

Doc smiled and nodded. "Yui and he are great kids. When I caught them bumming around the docks, I felt like I was rescuing a couple of wayward kittens."

His mother slowly turned to skewer Terry with a jaundiced stare. Terry smiled and looked down at his hot chocolate. "Bumming around the docks, eh?"

"We were looking around, you know?"

"I'm sure," his mother said, then smiled. She chuckled, and Terry let his breath out.

"Mrs. Clark?" Doc started.

"Madison is fine," she said.

Doc smiled and continued, "I don't want to spoil the mood, but can you tell me how the court case is going?" Her mouth thinned, and she looked at Terry.

"He means the one to take the cetaceans away," Terry said quickly.

"Oh, right," she said, casting another glance at her son. "Well, after the gag order was put in place, the press has been hounding us all pretty badly."

"I'm sure," Doc said, "I had one show up at school right before the break. Caught him trying to sneak into the cafeteria. Principal Landau wanted to press charges."

"We've moved through several motions, and right now both sides are in a discovery phase. I'm not a lawyer, but it involves a lot of questions. The high court hasn't tried many cases, and they're hesitant to create precedent. There are animal rights groups trying to get the cetaceans, all cetaceans, declared sentient beings with full rights under the Earth Republic Bill of Rights. The world FDA body is trying to get involved, suggesting the pinplants are unlicensed medical devices. Luckily the court dismissed their claim, because the cetaceans aren't 'people' by definition."

"Unless the animal rights groups win," Doc added.

"Yes, there is that. One of the problems we have now is that the religious nutjobs have gotten involved."

"The big churches? Like the Pope, and stuff?"

"No, thankfully. The Vatican has stayed out of it so far. There've been a couple edicts from the usual middle eastern sources, of course. I never thought I'd be glad Iran wasn't around anymore."

Doc grunted and nodded. He knew only too well.

"The problem with the religious types is this Faith of the Abyss," she said.

"The ones based on the orcas' god, Shool?" Terry asked.

"Yeah, them. They went from loons to well-funded loons almost overnight."

Terry remembered the birth of that—the people who'd show up every day to listen to Kray give a sermon on the god of the deep, how it had created the world, starting in the oceans, and gone on from there. "But Kray talks about Shool being a unifier," Terry complained. "How Shool wants all creatures on Earth to live together in peace."

"The Faith of the Abyss thinks cracking some skulls might speed things along. They've been protesting outside the courthouse in Sau Paulo, and here most days." She looked outside toward the ocean, almost like she expected to see them rappelling down the side of the institute.

"What about your husband?"

She glanced at Terry again, who was stirring his now-cold hot chocolate into a froth. "He's still in jail in Seattle. The feds have custody, and those charges are separate."

Doc looked at her for a long moment, glanced at Terry, then the empty chair where Terry's father would have sat. After a second, he nodded and finished his glass of wine.

"Well, it's been great, Madison," he said.

"You're welcome to stay," Madison said. "Plenty of wine."

"It's a bit of a drive back to *Krispin*," he said. She looked confused. "My boat."

"Oh," she said. "You live on it?"

"We're good friends," he said and winked. "It looks like it might rain, too." He got up, and she escorted him to the door. He took her hand and gently shook it. "Thanks for dinner."

"You're welcome in our home anytime," she said.

"See you at school after the break," he said to Terry.

"No time for a dive?"

"Other work," he said. "Sorry." With a wave, he was out of the apartment and heading for the elevator.

Terry turned to his mom as soon as the elevator door closed. "Mom, why couldn't you at least get dad out of jail?"

"His problems are his own."

"It's Thanksgiving, Mom."

"Yes, I noticed." She limped back and poured herself another glass of wine.

Terry made a face, but decided not to continue that line of conversation. He was learning, it seemed. "How long do you think before the court rules?"

"The lawyers say it could be as long as a year, or as little as two months. The high court is too new; there's no real precedent, as I said earlier. Our bigger problem is money."

"We still have people paying to talk to the bottlenoses and orcas," he said. She nodded. Terry had been instrumental in getting her to allow the encounters. The interest was many times higher even than when his father had charged for encounters. However, Terry had argued the chances for the cetaceans to meet and talk with people was good for them, and they'd agreed when Madison had asked them.

Eventually Dr. Hernandez and Dr. Patel had also asked her to allow the face-to-face meetings to continue, and for the institute to charge a modest amount for it. She contacted the government representatives through her lawyer and explained it to them. Dr. Taumata herself called and said it was permissible, as long as the time and number of visitors were kept within reason, so they'd begun again. Three days a week—on Monday, Wednesday, and Friday—for 2 hours. There were lines every day, rain or shine.

The bottlenoses were, of course, thrilled. The orcas seemed to enjoy company as well, the Wandering Pod more so than the Shore Pod. Terry decided to look for a chance to find out why. He got a chance the next day.

* * *

The institute was empty the day after Thanksgiving. Most of the staff were at home, so naturally Terry took the chance to feed on all three groups. It was the ideal opportunity to catch some private time with the orcas. There was only a single government intermediary on site, and he stayed in the security office, playing with his computer.

Nobody gave Terry a second look when he slipped back into the orca encounter area and spotted one of them lazily floating on the surface. It was a female named Moloko, whom he'd seldom spoken to. She had bright white markings that were probably the reason for her name, which meant milk in Russian. He gently slapped the surface, and she looked up at him with a huge eye.

"*What want?*"

"How come your pod is so sad?" Terry asked.

"*People want learn Shool.*"

"What people?" Terry asked.

"*People before.*"

"Before all the changes?"

"*Yes. Before. Now no come.*"

Terry understood now. The attendants who took admission now had digital facial recognition and were instructed to deny entry to a list of people who were members of the Faith of the Abyss, or just FA, as they were often referred to in the press. The group had held a protest outside the institute only the day before Thanksgiving.

"They were bad people," Terry tried to explain.

"*How bad?*"

That's not an easy one to explain, Terry thought.

"*Kray say they want learn Shool.*" Another orca on the surface nearby was looking at him. It was the male named Byk. "*Learn Shool good.*"

"They're hurting people," Terry said.

Kray surfaced right in front of Terry, making him gasp in surprise. Being only centimeters from a five-ton apex predator was disconcerting, even knowing the orcas had never treated man as prey. "*Why they hurt?*" Kray asked.

"They're desperate to get in here," Terry told him. "To see you."

The massive orca shook his head up and down. "*They hurt see me?*"

"Yes," Terry said. He'd been warned more than once about being *too* truthful with the cetaceans, but they weren't naturally schooled in subterfuge, or even misdirection. He wasn't entirely certain they didn't know how to lie. Dr. Orsage was constantly studying that aspect of their personality.

"*We no want see them,*" Kray said. "*Not see is good.*"

"We agree," Terry said.

"*Protect moms,*" Kray said.

"Moms?" Terry wondered aloud. "My mom isn't in any danger."

"*Not you mom, our soon mom.*"

Terry blinked and looked at the massive orca who slipped part of the way underwater, his pectoral fin slapping the water lazily. *Soon mom*, he thought. "Do you mean yours is pregnant?"

"*I can no be mom,*" Kray said, his translated words conveying a sense of amusement.

Terry felt his cheeks grow hot. "I know you can't get pregnant," Terry said. "Are one of the girls pregnant?"

"*I be mom,*" Moloko said.

"Oh, shit," Terry said. He got up and ran to the elevator.

* * *

"Nobody can know about this," his mom said. Within minutes of his running into her office with the news, she'd called all the senior staff to tell them. Terry stood aside, surprisingly not chased out of the office, and listened as the adults discussed what to do.

"I think it gives weight to the statement of their natural innocence in this," Dr. Patel said. "If we told the investigators—"

"If we told them, they might take it the wrong way," she cut the man off. "We can't predict what they would say or do."

More of the doctors nodded, then shook their heads. Terry knew how persuasive his mom could be. She got up and limped over to the window overlooking the orca tanks. Several were swimming in lazy circles around a sunbeam shining in through one of the many skylights.

"Have all the cetaceans tested," she said, "ASAP."

"I'll get right on it," Dr. Jaehnig said.

"Assuming none of the others are pregnant, I want them all on pregnancy suppressants."

"Do you think that's necessary?" Dr. Orsage asked.

"What do you think would be the results of a slew of births with their...*altered* personalities?"

"You know I have no clue," the woman replied.

"All the more reason to put the brakes on this," she replied and then looked at them. "I'd like to know why nobody witnessed the mating, and how long ago it was."

"I can answer that," Dr. Hernandez said. She looked a little surprised that the expert on their bottlenose dolphins was the one to talk. She nodded for him to proceed. "When I got your message, I was within earshot of the bottlenoses, who heard your call. They all knew about it."

"How?" she wondered.

"I don't know, but they also knew when the pregnancy happened. They gave me a number of days, so on my way down I ran the recordings back." He handed his slate to her, and she looked at the images. Despite the machine being largely transparent, Terry couldn't see anything on it. "The date they gave was precise."

"They're talking to each other somehow," she said.

"Not possible," Dr. Patel said. "They're never closer than having several meters of concrete between them. The two orca pods, possibly. But the orcas and bottlenoses? Impossible."

"Regardless," his mom said, looking down at the display, "this is interesting. Carry out the tests, and we'll go from there."

After a minute, they all left the office. Only then did she realize Terry was still there. "You've been here the whole time?" He gave a cockeyed smile and she shook her head before smiling herself. "Thank you for bringing me the information."

"What was I supposed to, keep it quiet?"

"Definitely not," she said and limped over to him. "You know the world government has been talking about convening a tribunal?" Terry nodded. "That doesn't mean anything will happen soon, but it does mean they're going to begin deliberating on what should be done."

"Are we going to testify, like in court?"

"Only if there's a trial," she said. "The meetings we had with Dr. Taumata were our only chance to talk it out. We're past that now." She sighed, moving over to a chair and slowly lowering herself into it. "The world court doesn't know what they're doing, so this will take time. In the meantime, we'll just do what we can, and hope."

That night at dinner, his mom picked up her phone when a message came in. "What's up?" Terry asked.

"Dr. Jaehnig has the data on the test." Terry put his fork down and listened. "Only the female Resident, Moloko, is pregnant. None of the other orcas or any of the bottlenoses are."

"Is that good?"

"Yes," she said. "They're going over all the camera footage, though, to see how much loving has been going on." Terry laughed, and she smiled at him. "Based on the date from our recordings, Moloko is 10 months pregnant. She'll be due between June and August."

Terry grinned. A baby orca would be cool. At least it was something to look forward to in the coming months, and would take his mind off of his parents' impending divorce. They ate the rest of their meal in silence, both wrapped in their own thoughts.

* * * * *

Part II

Exodus

Chapter One

Molokai Middle School, Molokai Hawaii, Earth
May 31st, 2037

The entire class looked up in alarm as a rattle rolled through Molokai Middle School. Several students yipped in surprise, and one boy gave a little scream. In the following silence, his friends gave the kid a good ribbing.

Terry listened and waited with the practice of a long-time resident of the Hawaiian Islands. Earthquakes were sometimes a daily occurrence. A single shudder shock, though? Unusual. It reminded him a little of the brief activity period from Wailau—or the East Molokai Volcano, as the tourists called it—five years ago. Only in that case, it was a series of intense shocks, not just one.

"Everything looks fine," the teacher said, holding up her hands, "probably just an earthquake." The kids who were native or long term residents all looked at each other skeptically, probably thinking the same thing as Terry.

An hour later at lunch, Terry realized a few kids were missing from his class. His school wasn't large—less than 50 seniors in all—but he wouldn't have noticed a few missing if someone else hadn't mentioned it as he was passing.

"Did you see Katrina Long was pulled out?" someone said.

"Yeah, Colin, too," another said.

"Earthquake fever," Yui said with a smirk as they found their customary table. The friends had only just started to eat when they felt the next tremor. This time Terry noted a long, low reverberation following the shock. Unlike an earthquake, this one he *heard* instead of felt through his feet. *What the hell?* he wondered. It was almost like an explosion, only it went on for several seconds before trailing off.

The second one was followed by several more over the course of his lunch hour. They seemed almost regular. He'd been trying to have a conversation with Yui about a dive they'd been talking about. Since it was the last day of school, Doc had offered to take them on a celebratory dive the next day. But every time they got into the conversation again, there was another shock and rumble. He looked up and saw several of the teachers by the exit, talking. Now he knew something was up.

"Yo, Terry!" Ben Stevenson called from the next table over.

"What's up?" Terry asked. Ben held up his tablet and waved for Terry to come over. Terry glanced in the direction of the teachers. Using computers during school was against the rules, even during lunch. The adults were in a huddle of conversation, and they had a tablet, as well. He glanced at Yui, who nodded, and the two slipped over next to their friend.

"Check this out," Ben said and clicked on the screen, bringing up the web page for a local television station.

"This video was shot live by an observer and sent to us at WFFV," a man's voice said. There was a moment of poor camera control, typical of someone shooting with their phone. The view jerked around before suddenly focusing on an unmistakable shot of the PCRI. Terry recognized it instantly; the view was shot from the road above and behind the institute.

For a few seconds he thought there'd been another protest by the Faith of the Abyss, which happened almost every day. Immediately, his fear evolved to thinking it was a bomb attack or something like that. When the camera swung around to show the main road up to the institute, it was blocked by a sea of flashing emergency lights. *Oh, no*, he thought.

"What's going on?" Yui asked.

"Wait for it," Ben said. A second later, a ship plummeted out of the sky, its engines flashing like stars as they fired. It slowed steadily as it descended. As it slowed to a stop, a thunderous *Booom* rolled across the person filming the events, and the recording jerked all over the place again.

"We're hearing sonic booms!" said another kid, who was watching the video over their shoulders.

"How do you know?" another kid asked. They'd apparently drawn a crowd.

"My brother's a merc," the kid said. "His outfit's in Houston, and he says ships make those sounds when they come down from orbit."

Terry watched the scene intently, trying to will the person filming to refocus on the action. He was about to yell at the tablet when it finally refocused, and he watched a huge ship settle down into the upper parking lot, the one used by staff. Even before the ship began to lower toward the ground, he could see the concrete was blasted black. It hadn't been the first ship to land.

"Terry Clark!"

He looked up at the authoritative voice. Doc, Mr. Abercrombie at school, was standing with the teachers, waving him over. He immediately walked over to him. Everyone around was watching him. "Yes, Mr. Abercrombie?" He was terrified.

"Your mother said to take you to the institute immediately," he said.

"What's going on?"

Terry hadn't noticed Yui had followed him over. "I don't know," he said and looked at Doc.

"She'll tell you when we get there. Come on." He gently took Terry by the shoulder and led him toward the lunchroom exit.

"What about Yui?"

Doc looked back at her, still standing by the other teachers, looking confused and afraid. He glanced down at Terry, then back at her. "Say goodbye," he said. "Quickly."

Terry went over to Yui, not knowing what to say. He finally settled on, "See you soon."

"What's going on?" she asked again. Her eyes were shinning with unshed tears. "Why won't anyone tell us?"

"I don't know," he said. "I'll call you as soon as I know." He held up his phone.

She took hers out and nodded. "As soon as you do?"

"Yes," he said. "Promise." Before he knew what to say, she grabbed him and hugged him. Doc's strong hands gently took him and pulled him back. Yui's lips brushed his cheek so gently he wasn't sure it had really happened. Doc led him to the door, and he looked back. The image of her standing there, tears now streaming down her cheeks, was etched in his mind's eye like a laser cut image.

Outside, Doc took him to the teacher's parking lot, and they got into his old 2016 Ford pickup. He'd bragged about it the one other time Terry'd ridden in it. "No damned auto-drive, just like I prefer."

After making sure Terry was buckled in, Doc fired up the engine and pulled out of the parking lot, heading down the coastal road faster than Terry thought was safe. As they approached the institute, he cut off the main road and up away from the beach.

"Where are we going?" Terry asked.

"Up to the employee parking lot."

"That's the next road down."

"Only if you use the road."

Terry was about to ask him what he meant when Doc slowed down. He turned off the road and right through somebody's immaculately-tended front yard. Terry let out an uncomplimentary squeak and grabbed the bar mounted to the dashboard. Doc called it the "Jesus Bar," and for the first time, Terry knew why.

The truck bounced over a hedge and onto a small dirt road. Doc drove the truck with casual confidence, managing to impress Terry, despite the terror from the ride. He no longer had any idea where he was, until the dirt road turned, and he was looking down on the institute. He'd looked up behind the buildings many times and had never realized there was a road on the rocky hill. The same ship he'd seen landing just minutes ago was squatting on the charred concrete like a big beetle.

"Hang on," Doc said and turned off the dirt road.

"Oh, shit," Terry said, afraid Doc was going to jump down to the parking lot 30 meters below. Instead, there was another dirt road. Or maybe more like a goat path? Either way, the already nerve-wracking ride became terrifying. Terry held the Jesus Bar like his life depended on it, which he was afraid it did.

Then they were skidding to a stop next to the institute's perimeter fence, and Doc bailed out. "Come on, young man," he said.

Terry unpeeled his fingers from the bar, his hands hurting from the force he'd been exerting. He unbuckled and got out of the truck.

By the time he'd come around to the front, Doc already had a big section of fence pulled back to reveal an opening large enough for both of them. "What about your truck?"

"Don't worry about it," Doc said and gently urged Terry through the hole.

Somewhere during the drive, Doc had put on a headset, which he was talking into. "I have him, we're north of the lot, don't lift off. I repeat, don't lift off." He turned to Terry. "Come on, we need to hurry." He took Terry's hand and ran. Terry wanted to know why they needed to run, but just concentrated on keeping up with the man's much longer strides.

In a short time, they were on the concrete, and the ship loomed above them like a building with rocket engines and landing legs. Terry wanted to gawk and ask a million questions. In every place the previous ships had landed, the concrete was charred into a series of small craters. He tried to imagine how hot those rockets must be to melt concrete. Where the ship sat at the moment were six smoldering burn spots. *Holy cow,* he thought.

They ran past the ship toward the institute. As they passed to the other side, Terry saw a big tracked machine moving from the bay door at the back of the main aquarium building. It wasn't going more than a slow, walking pace and was being followed by a dozen of the institute's staff. None so much as looked up as Doc and he ran by; they were far too intent on the vehicle. It reminded Terry of a gas tanker.

At the back door, his mother was standing with one of the alien slates and all the senior science staff. Here, more staff were moving dollies packed high with all manner of crates. They went by just like the earlier staff, not noticing Terry or Doc, and intent on their tasks.

"Mom!" Terry said when he saw her.

"Oh, Terry," she said and disengaged from the staff. They looked annoyed as she limped toward him. Terry noticed she was using her cane, a sure sign she'd been on her feet all day and was tired. She pulled him into an embrace. "Doc, thanks so much."

"My pleasure, Madison," he said.

"Mom, what the heck is going on?"

"The High Court's going to rule in a few hours," she explained, putting a hand on both shoulders. "They want to euthanize the cetaceans."

Terry's eyes widened in shock and horror. "Kill them?" His mom nodded her head. "But why?"

"Dr. Trudeau managed to successfully argue that the modified cetacean's quality of life was sufficiently damaged, and they were a danger."

"A danger?" Terry demanded. "How? They're just dolphins!"

"I know it, and you know it, but a lot of people fear the cult, the Abyss followers. They've attacked advocates of our cause."

"How does that mean the cetaceans are hurting anyone?"

"To us, it doesn't," she said, "but to the lawyers, it was a weapon to use against us in arguments."

"It just isn't fair." Terry insisted, "We need to do something."

"We are," his mother agreed. "Come inside and I'll show you."

They went into the main building, and Terry looked at the nearest orca tank. It was empty, with no sign of the huge whales anywhere.

"You're hiding them!" he said with an ear-to-ear grin. His mother looked at Doc, then back at him. "Aren't you?"

"Yeah, kid," Doc said. "Somewhere they'll never find them."

"Where?"

"We'll explain when we get there," his mother said.

"I get to go?"

"Absolutely!" She looked at the boxes going by. "Can you go inside and get your stuff together? I left a crate in your bedroom. Only what fits. Understand?"

"Why can't I take everything?"

She and Doc exchanged the same look. Doc shrugged. "We don't have time. The court will realize any moment now what we're doing, and they might send the police."

"We're breaking the law?" Terry asked in a hushed tone.

"Yeah," his mother said and nodded. "But it's an immoral law that would mandate the cetaceans' death because of what your father did." Terry's face darkened, and she shook her head. "Doc, can you take him up to the apartment?"

"Sure," he said. "Come on, kiddo, I'll lend a hand."

They went to the elevator. The doors opened just as they arrived, and four people came out with carts piled high. Terry saw everything from file boxes to specimen vials. They were emptying the labs upstairs. Doc walked in front of him up to the residence wing, reaching the apartment first, and keyed open the door.

Terry went straight to his room and, just like his mother had said, there was a plastic case sitting on the floor. It was about a meter long, half a meter wide, and more than half a meter tall. It wasn't big enough to hold all his clothes, not to mention everything else. "I'll never get everything in there," he said.

"Don't worry about it," Doc said. "Just get the important stuff."

"Like what?"

"Underwear and video games?"

Terry laughed, and Doc went over to open the case. Terry saw his name with some more information printed on a removable label. He wanted to know what was on it.

"No time, just pack. I'll help. I have lots of experience."

"How?" Terry asked, pulling open a drawer on his clothes chest.

"When you're a Navy SEAL, you move all the time, usually with no notice. We always kept the vital stuff in a duffel we called our 'Go Bag.' A lot of the guys on the teams never unpacked."

"They lived out of their go bags all the time?" Doc nodded. "That had to suck."

"All a matter of perspective, I guess." Doc helped him sort by making piles of what he thought was important to the Terry. He was right much more often than he was wrong. "You and Yui are really good friends," he said, not so much a question as a statement of fact.

"Yeah, she's my best friend." Terry tossed aside a pair of slacks and took jeans instead. "We were friends almost from the time we met in grade school." He stopped and thought. "She's just cool, and we get along great." Doc nodded but didn't comment. He handed Terry a pile of thin sweats. "It's hardly ever cold enough for those," Terry complained. "It's almost summer, too."

"You'll want them where we're going," Doc said.

Terry smiled and thought, *So we're going somewhere cold.* He was excited about seeing someplace new and being with the cetaceans. There'd be some great stories to tell Yui when he got back.

Doc put his hand to his ear over the headset. "Ship's taking off."

"Can I watch?"

Doc looked at his watch, then nodded. "For a minute."

Terry dropped the sweats in the case and ran out to the living room. The big window overlooked the ocean, but two smaller ones to the rear overlooked the tanks, and the parking lot, somewhat. He was disappointed he couldn't see the ship, but then the ground shook, and the building rumbled as he covered his ears against the intense roar. Outside, the beetle-like ship climbed into view, riding on six brilliant columns of pure blue fire. It was *incredible*.

"I'm going to get to ride on one of those?"

"You betcha," Doc said behind him. Outside the ship climbed into the sky, and the roar slowly dissipated. Terry lost view of the ship in the small window. "Come on, let's get back to it."

He somehow managed to get the case filled. In the end, Doc and he both had to sit on it and latch the locks with their feet. Terry laughed uncontrollably as the drama played out. He only managed because Doc said he could take his school backpack, too, which he stuffed with books, games, and his tablet computer. At the last minute, Doc took his dive computer, which Terry had left on the room's desk, and put it in the backpack.

"I won't have a chance to use it, will I?"

"You never know," Doc said.

They traveled down the elevator just in time for Terry to watch the big tank vehicle loading the bottlenoses, one after another, into its interior using an amazing flexible plastic tube with metal articulations. For their part, the dolphins appeared to be having the time of their lives.

His mother was still in the same place, by the doors outside the employee parking lot. Only now there were more people. A *lot* more people. There were men and women he'd never seen before, along with children, too. Many wore grim expressions, and the children looked confused or scared. A little of it began to rub off on Terry.

"Everything will be fine," Doc said, noticing his expression. "Your mom planned ahead."

"She knew this would happen?"

"More like a contingency plan. You know what that means?"

He nodded. "Who are all these other people?"

"Family and friends of the staff," Doc said. "Also some supporters who helped financially." He looked up and shielded his eyes. "Here comes the last one."

A brilliant flash of light was falling toward them from the sky, its engines blinking as it maneuvered. Terry watched it come, marveling at how such a huge thing could fall all the way from space with seeming ease.

Doc put his hand to his ear again. "Madison!" he yelled. She spun around, attentive. "A flyer is coming from Honolulu, where a suborbital just landed."

"They figured it out," Terry's mom said. "Everyone, ready to go! Doc, can your friends buy us some time?"

Doc's mouth was a thin line, but he nodded his head. He spoke into the tiny microphone by his mouth, too quietly for Terry to hear, then aloud to Terry's mom, "They want to come along afterward."

"Are they sure?"

"Yes."

"What about their families?"

"None of them have wives or kids; that's why they came."

"Okay, but they better hurry." The rest of the conversation was drowned out as the ship's engines roared to full power, burning off velocity.

Terry saw it was coming in to the side, over the water, and only began to slip sideways toward the institute after it had nearly slowed to a stop. He wondered if that was on purpose. Before he could ask anyone, it flew over the parking lot and landed on four columns of fire. This ship was different; it was more boxy looking.

The engine roar rose to an intolerable volume, and Terry again covered his ears. The blast from the rockets blew debris everywhere, and the wind was strong enough to push him back, even a hundred yards away. As its big, thick landing legs pistoned to bear its weight on the ruined concrete, Terry saw writing on the side near a big glass cockpit. "USS *Teddy Roosevelt.*"

As soon as the gear touched down, the engines cut out with a quickly reducing whine, and people raced into motion. Terry was swept along with the first group as Doc easily carried the case they'd packed together. He could hear voices yelling, children crying, the motors of the dolphin transport whining, and the distant sounds of gunfire. His eyes were as wide as dinner plates as he half walked and was half carried by Doc across the now crunchy concrete.

The closer he got to the ship, the bigger it seemed. It looked like a flying aircraft carrier to his untrained eyes. He wondered why it looked so much different than the beetle-shaped one earlier. His young mind wanted to ask a thousand questions, but there was no time.

Two ramps had lowered from the *Teddy Roosevelt,* one from under the front, and another much larger one under its rear. The dolphin transport was rumbling toward the rear one. Terry was at the front of a steady stream flowing up the front ramp.

"Take care of him, Doc?" his mother asked.

"You bet," Doc said and guided Terry to a ladder and up several decks.

The inside of the ship looked nothing like the sci-fi shows Terry had seen. It was rough, dirty, and there was rust in places. Nothing was white or padded. *What a dump*, he thought. A pair of crewmembers passed them, going down, while Terry and Doc went up. They looked just as dirty and rough as their ship. Neither seemed to be wearing uniforms, just oily coveralls and ballcaps which said USS *Teddy Roosevelt*. The logo on the hat was a fat guy with a big mustache riding a moose.

"Here we are, Terry," Doc said as they arrived at a room with lots of seats. It didn't look like it usually had a lot of seats; in fact, there was a man in the back busily clicking more to the floor. It appeared the floor was covered with places for them to be snapped into place.

"I want to stay with you," he said to Doc.

"No can do; I have to help outside."

"I can help," Terry insisted.

"Yes you can, by staying right here and helping the younger kids coming up." As if Doc had conjured them, a bunch of kids were shepherded into the chamber. "Please?"

"Okay," Terry said. Doc nodded, set the crate by another door, and was gone in an instant. Terry grumbled, then saw a pair of young boys—twins maybe—who looked scared to death. "Hey, you guys want to play a game?" he asked and fished out his game box. They looked skeptical but came closer. Terry smiled at them, and they smiled back. In minutes, there was a crowd around him, and Terry at least felt like he was helping.

He didn't know how much later it was when a crewman dropped in from the deck above and looked at the dozens of kids standing around in abject shock. "What the hell is going on here?" he gasped.

"Keeping them entertained," Terry said.

"We lift in one minute!" He raised his voice to a low yell. "Get in a chair, *now!*" The kids, being used to grownups getting excited, moved in response to the specific order. Well, most of them did.

Terry looked at the seat design and instantly joined in, helping the kids closest to him. Other older boys and girls saw what he was doing, and they began helping others. The crewman quickly showed him how to flip the buckles so they couldn't be unhooked by the occupant, then went around corralling a few children barely old enough to be in school, bodily stuck them in chairs, and strapped them in. Just as Terry helped the last boy buckle in, an alarm began to blare.

"Thanks," the crewman said, then pointed to one of the last empty seats. "Buckle in, space cadet!"

Terry threw the man a salute and got a smile in reply. He dropped into a seat and pulled the straps into place. "Lift ship!" someone yelled over the intercom. Just as he clicked the straps home, the world seemed to explode.

Pure transcendent rage assaulted his senses. It was like being in a hurricane and an earthquake at the same time. He'd been in some fast boats and flown a number of times, so he'd felt acceleration. None of it was like what he felt at that moment. Something was sitting on his chest, crushing the air from his lungs. He thought he was screaming, then realized it was all the kids around him. Some in shock, some in stark, raving terror.

His vision swam red, and he could see kids tearing at their restraints. The still-functioning part of his brain now understood why the buckles on the restraints were reversible so the person wearing them couldn't release them. He could barely breathe and could only try to imagine what would happen if the children unlocked their straps and crashed to the floor. *Is it ever going to end?*

Suddenly the pressure began to fall away. His vision cleared, and he looked around. Some of the kids appeared to have passed out. The sound of the engines' roar was greatly diminished. The crewman buckled in nearby was using a computer tablet and glanced at his young charges.

"When do we land?" Terry yelled at him.

"Land?" the man asked, looking confused.

"Yeah, when we set down to hide the cetaceans."

"I don't know what you're talking about," the man said. "We're set to rendezvous with a hyperspace carrier in eighteen hours."

The horror on Terry's face must have registered with the man, because he looked surprised. "Nobody told you we were leaving Sol?"

"We can't…" Terry said, his voice trailing off. The man looked sad, and Terry got mad. Then he remembered his last words to Yui. *"I'll see you soon."*

In a panic, he grabbed his phone from his pocket and clicked on Yui's grinning face. Of course it was a satellite phone, but would it work in space? It took the phone forever, but it did eventually connect, and he heard a ring.

"Terry?" Yui's voice spoke. It sounded distorted.

"Yui, it's me. I'm sorry!"

"Terry, where are…" the call broke into static. "Saw ships taking….police are everywhere!"

"We're going to another star! They didn't tell me!"

"…star?...Terry, I…you!" The phone disconnected.

"Yui! Yui!"

"Take it easy, kid," the crewman said. Terry stared at his phone in anguish, slowly letting it fall from his hand. It bounced off the floor and flew across the room, spinning lazily as it went. His tears didn't fall down his cheeks, instead forming puddles over his eyes. He was in space.

* * * * *

Chapter Two

Approaching the Stargate, Sol System

July 1st, 2037

Terry didn't speak to Doc when he came to get him. The older man floated onto the deck, looked at the devastated expression on Terry's face, and simply unbuckled him.

"Come on," Doc said. He gently took Terry by the arm and began moving him.

Part of him marveled at zero gravity, but that part was crushed by his sense of loss. *Why didn't they tell me?*

"I'm sure you're wondering why we didn't tell you," Doc said as he helped Terry through a hatch and up/down another deck. Terry had no idea where they were going. "Your mother was afraid you might end up in jail with everyone else when the government came for us."

"What do you mean?"

"Glad you're still with us," Doc said. Terry shrugged and almost hit a ladder. "Careful until you get used to this." Doc helped him get his own grip on the ladder before speaking again. "The court not only ruled against allowing the whales to live, it also ruled everyone involved in the project was guilty of illegal modification of an endangered species."

"I didn't do anything," Terry said.

"No, but you helped take care of them. In the eyes of the law, that's enough."

"They were going to put me in jail?"

"We don't know," Doc admitted. "As a minor, probably not. But they would have put your mom in jail, and you'd have probably been tried as a minor. Might even have been sent to some sort of juvenile detention facility." He shrugged. "So much of the new Earth Republic government is still unset, nobody knows what would have happened to you. Your mom thought it better you come."

"Without asking me," he said darkly. "No one thought about what would happen to *my life*."

"That's not fair," he said, "and not true. She was always thinking of you. In fact, she was thinking about staying and fighting it out, until we found out they were going to arrest you along with everyone else."

Terry looked away, but couldn't let go of his feelings of betrayal. They continued moving through hatches and long companionways until they reached a dome with windows all around. The Earth was a sphere off to one side and looked no bigger than a basketball. Terry gasped at the view. *I'm in space*, he thought, the spectacle finally overcoming his anger. In the dome were all the institute doctors, three strange people he'd never seen before, and his mom.

"I'm sorry," she said as soon as she saw him. "There wasn't time."

"Doc explained," Terry said. She could see he wasn't happy and frowned.

"So you know we had to do it this way?"

"No, I don't," he said. "I'd have understood."

"Would you?" she asked. "Terry, you're mature for your age, but you're still a child. The truth is, a lot more people than just you and I were in danger of going to jail, maybe forever. I had to think about everyone."

"And the cetaceans," Dr. Orsage said. His mom nodded in agreement.

"We also thought you deserved to be here," Doc said.

Terry looked around at the people and realized he was the only kid there. Everyone else was senior staff from the institute, Doc, and some of the ship's crew. At least, he guessed that was who the three strange people were.

"Terry," his mother said, "this is Captain Baker; she owns the *Teddy Roosevelt*." A woman with long grey hair pulled back was hanging onto a rail like she'd spent her life in space. She nodded to Terry and winked. He smiled despite himself.

"Glad to have you aboard, young man," she said. "This is Commander Ed Moore; he's my XO. If you need something from me, he's usually who you'll talk to." The man she'd indicated was considerably younger than the captain looked, despite being bald. He smiled a big, natural smile and nodded to Terry as well.

"Lastly, meet Ensign Drake; he's my purser and will see to all the passengers, including you, enroute." Drake was a young man, and nodded at Terry with no smile. He had short cut dark hair and sharp eyes.

Terry was about to ask what their destination was when something outside caught his eye. They were approaching another ship. Terry grabbed a handle and moved closer to the window for a better look. He didn't know much about spaceships, though just about everyone on the planet would recognize this one—a long, cigar-shaped ship with a ring of modules around the blunt rear.

"Is that *Pegasus*?"

"Yes it is," Captain Baker said. "*Teddy* and the other transports are catching a ride. My ship's capable, but she doesn't have her own hyperdrive."

"*Pegasus*," Terry said again. The famous ship of the Winged Hussars, one of the Four Horsemen. Eleven years ago, they were the last of the alpha contract merc companies to come back from deep space. Everyone had written them off for dead, but they came back, and in a different ship than the one they'd left with. Nobody knew much about the huge warship, only that it was incredibly powerful and rarely came back to Earth. "Why are they helping?" he asked.

"Your mom can explain better," Doc said.

"Well, the Hussars have helped us for years," his mom explained. "They were the ones who arranged to move the bottlenoses and orcas from the parks where we found them. They were also the principle financial backer. Amelia Cromwell, who's married to the Hussars' commander, Lawrence Kosmalski, has been extremely helpful, though it was Colonel Kosmalski who volunteered to get us out this time. He just happened to be here when everything fell apart."

"Where are we going?" Terry asked. All the adults looked at each other, but none of them answered right away.

Eventually his mother replied, "For now, we're riding with the Winged Hussars to a system called Karma. We'll wait there to see if this legal stuff can get sorted out."

"What about the cetaceans?" he asked.

"You can see them after we dock with *Pegasus*," his mom said. She looked at the captain. "We'll have a few hours before we go through the stargate?"

"We don't jump until 22:00 Zulu," she said. Outside, *Pegasus* grew steadily closer.

* * *

Docking with the Winged Hussars' huge warship turned out to be nothing special. A few minutes of bumps from the *Teddy Roosevelt*'s maneuvering thrusters, followed by a jolt, and the PA announced they were docked.

Terry realized he didn't know what Zulu time was after docking, but then a crewman helped him update his phone for the ship's network, and the time matched immediately. They had three hours. He spent the time in the observation dome, watching the proceedings in space.

They were one of four ships docking with *Pegasus*, all of which had evacuated the institute, cetaceans, and staff. He overheard one conversation his mom was having with the radio operator. Authorities on Earth were insisting they return to Earth immediately.

"Can they make us?" Terry asked Doc.

"*Pegasus* is more powerful than all the spaceships Earth has combined," he said.

"How do you know so much about this stuff?" he asked Doc.

"I was a merc for a couple years," Doc said. Terry gawked. "Yeah, I didn't tell anyone. I was with the Winged Hussars, and helped them develop marine tactics."

"I thought marines were for water and stuff."

Doc laughed and smiled. "These are space marines. More like SEALs in a lot of ways. But SEAL stands for Sea Air and Land. Sea, Air, Land, and Space?"

"SEALaS?" Terry asked. Doc cocked his head and shrugged, making Terry laugh. "Yeah, it doesn't work, does it?"

"No, not really. And space marines have been talked about in science fiction. It was too cool a name to pass up, I guess. Anyway, I helped develop some tactics to defend ships from boarding, and to board other ships. We trained doing some of that as SEALs. I spent some time with NASA learning zero gravity maneuvering." He flipped around a couple times, looking like a gymnast. "Afterward I put it all together and then taught the Hussars."

"That is, no kidding, cool." Doc shrugged. "Can you teach me some stuff?"

"Like what?" Doc asked, his mannerism suggesting suspicion.

"How to get around better in space," Terry said.

"Oh, sure. You don't feel sick at all?"

"No, why?"

Doc nodded. "A lot of people get sick in zero gravity."

Terry thought about it. His stomach had felt funny since they'd reached orbit, but not sick. He'd figured it was because he missed Yui, and thinking about her took away some of the fun he'd been having. Doc saw his look and frowned. "Let's go check on your dolphins?"

"I'd rather see the orcas," he said. Doc nodded and they set out together.

As the two moved through *Teddy Roosevelt*, Terry watched how Doc moved and began to copy him. The former SEAL seemed to unconsciously plan every single move. He would soar from one handhold to another, often only touching the next handhold before gently pushing onward. It was a ballet. Terry couldn't do half as well. Still, he tried.

Doc watched him as they proceeded, making suggestions and generally nodding in approval. "All your diving and swimming translates."

"You're right!" Terry said as he made a particularly good grab at a passing handhold. Then he missed the next one, and Doc had to snag him before he crashed into a wall. "Well, kinda." They both laughed.

"You'll get better." They continued.

"Have you been on this ship before?"

"Nope," Doc said.

"Then how do you know your way around?"

"All ships are similar in many ways," Doc explained. "This is a *Kuiper*-class, the first Human-made ships. I was on the *Donald Trump* shortly after it launched in 2031. The later iterations aren't as ugly as the first one, but it got the job done. They're working on a new class; *Comal Tramp* is the name. Those will be hyperspace-capable!"

"This ship is only six years old?" He looked at the beat up interior, the rust spots, bent ladder rungs, and other signs of neglect.

"This ship is more like five," Doc corrected.

Terry shook his head in amazement. "This thing is trashed."

"It's a working ship." Doc said, "I've been on a lot worse down on Earth." He swung around a corner, and there was a big doorway. "Here we are." The door said, "Transfer Lock #2." One of the *Teddy Roosevelt* crew was manning the hatch and saw them approach.

"Going over to *Pegasus?*" she asked.

"Yes," Doc said. "This young man helps care for the whales."

"Oh, I see," she said and pressed a button. The big door rumbled and rotated to the side, showing a tunnel to another door. "Press the green button at the other end."

"I know the drill," Doc said. She nodded, and they pulled themselves through. At the far end Doc pressed the green button, and the door rumbled back closed behind them. Terry felt his ears pop and put his hands up to them. "Pressure between the two ships equalizing," Doc explained. The door in front of them moved aside, much quicker and quieter than the other ship's lock.

Inside stood a pair of men in black coveralls Terry realized was a uniform. Both wore ball caps and there were red stripes down the outside of their sleeves and legs.

"Welcome aboard the EMS *Pegasus*," one of them said, a man in his forties. Then he looked closer at Doc and came more erect, not easy in zero gravity. "Lieutenant Commander Abercrombie, sir. Good to see you again."

"Sergeant Teal," Doc said.

"Lieutenant Teal now, sir."

"Congrats, my friend," Doc said, then looked at Terry. "This gentleman was a new recruit when I started training the Winged Hussars' marines. How has my training worked out?"

"Great, sir," Lieutenant Teal said. "We've had to make some changes, of course. We had a fight two months ago; a bunch of Zuul tried boarding. They weren't expecting the hairless monkeys to be able to put up a fight." The man's teeth skinned back in a feral smile. "They won't be expecting anything anymore."

"Glad to hear it," Doc said, then gave a little cough and glanced at Terry. "This is Terry Clark, the son of Dr. Madison Clark, head of the science expedition."

"Hello, Terry," the marine said. He introduced the marine with him. "I don't suppose you need directions?"

"No," Doc said. "Just tell me which docking port has which ship?"

"*Kavul Tesh* is at dock two, and *Kavul Ato* is at dock three."

Terry noted the one they'd come out of was dock one. Doc thanked his old student and set out. Right away Terry noticed the interior of *Pegasus* was vastly different—in every way—from *Teddy Roosevelt*. Its corridors were rounded and smooth, the metal carefully painted and tended to. They also curved around the ship. *Teddy Roosevelt* was like being in a building; everything had right angles. It somehow felt inHuman.

"Different kind of ship, right?" Doc said, looking at him.

"Yeah. Feels weird."

"It should," Doc said. "*Pegasus* was made by aliens before Humans learned the written word."

"Incredible," Terry said. It was only a rumor among people. Endless videos talked about the Four Horsemen, speculated, guessed, or sometimes made up stories. They all wanted to know how they survived and flourished. The most commonly speculated on rumors were about the Winged Hussars and their mysterious ship, *Pegasus*. The most common rumor was they'd made it from parts. That it was entirely alien was not a commonly held belief. The Hussars themselves didn't talk much, mainly because they weren't ever on Earth.

Doc led them around the circular corridor. A door to their right said, "Lift #2." The door opened. Inside was a woman and an alien who looked like a badger. Terry knew the race; they were called Cochkala. The Human had gold stripes on her uniform, the Cochkala blue. They got out and moved back in the direction Terry and Doc had come from.

A little further on, Terry saw two aliens working on an open panel. One was an elSha, like he'd seen before. The other looked like a big anteater. They both wore clothing appropriate to their races in black, just like the marines, only these two had green stripes. The elSha moved an eye to track them as they went by; the other didn't seem to notice.

"How many aliens are in the Hussars' crew?" he asked Doc.

"A lot," Doc replied. "They have to be at least half Human, according to the Merc Guild, so less than half."

They walked past one of the other locks. This one was unguarded, with a ramp going up and a ramp going down, and finally another lock's sign said #3. A pair of marines saluted and opened the door. "This is one of the ships holding your orcas," Doc said and went inside.

"Why do they always keep the locks closed?" Terry asked.

"Warship," Doc said. "It's protocol."

"But this is Earth; aren't we safe?"

"Nowhere in the universe is safe," Doc said.

Terry wondered why he would say such a thing, then realized Doc had been a merc and lost friends in the alpha contracts. He guessed Doc would know as well as anyone else.

The inside lock opened, and they entered the other ship. *Kavul Ato*, the marine lieutenant had called it. Its interior looked strange, like *Pegasus*, but different. The curves of the corridors were more unusual, as if whoever had designed it hadn't had a plan and had just wanted to build something.

Doc wasn't as familiar with this ship. He stopped the first crewman they encountered, a woman with short brown hair and bright green eyes.

"Where are the whales?" he asked her.

"Main hold," she said. "Two companionways over there; you'll see signs."

"Thanks," Doc said, and they floated in the indicated direction. It was a good thing there were signs, or they never would have found it.

"Who made this ship?" Terry asked.

"Some aliens," Doc said. "No clue which ones."

"Why are Humans using alien ships, anyway?"

"Because we're still figuring out how to make our own," Doc said.

The corridor opened through a big hatch into the hold. Inside, a massive glass wall had been installed and the space was completely filled with water. Four orcas floated inside, so Terry knew it was the Shore Pod even before he recognized Kray.

Terry was about to ask what was on their heads but he figured it out. A glass dome with machinery integrated into its rim was somehow stuck to the orcas' heads. There was no air in the tank, but since there was no gravity, it wouldn't have mattered. Terry understood—without gravity, the air wouldn't form a surface, it would just float around the water in bubbles. The apparatus on their head was a rebreather, related to the device Doc had brought them to dive with the previous year.

"Hello, Shore Pod," Terry said.

The four orcas lazily moved over to the tank wall and looked at him with their huge eyes. "*Warden Terry,*" Kray said, "*you in dark, Shore in dark.*"

Terry looked around. The hold was well lit. "It is not dark, Kray."

"*Is dark,*" Kray said.

"*Is all dark,*" Ulybka said. "*Beyond.*" All four orcas turned to face in different directions.

"In space," Doc said. "They mean in space."

"How do they know they're in space?" Terry wondered aloud. The orcas didn't answer.

* * * * *

Chapter Three

Hyperspace

July 3rd, 2037

Terry watched in amazement tinged with horror as the orca was born. Dr. Jaehnig, in a wetsuit and using an alien rebreather, assisted the birth. Terry knew in the wild, orca podmates helped in the birthing process. The problem was, none of the orcas were in any position to help.

Just over 36 hours ago *Pegasus* had gone through Sol's stargate and into hyperspace. The sensation was a nightmare given birth; you were ripped apart only to be reassembled a heartbeat later. He'd read that philosophers called it a transcendent moment of un-creation/creation. He just thought it sucked. He went through it in his cabin, with his mom. He didn't want to ever do it again. The crew was unimpressed. Everyone in their group—they now thought of themselves as refugees—felt the same way. Except Doc, of course. He seemed to think it was interesting.

Less than an hour after entering hyperspace, Terry found his way to *Teddy Roosevelt's* bridge to stare at the white nothingness of hyperspace. The opposite of normal space, it was the omnipresence of light. It didn't hurt to stare at it; there was really nothing there.

In school, he'd learned scientists believed the brain was incapable of understanding hyperspace, so it made the white you saw. It was curious, but he didn't have long to ponder it.

The orcas were becoming restless. He'd gone to *Kavul Ato* to see. The orcas were swimming around and around their tank, sometimes bumping into the walls, sometimes the glass, sometimes each other.

"*Beyond, beyond, beyond!*" they were saying repeatedly. They wouldn't respond to the Humans.

"*Shool!*" they also said intermittently.

"What do you think?" his mom asked Dr. Orsage, the only one of their number who specialized in cetacean psychology.

"I don't know," she admitted. "Maybe an energy field generated by the ship in hyperspace? It appears to be cumulative." Moloko, the pregnant female, slammed into the glass divider hard enough to make it vibrate. "We're going to have to sedate them!"

"That'll endanger her pregnancy," Dr. Jaehnig warned.

"If the glass breaks," one *Kavul Ato's* engineers warned, "the surge of water may shatter the bulkhead. A couple million liters of water crashing around…"

"What about the Shore Pod?" his mom asked.

"Same thing!" Doc said, floating in. "But the dolphins are fine. They're acting like they're meditating, but otherwise they're fine."

His mom turned to Dr. Jaehnig. "Do it. Fast."

There were two Selroth aboard *Pegasus*. The Humanoid aliens were aquatic, able to breathe underwater. They looked Human, but with shiny skin, similar to a dolphin, and their heads were hairless, with gills and big eyes. Colonel Kosmalski had agreed to loan them to the institute refugees to help with the cetaceans. They went into the tanks with straps, and with the supervision of Dr. Jaehnig, the process began to sedate the orcas.

The other three were easy; their weight was known precisely, and the correct amount of sedative was administered by the Selroth with a quick jab of a spear-like syringe. Every time they pocked an orca, the huge predator would spin around and try to bite them. Terry gasped, afraid the orcas were about to kill the aliens. However, the Selroth dodged the attacks with ease.

"Much easier to avoid than the *Oohobo* on our home world," one said after climbing out of the tank. They were just about to give Moloko her anesthetic when she arched her back and discharged some strange-colored fluid from her genitals.

"Oh, no," Dr. Jaehnig said. "She's giving birth."

The actual birth only took a few minutes. The baby's flukes came out, and before long, half the body was protruding. The Selroth both jumped into the tank and were joined by four big, strong researchers. The other three members of the Shore Pod were sedated and lolling around in the tank, their rebreathers keeping them safe. Together with the Selroth, the Humans struggled to secure Moloko by hooking dozens of fabric cargo straps around her flukes and midriff.

They managed to restrain her, though only just. The baby burst out in a cloud of blood and amniotic fluids. Terry was unable to stop gawking even as the researchers corralled the baby and slipped one of the dome rebreathers on it.

"It's a shame," his mother said, shaking her head. "Just a shame."

"What?" Terry asked. "The baby looks okay."

"It does," she agreed. "Dr. Jaehnig says it's only a couple weeks premature. But with Moloko crazy like the rest of the orcas, there's no way the baby can nurse."

"What does that mean?"

"We might have to euthanize it."

"Wait," Terry said, louder than he intended. "You're going to kill it?"

"It's going to die, Terry."

"Can't you feed it?"

"If we didn't have nine insane orcas to tend to for another five days, maybe. It's never been done, though."

"I'll do it," Terry said. He surprised himself; he had no idea what it meant.

"Oh, son…"

"I said I'll do it."

"Terry," Doc said, floating over, "I don't know much about these whales, but you really don't know what you're getting yourself into. There's no surface, you'll have to feed it underwater."

"I know how to dive; you know that. Damnit, don't let the baby die!" Terry floated over to the tank. The baby looked a lot like its mom, only smaller and chubbier. One of the Selroth was swimming alongside the baby as it tried to nurse. Moloko was spasmodically pumping her flukes, now drugged and unaware of her surroundings. The baby was pushed away without feeding.

Doc looked at his mom, who was exhausted and looked sad. "Could it survive?"

"No orca has ever lived without being able to nurse."

"Then there's nothing to lose," Doc said. Terry's mom looked surprised at Doc's approval. In the end, she relented.

"It's your responsibility," she said. "The assistants can make the milk—I checked—but they can't help you feed the baby."

"I understand," Terry said, nodding. "I can do it."

"Okay," she said, "let's try."

* * * * *

Chapter Four

Hyperspace

July 5rd, 2037

The crew of *Kavul Ato* ended up sealing a small compartment off the main hold for Moloko's baby. It provided better filtration and improved heat control. Terry spent several hours every day reading research files on rearing orcas. As his mother had said, a baby orca had never been successfully hand raised. The closest was one born in Vancouver Canada 35 years previously. The female calf only lived for 4 months.

There was a great body of research on orca milk. Modern autochefs, which were able to synthesize a wide range of alien dietary requirements, allowed the institute scientists to produce a perfect replacement. The problem was getting the baby to take it.

Terry spent every moment he wasn't sleeping, eating, or studying in the mini-tank with the baby trying to get him to feed. He knew the baby was a male thanks to some of the research.

The baby was listless from being separated from his mother at birth and was having difficulty swimming. "I think it's the swimming problem," he told Doc the first day after the baby was born.

"Why do you think that?" he asked.

"Well, I've watched hundreds of videos showing baby orcas feeding, and they all do it in motion. The baby's having trouble swimming; he keeps spinning around."

"We might be able to ask if they can spin the ship," Doc said, scratching his chin.

"What difference does that make?" Terry asked.

"It creates pseudo gravity." Terry stared. "You know the trick when you spin a glass of water over your head and it doesn't spill?"

"Oh, right, we did that in class one year."

"Yes, we'd be the glass of water out here. *Pegasus* would be the center of gravity."

"How do we ask?"

"Let's go talk to the captain."

Terry was used to passing though *Pegasus* every day. His quarters were in *Teddy Roosevelt* and he moved over to *Kavul Ato* every day. He even stopped for a few minutes to see the Sunrise Pod on his ship, and once to see the Wandering Pod on *Kavul Tesh*. Like the Wandering Pod, they were heavily sedated and closely watched.

Even transferring between ships, he'd never seen more than the one hallway on *Pegasus*. After Doc made a call to the warship, he took Terry back aboard and they went to the lift. "Where are we going?" Terry asked.

"The CIC."

"What's a CIC?"

"Combat Information Center, sort of the brain for a warship."

"What about a bridge, like *Teddy?*" The lift clanked and was pulled up in relation to the decks.

"*Pegasus* has a bridge, but they only use it for docking, when it's better to have eyeballs."

"Ships this big dock?"

"Sure," Doc said, "there are bigger ships, and space stations."

"What's bigger? This is huge!"

"Well, regular battlecruisers are 20% bigger. *Pegasus* is an old design, after all. Heavy cruisers are bigger, but there aren't many of those around. Battleships are freaking massive."

"How massive?" Terry asked as he watched several aliens move along a deck they were passing.

"Like a kilometer on a side! They're round, usually, or egg-shaped. Not fast, but bristling with guns, missiles, and shields."

"Half a mile," Terry said, letting out a low whistle. A Buma on the deck they'd just passed whistled back, and he was afraid he'd just said something funny. "Anything bigger?"

"I've heard about dreadnoughts, but never seen one. They must be a mile, at least. Probably just small enough to fit through a stargate."

The lift stopped and they floated out. Halfway around was a strange corridor going inward. It only went a short distance and stopped at a massive armored door. Two Winged Hussars marines floated there. Unlike others Terry had seen, these were completely alert and armed. Dangerous-looking laser rifles were slung on their backs, and pistols on their hips. They also wore armor. *This place must be very important*, he thought.

"Can we help you?" the older of the two marines asked.

"Yes, Sergeant, I'm Doc Abercrombie, here to see the colonel."

"Is he expecting you?"

"Yes, he is."

The marine nodded and spoke into a microphone connected to a minimalistic headset. He waited a second, apparently listening to the reply, then nodded. "Is this Terry Clark?"

How many kids are going to turn up here? Terry wondered silently.

"Yes, he is. I'll take responsibility for him." Terry glowered, but the marine nodded, then looked at him.

"Don't touch *anything* except marked handholds, do you understand?"

"Of course," Terry said flippantly.

Doc put a none too gentle hand on his shoulder. "Look him in the eye and say, 'Yes, sir.'"

Terry, while surprised, did as he was told. "Yes, sir, I won't touch anything except handholds." The marine nodded and allowed Terry and Doc to proceed. "Why so serious?"

"Because this is a serious place."

The inside of the CIC was spherical and reminded him more of old submarine war movies. Except old movies didn't have numerous Tri-V displays and aliens. Most of the crew was Human, and Terry was immediately aware of the man in the center. Probably Doc's age, he was covered in tattoos and sported, of all things, a blue mohawk.

Colonel Kosmalski was one of the most recognizable people on Earth, yet somehow Terry hadn't expected the blue mohawk to be real. It wasn't something you saw on military leaders. He thought the man would look more at home in one of the netgame parlors in Honolulu, or maybe Houston. Or perhaps a bar in an R-rated movie? Definitely not in command of the most powerful Human-owned starship in the galaxy.

"Welcome back, Doc," the colonel said. Terry thought the man's accent sounded strange, like maybe he was from Russia? The Winged Hussars always sounded exotic and strange to him anyway.

"Good to see you again, Lawrence," Doc replied.

"What can I do for you?"

"This is Terry Clark; he's Madison's boy."

"Welcome to the *Pegasus'* CIC," Colonel Kosmalski said. He had a boyish smile, which Terry found disarming.

"Thank you, sir." Terry was concentrating on hanging onto the handhold he'd nabbed when they'd floated in. An alien who looked like a big white rat was strapped to the workstation his grip was attached to. It eyed him suspiciously with little, black beady eyes.

"We have a request," Doc said. Colonel Kosmalski made a gesture, and Doc continued, "You might have heard that hyperspace is proving problematic for the orcas?"

"Yes, my physician mentioned it in our briefing. She said the dolphins appear fine."

"They're not 100%, but they aren't as weirded out as the orcas," Doc explained. "The effects were bad enough, but a pregnant orca gave birth prematurely."

"I'd heard about the birth, not about it being preemie. Is it going to survive?"

"We don't know," Doc said, then put a hand on Terry. "Terry here is trying to tend to it, but there's a problem."

"Gravity," Terry said. He swallowed before continuing, "The baby calf can't feed because his mom is catatonic, and I think the lack of up and down are just playing hell with him."

"Calf?" Colonel Kosmalski asked.

"You call a baby cetacean a calf," Terry explained, feeling uncomfortable trying to educate a commander of one of the Four Horsemen.

Kosmalski laughed and shook his head. "You learn something new every day in this big galaxy, but seldom about your own planet. So, what would you have me do to help this…calf?"

"We request you spin up *Pegasus* to give us some artificial gravity," Doc said.

"Please, Colonel, it might give the poor thing a chance."

"It's not exactly a simple thing," the Winged Hussars' commander explained. "We have to secure from zero-G stations and have everybody on all four ships ready for spin."

"I'm sorry," Terry said, looking at the deck plate.

"Don't be sorry, I'm just explaining that it's not an insignificant request." He looked at Doc. "You think it would work?"

"I don't know," Doc said. "I'm no marine biologist. Neither is Terry, obviously, but the explanation makes sense. I put it under 'it couldn't hurt,' myself."

Colonel Kosmalski ran a hand through his blue hair and grunted. Terry noticed one of the tattoos on the man's arm was *moving*! He'd never seen a tattoo move before, and lots of surfers on Molokai had them. He tried hard not to stare.

"Okay," the colonel said eventually. "I'll order spin."

"Oh, thank you, sir!" Terry blurted, and the colonel's smile returned.

"Best I can do will probably only give you one quarter gravity, though. Any more, and that hunk of junk *Teddy Roosevelt* is liable to come apart at the seams."

"Thanks," Doc said. "I owe you one."

Colonel Kosmalski snorted and made a dismissive gesture. "Means I still owe you a dozen. Get off my CIC, landlubber."

"Aye aye, Captain," Doc said and saluted. Kosmalski snorted again and flipped Doc the middle finger. Doc took Terry in tow and led him back toward the lift.

"Was he mad at you?" Terry asked, glancing back into the CIC as they left.

"No, grownups just talk that way sometimes."

I hope I don't act like that when I grow up, Terry thought. The two marines guarding the exit nodded to Doc and pretended Terry didn't exist. They were waiting for the lift a minute later when the ship's PA made a buzzing sound, and a woman's voice spoke.

"Attention all hands, attention all hands. Secure from zero-G operations and prepare for spin in 15 minutes. Repeat, prepare for spin in 15 minutes."

When they got back to *Kavul Ato*, the crew were rushing about, grumbling and wondering why the *Pegasus'* captain had decided to spin more than a day after entering hyperspace. Apparently, doing it that way wasn't normal procedure. Terry didn't offer to explain to them.

When the big warship started spinning on its cylindrical center of mass, the three attached ships experienced the highest gravity. As Colonel Kosmalski had said, a meter in *Kavul Ato* reported they were under 0.3 Gs. Terry quickly returned to where the orca calf's tank was and checked on him.

Doc warned him to be extra careful after a couple of days in free-fall. People sometimes forgot and injured themselves, which was no doubt part of the Hussar commander's concern. The inside of *Kavul Ato* seemed even more misshapen. Ladders were at odd angles, and some doors opened up or down, instead of sideways. Clearly the ship was not intended to be spun in this manner at all.

When he reached the tank, Terry was delighted to see the baby was swimming now, and no longer spinning much or bumping into the sides. He adjusted the lighting so it only came from 'up' in the compartment. That helped even more, and he saw the baby watching him through the glass. He loaded a big bottle, slipped into a wet suit, and grabbed one of several rebreathers hanging on the side of the tank.

Getting in was trickier now. He had to drain some of the water because the door would have dumped it all over the deck. The captain wouldn't appreciate that. When he did, it made an air space, and the baby surfaced even though it wore the rebreather. Acting on instinct, Terry removed the orca's rebreather. The calf immediately spent several minutes just circling with his little dorsal fin up in the air, breathing every minute or so.

"Okay," he said, "how about some food now?" He slipped into the water and the calf came over to push at him with his nose. As the newborn weighed more than 150 kilos, Terry was a little alarmed to be shoved around. For the first time, he was aware he was in the water with an apex predator. It was a newborn, sure. A newborn with 50 or so sharp teeth. He did his best to remember that an orca had never hurt a Human in the wild and brought the bottle around.

"Give this a try."

The orca calf pushed the bottle aside and nudged its nose into his ribs. "Oof," Terry said. "Why are you doing that?" The calf did it several more times. Then Terry remembered the videos of orca calves feeding, and he held the bottle against his stomach, the big blunt nipple pointing out. The next time the calf tried to nudge him in the ribs, the bottle was between them.

"Come on," Terry urged, and rubbed it against the calf's mouth. He gave the bottle a squeeze and rich, white milk spurted into the water. It was all the calf needed, and he latched onto the bottle.

The videos paid off again. Orca young didn't suckle. The mom's milk was under pressure, so the calf just bit down and the milk flowed into its mouth. Terry squeezed, and the liquid flowed. The calf backed away and paused. Terry watched for any sign that the little guy had spit it out. Nothing. In fact, he came in for more. "Yes!" he crowed and squeezed hard.

"Way to go, kid."

Terry looked over and saw Doc sitting on an equipment bench outside the tank, grinning from ear to ear, flashing a thumbs-up. Terry had never been happier in his entire life as the calf emptied the bottle in mere minutes.

* * * * *

Chapter Five

Karma Star System, Cresht Region, Tolo Arm
July 9th, 2037

"We're about to drop out of hyperspace, Terry." He looked up from the orca calf. His mom was standing in the bay's hatchway, leaning slightly to compensate for the ship's strange angle. Terry nodded and pulled the bottle from the calf, who snorted water from his blowhole and tried to snatch it back.

"Wow, he's really coming along, isn't he?"

"Yeah," he said, smiling. "He's nuts for this milk."

"You putting the extra antibiotics in?"

"Yes," he said. The previous morning, a blood test showed the calf had a slight infection. Apparently minor infections weren't uncommon for newborns in captivity. It might even be normal in the wild. Nobody knew. So Dr. Jaehnig had prescribed an antibiotic. The calf hadn't even noticed. "He doesn't care; he's just hungry. Hey, stop that." The calf had nabbed the bottle again.

"Here," his mom said and came over. With her help, he was able to get the bottle away from him. The calf gave Terry a playful shove with his big, wide nose. "Better get his breather on."

"Are we going to have to stop spin?"

"No, *Pegasus* said we'll continue spin. But Dr. Jaehnig's worried about the orcas' mental health, and the calf is an even bigger unknown."

Terry nodded and took the rebreather from a strap inside the tank where he'd been storing it. The calf floated on his side and looked at Terry with one eye.

"Have you had it back on him at all—oh!" She stopped in surprise when the calf swam over and helped Terry put the rebreather on. "Wow."

"Yeah, he's super smart." Terry made sure it was set properly, adjusting the strap slightly so the plastic dome was exactly over the calf's blowhole. Then he climbed out of the tank and sealed the door, in case zero gravity returned. "He's learning fast. Dr. Jaehnig was talking to me this morning and said you'd talked about the idea of performing implant surgery on him."

"We did talk about it," she agreed. "We want to wait until he's a couple months old and his mom understands."

"Have you figured out if she'll be able to take over nursing?"

"Probably not," she said. "We checked Moloko a few hours ago and verified she has almost no milk production." She shrugged. "She never successfully nursed. We'll have to see how it goes. You still okay to take care of his feedings for two years?"

"Whatever it takes," Terry said. "I promised." She smiled and pulled him into a hug. "You said we're coming out of hyperspace?"

She checked her watch. "In a few minutes."

"Will it suck as bad as going in?"

"No," she said. "Just feels like you're falling."

"What if you're in zero gravity?"

"Apparently it doesn't make any difference."

"Space is weird," Terry said.

His mom laughed and nodded. "It sure is."

"Prepare for hyperspace emergence," was announced over the PA on *Kavul Ato*.

Despite her assurances, Terry hung onto the hug. His mom didn't say anything; she just waited. Before long, he felt it, a strange falling sensation which made his stomach jump despite all the hours he'd recently logged in zero gravity. Just like entering hyperspace, it was gone in an instant.

"That's it," his mom said, and they both turned to see how the calf was doing. He looked at them curiously, seeming not to have noticed anything was different. "Welcome to Karma, little guy," she said. "Hey, he needs a name." She looked at Terry. "So, what is it?"

"I can name him?"

"Of course, you're taking care of him."

Terry looked at the calf, who was watching him. *Probably still hungry,* Terry thought. He took out his tablet computer and typed in some searches. The other orcas were all named using Hawaiian words. "How about Pōkole?"

"Hawaiian?" his mom asked. Terry nodded. "I don't know what it means."

"Short," he said. "The calf was born early, so I thought it made sense."

"I like it," she said, and went over to the tank. "Welcome to Karma, Pōkole. How does it feel to be the first orca born off Earth?" Pōkole spurted water on the tank hatch.

"Maybe that means he's happy?" Terry suggested.

"Probably just gas," his mom said.

An hour after they'd arrived in Karma, *Pegasus* cast the three transports off and bid them farewell. Terry heard the conversation where his mother and her senior staff thanked Colonel Kosmalski for coming to their rescue.

"I am happy to have helped," the colonel said in his thick Polish accent. "My wife Amelia has helped you many times, so how could I refuse when *Pegasus* was in Sol and you were in such dire need?"

"Did you hear what happened?" Doc asked Terry.

"No."

"When the Earth Republic demanded Kosmalski turn around and bring us back or they'd send the military, the colonel dared them to try."

"Holy cow," Terry said.

"Yeah," Doc said and chuckled. "These Horsemen are tough and independent. Nobody threatens them."

"What about the three transports?" Terry asked. "They don't belong to the institute, do they?"

"Oh, hell no. The institute couldn't even afford *Teddy Roosevelt*, and I doubt even the United States could afford *Kavul Tesh* or *Kavul Ato*. They're all leased for our use by the Winged Hussars. I think the captains all owed the Hussars a debt or a favor; I don't know. An awful lot of that kind of thing goes on with mercs."

"I always thought it was money."

"Lots of money, too," Doc said.

The orcas began to come out of their drug-induced slumber not too long after *Pegasus* cast them off. Pōkole's tank was connected to the Shore Pod's tank, and Terry watched as the adults began to come around.

"*Back…*" Kray said, the first to speak. "*Back beyond.*"

"Are you okay?" Terry's mom asked.

"*Back,*" Kray repeated.

One after another, the others came around, with Moloko the last to begin speaking.

"*Calf gone?*"

"You had your calf just as you and the other orcas began to…" she struggled with a way to say it. "After you lost control."

"*Beyond take calf mine.*"

"Your calf is still alive."

"*Alive? Where?*"

She nodded to the researchers, who opened the little tunnel, and Pōkole swam in. The calf swam over to Moloko and instantly began to nuzzle her, and everyone in the hold breathed a huge sigh of relief. Mother and calf were reunited and acted as if nothing was unusual. Moloko spoke to the calf in non-words, deep subsonic noises the translators didn't recognize.

"It's like she's singing to him," Dr. Orsage said, taking notes as usual.

"Pōkole," Terry said. "The calf is named Pōkole."

"*My calf Pōkole?*" Moloko asked.

"Yes," Terry said. "Is that okay?"

"*Sound right,*" the mother orca replied. "*I no milk,*" she said.

"*How long beyond?*" Ulybka, the other female, asked.

"Over five days," Terry's mom explained.

"*How feed?*" Moloko asked. Terry explained.

"Warden figure out," she said.

"*Warden everything figure,*" Kray agreed.

"We couldn't figure out what was happening to them," Dr. Patel said. The other doctors nodded in agreement.

"Can I help feed Pōkole still?" Terry asked.

Moloko nudged Pōkole over next to the glass and hummed at him, then bumped the glass in front of Terry. The calf nodded vigorously in an unmistakable gesture. *"Pōkole like Terry. I like Terry. This good."*

"Excellent," Terry said.

"I'm very proud of you," his mother said. He beamed up at her.

"What did it feel like?" Dr. Orsage asked the orcas. "Do you understand why you lost control?"

"Beyond," Kray said. *"Shool cry. Shool cry."*

"What do you think that means?" Terry's mom wondered.

"I have no idea," the psychologist said and made notes.

Later, the three transports docked together. *Teddy Roosevelt* was the only one of the three with multiple docking collars, so she served as the hub. It suited the marine biologists and staff just fine as it put them in the middle of all their charges. The conglomeration of ships was moored to the remains of an ancient mined-out asteroid named Karma Theta Two. The planet of Karma was thousands of kilometers away, a blue-green ball visible from *Teddy*'s observation dome.

With nothing more to do, Terry settled back into the cramped cabin he shared with his mother. *Teddy* was so filled with Humans, it smelled like sweat and pee to him. The captain said they were 20% over capacity, but said Human ships were made to take it. Terry wasn't sure he agreed, by the smell at least. Someone knocked on the door not long after he'd gotten there.

"Anyone home?" Doc's voice asked.

"Come on in, Doc," Terry said. The door creaked from rust as it opened.

"Hey, kid, how'd the reunion go?"

"Great! Moloko took to her calf right away, and vice versa. Moloko even wants me to keep feeding Pōkole."

"Is that the calf's name?" Terry nodded. "Awesome. Your mom said Moloko didn't have any milk." Terry nodded. "Hey, I just wanted to say I'm proud of you for standing up and helping after how bad it was leaving Earth."

"If I hadn't, Pōkole would have died."

"Exactly, but a little kid would have been too busy feeling sorry for himself. What you did was what a grownup needed to do, a man."

Terry smiled so hard he felt tears making his vision blurry and wiped them away. "He was so tiny, I couldn't let him just starve or get put to sleep."

"Four hundred pounds is tiny?" Doc asked. Terry laughed; he had a point. "I wanted to stop by and say goodbye."

"You're going?" Terry asked in surprise.

"For a while. I'm going over to Karma Station to talk to some friends, maybe see what I can do to put some pressure on Earth to let us come home without being arrested."

"Do you think it's possible?"

Doc shrugged. "I don't know," he admitted. "What I do know is that we can't stay here forever. Colonel Kosmalski said we could use the transports as long as we needed, but he didn't mean forever. So I'm going to go see what I can do. I made a few friends among the mercs."

"It sounded like Colonel Kosmalski pissed off the government," Terry said.

"Yeah," Doc agreed. "He has that effect on people. You keep helping out as much as you can, okay? Your mom depends on you."

"I'm still just a kid."

"Not in my eyes," Doc said, then gave him a quick hug.

"Hey, Doc?"

"Yeah?"

"How did you have the code to our apartment back at the institute?"

He gave Terry his appraising look. "You don't miss much. Probably make a good SEAL. Your mom and I have been seeing each other for the last month or so, after her divorce to your dad was final." He looked Terry in the eye. "We didn't tell you because we were afraid you'd take it the wrong way."

"I've known my mom and dad weren't happy together for a while," Terry told him. "Kids notice this stuff, even when we wish it wasn't happening. Are you in love?"

"Huh," Doc said with a grunt. "I don't know if it's that cut and dried. Let's say, we really like each other."

"Good," Terry said. "I like you, too."

Doc grinned. "Feeling's mutual, kiddo."

"You had a hand in getting Mom healed, didn't you?"

"What makes you think that?" Doc asked, his eyes twinkling in the cabin's low light.

"You sent a message to my dad saying you had friends who might be able to heal her. He refused, but she suddenly got better a couple weeks later. Was it those nanites I heard about?"

"Let's just say she got better and leave it at that. I gotta run."

"You mean fly," Terry said with a grin. Doc laughed and was off.

Terry slid into his hammock, hooked the straps across his legs, and pulled out his tablet. The ship had a network, and it was now connected to the GalNet. He grinned when he saw it was an unrestricted node, unlike the one back at his school on Molokai. For a second, he wondered about 'Adult Content,' then remembered the Galactic Union didn't care about such things. Besides, he didn't think he'd be too interested in pictures of naked aliens.

His mother had mentioned when they got to Karma that Terry would be able to send emails home. They just had to be under a certain size, which was one gigabyte, if he remembered right. It was like the Union's version of the postal service, only you never knew how long it would take to reach a destination.

Union free messages weren't like radio transmissions; the messages were bundled together and sent to every ship leaving the star system that was going in the right direction. Since they were just one transition from Earth, the captain said it would get there pretty quickly.

The first message was to his father. Terry still felt conflicted about leaving him behind. Of course, everything his mom and Doc had said about him looked to be spot on, but that didn't change the fact that he was his *dad*. Terry had done some pretty boneheaded things, too, and Dad had always forgiven him.

"Dear Dad,

I'm sorry I didn't have the time to say I was leaving, or even say goodbye. We found out they were coming to arrest us. I know you must have done what you did for a good reason, only I wish you'd told me. I feel sad, like maybe you did it on purpose."

He erased the last sentence.

"I wish you'd said something. Please write back, I want to know how you are.

Love, Terry."

Next he wrote a quick note and group addressed it to his friends at the middle school. He was well, and nobody better be saying he'd been kidnapped by aliens. He smiled at his own wit. He said they were trying to figure out how to fix everything, and they'd left to protect the cetaceans.

The last one he wrote was the hardest; it was to Yui. He decided to record it on video, which meant it had to be short.

"Hi, Yui," he said, and waved lamely at the tablet's camera. "I didn't know what was going to happen. I'm sorry. The government was going to have us arrested and kill the cetaceans. So my mom got the Winged Hussars to take us off planet. If I'd known, I don't know if I would have gone. You're like my best friend in the whole world." He shook his head. "In the whole galaxy now!

"The orcas got really sick in hyperspace. Moloko gave birth early, and I had to help save the baby. It's a boy, and I named it Pōkole. I saved him, Yui! I watched all these videos and figured out how to get him to feed. Hyperspace didn't bother him like it did the adults.

"Moloko and the others came out of it after we got here, and she likes the name, and I get to keep helping feed him because Moloko's milk isn't working anymore." He glanced at the file size and saw it was already more than half filled.

"I only have a few seconds more video, so I'll say bye. I miss you. Please send a message back? Bye." He stopped recording. The computer said it was the correct size, and he used the ship's GalNet node to properly address it to her. It felt strange addressing it to Tolo Arm, Cresht Region, Sol System, Earth, then her actual address. Before, he'd just used her email address. Then he hit send.

The free message system only let you send one message per day per star system. Sending bigger messages, or one guaranteed to reach its destination via the most direct route, cost 15 credits and up. He whistled. Fifteen credits translated to $450,000 dollars! He had about $150 on his Yack, so that was out of the question. He decided to send the group email the next day.

Terry stowed his tablet, reached back over his head, and shut off the little LED light, throwing the cabin into absolute darkness. He'd been surprised by just how dark it was in a ship with only a few windows. It wasn't quiet, though. *Teddy Roosevelt* was always alive with sounds. Fans were running, the distant fusion powerplant was always humming away, and often times the banging of crewmen fixing things could be heard.

In some ways, it was reassuring. He wasn't alone, despite being trillions of kilometers from home. Only, was the rickety Earth freighter now his home? He drifted off to sleep, hoping it wasn't.

* * * * *

Chapter Six

October 1ˢᵗ, 2037

Despite Doc's claim that he'd be back shortly, it turned out to be almost three months. On July 11ᵗʰ, Terry got an email from Doc. It was sent from Karma Station, and told Terry he'd be gone for at least a couple months, not to worry about him, and to help as much as possible.

"Where did Doc go?" he asked his mom at lunch. "Is he going back to Earth?"

"He's not going to Earth," she said, but she wouldn't tell him anything more.

Despite the orcas' recovery from the strange events in hyperspace, there was still plenty to do. More than there were people do to them, actually. He found himself learning how to maintain the tank filtration system and review computer records of water condition. Of course, those responsibilities were in addition to his taking care of Pōkole. Just keeping everyone fed and tended to on *Teddy Roosevelt* proved difficult. Terry had never thought about how much 125 people ate, drank, and more importantly, pooped every day.

The only thing he worried about was he'd yet to hear from his father or Yui. He checked with the Cartographers' Guild, who traced communications, among other duties. A week later, they confirmed the messages had reached Earth. His mother said not to worry, it was probably the government stopping their messages. She said when Doc got back, they'd find a way around the block.

Pōkole continued to thrive, and all the marine biologists congratulated him on his great work. He was gaining weight at more than a kilo a day. Pōkole also continued to bond with his pod, and they reveled in his young energy. At Terry's urging, the captain of *Kavul Ato* was convinced to open another adjacent cargo bay, and the orcas got more room to swim.

As he was working on the water systems as part of his job, he found himself finally spending some time around the bottlenoses, and was surprised at a profound change. They'd been strangely motivated by their trip through hyperspace. They were discussing how they couldn't wait to go back.

"Why are you so eager to return to hyperspace?" he asked Skritch, who appeared to be the de facto leader of the Sunrise Pod.

"*Like beyond!*" was the answer.

"What do you like about—" he'd stopped in mid-sentence, his mouth hanging open. "Beyond? You call hyperspace beyond?"

"*It beyond,*" Skritch agreed.

"*Beyond, beyond, beyond!*" The entire pod had surfaced, and was chanting the word repeatedly.

"Do you know the orcas call it beyond also?" Terry asked them.

"*Dark Killers blind beyond.*"

"*Afraid Shool is beyond,*" another said.

They'd taken to calling the orcas dark killers not long after they'd received their implants, though they preferred not to talk about the orcas at all. The orcas called the bottlenoses 'Swift Brothers.' Dr. Hernandez found it interesting as he'd studied their psychology. After all, orcas were more closely related to dolphins than other whales, though they were all considered toothed whales.

"Is *Shool* beyond?" Terry asked.

"*No*," they all agreed.

"Mom, did you know the orcas and the bottlenoses both call hyperspace beyond?" he asked her later.

"Yes," she'd said, "Dr. Hernandez mentioned it in a meeting a couple of days ago."

"They don't see each other anymore. How could they both come up with the same name?"

"The theory is, someone said something to the bottlenoses."

"I don't think so," Terry said.

"Can you support that theory?"

Terry loathed when his mom did that. The scientific method required you to be able to prove a theory. Of course he couldn't prove it. "I can't," he mumbled.

"Then tell me when you can."

Unfortunately, his duty required him to stay too busy, so he had no time to pursue the source of their terminology or how it might have come about. The closest he got to more information was discussing the idea with Dr. Hernandez briefly.

"I think it had something to do with the origins of words to the cetaceans," the doctor explained. Terry caught him in a hallway heading for a meeting and floated along with him.

"What do you mean?" Terry asked.

"Well, Klaak, the Sidar who specialized in pinplants, said that words are often created by the translation matrix and are assigned in some cases. Maybe that just means the matrix of both cetacean species found similar results and came to the same conclusion. Excuse me, I'm late."

Terry had plenty more questions, but grownups were always in a hurry. Mostly, he wanted to argue his case. How could the orcas and bottlenoses both settle on the word "beyond" for hyperspace when they had different experiences? The bottlenoses came out of hyperspace like they'd been to a summer camp, the orcas like they'd been tortured. Then Pōkole ended up with another minor infection, and he was too busy to worry about it.

When July gave way to August, his mother materialized out of nowhere with a tablet full of lessons.

"I have to do school work, too?" he complained.

"Yes, you do. Furthermore, I've assigned you extra learning, since we'll be living in space for a while. Two of *Teddy Roosevelt*'s junior officers have volunteered to help teach classes. You and all the other children will attend for five hours a day, five days a week. You'll have two hours a week with a tutor as well."

"What kind of tutor?"

"You'll be learning about Union pinplants."

Terry gawked. "Really?"

"Yes," she said, then grinned. "Your insights are excellent. Both Doctors Hernandez and Orsage said as much. Let's see if you take to it." After that, the time flew by. So much so that when Doc returned, he didn't notice for two days.

"Hey, kiddo," Doc said as he floated into *Teddy Roosevelt*'s galley, the only large space left on the freighter not full of water.

"Doc!" Terry said and slipped out of the strap around his waist holding him to the bench. He pushed over, then gave his friend a hug. "When did you get back?"

"Two days ago."

"You didn't say hi?"

"I've been pretty busy," he said.

Terry smirked. "I bet, smooching my mom?"

"Mind your own business, Squirt," he said and smacked him on the arm. Terry caught himself before he sailed away without thinking about it. "No, we've been talking about what we're going to do now."

Terry was about to ask what that meant when he saw Doc was wearing a uniform. "Wow, what have you been doing?"

"Working," he said, and showed Terry the patch on his uniform sleeve.

"Woah, Golden Horde? I didn't think they hired anyone who wasn't from China, or something."

"They had a change in ownership, so to speak," Doc explained.

Terry looked at the two gold bars on Doc's collar and his still heavily-suntanned face. The man looked a little older, somehow. "Why did you join a merc company?"

"For this," Doc said, and held out a credit chit.

Terry took the plastic Union credit chit and examined it. In school they'd learned a little about them, in particular how to understand one of the more common Union numerical systems. "A thousand credits? Holy crap, that's $35 million dollars! They paid you that much?"

"No, they paid me and my team $4 million credits for the first contract, $2.5 million for the second one, and a $1 million credit bonus after we finished up."

Terry was as flabbergasted as he ever remembered being. He added it all up in his head. "$7.5 million credits in just a couple months?"

"Merc work pays really good, kiddo. If you survive, that is."

"The other SEALs who came with you went too, then?"

"Yes, there were eight of us."

"Were?" Terry asked, knowing the answer.

"Yes, two didn't make it. But the money's what we needed."

"What for?"

Doc grinned and winked. "You'll find out in a little bit." Terry went to hand the credit chit back. "No, that's yours."

"What for?"

"Your mom told me how hard you've been working. You deserve something for that."

"This is too much," Terry said, and tried to give it back to him again.

"Don't be ridiculous. We're not on Earth anymore. That doesn't go as far out here as you might think. Tell you what. Let me finish up a few things, and tomorrow we can go over to Karma Station. How does that sound?"

"Mom said nobody from the ship was allowed to go there," Terry said.

"Yeah, well, we're back now, so leave has been granted."

* * * * *

Chapter Seven

Karma Star System, Cresht Region, Tolo Arm
October 2nd, 2037

"I don't entirely approve," Madison said, scowling.

Terry knew better than to get involved in such a conversation. He'd learned over his short life that opening your mouth at the wrong time when grownups were having a discussion involving something you wanted to do often resulted in things not working the way you wanted them to.

"I'll be there," Doc said, "and my men are there as well."

"Karma Station is a den of killers," she insisted, her mouth set in a thin line.

"Mercs," Doc corrected her. "Am I a killer?" Caught off guard, she looked away, and Terry knew he'd scored. "You've got four million credits at your disposal, thanks to us. Call it what you will, but merc life is a reality to humanity now, and will be forever. It's no different than all of our history, really. People have always sold their swords for money."

"But why does my son have to be exposed to that?" she insisted.

"I'm not making him part of the company," Doc said. "I need to meet the men, and afterward Terry can see some of Karma Station. The station is a huge transportation hub. Merc business is only a percentage of the commerce that goes on there."

"Commerce," she said and snorted. Doc sighed.

Terry decided to play one of the only cards he had. "Mom, my birthday is in 10 days."

"And I suppose you think a trip to a…a…*mercenary den* is a suitable birthday present?"

"Merc pit," Terry corrected, then cringed. *Shit.* His mom looked at him, then turned her head to glare at Doc.

"Madison, the kid's been confined to three freighters for months, exercising every day to avoid losing bone mass. Don't you think he deserves a chance to feel some gravity and maybe see some of the Union before we're off again?"

She looked at the former SEAL for several moments before sighing, and Terry knew he'd won. "You won't let him out of your sight for even a minute?"

"Promise."

"Okay," she said, looking at her son.

"Woohoo!" Terry crowed.

"You be careful," she said, and gave him an awkward zero-G hug.

"I will, Mom."

"I'll be sure one of the assistants takes up your jobs today, but you still have to do your studies tonight. Understand?"

"Yes, mom," he yelled over his shoulder, because he was already heading back to their shared compartment.

"Take good care of him," she told Doc.

"Guaranteed."

In their room, he grabbed his backpack and a light jacket. He'd read that often space stations were cooler than most Humans preferred. Afterward, he rushed to *Teddy Roosevelt*'s hangar deck. Doc was waiting in the lock, a bag on his back and a gun around his waist.

"Ready, kiddo?"

"You bet," Terry said.

"First, a word." Doc moved so he was only a short distance away and face-to-face. "If I tell you to do something, you do it. You understand?"

"Yes, sir."

"Good. Second, alien mercs are dangerous. Some are simply hostile for the sake of being hostile. Humans are a new factor in their trade, and we're already getting a rep of being trouble. Don't talk to any aliens unless I say you can." He pointed to the translator fixed to Terry's coat.

"Got it."

"And last," Doc said, "don't spend all those credits on the first interesting thing you see."

Terry laughed and nodded. "I won't."

"Good, now come on."

They boarded the shuttle through an airlock. Inside, one of the *Teddy Roosevelt*'s pilots was already working at the controls. The woman looked back as Doc and Terry entered and found one of the dozen open seats. Two other people were already on board; Terry didn't recognize either of them.

"All set?" the pilot asked.

"Good to go," Doc said. Terry said he was, and the other two did, as well.

"Undocking, buckle up," the pilot said. There was a bump and a dull clang through the hull, followed by the sensation of the shuttle rolling around. "Thrust," the pilot said, and they were gently pushed back into their acceleration couches.

"How long to Karma Station?" Terry asked Doc.

"Oh, an hour or so."

Acceleration built up until Terry guessed it reached a half a G. He glanced at the uniform and other accoutrements of Doc's gear, in particular the gun. He'd never seen anything like it. "That's not a Human gun, is it?"

"This?" Doc asked. He drew the pistol, checked its condition, and removed a cassette from the handle. "Here." He handed it to Terry. "Safety's on, it's unloaded."

"Uhm," Terry said and took the weapon, "are you sure it's unloaded?"

"Smart kid," Doc said. "Never take another person's word for it; no matter how much you trust them, check yourself." He pointed at the controls. "Pull that back and look at what the display says."

"There's a red zero," Terry said.

"Then it's unloaded."

Terry examined it. It looked like a gun; the basics all seemed the same. The barrel didn't end in a hole, but rather a strange piece of glass. There were several controls on the side and the handle, along with writing he didn't recognize.

"This isn't from Earth," he realized.

"No, it isn't," Doc agreed.

Terry continued to examine it. "And it's not a firearm."

"Correct again. It's a laser pistol. One of the lessons from the alpha contracts was that our weaponry was sadly insufficient. We have cartridges that can kill most alien mercs, but you just don't get many shots."

"So this is an alien-made gun?"

"Yes, it is."

"How many aliens have hands like ours?" Terry asked.

"Not many," Doc confirmed. "Only one merc race is really close."

Terry gripped it in his hand and tested the feel. It was too big, of course. He was about to turn 12, but his hands weren't as long as an adult's. Even so, the handle looked rough. "It looks like it's home-made."

"Pretty close," Doc said. "My friend Janet Cross, who's in our unit, is an armorer. We got ahold of a case of Pushtal laser pistols." Doc saw the confused look on Terry's face. "Pushtals look like Bengal tigers, though luckily not as big, and tend to be black and white instead of orange and black. Anyway, the handles were all wrong. Janet used an alien machine called a manufactory to take the Pushtal guns apart and make new handles for these." He held up a hand. "Bonus is we sold a bunch to another Human unit we ran into."

Terry handed the gun back and watched Doc's movements. Just like he'd shown Terry, he verified it was empty, then slid the cassette back in place. Terry guessed it was a power pack. Doc flicked a control and slid the weapon back into its holster. "They're serviceable," he said. "Someday an alien manufacturer will be making new ones for us." He shrugged. "Maybe even a Human manufacturer."

Doc changed the subject, and they talked about Terry's studies, passing the time in conversation until they finally arrived at Karma Station. Terry watched the multi-wheel shape of the station approach from his tablet, linked to the shuttle's cameras, with awe and wonder. It just kept getting bigger, and bigger, and bigger!

"How big is that thing?" he finally asked Doc.

"Just over five kilometers across the outer ring," Doc replied. Terry whistled. "Yeah, and a couple hundred thousand beings live there."

The closer they got, the more traffic Terry spotted. From tiny darting shapes like their own, to huge donut- and egg-shaped transports, and even dart-shaped warships. It was like when they'd looked at a drop of pond water in a petri dish; everywhere there was life.

"Is this the busiest place in the galaxy?" Terry asked.

Doc laughed and shook his head. "No, Terry. Karma's in the middle of nowhere, just like Earth. I've heard about systems in the center of the galaxy, known as the core, where a trillion beings live, and you have to wait weeks for a chance to use the stargate." Terry kept gawking.

The shuttle soon got so close to the station that Terry couldn't see it all on the tablet, and he truly realized the scale. He thought of the old movie *Star Wars* as they flew toward the Deathstar. Three concentric rings were spinning around a central hub. The hub stayed unmoving in the center, where dozens of starships were docked. Their shuttle was heading toward a rectangle of light. After a few moments, he could see it was a big open space with ships hanging on all the walls.

"Docking bay dead ahead," the pilot told them. The shuttle had been coming in tail-first for some time. The pilot increased thrust for a few seconds, then it cut altogether. They drifted slowly until Terry could see they were inside. The shuttle's maneuvering thrusters fired several times, and there was a jolt. "We're docked. Stand by for boarding collar."

The pilot came out of his chair and floated back to the airlock. He watched the displays until there was an audible beep, and a status light turned green. "We're good to disembark," he said and cycled the doors open.

An elSha in a spacesuit floated there, looking inside the shuttle. "Cargo?" it asked the pilot.

"Passengers only," the pilot answered.

The alien floated inside and looked around. It had a slate it tapped on, and after a minute, the alien nodded in approval. "That will be 25 credits docking fee. Fuel is extra."

"Refill the tanks, please," the pilot said and handed the alien a card. "Purified hydrogen, if you would?"

"No problem."

"Come on, Terry," Doc said, and Terry realized he'd been staring.

"Sure," he said and floated toward the door.

The connecting collar was a big metal reinforced plastic tube designed to dock with hundreds of different kinds of shuttles. Terry thought he saw rust and cracks in the plastic and tried not to think about why the elSha wore a spacesuit. Not encouraging. He didn't breathe until they passed through the lock at the other side and entered Karma Station proper.

"Where's the pit?" he asked Doc.

"Out in one of the gravity rings," Doc replied. "Glad your mom didn't hear how eager you are." Terry gave an embarrassed grin in reply.

Doc took him through a series of corridors that led them to something he called a glideway. To him, it looked like a plastic tube.

"When you get in, the air will lift you up. After you get in, spin around so you're going feet first."

"Why?"

"Because we're going to be basically falling to the higher gravity areas of the station. If you go head first, it's gonna hurt when you try to get off."

"Oh." He did as Doc said, and a gust of air pushed him up. As soon as he was moving, he spun around feet first. It was a little like a water slide, without the water. For a second, as he began to accelerate, he was afraid it would go bad quickly. Then he felt Doc's hand on his arm.

"Don't worry, it's only scary the first time."

Terry tried to relax and look around. They were passing between decks, and he saw other tubes nearby with a variety of aliens. One or two he recognized; most he didn't. There were tubes where the occupants were going back the way he'd come, too. The glideway was kinda fun.

"We're getting off on Ring B, Deck 12."

"How do I tell where that is?" Terry asked.

"Right, I forgot you don't read the lingo yet. I'll pull us off, don't worry."

They passed through a long section without decks, or even windows. He was aware that now air was blowing up at him, keeping his pace from getting too quick. A couple of signs went by in glowing languages he didn't recognize, and he felt Doc gently pulling him to the side. Before he realized it, they were on a cut off, like a train moving onto a new track. A floor appeared below their feet, moving with then. Their feet touched, and the floor slowed them to a gentle stop.

"That was cool!"

"Told ya," Doc said.

"What if the air goes off, or the floor doesn't work?"

"It could get messy, I guess. But the tech is actually kinda simple."

Doc led him out of the station where they'd landed. You could get on or off a glideway there. Outside was a long, wide avenue lined with shops and a myriad of aliens moving in all directions. Above them was a continuous window through which he could see the ring closer to the hub. He was somewhat aware that the floors curved upward in the distance in both directions. They were standing on the floor of the spinning station. Unlike when *Pegasus* had spun them, he didn't have a slight dizzy feeling, either. Karma Station was beyond massive.

"There are bigger stations, aren't there?" he asked.

"How do you know that?"

"Well, every time I think I've seen the biggest thing around, I'm wrong."

Doc laughed and shook his head. "Yeah, this is big, but not huge. Come on, it's not far."

They walked along the promenade, as Doc called it. He said there was one on all three rings, and they served as a big business district. You could buy anything from food to missiles, according to him. Terry had a hard time understanding what any of the little shops were selling, or if they were selling anything at all. The bigger ones were sometimes two or three stories tall, reaching up to the glass roof. The scale had him dizzy in just a minute's walking.

"Here we are," Doc said outside a doorway with a symbol over the top. It looked like a gun, a sword, and diamond, and again he couldn't read the other writing.

"What's that mean?" Terry asked.

"Symbol for the Galactic Mercenary Guild," Doc said. "The place is called the Pit of Occo."

The doors opened, and a spider the size of a family sedan came skittering out. Terry squealed and jumped out of the way. It was one of the Tortantulas he'd read about, but there was no chipmunk on its back.

"Move it, meat sack," the Tortantula said. Well, it made clicks and rasping sounds, but its translator said the words.

"Pardon the hatchling," Doc said, and the Tortantula trundled past without another word.

"Is that one of the dangerous ones?" he asked after the spider was out of sight.

"Very," Doc confirmed. "It didn't have a Flatar, so that probably means it's a small one, likely a courier."

"D-did you say *small* one?"

Doc took him by the shoulder and guided him into the pit. He didn't know what he'd been expecting. Maybe the Star Wars cantina crossed with a wild west saloon? It turned out to be a big open room with a service area off to one side, Tri-V screens in the center showing all kinds of data, and small private rooms all along the walls.

"This is a pit?"

"Yup," Doc confirmed. A man, the first Human Terry had seen since they'd left the shuttle and its other occupants, popped out of a private room and waved.

"Yo, Doc, over here, Captain!"

Doc waved back and patted Terry on the shoulder. "Come on, kiddo, meet the crew."

They walked over to the room, and Doc went in first. Inside, five men and a woman sat waiting. They all greeted Doc, then looked at Terry.

"Men, this is Terry Clark. I've been telling you about him."

"Who the hell are you calling men?" the woman asked.

"Don't let her fool you," one of the men said, "she's got a bigger dick than any of us." Terry turned bright red, and everyone laughed uproariously.

"That foul-mouthed *lady* over there is Tina," Doc said. "Watch your mouth, Sergeant."

"Sorry, sir," she said. "Hi, Terry." He smiled and said hi back.

"That's Honcho," Doc said. A dark-skinned man with a cowboy hat touched the brim and nodded. "Over there is Toothpick." A man smiled back, missing several teeth.

"Why do they call you Toothpick?" Terry asked. The man pulled out a pair of shiny knives, grinned, and made them disappear. "Okay," Terry said, and more laughter broke out.

"That's Piano," Doc said. A thin Asian man with sharp, hard eyes nodded slightly. "And the two who can't stop playing cards are Hutch and Peyto." Two men wearing ballcaps who looked like brothers waved without looking up from their cards. One hat was the Boston Red Sox, the other the Chicago Cubs. They both looked more like football players, with necks thicker than Terry's waist.

"Welcome to the Last Call merc company," Tina said. Everyone raised a glass. Doc picked one up, apparently waiting for him, and raised it as well.

"Do I get a drink?" Terry asked with a mischievous grin.

"*No!*" they all barked. Terry turned red again, and they all laughed.

"Any word on that contract?" Doc asked after the laughter died out.

"Not yet," Piano said, his voice rich with the accent of whatever Asian country he was from.

"You catch the spider just leaving?" Tina asked.

"Yeah, almost ran us over," Doc said. All eyes turned to look out into the pit, searching. "Wonder what's going on?" They looked at each other and nodded.

"Toothpick, see if the bar has something the kid can drink?"

"Sure, Captain," the man said and got up to leave. "Whatcha like, kid?"

"Soda, or water is fine."

"Be right back."

"Pop a squat, Terry," Tina said and patted the bench next to her. Terry sat down. It wasn't comfortable, more like a padded steel plate, he guessed because the pit probably catered to dozens of different races. "Doc says you're studying to be a marine biologist?"

"Not really," Terry said, "but I've been studying pinplants."

"No shit?" she said.

"Hey," Doc growled.

"Crap, sorry kid. We've seen a lot of aliens with them, especially pilots. I heard some are researching making them work for Humans. Maybe you'll figure it out?"

"I'd like to," Terry said. "Our cetaceans all have them."

"We know," Honcho said and took a drink. "That's why we're all stuck out here."

"I'm sorry about that," Terry said, looking away from the man's hard stare.

"It's not the kid's fault," Doc reminded his man. "Not anyone's fault, really. Aliens pulled one over on them, from what I hear."

"Even the kid's old man?" Honcho asked.

"Drop it," Doc said.

"I was just—"

"I said drop it, Sergeant."

"Yes, sir," Honcho said and went back to his drink. It was uncomfortably quiet for a minute until Piano came back. He was carrying a bottle of Coca-Cola.

"Holy cow," Doc said, "where the hell did you get that?"

"Bartender said it was stocked by Jim Cartwright!" Piano said and handed it to Terry.

It was a glass bottle. He'd never seen one like it. He looked at the label and saw it had been bottled in Saudi Arabia, and there was Arabic writing as well. He couldn't figure out how to get the metal top off, either.

"Here," Doc said and took the bottle. He pulled out a tool from his belt and *pop*, the top came off with a fizz. Terry took it back and drank.

"Holy shit!" he said as the carbonation and sugar went down.

"Hey!" Doc barked.

"Oops," Terry said. The SEALs cheered and raised their drinks.

"To Terry," Tina said, "we'll make a no-shit SEAL out of you yet!"

"*Salute!*" they called out and downed their drinks. Even Honcho gave Terry a wink.

Doc did a facepalm. "Madison is going to kill me."

Terry sat and listened as the seven mercs talked. They went from weather in Houston to scuba diving, parachuting, driving cars, and on to fighting aliens. He stayed quiet, and they almost forgot he was there. Until Tina let out a string of profanity, and Doc yelled at her.

Then Tina looked up and tapped her ear. Terry hadn't even noticed she was wearing a radio. It was the tiniest thing he'd ever seen, and he wondered if it was alien origin like the laser pistols they all wore.

"Whatcha got?" Doc asked.

"Someone down at Peepo's said she's coming this way," Tina said.

"Got it. Okay, Terry, someone's coming I need to talk to. You can stay because there's nowhere to stash you. So sit back there between Honcho and Piano and keep quiet, okay?" Terry nodded. "Cover him, okay?" he asked the two.

"Will do," Piano said. Honcho just nodded.

Terry slipped around the rear of the crowded room and sat where he'd been told. Despite being surrounded by big armed men and women, he felt a jolt of fear.

"Don't worry," Honcho said in his gruff voice, "we got this, kid."

Terry watched out the door into the Pit of Occo, breathing faster than he liked. After a few seconds he called on the dive training Doc had given him way back when they first met. "Never let fear win. If you do, you die." He closed his eyes and took a deep calming breath, and it helped. When he opened his eyes, it was just as a dozen MinSha came into the pit.

Their red compound eyes moved as they spun their heart-shaped heads to take in their surroundings. They all wore black combat armor over their green chitin, the same as the ones who'd blown the hell out of the Middle East eleven years ago, within weeks of his birthday. The mercs around him didn't so much as budge.

The leader of the MinSha looked directly at Doc, who was now standing in the doorway to their room, and pointed a viciously serrated arm at him. The others headed in the Humans' direction. "You are the Last Call?"

"That's us," Doc said, his hand falling casually to his belt, mere centimeters from the holstered laser pistol. "Who are you?"

"We are Viscou Ak, and you killed our mercs on Shlee Prime!"

Doc looked at Toothpick, who was just to his side, his eyebrows going up. "Did we kill any bugs on that world?"

"Yeah, but I can't be sure."

Doc grunted and nodded before turning back to the MinSha. "Killing bugs is more of a hobby than a profession for us."

The MinSha leader made a hideous rasping hiss and its troopers spread out to either side. They fairly bristled with weapons, but none were being aimed…yet.

"No fight in my pit!" an alien screeched and ran between the two sides. This alien looked a little like a sloth to Terry, and he wondered if it was a Caroon.

"Get out of the way, Occo," the MinSha chittered.

"If the shooting starts, just dive behind these seats," Honcho said to Terry.

Terry nodded in reply and began to wonder if his mom had been right. Staying on *Teddy Roosevelt* might have been a good idea after all.

"You Humans are in over your heads," the MinSha said. "We should have sterilized your miserable world instead of a small part of it. Worthless, miserable mammals."

"Here's your chance to get rid of a few more mammals," Doc said, patting his chest. "Your move, bug."

"If you wish," the MinSha said.

Oh, hell, Terry thought. Occo fled, squealing. The MinSha watched the pit owner go, then nodded to its partners.

"Is there a problem here?" said a woman's voice behind the MinSha.

The alien's head spun around to observe dozens of Human mercs spreading out behind them. Unlike Doc and his people, the newcomers wore light and efficient-looking combat armor, complete with helmets and tinted visors. They also carried short-barreled rifles that Terry suspected were lasers. Each of the MinSha had at least two pointed at them.

"This argument isn't with your company," the MinSha said, turning its head so it could see both groups of Humans. The armored antennae swung in a circle like helicopter blades.

"You aliens are going to have to figure something out about Humans."

The MinSha snorted. "What do we need to figure out?"

"You mess with one of us, you mess with *all of us*."

"Like I said," Doc said, "your move, bug."

"This isn't over," the MinSha said, and his team moved as one toward the door. The new arrivals closest to the exit moved aside just enough to let them through.

"Better hope it is," said the woman who'd spoken as the alien leader left.

"Thank you!" Occo screeched, and Terry realized the screeching was its normal way of speaking. "You drink on Occo."

"With thanks," the woman said and removed her helmet. Long hair as black as night fell down her back, and small but intense eyes examined the room. *She's beautiful!* Terry thought. Hutch and Peyto picked up their cards and resumed the game where they'd left off.

The woman looked at one of her men. "Sergeant Chang, make sure our guests actually leave the vicinity."

"Yes, Colonel," a man said and bowed. Six others fell in with him as he exited.

And a colonel?!

"Terry," Doc called. "Come on out here. You've met one of the Four Horsemen, meet another."

As he came out from behind the table, Terry got a better look at one of the newcomers. She wore advanced camouflage fatigues, and all her equipment looked new. On her shoulder was a golden patch with a black embroidered horse archer charging.

"This is Colonel Tuya Enkh, commander of the Golden Horde. Tuya, this is Terry Clark, the son of the woman I told you about."

Tuya's eyes screwed up into a smile, the epicanthic fold turning her dark eyes into almost pinpricks. "I am pleased to meet you," she said. "The Golden Horde is at your service." She gave a little bow as she smiled at him. The helmet had modulated her voice so it sounded neutral. Now, without the effect, her accent was clearly Asian.

"Nice to meet you too, Colonel," he said and awkwardly returned the bow. She grinned even wider. "Not to be rude, ma'am, but I thought a man was in charge of the Golden Horde."

"Yes," she said and shrugged. "Borte is no longer in command. A change in leadership was necessary for the Horde to thrive." Terry wondered what she meant. "Now if you will excuse me, young man, I have need of Colonel Abercrombie."

"Just Doc is fine," he said, "you know that." Doc turned to Tina. "Do me a favor and take Terry shopping?"

"Sure, *Colonel*," Tina said, her voice full of amusement.

"Stow that shit right away," Doc growled. All the other men snapped to attention and saluted. "Oh, for the love of God."

* * * * *

Chapter Eight

Karma Station, Karma Star System, Cresht Region, Tolo Arm
October 2nd, 2037

"Sergeant Tina?" Terry asked as they walked.

"Just Tina, kid."

"Okay, Tina. What the hell was that all about?"

The older woman laughed and flipped her short blond hair over one shoulder before answering. "We—Humans, that is—and the MinSha don't have a good relationship."

"They blew up a lot of people," Terry said.

"And not without provocation," she agreed. "However, they lost two troopers; they didn't have to kill a couple million. That kind of soured our relationship from the beginning. Well, since day one, Asbaran Solutions has taken every contract they can get that lets them kill MinSha, even if they lose money."

"That's just one Horseman though," Terry pointed out.

"Aliens don't differentiate one hairless ape from another very well."

"Ah," he said. They walked on for a bit before he said anything else. "Were we in danger? I mean, really?"

"Humans are always in danger off Earth, young man." She looked down at him. "Don't forget that, okay?" He nodded. "Seriously, most aliens don't believe life is nearly as important as we do.

To the bugs, glassing Iran was just tit-for-tat. We killed two of theirs, they killed two million of ours."

"But aren't we making it worse by being mercs?"

"Maybe," she admitted, nodding slightly. "But some believe if we don't learn to fight them, we might not be around for long."

"We learned in school there are rules against that since we joined the Union."

"Oh, yeah," she said in mock seriousness. "Rules, right."

"You're making fun of me."

"Maybe," she said. "Sorry, but you have to understand that rules are made to be broken. You only get in trouble if you get caught."

"Won't the Peacemakers punish someone who kills us?"

"The Peacemaker Guild are a weird bunch," Tina said. "Who'd have thought a libertarian society with fewer rules than a street fight would have all powerful law enforcement. Shit, kid, they don't even have a single jail in the Union, did you know that?" He shook his head that he didn't. "If you do something the Peacemakers can ding you for, you either pay a hefty price, or…"

"Or what, Tina?"

"You pay the ultimate price. All I know is, don't even screw around when there's a new rule."

"What rule?"

"Well, the rules have always been; One, don't step on Superman's cape. Two, don't piss into the wind." Terry giggled at that. "Three, don't take the mask off the Lone Ranger. Now the fourth rule is don't piss off a Peacemaker."

"I'll remember that," he said. She gave him a rueful grin that made him wonder if she meant it. He'd have to do some reading on the Peacemakers, now that he had a full GalNet node at his disposal.

They approached a long line of carts set up in the promenade. These weren't permanent and weren't selling big things. It looked like they were meant to deal with tourists. *I'm a tourist,* he decided, and he slowed down to look over each cart. Tina stayed within a few meters and let him find his own way.

The first few seemed to specialize in food and drinks. Terry knew so little of the written languages he had to go by what he heard from vendors or customers. His translator was on automatic, and it converted whatever it heard and was capable of rendering into English. The tiny device could translate more than 100 simultaneous conversations. He'd learned that from his studies on Union pinplants. If he possessed pinplants, he could have programmed them to sort the multitude of conversations to search for something he was interested in, like his name or species being mentioned.

Lacking pinplants, Terry was forced to use his own perception to pick up on what was being said. He knew most of the foods wouldn't be palatable to him, or worse, could be poisonous. Human digestive systems were one of the most delicate, he'd heard.

He continued past those vendors and came across one selling guns. Right out in the open, racks upon racks of guns, ammo, and a case full of what looked like grenades! He stopped and stared. There wasn't even a living attendant, just a robot and a slate to enter your order and pay. Tina noticed he'd stopped and looked at him.

"You've never seen a robot kiosk before?" she asked.

"Those are guns! And grenades!"

"Yup."

"But what if I wanted to buy a gun, a kid?"

"Go for it."

His jaw fell open and he gawked at her. "But…"

"But what, junior? This isn't Earth, not everything is against the law, and there aren't cameras on every street corner watching you. Karma Station is a trade zone and a merc zone. A lot like the startowns around starports; only Union laws hold sway, and there ain't many of those. Don't they teach you this in school?"

"Yeah, but…"

"But what?"

"I guess it's not quite the same as seeing it for myself."

"There have been people on Earth who think like this for a long time. They're called libertarians. Whatever you want to do is okay, as long as you don't try to hurt other people."

"But if I buy that gun, I could hurt someone."

"And you'd be shot dead in short order. Look around you, kid. I mean, really *look*."

Terry made a face but looked around at all the aliens walking by. He wasn't sure what Tina had expected him to see until he noticed one had a gun. Then another, and another, and another! It looked like more were armed than weren't. A lot of them he was certain weren't merc races. Maybe even most.

"It looks like almost everyone has a gun!"

"Bingo," Tina said and mussed his hair. "I bet all of them do; you just can't see the ones who conceal."

"Aren't there any cops at all?"

"Karma employs several merc companies for security," she said, "though they're only lightly armed. You don't want anyone pulling off a major firefight inside a big pressurized tube in space."

"What if those MinSha had attacked you back in the pit?"

"Then we would have fought, though only with small arms and laser pistols. Don't want to piss off the neighbors." She winked at him, and he shook his head.

"It doesn't sound safe," he said.

"Nowhere in the universe is safe, kid."

Terry grunted. Doc had said the exact same thing quite a while ago. He'd shrugged it off, but it looked like the man had been more honest than Terry had thought.

Out of curiosity, he went to the kiosk and scrolled through the selections on the slate. He could read the numbers, though not most of the words. He recognized an 'audible' selection and pressed it. The slate spoke in various languages. When his translator understood one, he pressed the icon again.

"Welcome to Z'hhk'l's Weapons Emporium. Please select your category of weapon." It went on to list those categories: blade, blunt force, ballistic, energy weapon, high explosive, and a selection of defensive armors. The last was short.

Terry clicked on handgun, and pictures began to scroll by. Like Doc had said, their designs weren't for Human hands. Far from it. He picked one anyway. The gun enlarged to take up the entire screen, and a Tri-V popped up showing the various features. The kiosk said it had three in inventory, and the price was 75 credits, or 110 including a hard-shell box, two extra magazines, and 150 rounds of armor-piercing ammunition.

"Thing has quite a kick," Tina said over his shoulder.

"I was just curious," Terry said, his face turning red.

"Don't blame you. That gun is favored by the HecSha. They look a little like bipedal dinosaurs with flattened heads and a bad attitude." She took out a slate and tapped on it. A second later the Tri-V came on with a HecSha displayed. Obviously a merc, the alien carried all manner of guns, knives, and explosive devices. It looked at him and sneered, its mouth full of blunt yellowed teeth.

"Ugh," Terry said. He looked back at the gun and noted the price again. Doc had given him enough credits to buy a dozen of them. He began to understand what the man had meant by credits not being the same in value out there as dollars.

"Come on kid, if you want a gun, we'll get you one."

"No!" he said a little too defensively. "I don't want a gun, I was just…"

"Seeing if I was full of shit?" Terry spluttered. "It's cool, I usually *am* full of shit." He looked up at her, and she winked. Terry laughed, and they continued down the line of kiosks. In a little bit, he came to one he liked.

"Hey, now this is something!" he said. The kiosk had a Tri-V running over the booth showing a variety of slates and other computer equipment. "Do you think I can afford one?" he asked Tina.

"How much you got? I doubt dollars will convert out here; we're not common enough yet." Terry took out the 1,000 credit chit and showed her. "Woah, dude! Where'd you get that?"

"Doc gave it to me for working so hard while he was gone."

"Guy likes you, that's a nice little payment. Let's see…" she said. "I don't want to sit here all day while we do this slowly." She used her slate to interface with the kiosk. The computer was linked wirelessly to her own translator, allowing for text conversion. She knelt down so he could see the written inventory and prices.

The kiosk had slates ranging from ones it called 'Routine' to ones that were 'Industrial." Terry clicked on Routine, and it showed a list, varying by size and configuration. He'd only seen the ones a few aliens carried and that his father had bought for the institute. They'd all been rectangular and transparent. He realized that was only one of a thousand variations. Many were hexagonal, or hourglass shaped. They even had some that were as thin as a pencil.

"I didn't know there were so many," he said, shaking his head.

"You just want one for yourself?"

"Yeah," he said.

"Let me." She clicked on the slate, and in a second three were displayed. All were similar to the ones he'd seen his mom using, though in three different colors, and one wasn't transparent. However, the cheapest was, and labeled as 'reconditioned'. He was used to that on Earth; a lot of high-end electronics were recycled. He clicked on the one at the bottom of the list. It was 19 credits.

"That's it?" he wondered.

"Sure," she said. "There's probably a thousand companies making a million of those every day. They're like water bottles back on Earth, cheap and everywhere."

Terry clicked on a new version of the same slate. It was 53 credits. "Can you show me one of the Industrial type?"

"Sure," Tina said. She clicked a few times. The selection there wasn't as large. "These aren't always made to be easily portable," she said and pointed to the dimensions. "That's translated into English meters."

Terry could see what she meant; most were pretty big. The smallest was 34 centimeters by 19. He conjured up a mental image. It would be a little bigger than his tablet back on *Teddy Roosevelt*. He clicked price. That model would cost 198 credits. He looked at Tina and grinned.

"Go for it," she said, "it's your money after all!"

Terry gleefully pressed the select button. A little window lit up on the side of the kiosk where a door opened. He placed the chit inside, and the door closed. "What if it doesn't give me the slate?" he asked suspiciously.

"That would be how you got your expensive robotic kiosk shot full of holes," Tina said and winked. "Remember that HecSha? What do you think it would do if a slate didn't pop out?"

Terry laughed and imagined the alien merc eating the kiosk. *Crunch, crunch, yum!*

The machine displayed some words on the screen above where he'd put the money. Tina held up her slate for him. "Processing Request," it said.

"It's probably verifying the credit chit is genuine. Takes a few seconds." The machine beeped and new words appeared.

"Would you prefer cash or credit in change?"

"Cash," Terry said. Tina pressed the selection for him. The same door he'd put his money into reopened. Inside was a box and a small stack of credits. He took the slate and tucked it under his arm while counting the credits. There were eight 100 credit chits, and two little 1 credit chits.

"Are you satisfied with your transaction?" the machine asked.

Terry opened the plastic box and found exactly what he'd ordered inside; a shiny new silver-backed slate. He found the activation plate at the bottom, just like on his mom's, and pressed it. The slate came alive with sliding alien script.

"We can get it configured in a minute," Tina said, then pressed "Yes" to answer the machine.

"Thank you for your transaction."

"Holy cow!" Terry said, and turned the slate over and over in his hands.

"Score, kid," Tina said. "Come on, there's a little place just over there that serves drinks. I have a program code for a few you might like. We can have a drink, and I'll get that slate working in English."

Terry nodded and followed her like a puppy dog, never taking his eyes off the amazing machine he'd just bought for only 20% of his money. He was also thinking, *What else can I get while I'm here?*

* * * * *

Chapter Nine

For the first time, Terry was in a hurry to return to his quarters after doing his chores and giving Pōkole his morning feeding. He didn't have a lot of time because he needed to get to his studies. Regardless, he was committed to spending some time with his new slate.

Her familiarity with the technology, as well as an understanding of some Union languages had enabled Tina to set up his slate in just a few minutes. It had been hard for him to sit on the little shop bench and wait; he'd clenched his hands under the table as she worked. Finally, she spun it around on the table and the writing was in English.

"I interfaced it with my own tablet and uploaded an English matrix. You can add other languages later."

All thoughts of seeing where he could spend some more of his loot was gone as he began to explore the slate, and he quickly realized it wasn't just a fancy computer. It was more powerful than the most capable Human-manufactured computer ever made.

He did make one more stop before heading back to the Pit of Occo. He went to the same kiosk he'd bought the slate from and also bought a carrying case designed to fit it perfectly. Thanks to the new slate, he didn't need Tina's help ordering, either. It cost him another five credits for the case, and one credit for an adjustable strap. At the same time, he dropped 100 credits into his Yack. Now he had some digital money to play with as well. US currency was less than useless out in the galaxy.

Comfortable in the cabin he shared with his mom, Terry linked the slate with *Teddy Roosevelt*'s computer, and through it to the Gal-Net. The slate instantly began an update cycle, telling him it was copying 11 petabytes of data.

"Oh, no," he said, gawking at the number. He went into the slate's internals and checked on available memory. The slate had four exabytes. "Exabyte?" he wondered, and accessed the ship's computer for a reference base he'd understand. In a second he had the answer and gasped out loud. An exabyte was 1,024 petabytes, and of course a petabyte was 1024 terabytes. The little silver slate had 11.5 million *terabytes* of data. His old slate had 10 terabytes, with just 2 available for downloaded data. In short, the new slate was a *beast*.

"It isn't even the best," he said as he clicked around. He'd bought it from a kiosk in a tourist area of Karma Station. That must mean the really powerful ones were sold in other locations where serious customers could be expected. Tina and Doc had said Karma was only a minor trading hub, which meant they wouldn't have the best computer technology available. Of course, he'd spent almost 200 credits, which on Earth would be $7 million.

He went back to the main screen and checked the download status. "Time to complete—65 hours."

"Crap," he said. It must be the *Teddy Roosevelt*'s computer causing the bottleneck. "So, can I just connect to the GalNet directly?" He tried. The slate informed him three GalNet nodes were available with a transfer rate of one petabyte a second, ten petabytes a second, and twenty-five petabytes a second. Of course, having his own connection would cost him. He checked how much, and grinned. Even the slowest, one petabyte a second, only cost two credits per day.

Terry pulled out his Yack and bought a months' worth of access and got a discount to 50 credits. Money well spent, he decided, and resolved to put most of the rest of his credits on his Yack. He was beginning to understand what Doc had meant about the economies being different once you got off of Earth. His 1,000 credits wouldn't go far.

With his own personal temporary GalNet node, the download took 11 seconds. Afterward he had a completely up-to-date and working slate, just in time to do his school work. *Crap.* He wanted to use the slate for the work, but he had some trouble getting the slate to interface with his tablet. It seemed the tablet was so slow, the slate didn't think it was even working.

Terry went ahead and did his classwork on the old tablet, all the while chewing over how to get the new slate to behave with his old tablet. He was just about done when his mom floated in, yawning and half asleep.

"Hey," he said.

"Oh, hi. I wondered where you were." She slid over to their wardrobe and grabbed her towel and a clean pair of sweats. The ship never quite kept up with their laundry needs.

"Yeah, I wanted to work here. You're back late."

"The orcas are starting to show some negative effects of extended zero gravity," she explained.

"I thought that wasn't a concern because they don't need the exercise we do."

"Sort of," she said. "They get their basic exercise from swimming around. There isn't much room, but we've got all the cetaceans doing laps twice a day. The bottlenoses understand better than the orcas." She got a curious look on her face. "Anyway, it isn't physical strength or bone, it's digestive. Something nobody expected."

"What can we do about it?" Terry asked.

She smiled, glad he was so engaged. "Dr. Jaehnig's working on it, but he's worried there's nothing we can do except get them out of space as soon as possible."

Terry knew all too well that keeping them all supplied with fish was also becoming an issue. *Kavul Tesh* had been positively *crammed* with frozen fish, hundreds of tons. But they'd been in space for months. They'd managed to buy some fresh fish from traders on Karma Station, after extensive testing of samples to verify it would be edible by their charges. Even so, supplies were getting slim.

"What are you working on there?" She'd noticed his new slate.

"I bought it over on Karma Station with Doc yesterday!" He held it out for her to see.

"Holy cow," she said, looking at it with wide eyes. She rolled it over in her hands, examining its build, then tapped on the controls icon to see capacity. "Damn!" she said. "This is 10 times better than our best ones. How much did Doc give you?"

"That one cost 198 credits," he said. "I got a few extras with it."

"Most of ours were under 20 credits," she said, her mouth turning into a frown. "He gave you 200 credits."

"No, he gave me 1,000."

Her eyes went wide. "That's like 30 million."

"More like 35 million," he said, but he was getting suspicious.

"Terry, we're struggling to make ends meet."

"I know, I didn't spend it all. I thought a new slate would be a good investment. They practically last forever."

"I know, ours are like 300 years old," she mumbled under her breath.

"You're not going to take away my money, are you?"

"No, you earned it." she said, though he could see she'd thought about doing just that. "I think I need to talk to Doc about this, though. Take extra good care of that slate, ok?"

"You know it," he said, breathing a little easier. "I got a custom carrying case for it, too."

She made a face and headed out into the corridor with her clean sweats and a towel. She came back a minute later, her mood even worse. There was no hot water.

* * *

The next morning he ran into Doc and his team in *Kavul Ato*'s equipment bay. They were working on some kind of metalworking gear. Terry was there for a new seal on one of the water transfer pumps and hopefully a Union-designed electronics diagnostic tool. It would interface with his slate and help figure out why one of the pumps kept chewing up seals.

"Hey, kiddo," Doc said as he watched Honcho and Peyto swear and fight with a fitting.

"Hey, Doc," Terry said and floated to a stop. He watched the two big beefy SEALs struggle to get a good bracing in zero G, while also trying to apply force in opposite directions. "Did mom talk to you?"

"About your money and slate, oh yeah."

"Uh, oh," Terry said.

"Don't sweat it," Doc said. "She's honked I didn't tell her about the money I gave you."

"What did you say?"

"I said what I gave you was my business, not hers."

"Wow," was all he could manage.

"You gotta keep 'em in line," Tina said and winked.

Terry blushed, though he didn't know why. "What did she say to that?"

"What could she say?" he said, and shrugged. "She asked me to tell her next time I gave you money, and I said I would. That much was her prerogative."

Terry didn't understand how that worked, but he did understand getting between grownups having a disagreement was a *bad* idea. Peyto let out a grunt, and the nut broke free. The huge man managed to not crash into the wall behind him, mainly through an amazingly acrobatic move. After he recovered, Honcho slapped him a high-five while Toothpick slid in and removed the bolt. It looked for all the world like they were working on a tiny spaceship.

"What is that?" Terry asked. Tina glanced at him and looked away. Was there a hint of a grin on her face?

"I can't tell you right now," Doc said. To make it worse, Piano moved between the thing, whatever it was, and Terry. Peyto already had a deck of cards out and was back to playing with his buddy Hutch.

Terry made a face and thought about trying to use his slate to get some pictures, then decided against it. Instead he gave up and went to the stores area to look for the parts he needed. The SEALs continued talking but kept the volume down too low for Terry to hear anything. He got what he needed and headed out the door. Doc watched him the whole way, nodding and giving him a half smile. Terry just frowned.

He returned to the pump room, floating down the corridors from memory without thinking about it. One of *Kavul Tesh*'s maintenance techs was looking over the technical manual on his personal slate, trying to make sense out of what was wrong. Terry took the diagnostic tool, connected to the pump, and linked it with his new slate.

"That's an impressive slate," the tech said.

"I just got it," Terry said and loaded all 22 diagnostic subroutines. With a click, he ran them simultaneously. "And yeah, it's pretty cool."

"I'll say," the tech said. "I can only run two of those at the same time; and it's slower, too."

Terry grinned as the machine worked. He had the results in only a few minutes, and the tech was able to adjust the parameters.

"I would never have guessed the pulse rate would cause the seals to fail," the man said. "Thanks, kid."

"No problem," Terry said and went happily back to the hold to see how the bottlenoses were doing.

Because his duties mostly revolved around Pōkole, Terry seldom got to see the Sunrise Pod. Because there were so many of them, they had more space than either of the orca pods. All three holds within *Kavul Tesh* had been converted to tankage and interconnected to provide thousands of cubic meters of tank space. Water was purchased from a tanker—normally used for reaction mass—and loaded aboard. Converting it to the right chemical structure wasn't difficult.

"Terry, Terry, Terry!" they greeted him in their traditional manner.

"Hello, Sunrise Pod. How are you doing?"

"*Miss sky, miss beyond,*" Skritch said.

"I know," Terry said. "I miss the sky too." *Though I don't miss hyperspace,* he thought.

"*How long?*" Hoa asked.

"You mean how long have we been here?"

"*How more long?*" Skritch said.

"I don't know," Terry admitted.

"*Understand,*" Skritch said, and he went off to swim through the various tunnels connecting the sections together.

"They're worried."

Terry turned and saw Dr. Orsage floating by the door with his ever-present slate, taking notes. "About what?"

"Three of the females are pregnant."

"Oh!" Terry said, surprised. "I thought they were getting drugs to suppress that."

"They were," the cetacean psychologist said. "It doesn't seem to have worked. When a routine test showed the pregnancies, we discontinued the drug."

"When are the babies due?"

"In about 7 months is our estimate."

"They're worried about having the babies here on the ship?"

"Yes," Orsage agreed. "So are we, actually. Now, excuse me."

Terry went back to his room after he finished Pōkole's late feeding. The calf was growing at a phenomenal rate and showed no negative signs of zero G, unlike the adult orcas. In his room, he logged into the education network and checked for classes he needed to work on.

Several of the other kids were getting together to swim later. He wasn't as interested as he would have been before leaving Earth. Yui wasn't there, and he spent half the day in the water already. He thought he might go this time; it was usually fun to play with the bottlenoses. Then he found something that changed his plans for him. Messages from Earth!

* * *

T erry opened the packet from his mom's account. There was a brief note attached.

"Terry, these came in a couple of days ago. We weren't keeping them from you; we just wanted to be sure no virus or anything else was attached. If you want to wait until I get back to our compartment before reading them, I'll be there on time tonight. If not, well, you're grown enough to make your own decisions. Just know the Earth Republic has been intercepting our messages, just like we thought. This got through because we paid a trader to bring them. Love, Mom."

He stared at the email packet for almost an entire minute. Eventually, he elected to open it. There were 32 messages inside. Terry yipped with excitement, until he realized only 11 of them were personal messages.

A bunch were from the middle school informing him he'd been suspended, and threatening disciplinary action if he didn't report back to school. Those messages made him laugh. "Come and get me!" he said, and moved the messages to the archive. The next were more worrisome. The World High Court had tried the staff of the PCRI in absentia.

Terry used the Human internet and looked it up. It meant they had been tried without being present, something apparently allowed in the Earth Republic. Everyone on staff was found guilty of various crimes, ranging from illegal experimentation on an endangered marine mammal to destruction of evidence and contributing to the delinquency of a minor. He was mentioned prominently in the last.

While he hadn't been directly tried because he was a minor, he was remanded into the custody of the state for psychological evaluation. Parental rights were stripped from his mother and father, and he would be tried in juvenile court once he returned to Earth. Apparently the ability to try people without being able to defend themselves didn't extend to kids.

"We're all criminals," he realized. Attached were a slew of news articles dating from a month ago up to only a week ago. Huge banner stories proclaiming that "The Hawaiian Mad Scientists" were found guilty. "Bastards," he said. The press had tried and found them guilty long before the courts, apparently. There was even a picture of him and his parents taken two years ago, long before all of the events that had led him hundreds of light years from his home.

One video showed the press trying to get into his old middle school to interview his friends. He had a second of video showing a teacher escorting Yui away as the staff tried to stop the press from getting to her.

They'd prosecuted Doc and his men, too. They'd gotten him on the same contributing to the delinquency of a minor charge—for him, of course. The other men, including the two who were now dead, were tried as traitors to the Republic and found guilty as well. They'd still been on active duty. That explained why Doc hadn't been back to Earth in all these months, too.

Afterward, he went looking for personal messages. There were three, one from his father, and two from Yui. Just two messages in the months he'd been gone. He opened the one from his dad.

"Son,

I don't know how to say I'm sorry. Everything just went wrong. I know people are telling you I hurt your mom, but I didn't. Please believe me, I did it all for her. I just got carried away. Do you understand? Of course, you know the pinplants on the cetaceans were an accident. We should have waited and got outside help. Again, your mom was right, and I was wrong. I made more mistakes than I did things right. I only wish I'd been able to go with you. Please, write back?

Dad, I love you."

He'd never really apologized for what he did, only how it went wrong. Terry could clearly see his dad trying to justify his actions and avoid the truth. It made his dad more guilty in Terry's mind. He knew for a fact that Doc and his SEAL buddies had gotten the alien nanite treatment to his mom, and his dad wouldn't allow it, so they did it in secret. Not allowing Doc's friends to try, more than any other act, convinced him his father was lying on some level. Maybe on all of them. He didn't write a reply. Maybe later. He opened the first message from Yui. It was marked only a day after he'd been spirited away.

"Terry, OMG, I can't believe what just happened! It's all over the news! There are like a million reporters all over Molokai! I tried to talk to you longer, but the phone cut out. I wanted to say...I wanted to say how much...how much of a friend you are. We know you're on a ship and the Winged Hussars are taking you out-system. The government is *pissed!* It's funny. LOL. Everyone at school knows you guys didn't do anything wrong, so don't worry about it, okay? I'll write again soon, and hope you can, too.

Bye, I miss you."

"I miss you too," he said, even though he knew she couldn't hear him. He opened the second email.

"They convicted you guys in court. I'm sneaking this message out, but it's the last one. My father's forbidding me to send any others. I'll try, but I don't get an independent account until I turn 16. You know Dad's a government contractor; if I get caught...well, he could lose his job. I wish you'd sent something, or someone came back to fight in court? I...goodbye."

"No," he said, "what?" He reread it, wondering if she'd put in a hidden code. No matter how he read it, the message came out the same. Goodbye forever from his best friend. He was still staring at the message when his mom came in. The look on his face told her he'd read the messages.

"I'm sorry," she said.

"It wasn't your fault," Terry said. He was surprised he wasn't more emotional. Maybe there weren't any more emotions left in him. "Maybe it will all get fixed down the road."

"Maybe," she said. The sad smile on her face told him the truth of it; she didn't believe it would ever be fixed. Terry would never see Yui, or Earth, again. Terry went back to his school work.

* * * * *

Chapter Ten

erry turned 12 years old with Doc away again, working a contract on which none of the details were shared. It had something to do with the machine they'd been working on in the mechanical area aboard *Kavul Tesh*. Thanks to the huge infusion of credits, they were no longer in any danger of losing a place to stay, either. Doc's Last Call merc company sent millions more, and the captains of the three ships were just as happy to float near Karma and get paid as they were to fly around the galaxy. "Less risk," Captain Baker said with a wink.

Terry pushed his lessons hard. The lessons and taking care of Pōkole kept his mind mostly off the loss of Yui as a friend. Before her message, he'd been able to tell himself it was only temporary, like a long summer vacation, and they'd be diving off Molokai again sometime soon. The illusion was revealed now, and the bitter truth hurt. He buried his feelings in his duties and studies. Pōkole enjoyed the attention, and Moloko even began referring to Terry as a member of the Shore Pod. Of everything, having them think of him as a member of their pod helped. It helped a lot.

Thanksgiving passed, and his mom was pretty sad. Terry could tell she'd become quite attached to Doc, and he was off on some alien world fighting to make them money. She was quiet the entire

239

time they ate. Besides, zero gravity turkey wasn't as fun as the regular kind, or as tasty.

It wasn't just his mom, Terry noticed, the general mood of the staff was down. Of course everyone knew they weren't going back to Earth any time soon, or possibly ever. He wondered if those feelings were at all blunted by the knowledge, had they been still on Earth, most would now be in jail. Terry decided it was best not to ask anyone.

On the morning of the 4th, he was awoken to the sounds of more activity on *Teddy Roosevelt* than he'd heard in quite some time. Sounds he knew meant they would be getting underway. He dressed and quickly headed for the big dome observation blister, the location he knew his mom would be running things from.

Terry floated in through the hatch and immediately saw Doc talking with his mom and Captain Baker. Doc noticed him come in and threw him a wink. Terry waved and stayed by the door. Adults talking usually meant they didn't want kids in the middle of it all. He caught a handhold and waited. In addition to the captain, his mother, and Doc, all the senior scientists from the institute were there.

He didn't wait for long. The conversation finished, and his mom turned to him and beckoned for him to come on over. Terry pushed off the wall and expertly grabbed a hold next to them. "Hey, welcome back!" he said to Doc.

"Good to be back, kiddo."

Terry turned to his mom. "I heard all the noise; we're getting ready to move?" He tried to control the surge of hope flowing through him at the slim chance everything was fixed on Earth, and they were heading home.

"We found a place to go while we figure out what to do long term," his mom said.

Not home. "Is it nearby?"

Doc and his mom looked at each other, and Doc said, "It's about 8,000 light years from here." Terry's eyes bugged out. "That isn't as far as it sounds."

"Sounds pretty damn far to me!"

"Watch your language," his mom cautioned.

"Sorry," Terry said.

"We can get there in one jump," Captain Baker told him.

"Why are we in such a hurry?" Terry asked.

Doc looked at his mom, who nodded, so he explained. "Just before I got back, an Earth Republic corvette jumped in-system. They had orders to board *Teddy Roosevelt* and take as many of us into custody as possible."

"I didn't hear about it," Terry said in surprise.

"We didn't tell anyone," Captain Baker said. "Or how all three of our ships powered up their weapons and shields, refusing to be boarded."

"What happened next?"

"The Earth ship tried to send over boarding parties," Doc said. "My men and I got in a shuttle and were going to return the favor. They were less skilled in such tactics and only had a few security forces."

A small smile appeared on the captain's face, and she winked. "They decided it was in their best interest not to enforce those orders."

"But it's a warship, right?"

"A small one," Doc said. "All ships carry some form of weaponry. The corvette might be more than a match for a single merchant, but not three of them. They were outmatched on all fronts."

"So they went back to Earth?"

"No, they're still here, waiting." Captain Baker said.

"We'll be leaving," Doc said. "Catching a ride in a few hours."

"How?" Terry wondered.

"On a Behemoth."

The captain pointed out the observation dome, and Terry could see a growing shape in the distance, a huge round structure growing steadily closer. To his shock, he realized it was a spaceship.

* * *

Its name was *Second Octal*, a 29,000-year-old ship that had plied the galactic space lanes while Earth was still held in the grasp of a global ice age, and man had yet to learn how to read or write. At a diameter of just over two kilometers, *Second Octal* was a medium-sized *Behemoth*-class transport.

Terry spent the hours before they docked digesting all he could on the *Behemoth*-class transports. He learned they made a large part of their income from simply carrying non-hyperspace-capable transports like theirs from system to system. They also carried untold billions of tons of freight every year. Everything from huge automated factories known as manufactories, to shipments of the tiny robots known as nanites, like the ones that had healed his mom. They also never, ever, stopped moving.

The vast spherical ships contained entire families who spent their entire lives on board. They would be born, grow up, live, and eventually die there. The ships maintained a constant spin, producing gravity on the inside of the outer hull. What they didn't have was powerful engines. A *Behemoth* was lucky to generate $1/10^{th}$ of a G in thrust. They moved from system to system on courses planned years, sometimes centuries, in advance. Using this method, they could arrive at just the right time, and in the right direction, so they didn't have to use their engines at all, simply coasting from one emergence point to the system's stargate, and onward.

In each system, ships would meet them to transfer cargo and passengers. It was extremely efficient, if not always easy to coordinate.

As *Teddy Roosevelt*, *Kavul Tesh*, and *Kavul Ato* accelerated toward the *Behemoth*, Terry was in the observation dome watching the ship get closer. It was like the old movie *Star Wars* in some ways. The closer they got, the more details he could see. It began as a featureless form and slowly gained more detail.

The ship was shaped like an elongated sphere, spinning with its narrow ends facing perpendicular to its angle of rotation, so it flew through space almost sideways. He began to see bands around the widest part in the middle and could see large structures on the bands. Then, as they got ever closer, he realized there were ships, like his, docked along the outside.

"How are we going to dock with the outside spinning?" Terry asked.

"Carefully, lad," Captain Baker said and shook her head. "Very, very carefully." She left a short time later to go to the bridge, leaving the rest to watch from the dome.

Doc talked with his mom, describing the merc contract he and his men had completed while they were gone. No fighting was involved, which greatly relieved both Terry and her. They'd scouted an old abandoned industrial complex on an out-of-the-way world. Terry didn't know mercs did those sorts of jobs, but Doc said they'd do whatever paid them. The bonus this time was they'd gotten an opportunity to live on the same location.

"What's it like?" Terry asked.

"It's hard to explain," Doc said. "We'll be having a big meeting once we're back in hyperspace."

"We'll have nine hours after we dock with *Second Octal*," his mom said.

"If we dock with it," Dr. Patel said.

"What do you mean, sir?" Terry asked.

"I've seen this operation before. I've made two trips to space before this, both for research. The second time we saw one of those," he pointed at the approaching ship. "This freighter was trying to dock with it. They tried three times, and missed every time. It's a little like trying to jump on a moving train from a moving car. There isn't much margin for error."

"What happened?"

"Well, they tried a fourth time and missed again, badly. They hit the *Behemoth* and a big chunk of their hull was torn out. A bunch of their crew died. I think they had to pay the *Behemoth* for the damages, too."

"Suck city," Terry said.

"I concur, young man."

An hour before they met up with the bigger ship, their three vessels undocked. The scientists split up and left to tend to the various pods. Terry's mom asked him to stay with Doc in the observation bubble.

"You'll be safe here and have a great view," she said. *Teddy* only had the one docking collar capable of mating with the *Behemoth*, but it was on her belly. Sadly, their safety would be paid for with the worst seats in the house.

"I'll keep an eye on him," Doc said; Terry made a face. "We'll have a good view of the other ships docking, though," he reminded Terry. Then the ships were undocked and under power for the first time in months.

The trick was to match courses with the *Behemoth*, approaching at the larger ship's velocity *and* its speed of rotation. You came along-side, perfectly timed with your docking collar rotated into the exact position, clamp on, magnetically lock yourself to the hull, and hang on. The stress on your ship could be substantial as you were pulled into their rotation. Captain Baker said a couple seconds of three Gs would be about it.

"The docking collar flexes to take up the forces," he explained over the PA as they approached. "Unfortunately, nothing can be done about the inertial forces of being slung around. After we dock, we can enjoy half a G all the way to our destination."

Kavul Tesh was first. The three ships were strung out in a line, with *Teddy* second, and *Kavul Ato* last. In the middle they had a good view of the insectoid shape of *Kavul Tesh* rolling so it's back was to the *Behemoth* as it caught up to it. The huge spinning transport loomed over the other ship like an elephant over an ant. Terry real-ized he was shaking his head and holding his breath at the same time.

It was anticlimactic when it happened. One moment *Kavul Tesh* was directly alongside, the next she was accelerating away and quickly lost around the middle of the *Behemoth*'s bulk.

"Our turn," Doc said.

The three transports had requested adjacent docking positions, and had been granted them. Thus they were spaced so as to be in position at exactly the time it took for *Second Octal* to orbit around once. Terry and Doc saw *Kavul Tesh* coming around just as the captain rolled *Teddy Roosevelt*'s belly toward the *Behemoth*, blocking their view.

Doc made sure Terry was secured in a chair, then himself. The seconds crept by.

"Standby to dock," the confident voice of Captain Baker came over the PA. Terry tensed. There was a bump followed by a resounding *Clang!* though the hull, and suddenly they were thrown upward in their chairs.

Terry looked up at the dome, which was now decidedly *down*, with alarm. The straps held firm as it felt like his eyeballs were going to pop out. A second later, the force fell off.

"There we go," Doc said. He unclamped his harness and did a graceful flip, falling a couple meters to the glass dome with a thump. "Come on, kiddo."

Not to be outdone, Terry unlocked his. It came undone much faster than he'd expected, and he fell face-first toward the glass. "Shit!" he yipped.

"Gotcha," Doc said and caught him easily, then spun him around and put him on his feet. Terry wobbled at bit. Months in zero G with only a single day on Karma Station had left his legs wobbly. They all exercised every day, but it wasn't the same thing.

"Sorry," Terry said. Doc patted him on the shoulder. Terry looked down and out into the spinning abyss. He swallowed. "Is this safe?"

"As safe as space gets," Doc said. Terry's eyes snapped up to his, and he saw the man smiling, then laughing.

"Jerk," Terry said, and punched him in the stomach as hard as he could. It was like punching a bag in the gym.

"Hey, easy there, I'm old and frail. Help me out; these chairs can be repositioned so we can watch *Kavul Ato* dock."

Just like Doc said, the chairs were designed to be dismounted from the 'roof,' where they were now, and relocated to numerous places in the observation dome. None of them would make the seats perfectly upright, like they would have been if the ship was sitting on the ground. It was enough to sit at a 20-degree angle, though, especially in the low half-gravity, to allow them to watch their last ship dock.

Terry could tell right away something looked wrong. *Kavul Ato* wasn't quite on the right course. The captain tried hard to change courses, but there wasn't enough time. Suddenly they stopped trying and fired braking thrusters to slow down. As *Teddy* orbited away, *Kavul Ato* fell back.

"Why'd they stop?" Terry wondered aloud.

"Probably waved off by the *Behemoth*." Terry looked at him uncomprehendingly. "It's a signal you give to someone trying to land if it's not going to work." He waved his hands back and forth. "Wave off, get it?"

"Oh, sure. But what now?"

"I suspect they'll try again."

They did, and the two watched the transport orbit into view again. This time they were coming in too quickly, and overshot.

"What do we do if they can't dock?" Terry asked. Pōkole and the Shore Pod were on the other ship. They wouldn't leave them in Karma, would they?

Doc used his communicator to call Terry's mom, who was with the bottlenoses on their ship. After a brief conference, he turned to Terry. "If she can't dock, we're going to undock and rejoin her."

"What about the planet we're going to?" Terry asked.

"That would be off the table," Doc said. "We have a limited window, and this *Behemoth* is the only ship going there for the next three months."

Terry blew air out between his lips and watched as *Kavul Ato* again orbited into view. He thought it looked out of position again, and he saw some of its maneuvering thrusters firing. However, this time the corrections worked. The ship fell in directly behind them, and he felt a slight reverberation through the hull.

"*Kavul Ato* has successfully docked," the captain announced.

"Yes!" Terry cried and gave Doc a high five.

Doc put his hand to his headset. "Your mom says I'm to take you to *Kavul Ato* so you can help with the orcas there. Ready to go aboard *Second Octal?*"

"You know it!"

* * * * *

Chapter Eleven

Kavul Ato, Karma Star System, Cresht Region, Tolo Arm
December 4th, 2037

Moving through *Second Octal* turned out to be anticlimactic. Terry and Doc climbed out of the belly of *Teddy Roosevelt* on rungs intended for the other direction. The crew was busy reconfiguring their ship for its unusual gravity orientation, so nobody was at the lock when the two moved through it. It was the same at the other end when they cycled into *Second Octal*.

"You'd think they'd have some security," Doc noted.

Terry nodded; that would have made sense. On the other side of the lock, they climbed onto a wide corridor with a slight curvature in both directions. It reminded him of Karma Station's promenade, which made sense, as *Second Octal* had nearly the same diameter. *Only this is a starship,* Terry thought.

He didn't know which way to go, but Doc set them off in the direction he was sure would lead to *Kavul Ato*. Unlike Karma Station, there were no shops or aliens moving about on their business. It was completely empty.

They moved along until they saw an elevator shaft going up. Doc examined the sign. "This lift goes to the other areas of the ship," he said. "You need an access card."

"Still surprised there's no real security," Terry said. Doc nodded, and they continued on until reaching the docking location of *Kavul Ato*. A crewman from the ship was waiting for them; apparently the same lack of security that didn't keep someone from entering *Second Octal* would also not have prevented them from entering the ship without invitation.

"Dr. Clark said you were coming," the man said and followed them into the lock.

Once in the ship, Terry quickly made his way to the hold where the Shore Pod was. Two marine biologists were already in the tank giving the orcas anesthetic. One of the ship's crew, a cargo handler, was standing by watching.

"The whales asked to be knocked out," the crewman said, shaking his head. "They don't like hyperspace, do they?"

"Not at all," Terry agreed and he quickly got into his wetsuit and grabbed a rebreather. Pōkole was swimming around his mother, circling over and over nervously.

Once he was in the water, he went to the calf, who immediately turned and nuzzled Terry nervously. "It'll be okay," Terry said and stroked the infant's long, smooth side. He looked to see who was administering the sedatives. "Dr. Patel?"

"Yes, Terry?" the doctor replied a few meters away.

"Are you going to drug Pōkole too?"

"Your mother said it's up to you."

"Oh!" Terry said, surprised. He looked at Pōkole floating next to him, and then at the calf's mother, who was slowly falling asleep. The adults couldn't handle hyperspace, but Pōkole had been born there, and had shown no signs of trouble for the following four days.

"Don't give him anything," Terry said, "but you better give me the dosage necessary and show me how to use it, just in case."

Dr. Patel met him outside the tank a few minutes later. The ship's techs were pleased with themselves, having installed exits to the tanks on the ceiling and the floor, just in case the ships were forced to dock in unusual orientations. Once they were out of the water, he showed Terry the injector and how it operated.

"Make sure you inject at the base of the flukes," he told Terry and showed him with a slate. "If you're smooth with the injector, he'll hardly feel a thing. Maybe do it while he's feeding." Dr. Patel checked the time. "We're due to enter hyperspace in two hours, so be ready."

"Yes, sir," Terry said, and took the injector. "I hope I don't need it."

"Me too, son."

Terry got back in the tank and spent time keeping Pōkole calm and reassuring him. The young orca was confused, wondering why none of the orcas were responding to him. He didn't remember a few months ago just after he was born. The body language of an orca was easy to detect and uncomplicated. Terry could tell Pōkole was scared.

"Entering the stargate in five minutes," Terry heard over his underwater earphones.

Here we go, he thought. He swam to the surface and got the milk bottle from its warmer. Pōkole saw and immediately darted over for some food. The calf had long since gotten gentler about his feeding habits, not knocking Terry all over the pool in his impatience. Pōkole used to be nearly three times the Human's size, and had since grown to over four times.

Based on the medical staff's analysis, Pōkole was gaining 1-2 kilos a day. Drinking five liters of the fat-dense milk a day certainly helped. There was so much fat in the milk, it was more the consistency of toothpaste than what Terry thought of as milk. Some of the stored and purchased fish was being processed into the milk each day.

"Entering hyperspace," Terry heard.

He felt the jolting sensation of being destroyed and rebuilt again. Instantly all four adult orcas spasmed in their drug-induced slumber, then settled in the simple fabric slings rigged to keep them at the tank's surface so the rebreathers weren't necessary. Pōkole stopped feeding and rolled to look at Terry. His eye was already the size of an adult Human's fist. The calf blinked and focused on his benefactor.

Oh, no, Terry thought. His instinct was to back away, just in case. Instead, he let the bottle float free and ran both hands along the orca's side. "It's okay, baby," he said, sure the sounds would transfer in the water despite the rebreather in his mouth. "You're safe."

Pōkole looked around, swimming a slow circle around Terry and observing his surroundings as if he sensed something was wrong. Terry reached back and took the injector. It was too big to hide, but he kept it against his stomach and covered it with the bottle in his other hand to make it less visible. He doubted the calf knew what it was.

Eventually Pōkole drifted back over to Terry and nuzzled against him uncertainly. Terry moved along the calf's body toward the tail. He kept the mental image of the spot Dr. Patel had said to use as the injection point firmly in his mind, all the while praying he wouldn't have to do it.

Finally, Pōkole poked the bottle with his nose, a sure sign he wanted more food. Terry exhaled a line of bubbles, then offered it to the calf, who began to eat contentedly. He was going to be alright. Terry tucked the injector behind his back and concentrated on feeding Pōkole.

* * *

"How's Pōkole?"

"He's fine, Mom," Terry said as he walked awkwardly into *Teddy Roosevelt's* galley. The crew had done as good a job as they could configuring it to operate upside down. It hadn't been designed with the same flexibility as *Kavul Ato* and *Kavul Tesh*. Regardless of how you looked at the room, it appeared like they were eating on the ceiling. Even the little autochef was held to an exposed support beam by clamps. "He doesn't show any signs of the adult orcas' reaction to hyperspace."

"Good," she said. Terry got some food from the autochef and joined her. "The bottlenoses are practically drunk with excitement," she said after he'd sat down on the awkwardly mounted bench.

"I'd like to find out why," Terry said after he'd had a bite of food. He made a face at the bland concoction. He couldn't tell what it was supposed to be.

"I think you have enough to do with your studies and Pōkole," she said, glancing up at him.

"Aw, Mom…"

"Don't 'aw Mom' me," she said. "Your grades in math last week weren't great."

"They were 92%," he complained.

"Your tests the previous week were 98%."

"Doc says even the best have an off week once in a while."

"Doc isn't your dad."

"Not yet," he said, and glanced up at his mom. She was decidedly looking down at her food with a slightly rosy glow to her cheeks. *Gotcha*, he thought. "Doc and his crew are going over to explore the *Second Octal* tomorrow. Can I go?" She'd never heard the details of their encounter with the MinSha on Karma Station, and if Terry had his way, she never would.

"I want to go over, too. Can you boys control yourselves until midwatch?"

Terry smiled; it sounded like fun.

* * * * *

Chapter Twelve

I t turned out getting onto the *Behemoth* was simply a matter of asking. All docked non-merc ships were allowed free access to the ship's various common areas. Since it was a kilometer and a half across, those common areas were enormous.

Terry was able to read up a bit on *Second Octal* specifically. Its crew was listed as "Approximately 4,000" and mostly Maki. While he'd seen Maki on Earth, they were a race he wasn't familiar with, so he looked them up before bed. They'd reminded him of monkeys when he'd first seen them back home. Now, as he looked at the GalNet images, they were more like lemurs. Only these were much bigger, though somewhat smaller than Humans, had split tails, and were also a merc race. "I wonder what they're doing running big space freighters?" he had wondered before drifting off to sleep.

"You guys ready for a day on the town?" Doc asked at *Teddy Roosevelt*'s airlock.

"Town?" Terry asked.

"Yeah, these *Behemoths* are small cities in space," he said. "I might have slipped over last night for a couple hours, just to look around."

"You know the crew are Maki, and they're mercs?" Terry asked. Doc gave him the appraising look again.

"Mercs?" his mom asked, looking at Terry in alarm.

"I knew they were a merc race," Doc replied. "I've been shot at by them a couple times. However, the Maki aren't like some merc races."

"What do you mean?" she asked.

"Well, they're more like us."

She had her slate out and was looking at the GalNet image of a Maki. "Doesn't look a lot like us," she said. "More like a monkey."

"Lemur," Terry corrected.

His mom rolled her eyes. "Same thing."

"I didn't say they looked like us, just that their societal structure is more like ours and less like other merc races." They'd climbed into the ring hallway around *Second Octal*, where all the ships were docked. This time there were others there. Terry listened to Doc with half his attention as he looked at the aliens. "The Maki society isn't built around mercs, like the Tortantula or the MinSha."

"I know what the MinSha are," she said. Terry glanced at Doc, who winked at him. "What are Tortantula?"

"Giant 10-legged spiders with a gun-wielding chipmunk on their backs," Terry said. She gasped.

"Close enough," Doc said. "The point is, their societies are completely structured around a merc life. If you aren't a merc, you work to support them. Your race gains almost all its income from mercs, and if you aren't one, you're a second-class citizen, or worse."

"How are the Maki different?" Terry asked, also curious. A bunch of lizards, more like snakes, but with six legs, were motivating by. Behind them were tall, Humanoid aliens with water-filled helmets he immediately recognized as Selroth, like the ones on *Pegasus*.

"I don't exactly know," Doc admitted. "Only that they're a race big into starships, both military and transports. They make warships, too, as well as operate merc space navies."

"Do they make these?" he asked.

"I don't think so," Doc said. "I don't think anyone's made these for eons."

Terry looked around as they approached the lift from the other day. The ship looked worn, certainly. However, it didn't look as old as it was supposed to be. How could a ship operate for thousands of years? More, *tens* of thousands of years.

"Then where did they get them?" Terry asked.

Doc shrugged and punched a code into the lift's control panel. It flashed blue. Terry had begun to learn color coding wasn't the same as Earth in many places. Lots of races used blue as an 'okay' color, and green as bad. Doc had said once it was because not all aliens bled red blood; many were green. He guessed it made sense.

The lift opened, and Doc put out a hand to delay Terry. He wondered why, but then a massive brightly purple bulk moved out of the elevator. The Oogar's beady black eyes regarded the much smaller Human's as it shambled out. It roared, which made his mom squeak in surprise.

"Greetings," their translators said.

Doc touched his translator and replied.

"Greetings," he said in reply. Satisfied, the Oogar shambled off.

"I'd hate to hear it angry," his mom said.

"It doesn't sound a lot different," Doc said. "I met a guy who said the Oogar don't have an 'indoor voice.'" Chuckling, the three entered the lift. It had probably been a bit crowded with a single

Oogar. It fit all three of them handily. Terry tapped the controls, and the doors closed.

"They kinda smell," Terry said.

"I bet we don't smell good to them, either," his mom said. Doc nodded in agreement.

It seemed like a foreign concept to him, until he thought about it. What would the Oogar think of Humans? Hairless monkeys from a backwater world? Oogar were mercs, but had the Oogar been a merc itself? Did it even know they were Human? Every day he spent out in the galaxy, Terry felt like his perceptions were being altered.

No, he thought, *not altered. Improved.* He was about to tell Doc when the lift slowed to a stop. He noticed immediately they were lighter than before. It was similar to what he'd heard the moon was like, a sixth of a G.

The doors opened, and they shuffle-stepped out. Months of living in space had made his reflexes as flexible as his mind was becoming. If you lived in space, you adapted to varying gravity quickly, or got used to bruises. He didn't like bruises, so he worked hard to adjust quickly.

The lift doors opened. Terry expected to see a corridor like on Karma Station, maybe a wide promenade. Instead, it was more like the inside of a shopping mall. The area was curved and reminded Terry of a sports stadium. There were aliens everywhere he looked. He'd been expecting mostly Maki, but there were hardly any in sight.

As they moved into the open, there was a large interactive Tri-V. It would have been called an information kiosk in older times. Here it was part display, part directory, and part advertisement. Terry couldn't put his finger on what the place felt like. His mother did it for him.

"It's like a cruise ship!" she said, a laugh in her voice.

"Yeah, I suppose so," Doc agreed. "These *Behemoths* make a lot of their money carrying other ships from system to system. I guess they also make money off the ship's passengers."

They quickly learned the area was called the Pavilion by their translators. Terry recalled how the translators worked with a matrix of meanings and only assigned a word if the context was closer. He would have called it a mall.

The space was organized into levels, each one providing different products and services. On the bottom floor where they entered were mostly ship's services and the most Maki. The busiest was the ship purser's office, which handled the contracts of carriage between *Second Octal* and all ships docked for transit. Terry found out the purser also managed the ship's accounts in relation to cargo and any inside passengers. The latter turned out to number in the thousands as well. Billions moved around the galaxy on various starships. The cheapest way was via a *Behemoth*.

"They're more like balloons than airliners on Earth," Doc said. "You don't tell a *Behemoth* where to go, you just climb on and enjoy the ride."

Also on the first deck was a sizeable dining galley for passengers. You needed an inside ticket to access it. There was a sizeable store where you could buy supplies for your ship as well as passengers, while one more handled booking to extend a trip or arrange future ones. Outside the office was a Tri-V of the galaxy showing hundreds of sparkling yellow dots connected by a vast web of green traces.

"I wonder what it's for?" Terry wondered.

"Those are all our clans ships," a Maki who was standing nearby answered. They all turned to look at the alien.

"That's a lot of ships," his mom said. Terry nodded.

"How many?" Doc asked.

"Our clan boasts 122 ships," the Maki said, turning and gesturing at the Tri-V with all the flourish of a ringmaster at the circus. "A full 82 of those are *Behemoths*, like our beautiful *Second Octal*. Are you interested in booking further passage?"

"No, thank you," Doc said, and the Maki bowed before turning away. "Hey," he said suddenly, and the alien turned back. "Your translator has our language?"

"We have done business with Humans," the alien said. "It is only good business to be prepared for future business."

"He thinks we'll be around a long time," Terry said after the Maki left.

"Or at least be customers for a long time," Doc pointed out.

They moved up to the second level of the pavilion and found it contained a vast number of shops like what Terry had seen on Karma Station. Not quite as diverse, but many products were available, from day-to-day living devices such as cooking or cleaning, to electronics. Terry noticed a shop selling slates like the one he'd bought.

"Why do you want to go in there?" Doc asked. "You already have a new slate."

"I'm curious," he said. The storefront contained a Tri-V customer interface. To his amazement, it automatically changed to English as soon as he got close to it. "Excellent." Terry began clicking icons until he found his own model slate, if not a perfect match. He picked it, then gasped at the price. "They want 600 credits for the one I paid 190 for on Karma Station!"

"Nice markup," Doc said.

"I'll say," his mom agreed.

"How can they get away with it?" Terry asked. He looked at the description and, sure enough, it was even the same manufacturer. He couldn't read the writing, but he recognized the symbol.

"How can they do what?" Doc asked.

"That's...what's it called? Scalping!"

"Not really," Doc said. "Scalping is having something somebody else needs and charging through the nose for it because they have no other choice. And before you say anything, we're not in such a case here. You can always wait six more days and buy it at our next destination. Regardless, though, there's no laws in the Union to stop predatory buying or selling practices."

"Then how do they stop it?"

Doc laughed. "They don't!"

"How's that fair?"

"It isn't," his mom said.

"You agree with that?" Terry asked her.

"No, of course not. This is just the world we live in now. Besides, I see Doc's point. If you don't like the price, go somewhere else. You already found your slate for sale at another place. I bet they're available all over the galaxy at vastly different prices." She glanced at Doc and got a nod in agreement. "It looks to me like the Union depends on competition to keep prices down."

"You'd be right," Doc said. "It doesn't always work, of course. There are some things nobody else sells. In which case, the manufacturers suck as much of your blood as they can before giving you the product."

"But that's not—"

"Fair," Doc finished for him. "I know, kiddo. However, minus a governing body like some agency telling you what you can and cannot manufacture, there's also nothing stopping you from going into business to make the same product cheaper."

Terry grumbled. "Maybe I'll just hire some mercs to put you out of business." He wasn't expecting the response he got.

"Now you're thinking the way the Union operates."

"Wait, you mean that happens?!"

"You bet," Doc said. "That was one of the jobs we did. One company didn't like how another company was trying to take away their business, so they hired us to send a message."

"What happened?" his mom asked.

"Message delivered," Doc said and winked. "Don't look at me, the other guys should have hired some of their own mercs."

She shook her head in bewilderment. "With things operating the way they seem to, everyone must have to hire mercs to protect themselves."

"They do," Doc agreed. "How sweet it is."

"Why doesn't a big merc ship come along and attack this one?" Terry asked.

"Ah," Doc said and pointed at him. "Now that's an interesting subject. This ship is licensed under the Merchants Guild; attacking it would probably be a bad idea for the mercs. Without a contract, they'd be pirates. Which means they wouldn't be mercs for long. You see, pirates are galactic target practice. Normal ROE don't apply."

"ROE?" Terry asked.

"Rules of engagement. However, I think there've been wars between clans within the Merchants Guild. In which case, mercs got involved legally."

"Everything is so confusing," Terry said, shaking his head.

"Lots of people think the Galactic Union is a huge free-for-all, kinda like the old west. Nothing could be further from the truth. The great guilds sit astride the entire ballgame. The Merc Guild provides firepower and a way to settle the score, or get ahead. The Merchants Guild moves stuff around. Mess with them, and you could find it hard to get from A to B. The Cartography Guild controls the stargates. Don't pay their fees, you can't even leave the neighborhood. The Trade Guild manufactures things; upset their applecart and you might find nobody will sell you new equipment. The Information Guild maintains the GalNet and keeps data flowing around the galaxy. Piss them off, and your slate could find its data gone. Then we get to the syndicates, who operate under various guild licenses..."

"Okay, okay," Terry said, holding up his hands in surrender. "Damn, Doc, where did you learn all this?"

"Out in the galaxy," the man said and waved his hands in an expansive gesture. "That's why I agreed to teach the class. Being a merc and surviving means a lot more than just killing aliens and getting paid. If you jump on a starship and go to another part of the galaxy, you damned better know a bit about how things work beyond the barrel of your gun." He got quiet for a bit. "I hope they found someone good to teach the class after I left."

"I'm sure they did," Terry's mom said, and put a hand on Doc's muscular arm. The man smiled at her in a way that made Terry happy, while at the same time he missed his dad. Everything was so damned complicated.

"I still think the price is nuts," Terry said, looking at the display.

"Price too high?" the store's computer asked in English. "How about this?" The price changed to 500 credits.

"See," Doc said and winked at him. "How many stores back in Molokai would cut you a 20% discount just because you said their stuff was too expensive?"

"None," Terry admitted. They walked away, but he could hear the computer calling after him asking if 450 was a better price. *Strange world I live in*, he thought.

The next level up was designed for the convenience of the passengers, both on and off the ship. Various robotic vendors offered food, drink, and entertainment. There wasn't an awful lot of entertainment they found interesting. There were a dozen Tri-V galleries, though. Terry had heard about them on Karma Station.

A Tri-V gallery was a big room with dozens of Tri-V projectors. The floors were covered in millions of tiny ball bearings, which could be moved in any direction to simulate walking without moving. The floor could also raise and lower as you walked. The effect was the most immersive virtual reality imaginable. At least, the vendors claimed it was. No Humans took advantage of them because they needed to be programmed for a Human.

They found a food vendor whose kiosk responded in English when they approached. The selections were limited; however, they offered various juices and, amazingly, applesauce.

"Real applesauce?" his mom asked.

"Yeah, looks like it," Doc said. Then he pointed. "They have corn, too."

"Why would they have fruit juices, apple sauce, and corn?" Terry wondered.

"Merchant ships make a lot of their money speculating," Doc explained. "They'll buy something in one star system on the gamble somebody else will pay more for it than they paid." He touched the icons and grimaced. "Yeah, they're winning on this one."

Terry leaned in to read. The fruit juice was 10 credits a liter, the applesauce 25 credits a liter, and the corn 5 credits a half kilogram.

"Want a million-dollar meal?" Doc asked.

"Corn, applesauce and juice for a million bucks?" she asked, then laughed.

"We're not on Earth anymore," he said.

"Money doesn't work the same," Terry agreed.

Doc touched the control on a table with a long bench and ordered some of the juice, one liter split between three containers. The table opened a box, and three plastic glasses with brightly colored fluid inside rose up. Terry took one right away and had a sip. His mom's eyes went wide.

"Mango," Terry said and smacked his lips. "Ice cold and yummy!"

"I was going to suggest we go carefully," his mom said darkly.

"They just came from Karma," Doc reminded her, "one jump from Earth. This is on the trade route. Besides, remember, they knew English. I suspect this clan has traded with Humans a few times already." He took a drink of his own juice and nodded. "Since they probably paid a credit a ton, profitable transaction, too."

Terry's mom looked at the glass for a second, then took a drink, too. Her eyes widened and she moaned. "Oh, good," she said. All they'd had on *Teddy Roosevelt* was powdered drinks.

Doc played with the ordering system. In a few seconds, a bowl filled with applesauce rose into view. Everyone laughed when it arrived with straws instead of spoons. "When in Rome," Doc said and took a messy slurp. Soon they were all trying to suck the thick sauce through the straws and laughing uproariously.

Terry was glad his mom was having a good time and got an idea. While they ate, he used his slate to access the *Behemoth*'s computer. As he'd thought, all the various services they'd found in the Pavilion were also available through his computer, including the Tri-V gallery. Doc and his mom were chatting as they enjoyed the applesauce; neither of them noticed the grin on his face as he worked on his slate.

The corn proved more difficult. Doc was sure it would be raw, and even if it were sweet corn, it wouldn't be too tasty. So he dug into the ordering system and found a way to get it cooked. Terry helped by telling him how long it needed to cook and at what temperature, then had to convert the temperature into kelvin so the alien autochef understood.

"Add some salt!" his mom suggested as Doc was finishing.

"Good idea," Doc said, and found sodium chloride as an option, adding 5 grams to the order during cooking. Then he also remembered something other than straws to eat it with. They waited for a couple minutes while it cooked, not knowing what to expect. Then the little door opened, and a dish piled with steaming corn rose up. The smell was fantastic.

Doc picked up one of the spoons, more like a plastic dugout really, and scooped up some. "Here's mud in your eye." He blew on it, popped it into his mouth, and cautiously chewed. "Hmmm…" he said.

"Well?" Terry's mom demanded. Doc's serious face cracked into a wide grin.

"It's sweet corn," he said, "and perfect.

Terry and his mom dug in with a vengeance. It only took them a couple of minutes to devour the corn. Doc ordered more. At the same time, he found something else and ordered it.

"What's that?" she asked. He held up a finger for patience. She made a face but waited. Eventually the door opened, and another tray came up. This time it had a pile of corn and some steaming meat. "I didn't see any meat from Earth anywhere on the menu," she said.

"No," he said, "this is Kluup; it's from somewhere out there. My crew and I had it on a contract a while back. Tastes a little like chicken." The meat had a slight tint of orange and smelled a little like cooked tomatoes. Both Terry and his mom gave him a dubious look. "Oh, good lord," he said and speared a piece with the plastic skewer the meat came with. He blew on it and popped it into his mouth, chewing busily. "Okay?"

"Good enough for me," Terry said and got his own piece. It did taste kind of like chicken, with a slightly unusual sweet quality about it. Before long his mom gave it a try, eventually pronouncing it satisfactory. As the two grownups were finishing off the last of the fruit juice, Terry looked up the Kluup on his slate. It was from the far side of the galaxy. It would take months to get there, probably, and then get back. The thing looked like it was half worm and half squid. *Yuck!*

They looked around for a bit longer before heading back. Terry glanced at his watch and saw he needed to hurry to take care of Pōkole's feeding. The orca just got hungrier and hungrier as he grew. But as they left *Second Octal* and entered their ship again, he got a second to talk to Doc where his mom couldn't hear.

"Kluup comes from halfway across the galaxy," he said. "How did you get a chance to try it before?"

"I lied," Doc said and winked. Terry gawked. "You two were being such candy asses, I had to say something."

"You could have poisoned us," Terry said.

"Naw," Doc said. "If you look closely, the autochef had Human digestive requirements programmed. The meat was compatible."

"It could have been wrong," Terry mused.

"Yeah, maybe. But sometimes you have to take a chance in life, or what fun is it?"

* * * * *

Chapter Thirteen

Teddy Roosevelt, Hyperspace
December 11th, 2037

As it had in Karma, life fell into a routine in hyperspace. The spin provided by *Second Octal* made some aspects better. The Humans didn't have to spend as much time in the gym exercising and taking special medications to avoid losing bone density. Care for the drugged orcas was handled by the trained medical staff. However, the strange orientation of the ship made many routine tasks twice as difficult. This included a slew of water circulation and filtration pump failures on *Teddy Roosevelt*.

The malfunctions became enough of a problem that the biologists considered moving the cetaceans to one of the other ships. As a last-ditch effort, a small engineering team was hired from *Second Octal* to look at the problem.

Six Maki showed up one morning, all with tool kits and various diagnostic instruments. They examined the Human-made ship's systems for an hour. Much yipping and chittering followed. Terry watched and was curious as his translator didn't want to render what they were saying into English. After a time, they began making modifications.

The engineer on *Teddy* was alarmed when one of the aliens simply cut a power circuit and all three pumps went down. However, a second later, a new controller they'd built on the spot was installed, and the pumps came back online.

"The charge is 300 credits," the leader said, the translator understanding it.

"What if there are problems later?" the engineer asked.

The alien smiled. "There will not be."

Terry's mom paid the bill, and true to their word, no more malfunctions occurred.

"I wonder why we couldn't understand them," Terry asked her.

"I don't know," she said.

He did some of his own research. The only thing he found was about the Maki merchant clans. An entry in the GalNet mentioned clans appeared to have individual languages which didn't fit any of the translation matrixes. To further complicate matters, the Maki could produce varying tonal modulations in their vocal cords, which in turn meant they were able to alter the frequency of their speech.

They have built in scramblers, Terry thought. Handy.

In what time he could find between lessons, taking care of Pōkole, and helping out wherever he could, Terry worked on his pet project. He quickly realized in order to do what he wanted to do, he needed to learn some programming in the Galactic Union's standard computer language. Luckily it didn't require learning their spoken language. All programming was done in numbers, or some special symbol variants.

Within a day, he was writing simple programs that could respond to inputs. In two days, he was writing fairly complex decision tree routines. After three days he was learning how to integrate Human standard image files to Union programs so they could display and encode them in Union formats. On the fourth day, he finally got the program he'd downloaded to do what he wanted it to do, and quickly created his masterpiece.

"Hey, Mom," he said on the evening of their last day in hyperspace.

"Yeah, what's up?"

"Can you come with me aboard *Second Octa*? I have something to show you."

"Terry, I'm pretty busy. We come out of hyperspace tomorrow, and—"

"I know," he interrupted, "this is really important."

She looked at him and sighed. "Okay, but only for a couple of hours."

"Thanks, Mom!"

Terry led her out of their ship and into the alien transport, then up to the Pavilion. Doc was waiting there. She looked at him in surprise, then at her son. "What's going on?"

"The kid is sneaky," Doc said. "Come on, you'll want to see this." She looked suspiciously at the hand the man held out but took it anyway. Terry took her other hand, and they led her upstairs to one of the Tri-V galleries.

"I thought these didn't work for us," she said.

"Come on," Terry urged her. The look of suspicion changed to confusion as they walked into the entry area. Terry took a computer chip from his pocket and slid it into the kiosk. It beeped, and a price of 25 credits popped up. He inserted the money, and the doors opened.

"You may enter," a voice said in English. "Welcome, Madison Clark."

She looked at Terry in open-mouthed astonishment as they walked in. The floor felt slightly bumpy, but only a little. The lighting was dim, just enough to see there were walls a few dozen meters away, and the room was circular, with a domed ceiling as far away as the walls. "What's going to...woah!" She stopped as the light disappeared, and a complex maze of three-dimensional grids appeared. It almost instantly resolved into Kapukahehu Beach at sunrise. She gasped.

"Happy birthday, Mom," Terry whispered.

"Oh, my God," she said. The air was filled with the sound of Pacific Ocean waves lapping up a few meters away. Seagulls cried their mournful wails. There was a hint of salt in the air, and a breeze suddenly wafted across them. Somewhere down the beach, a dog barked and ran into the surf after a frisbee. Terry realized she was crying.

"Mom, are you okay?"

She turned to face him, and despite the tears, she looked as happy as he'd seen her in months. "I'm fine," she sobbed, and then grabbed him in a rib-creaking hug. "How?"

"Your incredibly brilliant son," Doc said. She gestured him over, and he joined the hug.

Terry sighed himself. It felt right.

After a minute, she let them go and turned around. The cliffs behind them were full of the same expensive houses as before. She took a couple steps, marveling at how the beach felt. "I don't understand," she said. "This isn't real, of course."

"No," Terry said, "it's just a really impressive Tri-V."

"Yeah, I understand what you did, but not how you did it."

"I just figured out how to set it up."

"Your son is far too modest," Doc said and put an arm around Terry's shoulder. "He learned how the Union's image processing software works, adapted it to use our software, and fed in a few thousand primitive Human images. A bunch I had from our diving trips, and even a few from publicity shots of Molokai."

"The alien systems are intuitive," Terry said, and shrugged. "It wasn't all that hard."

"As I said, overly modest."

"Terry," she said. "My brilliant son."

"You like it," he said, blushing despite himself.

"It's the most beautiful thing I've ever gotten for my birthday." She leaned over slightly, not too far because he was getting taller, and kissed him. "Thank you." He was smiling so hard his face hurt.

His 25 credits bought them an hour in the Tri-V gallery. When the time was running down, the sunset flashed green as a warning. Terry offered to buy another hour. The sun was falling below the horizon and appeared to match the end of the hour. They sat on the edge of the surf. The Tri-V couldn't simulate water.

"No," she said, "this is perfect." As the sun dropped out of sight, Earth faded into fractal patterns and was gone. "Perfect," she said. Another tear ran down her cheek. "Time to get back to work."

As they left, Terry caught Doc's attention. "I think I screwed up," he said.

"No," the man assured him. "You freaking nailed it."

"But she looked so sad."

"Women's hearts are a deep sea of emotions," he said. Terry looked confused. "Don't worry, kiddo, you'll understand one day."

"Excuse me," a voice said by the door.

Terry turned and saw a Maki waiting patiently. "Yes?"

"I am Esckyl, Primus of Entertainment on *Second Octal*."

"Terry Clark," he said.

"Dr. Madison Clark," his mom said.

"Just Doc," Doc said.

"I viewed a corollary image of your Tri-V program."

"You guarantee those are private," Terry said, his eyes narrowing. He'd read the contract carefully.

"As I said, it was a corollary image. All I could see was what was projected, not who was inside. You'll see the contract guarantees the merchant this, as a means of protecting against any liability we might incur."

"What can we do for you, Esckyl?" his mom asked.

"The program you wrote is of excellent quality. We've tried to create simulations for your race and have largely failed. Many adjectives were used to describe them, none of them complementary."

"I didn't write the program," she said and touched Terry on the shoulder. "My son here did."

"Son?" the alien tried the strange word. "Offspring?"

"Close enough," Doc said.

"I see. Well, even more impressive then. I was wondering if I might have a copy of the program, for instructional purposes?"

Terry was flattered and halfway to saying, 'Sure, why not?' when he felt Doc's gentle but firm hand on his shoulder.

"How much?" Doc asked.

"Sorry?"

"What's it worth to you?"

"It is just a simple program," the Maki said, effecting a convincing shrug. "I merely hoped to see it for some insight."

"Insight?" Doc said, nodding slowly. "Sounds like you need a lot of insight if all the Humans you tried your programs on thought they sucked."

"An exaggeration," Esckyl complained.

"No complementary adjectives," Terry repeated the alien's own words. While Terry was only 12, he was still five or six centimeters taller than the bipedal Maki. He rather enjoyed looking down on him. He also now knew from Doc's lead he had something. "Like the man said, what's it worth to you?"

Esckyl spluttered, his tiny eyes darting between the three Humans with what Terry now realized was obvious nervousness. They might be a merc race, but this particular Maki was no merc. He wondered why the alien hadn't just taken a copy from the computer. In fact, when he'd loaded it, the data was all there. His mind went back to the contract. Of course, it didn't copy the actual program, it merely took the data from the program he'd written on the chip! They wanted the program.

"I'll offer you a refund on your hour of time, and another 100 credits!" Esckyl tried hard to make it sound like a generous offer. Now with a good sense of what a credit could buy in space, Terry knew otherwise.

"I don't think so," he said.

"It really isn't as important as you think," Esckyl said. Terry took out his slate. The alien's eyes widened slightly when he saw it. "That's a good model."

"I know," Terry said without looking up. He quickly accessed the GalNet info on Maki and looked up Primus. *A senior leader with a Maki clan, often empowered with financial or military power*, he read. *Ah hah, gotcha.* "Not as important? Funny they sent a Primus, then."

The alien's eyes darted around as if looking for help. Of course, there were only the three Humans. "Okay, 500 credits."

"Five hundred," Terry said. The Maki grinned. "Thousand." His voice held a little quaver and he hoped the alien didn't catch it.

Esckyl blanched, the fur on his strange split tail stood up on end, and his entire body quivered as if Terry had delivered his offer at the end of a taser. He said several words in his clan's special language before he realized it and switched to one their translators would understand. "Ridiculous!"

"Fine," Doc said. "Bye."

Terry nodded, and they headed for the Pavilion exit. He was afraid he'd severely overplayed his hand when they got to the bottom floor and halfway across the Pavilion. The complex was nearly deserted since they were due to exit hyperspace in a few hours. Esckyl's feet made little flapping sounds as he ran up and around them to block the way.

"Wait, wait, gentle Humans. Will you negotiate?"

The three glanced at each other. Terry looked amused; his mom had a somewhat surprised and amazed expression on her face. Doc smiled like a grinning crocodile.

"Sure," Terry said. "I'll go down to 475,000."

* * *

The three climbed down from *Second Octal* together, the *Teddy Roosevelt's* crewman dogging the hatch behind them and sealing the airlock in preparation for undocking. Safely back in their own ship, Terry took out the little fabric bag and opened it. He removed one of the three 100 thousand-credit chits. The red diamond inside was the size of his little fingernail.

Each one of them was worth $3 billion dollars on Earth, making the whole pile $9 billion.

"Did that really just happen?" he asked.

"Yeah, it did," Doc said.

"I can't believe it," Terry's mom said. "Son, you really caught him off guard. You had a great-uncle who was a used car salesman. Maybe some of his genes rubbed off on you!"

"Well played, kiddo," Doc said. He removed a pistol from his pocket Terry hadn't even noticed he had. He set the safety back on and made it disappear again.

"Do you think we were in danger?" she asked.

"Probably not," Doc said. "Three hundred K isn't exactly killing money, but the Maki looked like he'd been filleted alive. Probably trying to think of how he was going to explain it to his captain and hoping it paid off." He looked at Terry. "You might have given him millions of credits in profit, you know?"

"I don't mind," Terry said, holding up one of the chits to see how the ship's light shone through the red diamond. He'd seen red diamonds before. All credits had one. Only the diamond in a one credit chit was nothing more than a grain of sand. Even the 1,000-credit chit Doc had given him wasn't more than the size of a grain of rice. The fingernail-sized one seemed enormous, and it really was beautiful in the light. "It only took me a few days to code."

Terry examined all three chits for a moment, then took two and handed them to his mom.

"Terry, why are you giving me these?"

"To help out," he said.

"No," she said and tried to hand them back to him. He moved away and held up a hand. "Terry, you earned these."

"And you've worked like crazy for months on end. If this helps us, helps the cetaceans, then that's cool." He held up one and looked at it. "I don't know what to do with 100,000 credits; what the heck am I going to do with 300,000?"

"Hire a merc unit?" Doc said with a chuckle.

"No, you keep it, Mom. If you want, call it one hell of a birthday gift."

"You're the best birthday gift a mom could ever have," she said and folded him into her arms. "I'll keep it just in case you change your mind."

Terry sighed. In a dingy starship corridor, racing through another dimension, for a minute, he was content. Doc gave him a wink, making Terry smile even bigger. With a credit chit worth $3 billion dollars, he was also the richest Human kid in the galaxy!

* * * * *

Chapter Fourteen

Teddy Roosevelt, Lupasha System, Coro Region, Tolo Arm
December 12th, 2037

Shortly after emerging from hyperspace, *Teddy Roosevelt* and her two accompanying ships were cast free from *Second Octal* one at a time, conveniently hurled in the direction of their destination. As was the way of the *Behemoths*, her arrival was timed so she was coasting toward the stargate.

The orcas were awoken from their chemically-induced slumber and rebreathers were affixed. It was the second time they'd undergone the procedure, and the first time they were ready for it. They came out much less disoriented than the previous time, showing no signs of stress or illness. Moloko reunited with her calf, and all was good.

Terry watched their ship detach from the observation dome on *Teddy Roosevelt*, now configured once again for standard operations. Captain Baker seemed happy her ship was no longer spinning around upside down.

"Welcome to the Lupasha system," she said.

Terry couldn't see much. The star was more orange than Sol was yellow, and it seemed dimmer or smaller, he couldn't make up his mind which. "Doesn't look like the kind of place we'd find a world the cetaceans can live on," he remarked.

"Looks can be deceiving," Doc said as he floated into the observation dome, his mom right behind.

"You've been here?" Captain Baker asked. Doc nodded. "Dead end, if you ask me."

"What's here?" Terry asked.

"Lupasha was supposed to be a massive trade hub," Doc said. "The star's an orange dwarf, or K-class, as the astronomers called it. On Earth, astronomers had it tagged as a possible exoplanet system."

Terry nodded. "We learned about those. We also learned, after we got stellar data from the Union, most of our guesses were less than accurate."

"Correct," the captain said. "There weren't any inhabitable planets here. At least, sort of." She touched a control and a low-resolution Tri-V came up. Terry saw it was far lower resolution than the miniature one on his slate. Displayed was the Lupasha star system, primary in the center, and planets projecting white rings to show their orbits. There were only three.

The captain continued her description, "The planet furthest out is a rock ball, gathered up from the system's Kuiper belt over billions of years. Not much there, and too hard to mine. Too unstable. The next is in the middle zone, and should have been one of those so-called Goldilocks planets. Only it turned out to be a dwarf planet. It does have an oxygen atmosphere, but because Lupasha is so dim, what water it has is frozen, and there's no active core." She shrugged. "Some minerals, but again, not worth it.

"The surprise turned out to be the last planet, closest to the sun." The Tri-V's grainy image centered on a gas giant. It somewhat resembled Jupiter, with numerous titanic gaseous vortexes raging in its atmosphere. It also had a prominent ring like Saturn. "It's big, too. A little bigger, and Lupasha might have been a binary system. Instead, we were left with this big-ass gas ball.

"Like gas giants in Sol, this one has multiple moons. Jupiter has 79, Saturn 53, Uranus 27, and Neptune 13. Some big, some small. Lupasha 1 here only has 11. But one of those 11 proved interesting." She looked at Terry. "Did you study Jupiter's moons?"

"Yes, ma'am."

"Excellent. Can you tell me which one turned out to have life?"

"Trick question," Terry said and smiled. "Two of them did; Ganymede has a strange spongiform life."

"An exotic," the captain said. "Even the Union doesn't understand it."

"Then you mean Europa." The captain nodded. "They're just tiny multi-celled organisms, and some plants living off the volcanic sulfur vents."

"Elegant little closed system," Captain Baker agreed. "Still, it was life, and it proved you didn't need sunlight for life to evolve. One of the moons here is just like Europa, only larger."

The Tri-V view moved to show a white planet in the foreground, the surface a latticework of cracks and impact craters. Data appeared next to the image, showing orbital speed, albedo, gravity, and surface temperature.

"Surface temp?" Terry's mom asked.

"Yes," Doc said.

"Insane," she said.

Terry examined the display. "52 degrees isn't cold," he said, "it's hot!" All the adults looked at him with the expressions they used when he'd missed something. "What?"

"Fifty-two kelvin," his mom said.

"Oh, hell," he said, both amazed and feeling embarrassed. He wasn't sure, but thought 52 kelvin was around 300 degrees below zero. Barely above the temperature of liquid nitrogen.

"Frozen hell," his mom said.

"It might be frozen, but it also had potential," Doc said. "It all has to do with the Izlians. They had an interest in Lupasha 1, the gas giant. It showed potential as a home for them."

"What race could live on a gas giant?" Terry asked.

The captain smiled and touched the Tri-V controls. The gas giant was replaced by what Terry thought was a fuzzy image of a Humboldt squid. "This is as good an image as we have of them," she explained. "Like the life forms on Ganymede, the Izlians are exotic. Their lifecycle isn't based on carbon, like ours. They live *inside* gas giants and would find our atmosphere just as lethal as we find theirs."

"The Izlians are starship builders," Doc said. "Some people say they basically wrote the manual on space combat. They've got huge fleets of ships, shipyards, and industrial operations. This moon was ideal to provide the elements needed to construct some parts of starships, right next door to a gas giant they could live in."

"So, what happened?" Terry's mom asked.

"I'm getting to that," Doc said. "The moon has the same liquid oceans under the ice as Europa, if deeper. They also have a much richer variety of life, as well. More than a few surprises. Well, the Izlians contracted with the Selroth, who would do the mining of the moon while they built their little colony. The problem arose when the Selroth backed out; they didn't like the chemical composition of the moon's oceans. Apparently there weren't enough minerals to make it worth it for the Izlians to perform remote or robotic mining. They gave up."

"But not until after they had the stargate installed," Captain Baker said. "Also a space station." She laughed. "Must have cost them a fortune."

"How do we factor in?" Terry's mom asked.

"The Izlians still want some of those resources and were willing to pay for a quiet exam. The leasehold is open on the planet/moon, but if they made a big show over interest, it might turn into a contested situation."

"How do you get these leaseholds?" she asked.

"You can slap down a huge pile of money to the Cartography Guild, fight someone to gain control, or use the planet to extract a certain amount of resources for a certain period of time without anyone else doing the same thing."

"Those are pretty vague situations," she said.

"It can be," Doc agreed. "Since this was an established mine at one point, the quantities are established; 20 million kilos of any ore within five years, then a 1 million credit fee. Or a 5 million credit fee up front. The Izlians are nothing if not cheap; they want to go for the mining, so the fee is paid for in profits."

"You and your men came here to scout," Terry said.

Doc nodded. "Yes, we did. We built a submersible and went down to recon the mining and habitat facilities for the Izlians. After we verified it's all still there, they offered us the contract to prove the claim."

"If the Selroth couldn't live there, how are we going to?" Terry asked.

"The ocean's chemistry is nearly identical to ours," his mom explained. "This also means the cetaceans can live there." Terry nodded in understanding. Now it all made sense. "We can, too, with some adaptations."

"Like what?"

"We're still working on it," she said, glancing at Doc.

Terry looked at Doc and then his mom. Of course, adults loved keeping secrets from kids. A lot of times it was because they thought kids couldn't handle the truth, which was completely wrong. Maybe little kids couldn't. Twelve wasn't a little kid. Terry had enough details, and the GalNet; he'd get his own answers. "We going down there now?"

"We're going to the space station first," Doc said.

"Where we'll be parting company," Captain Baker said.

"You aren't taking us to the planet?"

"Can't," she said, and shrugged. "No way to refuel, so we couldn't get back into space."

"We're going to hire local talent to get us down to the moon."

"Does the moon have a name?" Terry asked.

"It did in the Selroth language," Doc said. "Sounded like a hiccup underwater." Terry laughed. "Tina came up with its new name: Hoarfrost."

* * * * *

Chapter Fifteen

Lupasha Independent Trading Station, Lupasha System, Coro
Region, Tolo Arm
December 13th, 2037

Placed on an effectively free approach course to Lupasha's space station, *Teddy Roosevelt*, *Kavul Tesh*, and *Kavul Ato* drifted silently through space. Captain Baker remarked that *Second Octal* had released them so efficiently, she wouldn't have to use her engines to do anything except slow upon approach.

Only a single ship stopped in the Lupasha system with them, a tanker many times larger than the three ships from Earth. It was already firing its engines to slow down and park around the approaching station, which left the other three ships effectively alone on their approach.

Terry stopped off in the observation dome several times over the following day, enjoying the view of the approaching station. He'd found visiting stations in other systems was something to look forward to.

He'd seen Earth's tiny orbiting stations many times on TV and Tri-V. Then the massive triple rings of Karma Station showed him what was possible. He was filled with excitement as they fell toward Lupasha 2 and its orbiting station.

The planet Lupasha 2 was visible almost immediately, a mottled white/brown dot which grew hourly. When the ring of a space station became visible, the planet was still quite small. Terry remembered the captain had described it as a dwarf planet, like Pluto. A dwarf planet was often smaller than many other planets' moons. Of course, he wasn't looking forward to seeing the planet. The station came into focus.

"Wow," he said as he used a small telescope to examine the station. "Pathetic."

The station visible in the telescope was a sad echo of the massive Karma Station. It was obviously meant to be a similar design, only it had never been completed. The stationary hub in the center sported four spokes radiating out to a single completed ring. The framework of two more rings were in place between the hub and the one completed ring, almost resembling ghosts of what might have been.

The three ships spun around and used their engines to gradually slow until they were only a kilometer away from the half-built station, and then stopped in relation to it. It was big compared to their ships, but nowhere near as big as Karma Station.

Terry met up with his mom, Doc, and the other six mercs of Last Call in one of *Teddy Roosevelt*'s shuttles for the short ride over to the grandiosely named *Lupasha Independent Trading Station*. It was a surprisingly quiet ride, for many reasons. The mercs looked intent and businesslike. His mom looked concerned. Terry realized this was the end of the line. Lupasha was his new home for the indefinite future.

The inside of the station proved to be as slapdash as the exterior. There were no glideways like on Karma Station; instead there was a cluster of six traditional lifts in each spoke of the hub. Everyone in their party fit in the lift for their five minute ride.

As gravity slowly climbed, they passed through what would have been stations on the two rings. Instead, they were merely long-enclosed sections with nothing to see. It was a little sad.

Arriving at the ring with its half gravity—also less than Karma Station—Terry saw ample room for untold businesses existed in the promenade, yet most were empty, having never been completed. They were merely holes in the walls with nothing inside. Some played host to what could only be homeless families. Seeing one of the biggest problems Humans seemed unable to eradicate among aliens thousands of light years from home was a shock to him.

"Are they homeless?" Terry asked.

"Well, they don't have any way to leave," Doc confirmed.

"We ran across them in a few places during contracts," Tina told him. "Usually they're refugees from fighting. These are financial casualties."

"What do you mean?" he asked.

"Left here after the Selroth bailed and the Izlians gave up," Doc said.

"Isn't there any way they can get help?" Terry wondered. A big family of elSha watched him dispassionately from their dilapidated surroundings. They were cooking food on an improvised electrical grill, which looked like it was made from a lighting fixture.

"The universe isn't a fair place," Doc said.

Terry frowned. He'd heard Doc utter those words before, and he hadn't liked it then. The other Last Call mercs grunted in agreement, except Tina, who was watching Terry.

"It bothers you?" she asked. He nodded.

"Bothers me, too," his mom agreed.

"Maybe if we do well on Hoarfrost, things will get better for them here," she suggested.

"How?" Terry wondered.

"Prosperity has a way of spreading. Most of these aliens came here for work. If we do well, there will be more work."

"How many of them are there?" he wondered.

"Here?" Tina asked. He nodded. "Probably a few thousand, at least. Beings in this situation in the galaxy? I wouldn't be surprised if a million starve to death every day."

"Maybe if the Union didn't ignore them, less would starve," his mom said. Terry found himself nodding in agreement.

"Sorry to say, it's probably the opposite," Doc said. "They spent hundreds of trillions on Earth in handouts, and poverty stayed exactly the same, or got even worse. Places where industry grew and businesses flourished, poverty decreased. Usually precipitously."

"People still starve in places with lots of businesses," she said mulishly.

"And they always will," Doc replied. Terry could see his mom's jaw muscles bunching and knew she was struggling with herself.

The group of Humans moved through the station based on directions Doc and his people had obtained on their previous visit. The destination was a leasing office that appeared almost as dingy as the station itself. A bored-looking Buma was perched by a series of mounted slates, looking as worn out as the station. The office smelled like a birdcage in dire need of cleaning. The alien's owl-like head turned to notice them as they stopped in the entrance.

The Buma chirped and clicked. "You looking for something?" came out of Terry's translator.

"A ship," Doc said. He'd set his own translator into active mode, so it replied in the Buma's own language. It was a useful feature, as few aliens had English matrixes in their own translators.

"Oh!" the Buma chirped in surprise. It spent a minute shuffling computers and chips before looking back at Doc. "What are you in need of?"

Doc spent a minute detailing their requirements, which were considerable. Besides being able to temporarily house the 10 orca and 19 bottlenose dolphins, it had to have landing-capable small craft able to set down on a planet that couldn't refuel them.

"Not asking for much, are you?" the Buma said. The translator managed to convey scorn.

"It's what we need; can you do it?"

"How are you paying?" Doc flashed a pair of 100,000 credit chits. "Won't be enough."

"We have more."

The Buma's beak worked and huge eyes blinked. Terry guessed it was thinking about the possibilities. "How much more?"

The other six mercs moved into view of the Buma, who seemed surprised to notice them. None of them acted threatening in any way, yet they all carried weapons and wore armor.

"Enough," Doc said. "Can you help us, or not?"

"It's funny you ask," the Buma said in an unfunny way. "I got a message some time back requesting similar capacity."

"Interesting," Doc said dryly. Of course, he'd probably inquired before returning to Karma and getting the ball rolling. "You still haven't answered my question."

Terry was amazed he could be so cool about everything. If they couldn't find a way to move down to the planet, they were in big trouble. He'd heard the ships already had jobs elsewhere and needed to leave within two weeks. Even if they could be convinced to take their passengers and cargo back to Karma, the warship might still be waiting. Worse, there could be more of them by then. Going back wasn't an option.

"There's a heavy lift transport available," the Buma said. "Two orbital-class landers as well."

"Wonderful," Doc said, "we'd like to contract them."

"The ship isn't hyperspace capable," the Buma explained.

"Noted."

The Buma's huge eyes regarded Doc, then went over everyone else, lingering curiously for a fraction of a second on Terry before returning to Doc. "How long do you need these assets?"

"Four weeks will be sufficient."

Now the Buma's curiosity was obviously piqued. Its big head tilted almost 90 degrees. It took everything Terry had not to laugh. "The only ship capable of carrying the transports left the system a day ago."

"How about you leave the details up to us?" Doc said. "Will you arrange the lease, or not?" The Buma tapped at his slate idly for a moment, staring at Doc without saying anything. "Okay, let's look elsewhere."

"Nobody here on the station has the ships you want," the Buma snapped, clicking its beak angrily.

Doc shrugged. "With enough credits or firepower, anything is possible." His mercs stared the Buma down, and it ruffled its feathers and relented.

"Rate is 300,000 credits for one month," it said. "A one million credit damage retainer is necessary."

"Fine," Doc said. The Buma blinked twice and watched in amazement as Doc began producing more 100,000 credit chits. Lots more. "I want the contract in hard copy, and I'm affixing my Mercenary Guild license to the contract."

"You didn't say this was for mercenary work!" the Buma howled in outrage.

"You didn't ask."

"Ten days is cutting it dangerously close," Terry's mom said as they walked back to the shuttle bay. "Captain Baker said his next job is nowhere near Earth. If this doesn't work out…"

"What?" Doc asked. "We'll be worse off than here?" He gestured at the dilapidated interior of the station's promenade.

"He wouldn't dare fail to provide those ships now," Honcho said in a rare moment of speech.

"Why?" she demanded.

"When Doc put our merc registration on the contract, he upped the ante," Honcho explained. "Ole' hooter there doesn't come through, we can go to the Merc Guild."

"Better," Tina said. "We can take it out of his hide." Her grin was feral, as if she were hoping that situation would occur.

"Would beating him up get us down to the moon?" Terry's mom asked.

Tina shrugged. "It wouldn't, but it would be fun."

"Do you want to look around some more?" Doc asked Terry.

"No," he said. They were passing the elSha family, who were again watching the Humans go by. "Let's get out of here."

"Sure," Doc said.

"Wait," Terry suddenly said, and walked over to the family's home. The two adult reptilians watched him warily with both their independent eye turrets. Terry stopped at the edge of their space. Two of the young were hanging from the faded and dingy ceiling, also watching him. Terry didn't know much about the elSha, but he thought he knew hopelessness when he saw it.

He reached into his pocket and took a credit chit, sitting it on the floor just inside their door. One of the two adults—he couldn't tell if it was male or female—came closer, one eye darting to the credit chit and then back to Terry.

"Go ahead," he said, "I hope it helps."

The alien stepped over and picked up the chit, which was 100 credits in denomination. It examined it for a moment, then placed it in a pouch. "I thank you," the alien said, and bowed his head.

Terry nodded and rejoined the others. His mom put an arm around his shoulder and gave him an affectionate squeeze.

"Why did you bother?" Tina asked. "It probably won't help them get out of here."

"Maybe not," Terry said, "but it was fun." Doc glanced at him, and Terry winked at him. Tina cursed mildly, and they continued to the lift back down to the hub. Behind them, the elSha and its family watched them go in silence.

* * * * *

Chapter Sixteen

Hoarfrost, Lupasha System, Coro Region, Tolo Arm
December 24th, 2037

Lander 1 rode its descent motors like blazing pillars of hydrogen fire into Hoarfrost's atmosphere. The pilot, a huge snail-like creature with three eyes called a Bakulu, managed the craft via pinplants. When he'd come forward after checking on Pōkole, he'd marveled at the alien sitting glued to the pilot's area; the only discernable movement was its eyes, looking at three different displays at the same time while controlling the ship with its mind alone.

"Is it difficult?" Terry asked the Bakulu.

"Not at all," it replied. Terry's translator spoke in English, but for the life of him, he couldn't detect any sign the alien pilot had uttered a single word. "It takes only a tiny portion of my brain to operate the craft." One of its eyes rose over the huge pearlescent shell to regard Terry. "My species prefers serving in space; we are naturals in this environment. Most of our race is born in space these days. This merely enhances our natural proclivity to this environment."

"Living in space doesn't cause any physiological difficulties?" Terry's mom asked from behind them.

"No," the Bakulu responded. "Why would it?"

The transport used a combination of atmospheric resistance and engines to slow its descent, breaking through scattered cloud cover and skimming over the endless expanse of icy mountains. The surface looked like the Swiss Alps, made entirely of ice. The shattered ramparts towered kilometers into the sky in places.

Without warning, the broken mountains gave way to a vast plain extending for many kilometers below them. Terry looked out of the extra-large transport cockpit to try to get a feel for the plain. It didn't look natural.

"This is weird," he said, and pointed at the graceful curve of the plain.

"It looks the way it should," Doc said from the rear of the seating area. "It was created with orbital laser cannons."

"Holy cow," Terry said, glancing back at Doc. "Lasers?"

"Yup," he said. "Remember, the Izlians were in charge of this project." He pointed up. Above them through the crystal-clear cockpit, Lupasha 1 arced from horizon to horizon in swirling yellow/orange splendor. A line cut across the view, the plane of the great gas giant's ring, just below Hoarfrost's orbit.

"Why did they do it?"

"The ice below is two kilometers thick," Doc explained. "Ice of the sort you find on planets like this is more akin to rock, as I understand it. After the survey was complete, they parked a battlecruiser in orbit and set to work."

"How long did it take?"

"I don't know," Doc admitted. "Depends on the ship, I guess. Lasers vary from 10 megawatt to a gigawatt on warships. It could have had a couple, or a dozen. To answer your question, anywhere from a couple hours to days, I guess."

Terry tried to imagine a big alien spaceship in orbit, bristling with laser weapons, blazing away at the icy moon like in a sci-fi film. Attacking the surface of the world as if it were an enemy armada. Looking out over the nearly flat icefield, he had a hard time imagining why.

"So, why?" he eventually asked.

"Like I said, the ice was practically rock. When it gets that thick, the thermal transfer rates are tricky."

"True," Dr. Hernandez chimed in from the rear of the passenger area.

"They used the lasers to break up the super-hard ice and alter it to a more favorable form."

"Favorable to what?"

"Getting through," Doc said. He pointed out of the cockpit, and Terry could see the first artificial structures on the planet. They were perched on the edge of the first liquid water he'd seen.

"You've never explained where we're going to live here," Terry said and looked back at his mother. The landscape outside was dim, almost like twilight back on Earth. They were now only a kilometer above the ice, and he could see the laser-created plain wasn't as flat as he'd thought. It, too, was a cracked mess of mini hills. It looked like the ice fields in Antarctica they'd studied in school, where the icebergs were born. "Are we living in those buildings?"

"They're automated," his mom explained. "They're fusion power plants and big heat sinks."

"I don't understand."

She looked uncomfortable when she continued, "The power plant provides power to the mining and habitat facilities. Instead of dumping excess heat into the atmosphere, they dump it into the water you see via specialized heat exchangers. The exchangers heat the water and keep it liquid at the cost of 100 megawatts constant output."

"But why are they doing it?" he asked, feeling frustrated.

"Because it maintains a 19-kilometer cylinder of liquid water," Doc said, "which is the only access to the habitat and mining facilities."

Terry's brow furrowed as he tried to put the statement into context. Below them the facilities were coming into better view. A huge powerplant, like the fusion plants being built on Earth, dominated the largest part. He'd been wrong—the facility wasn't built on the ice; it was floating at the edge of the roughly circular lake of water. On the edge of the floating buildings was a ring of large landing pads and blocky structures. Nowhere for people to live, and no sign of vehicles.

Under two kilometers of ice, he finally realized. "We're living under the ice?" he asked, hoping he'd misunderstood.

"Yes," his mother said. Terry looked horrified. "Before you freak out, think about it. How is that so different from living in a spaceship, which you've been doing *for almost seven months?*"

"It's very different, Mom," he said.

"It's different for the cetaceans, too," she retorted, which brought him up short. "We're here because of them. For good or ill, all this has transpired for their welfare. We've been trying for half a year to find a place for them to live. This is the best we can do."

"I've been all over this arm of the galaxy," Doc said. "There are a few better planets, maybe, but they're all colonized, and would be problematic for us."

"This planet's ecology and ocean's chemical structure is almost ideal," Dr. Jaehnig said. The senior staff had been listening in the back of the passenger area. "We've been giving the cetaceans a drug therapy treatment designed to get them acclimated to the planet's ocean."

"That's why you built the submersible," Terry said, looking at Doc.

Doc nodded. The man was watching him closely, the ever-present appraisal stare Terry had seen him use so many times.

"What's the long-term plan?" Terry asked. He could tell by her expression his mother was caught off guard by the question.

"We get the cetaceans established, try to find a way for them to care for themselves in this environment, and if it works out, we consider going home to face the music."

"Won't they know where you've taken the cetaceans?"

"Unlikely," Doc said. "We used cash for everything, including these ships. The ships the Winged Hussars loaned us won't tell anybody where they went after Karma. Colonel Kosmalski assured us. As far as the rest of the universe is concerned, we simply disappeared."

Terry thought of baby Pōkole. What would happen to him if they were forced to return to Earth or were captured and brought back forcibly? Would he be killed like the adults, or end up in a side show? Child of the whale freaks.

"Then we'll figure out how to make it work," he said. His mom smiled and hugged him.

"I'm glad you're on board," she said. "You're our IT expert, you know."

He snorted but smiled. "I'm learning," he said.

"And we want you to keep learning," Dr. Jaehnig said. "I'll need some expertise if we're to implant the devices into Pōkole."

"You've decided then?" Terry asked, excited now.

"We were still considering," the doctor admitted. "It was Moloko who decided for us. She asked when her calf would get the implants. We said we were waiting to discuss it with her. She said the pod had agreed it would be good to do so sooner, rather than later."

"Surprisingly forward thinking for the orcas," Dr. Orsage said. "I've noticed as time has gone by, they're increasingly analytical in their thinking." She looked at Terry and pointed at him. "We need to learn more about these *pinplants*, so we can better understand their effects. We're depending on you, young man."

"I will," Terry said. Despite only being 12 years old, he felt 12 feet tall.

"Prepare for landing," the Bakulu pilot's voice said through their translators as the transport began a slow turn and started its landing sequence.

It took two trips of the lighter transport to bring down all the staff and their dependents. Terry had forgotten how many of them there were. He did his classes remotely because of other responsibilities, and he usually ate with his mom or Doc, and sometimes the other mercs. The small topside station, designed mainly for maintenance and providing just a few cots and assembly areas, was jam-packed with over 100 people.

The buildings next to the landing pads were stores, warehouses, and submarine pens. In the latter were their way to get down to their new homes. The cetaceans had been undergoing pressure acclimation for the last two days. The only one who wouldn't immediately be ready to dive down was Pōkole, who couldn't be separated from Terry yet due to feeding requirements.

The surface temperature was cold. Deadly cold. An unprotected Human would be instantly incapacitated; their eyes would freeze in a fraction of a second, skin in another second. They would be dead in under a minute. It was only 5 degrees kelvin above the temperature of liquid nitrogen. They all wore protective suits, like space suits, but without the need to compensate for vacuum. Tina called them hot pockets.

Having to spend a couple of minutes getting into a spacesuit for a one-minute walk from the landing transport to a building seemed like a waste of time, at least until he got into one and went outside. The suit's incredibly powerful heaters made it feel like he was in a rotisserie oven the second he turned them on.

"Do *not* turn off the heaters!" Doc warned them. He and his Last Call mercs were escorting them in groups of 10, as they only had 20 suits, and were keeping a few in reserve. "If you get a red light on your suit heaters, yell out immediately. You'll only have a few seconds before frostbite sets in."

"Will Pōkole be okay?" Terry asked.

"He'll be warmer than we are. Ready?" Everyone nodded.

Even through the visors, Terry could see everyone's eyes wide with concern. He thought he probably looked the same. Despite the searing heat from the suit, he bit his lip and waited as the lock cycled. A second later it opened, and the cold hit them.

Terry had been skiing a couple of times on Mauna Kea during the winter. He remembered how cold he'd been after several hours in the snow. It seemed to seep into his very bones. That was exactly how he felt after just a couple seconds of Hoarfrost's cold.

He coughed and gasped from the impact, and his suit instantly went to full power. He hadn't realized the heater wasn't on 100%.

He guessed full power outside the cold of Hoarfrost might have been as dangerous from the suit as it would be from the cold. As it was, the heaters pushed back the deadly chill to only a numbing cold.

They were all jogging by the time they ran into the building and through the double doors. Doc patted him on the back. "Good job."

"This is insane," he said to the merc.

Doc laughed in reply. "Young man, this isn't even winter here. Wait until we're behind Lupasha 1 for a week, and no sun reaches the moon. Pools of liquid nitrogen form, and the fusion plant can't keep the ice clear."

"I didn't think I'd be this excited to dive down two kilometers under water," Terry admitted.

"Soon," Doc said. "Soon."

Once all the people were down and safe in the buildings, landing the cetaceans could begin. Terry watched through the building's heated glass and a video feed under water as the heavy transport landed directly in the water. The cargo door opened, and out came the first five orcas. He recognized them as Wandering Pod.

The five sleek black and white orcas shot out of the cargo hold of the transport in a flurry of flashing flukes, which could only be described as pure joy. Around and around they circled each other, bumping and rubbing, rolling on their sides and looking up at the surface.

"Aren't they in danger?" Terry asked. "The cold."

"The water is around -10 degrees Celsius," he said and smiled. "Not too cold for an orca, from what I hear."

Terry nodded. That was true, of course. The water at the institute was kept at -2 degrees, not because it was ideal, but because it was expensive to refrigerate it. The water in the ship had been held at 0

Celsius. The arctic sea water could get considerably colder. The orcas were ecstatic.

He wondered what they would do. They'd been in captivity all their lives. None of their whales had ever been in the wild before. Would they run, or do something crazy? Instead, after their celebration, they simply waited.

A few minutes later the other transport landed in the water again. This was the one that had brought the Humans down. It opened its ramp just below the surface, and the bottlenoses shot out. It was like watching a machinegun firing dolphins. The ramp was narrow enough they were forced to go single file. Even so, all 19 were in the water in less than a minute. Unlike the orcas, they didn't spend their exuberance quickly. When the final big transport landed 15 minutes later, they were still racing around each other, around the orcas, and playing with half-submerged pieces of ice.

The doors opened on the last transport, and the five orcas of the new super pod raced out to join the others. It was the first time all nine adult orcas were together. Terry saw Dr. Orsage watching and, of course, taking notes.

The orcas swam next to each other, touching fins and brushing against each other. Then, almost before he realized it, two were fighting.

"What do we do?" he barked in surprise.

"Nothing," his mom said.

"We were expecting this," Dr. Orsage said. "They're deciding who's in charge."

Terry looked closer at the video image to try to figure out who was fighting. He thought it was Ki'i and Kray, the biggest males of each pod. Before he could be sure, it was over. Then he was sure it was the two he'd guessed when they swam side-by-side past the camera. Kray was in the lead, and Ki'i had a line of dark rakes down one side.

"Is he okay?" Terry asked.

Dr. Jaehnig was examining the footage. "Yes, it isn't serious. Common in wild orcas. Nothing more than a minor argument."

Terry looked at the deep gouges, which were bleeding, and shook his head. He hoped they never had a serious argument.

"There might only be one pod now," Dr. Orsage said, then shrugged. "We'll find out when we meet them down at the habitat."

Almost as if they'd been listening, all nine orcas formed into a line and slowly began spiraling down into the dark, dark depths. Thin lines of bubbles trailed from their rebreather domes and were soon gone from view, leaving no evidence they were ever there. As had been arranged, they would spend the next 36 hours slowly diving down the two kilometers to the habitat. It would give their bodies the time they needed to acclimate to the intense pressure.

The people left the gathering area and moved down a hall into a cavernous hangar. Inside were three cylindrical submersibles, each surfaced in a berth. Terry saw some of the staff were already removing cables and climbing inside. Soon lights came on as the vehicles came to life. Many in their entourage looked at the craft with mixed feelings. The younger children crowded around their parents. The older ones, like Terry, tried to look brave.

His mom and Doc led him to the closest one. People were loading what gear they could aboard. Most of the non-passenger space was being used by the module that held Pōkole, a long cylindrical container on wheels. The calf was asleep from a mild tranquilizer. Not much extra room would be available with so many people to transport down. The staff designated as pilots for the submersibles would take them back up after everyone was down and bring down gear the transports had gone back to space to get. Honcho from Doc's team was driving their sub.

They'd all said their goodbyes to the captains and crew of *Teddy Roosevelt*, *Kavul Tesh*, and *Kavul Ato*. As soon as the last load of equipment was offloaded, they would head for the stargate and the next job.

Captain Baker had wished him luck and given Terry a computer chip with some data to study on ships' computer systems. Baker thought he might make a good ship's computer officer someday. Terry took the data, of course, but he had no interest in being a ship's officer. Space was cool enough, sure. However, after half a year floating around the cosmos, he didn't think he'd want to do it for the rest of his life.

The submersible sealed up, and everyone managed to find a place to sit. Terry got to stay up front and had a view out of the super dense plastic windows as they dove under the waves. It was an alien-manufactured vessel, and looked quite high tech.

They maneuvered out of the submarine pen and out into the open, then Honcho programmed the vessel and it began its long, long dive. Doc's watch beeped, and he looked at it.

"Midnight," he said. "Merry Christmas."

"Oh, right," Terry's mom said. "I'd almost forgotten." She looked at Terry and frowned. "I'm sorry, I wasn't able to get you anything this year."

"That's okay," he said. "At least we're together." She looked at Doc, and they both nodded.

Dozens of people were crowded in the back, and someone sang, "The First Noel." Soon, they were all singing along as best as they could. Terry watched out the big windows. The subs lights were on, and he saw they were passing the orcas, slowly circling down into the night. The sub hummed with the sounds of singing.

Outside, the orcas seemed to be singing as well. Terry's translator didn't render any of it into English, except one word—*Shool.* As they descended into the abyss, the whales' song provided a mournful counterpoint to the hymns.

* * * * *

Part III

Exile

Chapter One

Terry rolled over in his bunk and stretched. After a week, his joints no longer ached with every movement. Unlike the cetaceans, the Humans hadn't been getting treatments to live at the extreme depths of their new home. Their bodies weren't designed to live at such depths. Orcas had been observed to dive more than 300 meters. That was nothing compared to the 2,000 meters of ice over their heads.

"I wish the place didn't smell like rotten fish," he said as his feet hit the deck. As usual, it was cold. He was always cold. After a lifetime in Molokai and always being warm, he thought they should have named the place Hell. He'd learned in school that the Vikings believed in a frozen hell, not a hot one. Made sense if you lived in the icy north.

The room's lights came on to show the stark grey walls. He had his own room again, 28.8 cubic meters of opulence. His bunk, a little desk, a chair, and a toilet that wasn't shaped for his butt. The toilet also converted into a shower, but it only sprayed cold water.

He went into the bathroom and washed up a bit, brushed his teeth, and used the toilet. The mirror was a highly polished piece of stainless steel. It worked well enough.

One level down, and he was in the mess hall. The sun wasn't visible to them, so day and night cycles had been established to match what they'd been used to on Molokai. Since it was breakfast time, the place was crowded. Conversations bubbled all around, some quiet, some loud. A few laughed, a couple cried. Adjusting to the pressure was a personal process. Not everyone experienced it the same way.

His mom came in and made her way over to him, standing in the food line. She was smiling, which got his attention. "What's up?" he asked.

"They got the first set of heaters working."

"Oh, thank god!" he said. "When?" She pointed up, and he tracked her gesture. A series of fabric tubes the engineers had strung the day they arrived in the hopes the heating system worked as planned had sat, unmoving, for days. As if her gesture was the cue, they began to billow, then stiffened. The first breeze of warm air blew across his face.

All around the room people looked up, some in confusion, many in amazement. They all wore just about every piece of clothing they had with them in order to keep warm. The habitat's atmosphere processing and basic power systems created enough heat to keep it from being freezing inside, but nobody in their right mind would call 10 degrees Celcius warm. They'd also been sleeping in shiny reflective space blankets to keep warm.

"Warm air!" someone yelled. A wave of applause rippled across the room, which quickly grew to loud cheering, and then a standing ovation. Terry's mom patted him on the shoulder and walked up to the front of the room where a low stage sat. The mess hall was also their meeting room, currently. When the people saw her, they fell silent.

"The staff hasn't had much sleep the last week," she said, "as I'm sure you all know." The door opened, and three people walked in, all looking oily and tired. "I think we owe Melissa and her men a round of applause."

The three new arrivals stopped in their tracks as everyone in the room applauded them, many yelling their thanks. The leader, Melissa, waved her hands to stop the applause. "This is just the start," she said. "We have the power transfers working properly now, so we'll have all the rest of the regular support systems working in short order." More applause. "But first we'd like some food, and some sleep."

"It feels so good," Terry said when she rejoined him. It was already warm enough that many were removing some of their extra layers. Terry set aside one of the two jackets he'd been wearing.

"It sure does," she agreed. "You get any food yet?"

"Still waking up," he said and yawned.

"How do you feel?"

Terry flexed his arms and nodded. "Better," he said.

She nodded and flexed her own arms. "Me, too. In fact, everyone seems to be getting there."

Their nominal medical staff had done everything they could to accelerate the acclimation process, but mostly it involved letting people adjust. Each day the pressure had gotten higher, until they were the equivalent of one kilometer down. Science had figured out how to allow people to acclimate much deeper, though it would take months. Coming up would be just as hard. The pressure would now only increase a few PSI per day.

"Any luck with the rotten fish smell?" he asked.

"They found a scent dispersal system," she said.

"You mean it stinks on purpose?" he asked. She nodded. They'd thought there must be a huge cache of rotten fish left behind by the Selroth. Now it looked like they *liked* the smell and had done it on purpose.

"They've turned one off, but there must be another."

Luckily for everyone, they'd brought their own autochefs and supplies. The food was at least pretty good, even if some of the pre-packaged stuff had imploded the previous day. Afterward, the cooks had taken measures to prevent any more losses until they could get local food processing properly.

After he'd eaten, he got up. "I have to go check on Pōkole," he said.

"Dr. Jaehnig says he's doing fine," she said.

"Yeah, he's used to the feeding system. Little guy just misses me."

"Don't forget, classes this afternoon." Terry rolled his eyes. "Be there, young man."

"Fine," he said and left. His mother yelled something after him, but Terry pretended not to hear her.

Leaving the mess hall, he went down two levels to the main floor, where he could see the dome. Their entire habitat was built inside a dome made from a single piece of ruby formed by the Izlians deep inside a gas giant. The technicians explained it was a molecular matrix that would handle almost any pressure difference. Regardless, it was hard to believe the water pushing on it was over 100 kilograms per square centimeter.

"One tiny crack," he said, looking at the dome.

Even so, the view was worth it. Thousands of lights were placed all around the dome at regular intervals, providing light during daytime hours. By projecting the light out, the brightly illuminated water created a more natural glow in the dome's interior. Outside, a pair of orcas swam past, too far away for Terry to tell who it might be. In addition, a dizzying array of native fish swam everywhere.

The native fish were blind, never having evolved eyes two kilometers under the ice. Instead, they possessed many varied ways of sensing their environment. These ranged from incredibly delicate pressure sensors on many, including the larger predators, to feelers. Many of the plant-eating fish sported a fan of ridiculously long feelers that reminded Terry of a mustache, used to find plant life along the many common volcanic vents.

The dome was built on the flattened top of an extinct undersea volcano. It was within a hundred meters of the ice, which extended for two kilometers above their heads; the melt shaft another hundred meters to the side. They weren't directly under the shaft, so if an accident happened, it wouldn't sink directly onto the dome, which wasn't indestructible.

As they were still working to get the habitat fully operational, the mines weren't yet a priority. They were scattered all around the habitat in every direction at varying depths, from a few hundred meters below them to several kilometers.

Inside the dome, their habitat was a series of buildings, varying from the five-story living quarters he was just leaving to the ten-story administrative and control systems building whose roof met the top center of the dome. Several smaller buildings were dotted around as well. He was heading for the one tasked as cetacean care, a two-story sprawling building with one of the habitat's three locks.

As he walked to the building, he passed a bunch of kids playing a kickball game. They were all younger, and seemed oblivious to both the view and the fact they were under the ice on an alien moon. They were just happy to be off the starships and to have ground under their feet, even if it was volcanic stone. The group noticed him and waved. Somehow, he'd become famous among the children.

The cetacean care building, dubbed the CC, was where Dr. Jaehnig had set up. As their sole cetacean-qualified physician, he was also their main Human doctor. Since he was forced to wear two hats, he wanted to be closer to those who would need him more.

The doors to the building were open, though a sign proclaimed, "The Doctor is Out." Dr. Jaehnig had a staff of five others, two fully-trained medical techs and three nurses, one of whom was learning to be a doctor. Terry knew the medical staff was one of their biggest concerns.

Terry went in and through the small waiting area into the back of the first floor, where Dr. Jaehnig had his office. The physician looked up and smiled when he saw who his visitor was.

"Good morning, Mr. Clark," he said.

Being called Mister made Terry feel strange. His father was Mr. Clark. "Morning, Dr. Jaehnig. How are your patients?"

"They're fine," he said. "The robot feeder is doing its job, and the cetaceans are continuing to eat their way through everything they can find that swims."

Despite being thousands of meters under the ice, Hoarfrost had evolved a wide variety of marine life. Most of it was various plants feeding off large amounts of nutrients ejected from deep sea vents, tiny animals feeding on those, and on up. The largest aquatic animal was a dinosaur-looking fish a meter long, which fed on smaller dinosaur-looking fish. At least until the Selroth had come along.

Terry caught movement out of the corner of his eye. One entire wall of the building was constructed against the ruby dome. Outside, one of the *Floot* flashed into view. It smashed into the wall and ricocheted off at an angle. No sound of the impact passed through the super-hard ruby wall. The *Floot* was classified as closest to the genus *Chelonia*, the green turtle. Except the *Floot* had six flippers and a long flexible neck, which could retreat into the shell, and a flippered tail for extra power.

A second after the *Floot* swam away, one of the orcas appeared in hot pursuit. Dr. Jaehnig shook his head and made a note in one of his slates. "They haven't figured out how to eat the *Floots* yet, but they keep trying."

Hunting the native life proved easy, since they were all blind. The *Floot* had been imported by the Selroth. Apparently they'd brought their own sea creatures for food and amusement. The marine biologists had been horrified to learn this fact, saying the damage to the biosphere was probably irreversible.

Dr. Patel was working on a study of the various Selroth species they'd encountered. He'd assembled a list from the GalNet of creatures from the aliens' home world and was marking them off as each was located. To this point they hadn't seen an *Oohobo*, a large predatory species native to the Selroth planet.

Terry looked at some of the Tri-V displayed details on Selroth marine species, noting their eyes shared similar characteristics—silvery with red rims and two irises. A strange and cool evolutionary adaptation.

Another of Dr. Jaehnig's Tri-Vs was showing a dissected local fish with descriptions pointing to various parts and organs. Terry could hear Dr. Patel's voice speaking as the dissection proceeded.

"Have they brought in any new fish today?" he asked.

"One of the bottlenoses, Hula, did a few hours ago. It was chewed up a bit, though." He gestured to a table, and Terry went over to look at it.

"It's got legs," he said.

"Looks like it," Dr. Jaehnig said. "Not my specialty. Patel will look at it this afternoon." The scientist glanced over at another slate. "You going to handle feeding Pōkole?"

"Yes," Terry said. Dr. Jaehnig nodded and went back to watching the video and putting bits of fish into test tubes.

Terry walked though several doors and down a corridor to the lock area. Of the city's three locks, only two were currently working. One of them was the submarine bay, which was still slowly transporting equipment down from the surface at the rate of one trip a day. The other was in CC, and acted as the center of all underwater operations.

As soon as he entered the moon pool room, he saw Doc and his crew were already there. "Hey, guys!" he said.

"What's up, kiddo?" Doc asked, glancing up from their project. All seven mercs were working on a series of big robots hanging from frameworks. They hadn't been there yesterday.

"Robots?" he asked.

"Not quite," Doc said. "We'll show you soon."

"Aw, come on?"

"Chill, kid," Honcho said, flipping up a welding mask to glance at him.

"Yeah," Hutch said. He and Peyton weren't helping much; they were playing cards, as usual.

"You never said if you'll be leaving for any other contracts," Terry said, hoping to change course and keep his eyes on what they were doing.

"Not sure yet," Doc said while looking at a slate Terry couldn't see.

"Going to take us three days to decompress from here," Tina said and shrugged. "Plus we have to rely on passive comms so nobody knows we're here."

"Go feed the fish, kid," Toothpick said, gesturing with his head toward the moon pool.

Reluctantly, Terry turned and headed over toward the moon pool. He glanced back once but still couldn't see anything. *What the heck are they working on?* he thought.

He reached the pool, and Pōkole immediately surfaced and chirped at him. "Hey, buddy," Terry said, "how you doing?" The young orca bobbed his head up and down quickly. He'd become much more expressive in the last few weeks before arriving on Hoarfrost, though Terry could tell he also missed his mom.

A movement drew his attention, and he saw Moloko floating just outside the lock. She had part of a dead sea creature and was playing with it. The life was so abundant around their habitat, the colonists were eating the stores put back for the cetaceans, because they didn't need it. Terry touched the transmit on his translator.

"Good morning, Moloko."

"*Morning, Warden Terry,*" she replied. "*How Pōkole?*"

"He is fine, but misses you." Terry took the ready bottle, and the calf greedily drank.

"*How now soon?*"

"Nine days," Terry said, after checking his slate to be sure. The pressure equalization was slower because of the Humans, which was hard for the cetaceans to understand. "Where are the rest of the orcas?" he asked.

"*They go.*"

"Where?"

"*Explore.*"

"Oh," he said. This was the first he'd heard about them exploring. "What are they looking for?"

"*Shool!*"

They're looking for their god? Terry thought. "How are they looking?"

"*Call into deep. Wait. Listen.*"

"Have they heard anything back?"

"*Not yet.*"

An hour later he was finished with Pōkole and headed back out. Doc and his people were nowhere in sight, and neither was their project. He made a face as he casually looked around the equipment bay, only finding random tools and testing equipment.

He must have still been scowling a few minutes later when he ran into his mom as he was heading toward the classroom area.

"What's wrong?" she asked.

"Nothing," he lied. She gave him her stern mom face. "The orcas are looking for their god, and Doc and the guys are up to something and won't tell me what."

"As for their god, that's up to them," she said and shrugged. "Dr. Orsage thinks it's therapeutic for them, being isolated from the sky and Earth."

"I guess that makes sense," Terry agreed.

"Yeah, it's probably harmless. As for Doc and his guys hiding things from you, how horrible," she said with a smile, which did nothing to reduce his saltiness.

"Everyone says I'm important. Why are they keeping secrets from me?"

"Only a couple get to know everything going on, and I'm sorry to say you aren't one of them." He looked down, embarrassed. "You're a huge help, but you don't have to know everything. You're not old enough to be responsible."

"I know," he said, feeling like a grade-school kid.

"As one of those who knows everything going on, I can guarantee you'll be quite excited by what the guys are working on." He brightened up, hoping she was about to spill the beans. "That said, aren't you going to be late for your first class?"

He checked his watch. She was right, class started in five minutes. "Yeah," he said.

"Get going, you'll find out soon enough." She continued in the direction she'd been heading.

* * * * *

Chapter Two

Hoarfrost, Lupasha System, Coro Region, Tolo Arm
January 13th, 2038

Life gradually got better in the habitat as more and more systems were made operational. The mechanical team under Melissa spent less time racing between urgent jobs and more time concentrating on long-term goals. The temperature and humidity settled into something more to the liking of the staff, who'd spent many years in Hawaii.

The orcas never found *Shool*, which was no surprise to their Human wardens. They also never stopped looking. Terry thought they were incredibly patient. If anything, they seemed more convinced *Shool* was out there, somewhere.

"Maybe Shool is beyond," the bottlenose Hula suggested one day.

Again with hyperspace, Terry thought. "What do the orcas think of that idea?" Terry asked her.

"They say we crazy."

School wasn't as lame as Terry had feared it would be. As one of the 12 kids who were high school aged, they were largely self-paced in their studies. He was assigned objectives and could complete them as quickly as he wished. He also got to work on his pinplant research and got credit for that as well, which was cool.

Despite missing Yui, he found himself making friends. He only recognized one of the boys from his age group; they'd played on different summer baseball teams. They all seemed to know him. Suddenly he was the *cool kid*, and he had absolutely no idea why.

Some of the things they got to do was help out around the habitat on work projects. The air was no longer filled with the smell of rotting fish, but a lot of junk had been left behind by the Selroth when they'd abandoned the place. Tons of it, actually. First the kids helped gather it in assigned areas. Next they helped clean, which wasn't as fun. Then they initiated a beautification project, which meant painting. The Selroth hadn't bothered with anything more than priming the metal buildings. Compared to the big ruby dome, the rest of the place was lame.

The adults handled the majority of the painting project because some heavy equipment was involved. Where the kids got involved was putting up murals on some of the buildings' larger walls. By the end of the second week, a dozen different designs were coming to life. The high schoolers' mural was on the side of the CC building, a stylized habitat inside its ruby dome with orcas and dolphins playing outside.

"Reminds me of that Captain Nemo movie," someone said. A short time later the movie in question was located. *Captain Nemo and the Underwater City*. Along with exabytes of data from Earth, they also had thousands of movies; the one in question was included. The same evening after dinner, a new tradition was born—movie night.

Some popcorn was produced, and the autochef made soda pop and candy for the kids. The main administration building still had a four-story wall painted white, and the movie was projected on the wall.

Terry found the special effects of the mid-20th century laughable, as you might imagine they would be. Still, having nearly the entire group together sharing snacks and watching the film together was a fun experience. Doc and his mom sat on either side of him, and he pretended not to notice when they held hands behind his chair. It felt good.

"Hey," Doc said about halfway through the movie. A giant manta ray was menacing a submarine. "I think we have the name of this place."

"What's that?" Terry's mom asked.

The view on the screen changed to show the underwater city. Sure enough, it looked a lot like what Terry and his fellow high schoolers were painting. "Templemer," he said. It was pronounced Temple-mere. She looked at him, then slowly nodded.

"I like it," she said, "not as pretentious as Atlantis would have been."

Terry had heard a few people joking about living in Atlantis. He had to think what would make Atlantis pretentious. Unable to figure it out, he decided he liked Templemer. "I think it's a great idea," he said. By the next morning, everyone was calling their home Templemer. The head doctors voted on it later, but there was really no need. They could've called it Mount Olympus, and everyone would have kept calling it Templemer. Their home had a name.

The next morning was the 13th, and a big day. All the head doctors met Terry in the moon pool, where Pōkole was swimming excitedly, around and around. Outside the lock, his pod floated, watching and waiting. Moloko was front and center.

Terry was already wearing his drysuit, as were his mother and Dr. Jaehnig. Both of them were already in the water trying to corral Pōkole.

"Can you help?" his mother asked in frustration. "The little guy is all worked up."

"Just excited about the big day," Terry said.

"How would he know?" Dr. Orsage asked. "The calf is only 7 months old."

"Oh, he knows," Terry assured her. "His mom wants him to get the pinplants now."

"We've been over this," Dr. Jaehnig said. "We want to make sure the calf is acclimated to Hoarfrost before undergoing the procedure."

"I know," Terry said, grabbing a rebreather and sliding into the water. "Explain it to them." He pointed out through the lock where the four massive orcas were watching intently. Terry smacked the water several times. "Come on, Pōkole," he said gently.

The baby orca, who was already 3 meters long and over 500 kilograms, spun around and shot toward Terry. His mother gasped in alarm. Terry turned sideways and reached out with a hand, catching the orca's dorsal fin as it slipped by, allowing himself to be propelled along with the powerful strokes of the calf's flukes.

"Atta boy!" Terry cried, smacking the young orca's side affectionately. "You know what's going on, don't you?" The orca slipped out of Terry's grasp, dove down, then shot straight up. Not quite managing to clear the water, he crashed down on his side with a huge wave. It was a pretty good approximation of the adult cetaceans' spyhopping, a behavior meant to get a look around the surface.

"Wow!" Dr. Hernandez said.

"Indeed," Dr. Patel agreed.

The calf calmed and allowed Terry's mom and Dr. Jaehnig to come closer. He rolled on his side and looked at them with one of his big eyes.

"He's thrived," Dr. Jaehnig said, slipping a stethoscope against Pōkole's middle. "Thanks to you, of course."

"He's strong and smart," Terry said. "I just gave him some love." He looked at his mom and winked. She beamed in reply. "Should I feed him real quick before he goes out? In case he doesn't come back for a bit?"

"Good idea," his mom said. Dr. Hernandez went over and got a bottle from the holding rack, and brought it to Terry. It took him a couple of tries to get the calf to eat—he was too excited— however, eventually food won out. The orcas outside continued to watch patiently.

Every few minutes a plume of bubbles would expel from their rebreather domes. The timing was good; the rebreathers would need new power cells within a couple of days. The nearest breathable air for the orcas was two kilometers straight up, a trip none of them would survive if they did it in less than a week to allow for decompression.

Pōkole only drank half of the fifteen-liter bottle before he wouldn't sit still anymore. "Good enough," Dr. Jaehnig said. "The little rascal doesn't want to wait."

"I can see that," Terry's mom said as the little orca did a quick lap, then stopped next to the lock. "Goodness, he knows how to get out."

"I told you," Terry said, "he's smart." He looked at the controls. "Can I do it?"

"Let's doublecheck pressurization first," she said, and Dr. Orsage walked over to examine the control panel.

"Am I late, Madison?" Doc asked. He was standing next to the moon pool entrance.

"Right on time," she said. "We're about to open the door."

"Pressure is within 20KSI," Orsage said. "Well within tolerance of the moon pool."

"Okay, Terry," she said, and nodded to him. "Go ahead."

He grinned widely as he swam over to the lock. It was situated a meter below the surface of the pool. It used the natural pressure of the room to keep water from flooding in when the door was opened. He'd learned how it worked days ago in preparation for this day.

He turned the key, bringing the mechanism to life. A horn sounded, then a click as the room's exit locked. If it were opened while the outside lock was open, the dome could partially flood. The status light turned blue, meaning all was well. He pressed the *OPEN* button, labeled with tape in English, and the lock ground into motion.

The door was a six-meter-wide iris valve. It began to cycle like an eye's iris opening wide for a dark room. A stream of water came in from the outside, raising the moon pools level a couple centimeters. Then it stopped, the pressure sufficient to keep it where it was. Pōkole looked at Terry as the door opened. "Go ahead," he said and pointed at the door. "Go see your mom."

Pōkole gave a screeching click and flipped over, diving down and rocketing through the door. In an instant, nine adult orcas surrounded him as he nuzzled up against his mother. The pod was whole again. Terry was grinning from ear to ear when he popped his head out of the water and shook the hair and water out of his eyes.

"You're not going out, too?" his mom asked.

"I can?"

"He's your responsibility," she said. "I think you're half orca by now anyway. We haven't seen anything dangerous, so just be careful."

Terry laughed and grabbed his suit helmet from next to the moon pool. It only took a few seconds to connect the power supply and activate the integrated heads-up display. The helmet had its own built-in rebreather, two LED lights, and the drysuit's integrated heater worked with it as well. Adding a pair of flippers and gloves completely insulated him from the bitter cold seawater outside. Doc handed him an equalizer belt for buoyancy and a dive knife.

He gave Doc and his mom a wave, flipped over, and dove down underwater. After hundreds of hours in the water, he was an incredibly powerful swimmer, and he was through the lock in a couple of seconds. Pōkole swam over and offered his dorsal fin. Terry took it, and he was quickly pulled over next to the other orcas. *My god, they're big*, he thought. He'd forgotten how much larger they were than Pōkole. Moloko gently brushed him with the dome of her head, and he felt a slight *bump* as she used her sonar on him.

"*Thank for care*," she said, Terry's translator pendant speaking inside the helmet for him to hear. "*Pōkole happy. Pōkole strong!*"

"I'm happy to help. We all love him," Terry said, again his translator booming the orca's reverberating vocalizations through the water. "Thank you for trusting me."

"*Part of pod*," Kray said. He was Pōkole's father. "*Want to fast swim?*"

"Not this time," he said. He couldn't explain that he wouldn't be able to tolerate the bitterly cold water for long. Despite the drysuit, he was already shivering. "Soon, maybe."

"*Terry Warden welcome always,*" Moloko said. Pōkole shoved him playfully, then the entire pod turned and swam away. The all-encompassing darkness of Hoarfrost's ocean swallowed them in seconds. Terry turned to swim back and stopped.

Templemer was a shining, multifaceted ruby with a thousand glittering points of light. He'd never seen it from the outside like this. When they'd come down, it had been completely dark; Honcho had homed in on a solitary sonar beacon. All lit up, it was one of the most beautiful things he'd ever seen. Seeing through to the inside was kinda hard, but he could see his mother waving him back.

The cold was really biting, so he swam toward the dome. On the other side of the ruby wall, he could see Doc running toward the moon pool, pulling off his light jacket as he ran. *What's he running for?* Terry wondered an instant before something slammed into him, and everything went black.

* * * * *

Chapter Three

Templemer, planet Hoarfrost, Lupasha System, Coro Region, Tolo Arm

January 13th, 2038

P ain. Soul-searing pain and the relentless rush of icy wa-ter over his body was all Terry felt. The headset inside his rebreather helmet screamed an alarm, and the little heads-up display showed his drysuit heater was failing. He felt ice-water needles spreading along his back, and ripping pain in his side and left leg.

What's happening? he thought, struggling to understand. One mo-ment he'd been swimming toward the dome, the next something hit him. Water was rushing past him, and he was bent over backward. Something had his side and leg. He struggled to look down. He was in near absolute darkness, only the two wildly spiraling LED lamps in his helmet providing any illumination.

A dark mass to his left blocked the light. He turned his head and saw an eye looking at him. His mind cleared with an electric jolt of adrenaline. Something had him in its mouth! For a split second his darkest fear came to life. One of the orcas had attacked him. Then his pain-fogged mind focused on the eye enough to discern details. It was silvery in color, with a red rim and two irises. *Two irises!* Selroth-native species had two irises.

It's gotta be an Oohobo, the little part of his brain still working on a logical level thought. None of the other Selroth-native carnivorous species were big enough to do more than nibble your toes. The water between him and the huge eye was momentarily tinted red. Blood. More specifically, Human blood.

"Not all aliens have red blood," Doc had pointed out anecdotally during an MST class discussion. It was one of those talks the other teachers back in Molokai wouldn't have approved of, but had the normally bored students on the edge of their seats.

He shook his head to clear it. The pain and cold were making him drift. Hundreds of hours of diving with Doc had driven home many lessons. One of them was, when you lost concentration, you were in the most danger. Another was sharks. The predators weren't common in the Hawaiian waters. However, Doc said the smartest thing to do was to avoid them. They were usually more scared of you than you were of them. But if they tried to attack, *hurt* them.

He couldn't use his left hand; it was pinned to his side. His right hand was free, and he stretched down. Tearing pain shot through his left side. He screamed and reached anyway, bending his right leg back to meet his hand. Fingers numbed with cold felt something hard, and he wrapped them around the object and pulled it free.

His vision was beginning to swim, and water was trickling into the helmet. The seal was failing. Terry fixed his grip on the handle, brought it around, and plunged the dive knife into the eye with a visceral scream and all the strength his 12-year-old, cold-deadened muscles could manage, driving it in to the hilt with a *Chunk!*

There was an explosion of pain, and he was flung free of the *Oohobo's* grip. A second later, the pain was mostly gone, replaced by the numbness of extreme cold. His suit's air heater had failed. He shook his head again, trying to clear his vision. The heads-up said the heater was out, buoyancy stability was unresponsive, power was down to 29%, and backup power was automatically tied into re-breather functions. Bad news all around.

He looked down, his helmet lights panning over his body, and gasped when he saw his left leg. The suit was torn, and shredded tendrils of flesh floated like ghostly fingers. Despite the training, panic hit him. He tried orienting with kicks of his legs, and the left one wouldn't respond. The panic grew into terror. He swung his head around, searching for the *Oohobo*. He found it only a few meters away.

The monster was easily 10 meters long, longer than an orca, but thinner. It reminded him of an alligator with an overly-long mouth full of too many teeth, and three sets of flippers instead of limbs. It was shaking its head furiously, trying to dislodge Terry's knife, which was still lodged in the beast's eye. Purple fluid jetted from the wound.

As it floundered, it turned onto its right side, and its good eye caught sight of him. Instantly it stopped shaking and locked eyes with him. Despite the pain, the fog in his brain, and the icy cold threatening to consume him, he fought the panic away and prepared himself as best he could. The *Oohobo* opened its mouth and shot toward him, but blurs of black and white rocketed past him to either side. A pair of 10-ton missiles composed of flesh and bloody vengeance collided with the *Oohobo* like hurtling freight trains. Brilliant white teeth flashed and tore at the monster.

Terry sighed and began to float downward. He feebly tried to correct his orientation to what felt like up and down, but failed. His arms didn't seem to want to follow his instructions. *Traitors,* he thought. The heads-up display said power was zero, all systems failing.

Something warmer than the water, a huge, soft pillow with dull, pointy edges gently engulfed him, and he felt the icy water begin to rush past.

"*Have you,*" he heard. "*Safe.*"

"I'm already dead," he whispered, and the darkness took him.

* * * * *

Chapter Four

Templemer, planet Hoarfrost, Lupasha System, Coro Region, Tolo Arm

March 19th, 2038

"*Must wake.*"

Leave me alone.

"*Must wake, or die.*"

I'm already dead, leave me alone.

"*Not dead, but be dead if not wake.*"

He struggled up a little and the *pain* tore at him. *No, it hurts.*

"*All life hurt. Life better than die. Hurt better than not. Mother needs you. Wake.*"

He felt himself pushed from behind, pushed up toward the light despite himself.

* * *

Terry choked and gagged around the tube in his throat, and his arms flailed.

"Grab him!" someone yelled.

"I got him, someone tie his leg down. Jesus Christ, what happened?"

"I don't know, he was spasming and talking gibberish!"

"Brain function?"

"Wait…oh, it's back, I don't know how, but it's back!"

"Impossible."

"You think I don't know?"

"Thank god, however it happened. Get that IV stabilized and give him a quarter grain of Isoflurane on a float drip."

Terry fought against the pain and confusion for another second until he felt a numbing coldness begin to spread through his mind. Then he was back in the darkness.

This time it only felt like a few seconds before consciousness returned. He opened his eyes and panicked when he couldn't see anything. After a second he began to make out details, and a face. His mother was standing nearby, and she was crying.

"Mom?" he said, his voice so raspy it didn't sound like his own. He coughed. Surprisingly, he wasn't in any pain, but instead felt all floaty.

"Terry," his mom cried and came closer. "Are you okay?"

"Yeah, I'm fine." The room was slowly coming into focus. He could see various medical equipment, as well as Dr. Jaehnig and his assistants. As slowly as his focus was returning, he realized they were there to take care of him. "I was dead," he said.

His mother collapsed, falling to her knees and nearly out of sight, completely racked by sobs and sounding of utter despair. "I'm so sorry," she said repeatedly.

"We really blew it."

Terry turned his head to see Doc on the other side of his bed. "I can't remember what happened, except I was dead."

"We want to get you better before we go into it," Dr. Jaehnig said, coming over to examine something Terry couldn't see. "Do you feel any pain?"

"No," Terry said, "but I want to know what happened." He closed his eyes and tried to concentrate. His brain felt like it was full of cotton candy. An image came to him of looking through Templemer's dome from the outside into the moon pool room. His mother with a look of stunned horror on her face, and Doc running toward the moon pool, stripping off his jacket and yelling soundlessly. The memory cut off as suddenly as it had returned.

"Sleep for now," the doctor said and nodded to the side. Terry opened his mouth to complain, but couldn't manage to say anything before darkness took him back.

* * *

"How you doing, Terry?"

He opened his eyes and blinked. Dr. Jaehnig was watching him a short distance away, holding a slate and glancing at its display every few seconds.

"Tired of sleeping," he said. Terry didn't know how long they'd kept him asleep, only that he'd been out for some time. His back hurt in the way it did when he'd been in bed too long. Despite just waking up again, he yawned. "Why do I still feel tired?"

"Your body's been busy healing," the doctor explained, again examining the slate.

"What are you monitoring on the slate?"

"Your blood chemistries. You see, we're trying to understand some things."

"Like?"

"Well, how you're alive mostly."

Terry nodded and felt something attached to his head. He also realized he was strapped to the bed. "I was dead, wasn't I?"

"Yes," the doctor said. "Dr. Clark doesn't agree with us discussing this, but she's not your physician." He shrugged. "It was obvious to me, you know. Frankly, I'm amazed and want to maybe understand how you came back."

"Can I have something to drink?"

"Of course." Dr. Jaehnig went to a nearby table and returned with a clear cup. There was a straw in it, and he put it to Terry's lips.

He wasn't happy with being fed like a baby, but he was too thirsty to argue, and he took a big drink. The doctor pulled it back far sooner than Terry would have liked.

"Let's not get too far ahead of ourselves, shall we?"

"First, tell me how long I've been in here, please," Terry said. "My back is sore, and nowhere in the habitat looked this good in my memory."

"No, it wouldn't," the doctor said. "You were injured 65 days ago."

The air went out of Terry's lungs with a *whoof.* He tried to comprehend what he'd just been told. Two months? He'd been hurt two *months* ago? "What have I been doing all this time?"

"You were in a coma with steadily decreasing brain functions." Dr. Jaehnig turned the Tri-V on for his slate and showed a date-indexed recording of graphs. As time went by, the numbers steadily decreased until it reached zero. "You reached zero a day ago, which was when we decided to…terminate life support."

"Let me die?"

"Yes," he said. "No brain functions. You were already dead. The fading of your higher brain functions was indicative of a cascade failure."

"Why," Terry said, not wanting to hear more about how they'd been going to let him die. "Why was my brain failing?"

"Do you remember what happened to you?"

"Only being out with the orcas, and something happened." His brow furrowed as he tried to remember.

Dr. Jaehnig nodded and tapped on his slate. "Understandable." He stopped and locked eyes with him. "Are you sure you want to see this?" Terry nodded emphatically. "Very well." He clicked on the slate, and the Tri-V came alive.

He was watching himself swimming out from the dome holding Pōkole's dorsal fin. The view was from a security camera, and he wasn't perfectly in frame as he met with the orca pod and watched the reunion of Pōkole with his mother and the rest of the pod.

"How's Pōkole?" he suddenly asked. As Dr. Jaehnig had said, the calf had been without his care for months.

The doctor paused the video. "He's fine. The other high school-aged kids pitched in, helping feed him after you were...after you were hurt." He unpaused the video.

Terry watched the orcas turn and swim into the darkness. After a moment, he spun around and swam back toward Templemer, moving slowly toward the bottom of the camera view. Then a flash of movement as a huge, sleek shape intercepted him, and he was out of frame. *That was the hit I felt*, Terry thought.

The Tri-V replay switched to inside the moon pool room, and Terry watched his mom scream and point. Instantly Doc burst into motion, running and stripping off his jacket as he went. The man's long frame translated into incredible strides as he leaped the last three meters into the water. Amazingly, he snatched the rebreather

Terry had left while donning his helmet as he was jumping into the water.

The view shifted again, this time to his own point of view just after he was attacked. The view was dizzying as he was dragged through the water. The rest played out in only a few seconds as he saw his hand appear with the dive knife and plunge it into the huge dual-iris eye.

"Incredible," he heard Dr. Jaehnig say.

"I don't remember doing it," Terry said.

"Well, I couldn't have done it. Not as injured as you were."

"How bad was it?" Terry asked.

"Just wait a second," the doctor said and pointed at the replay.

The monster let go and flashed away in a swirl of purple liquid. The view moved around, and eventually down to show his leg. It looked like a filleted fish with massive flaps of flesh, rubber from the ravaged drysuit, and jets of dark red blood. *Oh my god,* he thought. Then the view looked up to show the entirety of the creature attacking him. It was longer than an adult orca, but not as thick. Three sets of long flippers along its sides propelled it through the water. It had an incredibly long set of jaws, like an alligator, only thinner, and lined with shark-like teeth.

"The closest analogue we can find to it on Earth was a dinosaur named *Liopleurodon*. It's one of the Selroth transplants, an *Oohobo*. They're a natural predator from their homeworld the Selroth now keep as some kind of rite of adulthood?" The doctor shrugged. "We hadn't seen one yet, and with as much sea life as is around here, and the bottlenoses venturing kilometers in all directions, we were pretty certain there weren't any here. I'm sorry to say, we were wrong."

"With all the fish and stuff, why did it attack *me*?" Terry asked. The freeze-frame of the *Oohobo* sent a little shudder up his back despite the slight numbing of the drugs they had him on.

"Doc thinks it's because of your suit lights. The lights on the dome were installed by the Selroth, and likely a spectrum that doesn't attract the *Oohobo*. Our suit lights are a different frequency, and that must have been what caused it." He unfroze the image, and the *Oohobo* instantly noticed Terry with its remaining eye. He froze it again.

"Notice how it spotted you right away when you looked up?" Terry nodded. "Anyway," he let the replay continue, "we didn't have much left to work with."

The *Oohobo* shot toward the camera. Terry felt himself cringe. A split second later, two huge black and white shapes rocketed past him, jaws snapping; the orcas tore into the alien predator. Even from the horribly slewing images, Terry recognized Kray and Ki'i, the two dominant males from the super pod. He wanted to see more of the fight, but the fight began to fall out of frame, drifting lazily.

The last image was of an arc of bright white teeth above and below, closing slowly in on him, then the recording stopped. It started again a second later, showing Doc swimming through the moon pool lock with Terry in tow. His mother was screaming over and over as Doctors Orsage and Jaehnig leaned over the pool to pull the limp boy out. As his ravaged leg cleared the edge of the pool, he left a wash of bright red blood. His mother fainted, and the recording stopped for good.

"Did an orca bring me back?"

"Yes," the doctor replied. "Moloko brought you back. We got a couple of pieces of the *Oohobo*, but like I said, there wasn't much left. They tore it apart." He chuckled. "They were *pissed*."

"I'll say they were." Doc had come in at some point. Terry glanced at the old merc, who was in turn watching him carefully. "How you doing, kiddo?"

"Surprisingly alive," he admitted. "You came out for me without a suit. Are you nuts?"

"Do you remember what *you* did?"

"No," Terry said. "I just saw the movie, though."

"It's a blockbuster. The *Oohobo* was basically eating you alive, and you stabbed it in the freaking *eye!*" He laughed and shook his head. "God damn, kiddo, what you did was the most badass thing I've seen in my entire life."

Terry looked away, unwilling to meet his eyes. Mostly because he felt tears beginning to flow. "I didn't do anything."

"The hell you didn't." The man had walked up next to Terry when he wasn't looking. He felt the older man doing something and looked down. He was pinning something on the pajama top. It was an anchor with a trident through it, and an eagle. "You deserve it more than I ever did."

"Where's Mom?"

"She's sleeping right now," Doc said. "When you suddenly woke up after they turned off the life support, she kinda lost it. They gave her a sedative."

"How messed up am I?" Terry asked.

"We'll wait until his mother's here to explain," Dr. Jaehnig said.

"I don't think so," Doc countered. The doctor gave him a stern look. "This kid took on a dinosaur with a damn *knife*. The orcas risked their own lives to save him. I think he can handle the truth right now." Dr. Jaehnig frowned. "You tell him, or I will."

"Very well," the doctor said. He reached over and removed the strap holding Terry's arms down. They still felt like they had lead weight on them, but he could move.

"Thank you," he said.

The doctor nodded and pulled the sheet down the rest of the way. The left leg of his pajama bottoms was empty from mid-thigh down. "We weren't set up for this level of trauma when you were injured," Dr. Jaehnig said. "We had to use a tourniquet to save your life. By the time we could get a surgery set up, the leg was lost."

Terry nodded. He'd known from the minute he saw the injury recorded in his own helmet camera, and the better image of them pulling him from the water. It was more than a movie, this was real life. Despite telling himself he wouldn't, he was quietly crying. Doc sat on the chair next to him and held his hand.

"It's okay, kiddo, the hard part's over. You survived. We'll get through the rest together."

When his mom came in an hour later, he was out of tears. He got to hold her while she cried and tell her it was okay, not her fault, and he was going to be fine.

I survived, he thought. If I can kick a monster's ass, maybe I can do anything.

* * * * *

Chapter Five

Templemer, planet Hoarfrost, Lupasha System, Coro Region, Tolo Arm
April 5th, 2038

Of course, committing to doing something wasn't the same as actually doing it. Terry found out his injuries were more than just most of his left leg. His pelvis had been punctured by several of the 10-centimeter *Oohobo* teeth. Luckily, they'd missed his groin, which he was incredibly grateful for. However his pelvic bone had two hairline cracks. In addition, a tendon had been severed in his lower left arm, so his ring finger didn't work.

When taken as a whole with his lost leg, it all added up to several surgeries being necessary before they could deal with his missing leg. Because their medical staff was minimal, and Dr. Jaehnig wasn't a normal Human surgeon, the operations took two weeks.

As he recovered, several of the staff he'd come to know visited, as well as the other four high school age kids. They told him how Pōkole was doing. It was meant to make him feel better, but instead it made him feel sad, because he missed the baby orca.

"Quit feeling sorry for yourself," Doc said when he heard Terry say as much.

Terry gawked for a second, then frowned. "I wasn't."

"Yes, you were. Pōkole misses you, everyone knows, but the adults are keeping him safe, and he'll be waiting for you. Concentrate your energy on getting better and not worrying about feeling sorry for yourself."

Terry was mad at Doc's attitude for a while, then realized the man was right, and worked hard to stop pitying himself. He could be dead. A lot of the questions Dr. Jaehnig had for him revolved around the fact that he had been dead for 22 minutes.

"Do you have any memory from the time?"

"Something about a voice talking to me," Terry said.

"Talking to you? How?"

"I could hear someone speaking to me. That was why I came back, the voices made me." The more he tried to remember exactly what had happened, the hazier his memory became.

The cetacean physician wasn't impressed by his answer and gently pushed Terry for more details every chance he got. Eventually Terry confronted him about why the man kept pushing for more details if he didn't believe it.

"Because there simply must be another explanation," Dr. Jaehnig said. "Our equipment isn't the best. I'm leaning toward a sensor failure. You never did flat line. Damned good thing you woke up on your own, too, considering we'd terminated life support."

Terry didn't care what the doctor thought; he knew what he'd felt. The voices had been there. He was sure of it as if they were next to him, even though he couldn't remember what they'd said. He remembered the voice clearer than he remembered Yui's face. The thought threatened to drag him down again, so he dropped the entire idea.

After the last surgery on his hip to fix a lingering issue of the pain he'd been suffering, he was rewarded with a souvenir—one of the *Oohobo's* knife-like teeth. It was only a small one, 5.2 centimeters long; it had been embedded in his left hip socket where the scans hadn't discerned it from his own dense bone structure. Despite the pain from the incision, after waking from the anesthesia, the persistent pain was gone.

"Little something to remember the dead dinosaur by," Doc said and handed him the tooth. They'd drilled a hole in it and put a metallic necklace through the thick point.

"I think it's morbid," Terry's mom said. She'd continued to be morose at her son's injuries, though she was getting less so as he made continuous improvement.

"It's embracing the power that almost took your life," Doc explained. He pulled a necklace out of the neckline of his shirt and showed them a deformed bullet.

His mother shuddered. "I still think it's morbid."

Terry took the gift and immediately put it on.

In the last surgery, Dr. Jaehnig had also fitted his stump with a port. In the months since his injury, the colony had made great strides in getting on its feet. One of those strides was reactivating the abandoned ancient Selroth manufactory, a highly advanced automated 3D printing machine capable of producing all manner of parts and equipment, albeit slowly. They had also made the first trips to explore the mines responsible for Templemer being on Hoarfrost in the first place.

Dr. Jaehnig split his time working with the cetaceans, monitoring their progress in adapting to Hoarfrost's oceans, and studying the vast database of medical knowledge they'd brought with them to aid in Terry's treatment.

For his own part, Terry spent his time continuing his studies of programming and Union pinplant technology, which in turn led him down avenues of studies including biology, neurology, and physics. He didn't even notice how his studies seemed to be going so much better, even with picking up basic high school classes as well.

On the morning of the 5th, he was finally well enough to join class for the first time. His friends applauded when he rolled up in the motorized wheelchair Doc's people had put together for him. It was painted in gray and blue with shark's teeth, in honor of his battle with the *Oohobo*, and they all thought it was super cool.

The teacher, one of the institute's old educational team members who now handled most of the school programs, allowed everyone a few minutes to ask Terry questions. She carefully reminded them he wasn't a curiosity for their amusement, which Terry actually found funny. The questions weren't bad, mostly about how he'd been brave enough to stab it in the eye, and how much they'd enjoyed helping take care of Pōkole. He told them he hadn't been brave; he'd just done what he thought was right. He also agreed Pōkole was awesome, and he couldn't wait to see the calf again.

He only got caught off guard once. Katrina Long was a new member of the high school group. She was from a mainlander family and had long blonde hair, like many on Hawaii. He'd seen her before, of course; their population was quite small. She'd kept to the back of the class and asked her question last. The teacher pointed to her. "Can you go with us to see Pōkole after class?"

He was surprised, not only because he hadn't expected the question, but also because she was particularly pretty. "Sure," he eventually said. Then they went back to work.

Despite being out for two months, he found he wasn't behind. They'd continued the self-paced learning, and the teacher gave Terry a couple of quick quizzes on math and English. Satisfied, he was once again turned loose with the recommended lessons and reading list, which suited Terry just fine.

With the mobility his chair gave him, after classes he met with Katrina and three others; Colin, Dan, and Taiki. Together they went down to the moon pool. He sent a message to his mom through Templemer's new comms network, something they'd finished while he was out, and let her know where he was going. When he rolled into the CC building, she was waiting.

"Are you sure you're ready for this?" she asked.

"Oh, sure," he said. "Why?"

"Well, you know," she said and gestured vaguely toward the moon pool room.

"I'm fine, Mom."

The other four stood back quietly and waited. His mom glanced at them curiously, her gaze lingering for a second on Katrina, the only girl among them. "Okay," she said, and they went inside.

It was one of the assigned feeding times. Moloko and Pōkole were outside the dome swimming back and forth. Terry stared in amazement. Pōkole was at least a meter longer, and much thicker as well!

"He's gotten so big," Terry said.

"Yeah," Katrina said. "He eats like a horse."

"He's up to forty liters a day," Colin said.

"It takes all four of us," Dan agreed, and Taiki nodded.

Terry frowned slightly as he watched the four go into the changing rooms and come out in drysuits, wishing he could join in. His unhappiness was decreased slightly by the sight of Katrina in her drysuit. It fit her quite well. She grinned at him, and he caught himself grinning back.

The four each took a 10-liter bottle and slipped into the water. At the same time, Terry's mom activated the moon pool door control. Terry felt his ears pop as the pressure pushed the moon pool up a few centimeters before equalizing.

Both Pōkole and Moloko swam in, the calf quickly, and his mother more carefully. The door opening wasn't much larger than she was, and her mass took up at least half the volume of the moon pool. Her bulk entering the pool caused further water displacement, some running over the lipped sides into the runoff channels.

"*Terry!*" Moloko said. "*Pleased I am seeing Warden calf well.*"

"Hi, Moloko. I'm still healing, but better." He was interrupted by Pōkole doing a pretty good spyhop, standing on his tail briefly to see out of the water better. A series of snapping clicks were caught by Terry's translator.

"*Tear, Tear!*" It wasn't his name, but it was unmistakably the first syllable.

"Holy crap, he can talk?" Terry gasped.

"Sort of," his mom said. "I was saving it as a surprise. Dr. Orsage's beside himself. They're more like the vocalizations of a young child, but it's way ahead of when a Human baby would be forming more than baby talk. We're having to rethink how their brains develop."

"You did the surgery, too," he said, noting the telltale waterproof plug on the side of the calf's head in the white region called the eyepatch, which was, of course, located behind their eyes.

"Yeah, it went well. He's not using it yet, though. Dr. Jaehnig does downloads once a week to check how everything's going. He asked if you could look at the data when you felt up to it."

"I've felt up to it for days," Terry said. He wheeled his chair closer to the moon pool. "How you doing, little guy?"

"*Tear, Tear, good, good!*"

"A real word," his mom said, and pulled her slate from its bag around her waist. She quickly began making notes.

"Attaboy," Terry said.

Katrina offered her bottle to the calf. Pōkole instantly came over, and she activated the feed. Liters of thick milk substitute flowed, and he quickly emptied the bottle.

Wow, Terry thought, *he's a chow hound!* The little guy would probably be drinking milk for more than another year, though he was also likely eating some fish by now. Katrina's bottle empty, Dan took over, and the milk flowed. He finished it and rolled onto his side to look at Terry.

"*Pōkole want you feed*," Moloko said.

"I can't yet," Terry said.

Then Pōkole slid up the angled side of the pool and made a grab for Terry's motorized chair. He might well have grabbed it and pulled him into the water, chair and all, if Moloko hadn't in turn grabbed Pōkole by the fluke and gently pulled him back.

She issued a sonar beam at Pōkole. It was strong enough to disturb the water, and Dan yelped in surprise. Pōkole jumped and dove back into the moon pool, swimming down to the bottom and staying there.

"*Food later*," Moloko said, and turned and dove, pushing Pōkole out the door and the dome.

"What just happened?" Katrina asked.

"Yeah," Dan said. "It felt like I was hit by a huge bass-boosted speaker on 100!"

"What you felt was a direct sonar attack from Moloko," Terry's mom explained. "It was turned way down, though. It can kill at close range. They use them to hunt small fish."

"She was mad Pōkole tried to grab me," Terry said. "It's not his fault, he's just a baby."

"Agreed," she said, "but just the same, I want you a bit further back during feedings for a while."

Terry nodded. "Probably a good idea." He pointed at how Pōkole was swimming around outside, keeping a little distance from his mom. "I think we just saw the orca equivalent of a spanking."

* * * * *

Chapter Six

Using the manufactory, Dr. Jaehnig was able to build an artificial leg for Terry. Doc and his crew assisted in the fabrication process, which took an entire week and many test fittings. Back on Earth with the much-improved technology after First Contact, it would have been a single day with complex imaging systems and a quick build. As it was, his leg looked more like something from a bad sci-fi film. Terry thought it was awesome.

"Dude, your leg looks like a killer robot," Colin said the first day he walked into class.

"It's absolutely killer," Dan agreed.

"Badass," Taiki said.

"You can kick some real ass, I bet," Katrina said and gave him a wink. Terry felt his cheeks growing hot at her statement. Despite spending half a year with all the other kids who'd left Earth, he hadn't really made friends with anyone until now. It felt good.

The leg might have been an improvisation, but it worked perfectly once they had it fitted correctly. It hurt where his leg ended and the prosthesis began, though not as badly as he'd thought it would.

Besides finally being mobile, he gained the advantage of being able to feed Pōkole again. The leg was completely self-contained and watertight. Living in an underwater city, Doc had considered it a necessity, which had cost some extra time.

After months without being in the water with him, Pōkole was excited, of course. Terry spent a few minutes just stroking the calf's smooth side and letting the orca pull him around the pool.

"*Terr, Terr,*" he vocalized repeatedly. It sounded more like his name now than before. Moloko stayed at the back of the moon pool, out of the way, but mindful of her calf. His new friends helped by being in the water with him at the same time. He immediately realized the downside of the missing leg; his balance in the water was all messed up. The leg was heavier than his natural limb, pulling him down slightly. He couldn't swim; it was like an anchor.

He got through the feeding but was unhappy and frustrated by the end of it. Katrina gave him a hand out of the water.

"What's wrong?" she asked.

"I looked like a hooked fish out there," Terry grumbled.

"Takes time to get used to a badass battle leg," she said and gave him what was becoming her signature wink. He grinned despite himself.

"Yeah," Colin agreed. "Give it some time, buddy. They've got the swimming pool going. The junior high kids are painting Hawaiian scenes on the pool dome. It's supposed to be pretty cool. Let's get some swim time."

"Good idea," Dan agreed.

"We're all rusty," Taiki said.

"The kiddy pool?" Terry asked darkly. The others frowned, then he heard Doc's voice in his head asking if he was feeling sorry for himself again. He remembered stabbing the *Oohobo* in the eye with his dive knife and took a deep breath. "Sure. I'd like the help getting used to this leg in the water."

Katrina laughed and gave him a hug. Dan and Taiki both grinned at each other, making Terry wonder what they were grinning about. "It'll be fun," she said and winked.

* * *

"How was the first day back on your feet, kiddo?" Doc put down the slate in the shop he shared with other technical staff and his own people. He had an electronics loupe on his head, and a piece of equipment open on the table before him.

"It's working fine," Terry said.

"But?" Doc asked, hearing the hanging question in the young man's voice.

"It's swimming." Terry explained the problem. Doc listened as he spoke, then nodded.

"Yeah, makes sense. But I don't think we can do anything about it. Your friends' idea of practicing might have the most merit. Were you an expert the first time I took you kids diving?"

"Well, no."

Doc pointed at him. "Bingo. Your balance has changed. Walking is easy, because the leg's designed for it, and gravity here is a little less. We might be able to improve the leg with time, but right now we're getting the mines operational. Work with it, and we'll take you out next week to inspect one of the mines."

"Even after a week of practice, I won't be able to swim very fast," Terry pointed out.

"You won't have to swim fast, just swim well." Doc gestured for him to follow. "You were curious about something we were working on before you got hurt?"

"I remember," Terry said. "Ticked me off," he said.

Doc grinned and nodded before opening a door in the work area. Inside was a miniature submarine just big enough for a single large person, or a couple of small ones. "We built them for mobility and extended operations outside the door. The water's too cold for the drysuits."

"I noticed," Terry said peevishly.

"I'm sure you did. Even on maximum, you'd be hypothermic in less than an hour. Obviously wetsuits would be even worse. We've been using the full-size subs, but they're slow, cumbersome, and we still end up going out in drysuits and working in shifts on the ragged edge of hypothermia."

"How long have you been pushing it?" Terry asked.

"Since we got here. Lots of the science staff can dive, of course, but only a couple have cold water experience like we do." He shrugged. "SEALs have to be able to do extreme cold work from day one, or you can't be part of the teams. But we can't be the ones to do *all* the mine work."

"Why not?" Terry asked.

"Because there are only seven of us."

Terry turned and saw Peyto and Hutch lugging an air tank through the doors. Both men were built like tanks themselves, with necks so thick with muscle he didn't know how they could move. Peyto had been the one talking. The two looked like brothers, but weren't related.

"We have other stuff to do," Hutch agreed.

"Merc stuff?" Terry asked.

"You know it," Toothpick said as he came in behind the two big guys, carrying gear himself.

"What kind of contract?" Terry asked. Tina, the only girl in their group, was right behind Toothpick. She grinned at Terry as she helped Piano and Honcho manage a big crate overflowing with hoses and pipes.

"Don't know yet," Doc said and went to help his crew sort the gear.

"Where'd you find all this stuff?" Terry asked, going over to look at the equipment.

"The Selroth left a ton of shit when they evac'd," Tina told him. "There's a huge junkpile over on the far side by Lock #2, the broken one. Whatever they didn't want to take, they dumped."

"By the looks of it, they didn't want to take anything," Honcho said, taking off his cowboy hat to wipe sweat from his brow. He liked it cooler, and had said one of the downsides of getting the heating up and running was the damn Hawaiians kept it too hot. Doc said the man was from North Dakota and liked it right about 12 degrees. The dome was being maintained at what Terry thought was a bit cool, 22 degrees Celsius.

"How's the leg, kid?" Tina asked.

"It's just about awesome," Terry said.

"Just about?"

"He's having trouble in the water," Doc said and mentioned the buoyancy.

"Told you it would be a pain," Piano said. Terry had been amazed to find out the man had a doctorate in marine engineering.

"Couldn't get the system to balance on land *and* water," Tooth-pick noted. He was a marine mechanic, so the two had done most of the design work on the leg.

"Manufactory is an ancient POS," Tina said as she eyed an electronic circuit board from the parts they'd brought. She was an electronics specialist.

Doc had told Terry once that SEALs tended to come from all areas of expertise, so the teams would have the skillsets they needed for missions. Obviously he was a dive specialist. Honcho was a pilot of some skill. He'd never told Terry what Hutch and Peyto were good at besides carrying heavy loads and playing cards, which they were getting back to since the heavy stuff was done.

"Just going to take practice," Tina said.

"Doc said as much," Terry replied, trying not to sound surly.

"Us officers know what's good for you," she said and grinned at him. Over at the work bench someone made a farting sound, and the others laughed. Doc and Tina, the two officers of the team, rolled their eyes but didn't say anything.

Terry loved to watch the interplay between the former SEALs, now mercs. They were all so different (except Hutch and Peyto, anyway), yet at the same time they were closer than most families. *Maybe it comes from fighting together*, he thought. He figured he was probably too young to understand anyway.

"I told the kid he could come along when we test the minisubs," Doc said.

"Ain't scared to go out in the deep again, are ya?" Honcho asked.

"Don't needle the kid," Toothpick said, glancing up at Honcho from his work and brandishing a knife. "You might find yourself getting needled."

"Bite me," Honcho replied to his teammate, then glanced at Terry curiously.

"No, I'm not scared," Terry said. They all stared at him. "But there's something I'm going to need."

"What, your momma?" Honcho asked. Toothpick stopped working and glared at Honcho.

"No," Terry said and stood up straighter, the leg's drive motors whining slightly. "A new knife, asshole."

Honcho's mouth fell open as catcalls flew from his teammates. A second later he was forced to duck under the work bench as catcalls gave way to tools, parts, and empty drink cans. Doc nodded to Terry, a small grin on his face. Tina winked at him, and he smiled back.

"I like this kid," Toothpick said and walked over to Terry. "Here, son, you can have this one." He unbuckled a knife from around his thigh and handed it to him. "I got this after my first mission, a present from my brother. I want you to have it."

Terry took the sheathed blade and belt. It wasn't too heavy. He pulled it out, the sheath giving a click as the positive-retention released. The blade gleamed in the work lights, a solid five-centimeters thick and around 30 long. It had a false edge on the backside, as well as serrations for 10 centimeters before the hilt. The handle was rubberized and felt good in his hand. He tested the edge against his index fingernail, and a surprising amount of nail peeled away. It was as sharp as a scalpel.

"I can't take this, Toothpick," Terry protested and carefully resheathed it.

Toothpick shook his head and turned away. "It's yours."

"But," Terry said, and felt Doc's hand on his shoulder.

"It's good, kiddo. Come on, these guys got work to do." Doc walked him outside, where he spoke to him again. "Take good care of it."

"I will," Terry said. He turned and staggered a little. Doc steadied him with a powerful hand.

"You'll get better with the leg. I've found when it comes to life, you either stand, or you fall."

Terry listened and nodded, looking down at the leg and noticing the knife again. "This was important, wasn't it?"

"Yes," Doc said. "His brother was on the team with us. We lost him on our first trip after you were evacuated to Karma."

Terry stared at the blade for a long time before he turned to ask Doc why Toothpick would give it to him. But Doc had already gone back inside, leaving him alone with his thoughts.

Later, back in his quarters, Terry sat at the small living room table and stared at the knife, trying to fully understand the meaning of the gift. He was still sitting there when his mom came in.

"Hey," she said and hung the bag she habitually carried with her slate in it. "How'd the feeding go?"

"I had some balance issues with the leg," he said.

His mom looked at the leg and quickly away. She closed her eyes and took a breath. Terry knew she was struggling with his artificial leg and the injuries he'd sustained. He knew she was still blaming herself, but didn't know how to make her stop.

"Do you want me to tell Dr. Jaehnig to work on it?"

"No," Terry said, "I'm going to work on learning to cope with a couple friends by swimming every day in the new pool."

"Are you sure?"

"Yes, I want to figure it out myself. Everyone's worked hard enough already to help me."

"We'll work as hard as you need," she said.

"It'll be fine," he said. She walked over to him and grabbed him in a powerful hug. "Why the hug?" he asked.

"For being braver than I am," she said. "Where'd the knife come from?"

"Toothpick gave it to me." Terry explained how it had happened. His mom narrowed her eyes when he mentioned how Honcho had asked if Terry needed his mom to go swimming again, then smiled at his comeback.

"Giving knives and coins is a big deal in the military," she said. "It would seem you've impressed Doc's people more than you realize." Terry nodded in understanding. He'd figured, from Doc's reaction. "Just be careful, okay? I only have you now."

* * * * *

Chapter Seven

Hoarfrost Core Mine #11, Planet Hoarfrost, Lupasha System,
Coro Region, Tolo Arm
April 22nd, 2038

"How you doing in there, kiddo?" Doc asked over the radio.

"Great!" Terry replied, carefully feathering the control thrusters to stay within a meter of the seven figures in drysuits. "I'm watching the sonar, though."

"Good deal," Tina said. "We don't want you to have to stab some more *Oohobo* to death out here."

"*It okay, it okay!*" Hoa the bottlenose transmitted on their channel.

"*We watch good!*" Hoba, another of the bottlenoses, agreed. Ever since his attack, the bottlenoses had worked out patrols with the orcas to ensure no more of the giant predators got close. They acted as scouts, with their bigger cousins performing as interceptors. Since Terry's attack, Doc's team had encountered two more incidents of *Oohobo*, both safely intercepted by orcas, with only one minor injury on the whale's part. However, they remained a constant danger.

"We have no idea how fast they breed," Dr. Patel pointed out. "The GalNet files were detailed, but the orcas haven't left us much to work on. Based solely on the number we've encountered in only a few months, and the density of suitable prey, it's safe to assume there might be thousands."

"Thanks Hoa, thanks Hoba!'

"*Yes, yes, help!*" Skritch agreed. The entire Sunrise Pod was out helping today, since Terry was in the miniature sub for the first time. They found the device fascinating.

Dr. Orsage said it was good to see them interested in something, and to encourage it. The bottlenoses had been somewhat quiet after arriving on Hoarfrost. They talked about the "Beyond," which Terry knew was their way of describing hyperspace. They liked it just as much as the orcas appeared to hate it. They asked when they were going back to the beyond, but of course nobody could say. Terry knew it was likely never, but he'd learned to keep his mouth shut instead of providing random information to the cetaceans, especially since their implant surgery.

Terry wanted to ask them what they found so interesting about the beyond; he really did. He'd been about to ask several times, when his better sense kicked in, and he'd let it go. Maybe they'd volunteer the information one day with a little prodding.

The big submarine was parked on a rocky outcropping a hundred meters away as Terry followed the seven mercs moving through the water using small, yet powerful machines called Seascooters to jet along. Held in both hands ahead of their bodies, they could reach speeds of 10 knots in a pinch, though they cruised at around five.

Terry's new one-man submersible was more akin to the old wet subs he'd seen in a museum. Terry still wore a drysuit, but it was connected to the craft's built-in power source, and provided ample hot air circulation to keep him quite comfy. Plugged into the machine's impressive sensors and remote manipulator arms, he could go over 20 knots and lift 100 kilos! He felt a little like a superhero in the thing, even if he did look like an overweight torpedo with arms. Surrounded by reinforced plastic windows, he had nearly perfect forward visibility, and a camera let him see behind.

"This thing is great, Doc."

"I thought you'd like it," Doc replied.

"Keep an eye on the crappy Selroth power cells," Toothpick warned. "If it shits the bed, you'll only have five minutes of power."

"Yes, sir," Terry replied.

"Got the rover on sonar," Honcho announced. His Seascooter was more advanced than the others, allowing him to act as lead. Terry's systems were even more advanced, but this was his first time out in the new minisub.

"Lock onto Honcho's beacon," Doc ordered.

Terry called out "Roger" when it was his turn, which was last. He really didn't mind. It was cool just being part of the operation.

They sailed through the water for another minute. It was as clear as glass, yet even with their lights, they could only see a few dozen meters. Their lights were now set to the same frequency as those on Templemer's dome.

The scientists still didn't know if it was the Human's lights attracting the *Oohobo*. Retuning the lights was simply an expedient. The result was things appeared slightly orangish to them. To Terry, it lent everything a slightly fake feel, and he worked not to let it lull him into a false sense of complacency.

Finally, their target came into visual range. His sonar showed a large metallic object ahead. He squinted through his helmet to make sense out of it. The mine was designated Core Mine #11 on the Selroth records, and it was currently being worked by Extractor #3.

The habitat controlled six extractors, five of which were currently operating. One was lost and had yet to be recovered.

Perched on the lip of an underwater volcano's cone, the extractor looked to Terry like a bunch of treads with a collection of tanks on its back. It took another minute of buzzing through the water to realize just how damned big it was—at least the size of an apartment building.

"Wow," he said. "It's huge!"

"That's what she said," Piano said.

"That's not what I said when I saw it," Tina replied, and everyone cracked up.

Terry grinned. He'd been in grade school when he'd first heard the joke, and it was still funny. "How can we not find one of these?" Terry asked.

"It's a big ocean, kiddo," Doc said. "There are 92 of these little volcanos around Templemer within a 50-kilometer radius. The Selroth data showed 44 active mines the last time they were here, which was 320 years ago. The problem is, the alien morons didn't turn them off when they left, so the roving extractor just kept going around until something broke."

Terry silently whistled. The Selroth were on Hoarfrost mining before the Revolutionary War. He wondered if he could find it.

As he was thinking, they came within a few meters of the monstrous tracked machine. He realized he was sweating and checked his HUD. The water temperature had risen 20 degrees in only a minute!

"It's getting hot," Terry said.

"That would be because of the volcano," Peyto said.

"Oh," Terry said lamely and adjusted his suit's system. The hot air blowing between the tough neoprene covering and his skin cooled, and he instantly felt better.

"Found the lock," Honcho said.

"Let's see if Terry can get in there with his toy."

Excellent, Terry thought, and moved the sub forward.

Before they'd left on the mission, Doc had shared the security codes for the various extractors with Terry. He carefully maneuvered around the outside of the extractor, the sub's computer using sonar to build a Tri-V construction of his surroundings. He accessed the data on the extractor and found the access points. Each of the six extractors in the database was different, having been built on the planet from available parts. Number 3 showed six ways to get inside. Terry wanted one of the personnel hatches.

He activated the minisub's external LED floodlights and maneuvered to one of the indicated personnel access points. The sub's sonar showed the seven mercs nearby, keeping careful watch over their young charge.

At the lock, Terry activated the remote arms, using them to open an access panel and reveal the security system. A Union standard panel was there, able to be configured for a dozen different command script-oriented languages. A year ago he'd have been lost. Now he'd spent many hours learning various scripts, and he had his high-end slate secured within the sub's computer compartment.

Between his knowledge and the slate's augmentation, Terry selected a language he could work with and entered the access codes Doc gave him. The extractor didn't accept the code.

"Code's no good," he transmitted.

"I'm not surprised," Doc replied. "We figured the damned Selroth wouldn't have given the real access codes to the Izlians."

The mercs floated nearby and talked over their options, from trying to gain access to the extractor via a cargo hatch, to cutting their way in. The former was unlikely to be any more successful, and the latter could have catastrophic consequences.

Terry listened with half his attention as he examined the system's access interface. It was obvious the Selroth hadn't given the correct access codes. Of course, the code had been set hundreds of years ago. None of the Selroth alive then would still be around. *How would they keep those access codes for so long?* he wondered. The answer was, they couldn't. At least, not with any chance of someone down the road having them when they wanted them.

While the others were talking over their options, Terry began messing with the codes. Only a second later, the door flashed an accept signal and the door began opening.

"Got it," he transmitted.

"Holy shit, kid," Tina said. "Way to go!"

"How'd you get it to accept the code?" Doc asked.

"Well, I thought about how you'd keep a code for over 300 years with any chance of coming back later and not count on it being stored. You can't. So I tried the code backwards, and it worked."

"I'll be damned," Toothpick said.

"Probably," Honcho said.

"Come on," Doc said. "Let's check it out."

Terry hadn't known until then that they'd been unable to gain access to any of the extractors. The mercs gave him a pat on the back and told him how good a job he'd done when he got out of his minisub and joined them inside the extractor.

BLACK AND WHITE | 365

As Terry and the others began examining the extractor's interior, Tina used the code Terry had discovered to access the computer. The extractor had been operating without maintenance or instructions for three centuries.

The inside of the extractor made Terry think of old WWII submarine movies, or B rated sci-fi. Rusty hallways clogged with pipes, cable runs, and various ductwork. It felt like being inside a living thing, with pumps pulsing and power thrumming throughout the structure.

"What powers it?" Terry asked Doc.

"Fusion power, like everything else in the Union. They love throwing gobs of power around."

"But I thought they needed the stuff to contain the reaction?" He made a face as he tried to remember what it was called.

"F11," Doc said.

"Right, F11." Humanity had been trying to create fusion power for 75 years on Earth, only to find out after First Contact that their efforts were ultimately doomed to failure. The vital link to controlling a sustained fusion reaction was an isotope of Flourine with the amazing property of being able to absorb most kinds of energetic radiation. F11 contained and controlled the biproducts of the miniature stars held within a fusion reactor.

"But doesn't it have a limited life?" Terry asked.

"It does," Doc agreed. "We think the reactor in these extractors doesn't consume much power. Since F11 endurance depends on how hard you use it, it's possible they could last a long time."

"Like centuries?"

Doc grinned and nodded.

"That could also be what happened to the missing extractor, right?"

Doc gave him the appraising look and smiled. "Exactly our thought."

They walked around for a bit and eventually returned to the lock area. Terry's leg didn't hurt as much; he'd gotten a lot of time on it in the last week, and all the swimming practice helped. They found Tina sitting cross-legged on the floor tapping on her slate. "I've got access to the whole system," she said. "Terry the Terrible's code works on all the extractors' computers."

"Terry the Terrible?" Terry said.

"What else," Toothpick said. "You're a badass, even if you are a little squirt."

"So were you as a kid," Piano said. Toothpick flipped him a middle finger in reply.

"Are they making fun of me?" Terry whispered to Doc.

"No," the older man said with a slight smile. "They're actually giving you a compliment. It's maybe a little tongue-in-cheek." He grinned at the young man who gave a little grin back. "What did you find out about this monstrosity?"

"It's been a busy little boy," Tina said. "This extractor shows a 26% overall active work cycle for the last 320 years. It's claimed a total of 4,991 tons of targeted minerals from the ocean vents."

"What capacity does the extractor have?" Doc asked.

"Just 950 tons," Tina replied. "There's 102 tons currently on board."

"Where's the other 4,889 tons?" Terry asked.

"Still trying to figure that out," she said, glancing up at him.

"Sorry," he replied.

"Status of the extractor's fusion plant?" Doc asked.

"F11 is 88% saturated," she said. "There are a few hundred warning status indicators as well. This thing needs help. If its health is any indication, we know where #6 went."

"Yeah, but what about all those harvested minerals?" Doc pushed.

"I'm freaking working on it," she snapped back.

"Language," Doc said.

Tina glanced up at Terry then away. "Sorry, kid," she said.

"It's okay," he said.

Tina continued working for a while, her hands flipping back and forth on the slate, tapping icons, and moving virtual controls. Eventually she sighed. "I can't find it," she admitted. "The six extractors were working together cooperatively, but the programming is missing part of the command codes. I have to admit, I was never very good with Union coding."

"I know someone who is," Doc said and turned to Terry. After a moment the mercs were all looking at him curiously. "Yeah, he wrote a Tri-V simulation program when we were on the *Behemoth*. Sold it for 300,000 credits."

Nods and a couple of whistles from the mercs and Terry felt his cheeks getting hot. "It wasn't a big deal."

"Three hundred K is a pretty big deal," the characteristically quiet Hutch said.

"I'll say," Hutch's buddy Peyto agreed.

"Don't forget the money came from a Maki merchant clan, too," Doc pointed out. If anything, the mercs' level of respect increased.

Tina tapped at her slate and stuck a data chip into it. A second later, she pulled it out and handed it to Terry. "Here's the program, can you please check it out?"

"Sure," he said, taking the chip. "Let me go back to the minisub and get my slate."

"You can do it later," Tina said, laughing.

"Oh, okay," Terry said and slipped the chip into a zippered pocket on his drysuit.

"For now, let's look at getting the other sub back and beginning to unload what's here," Doc said. The mercs nodded. "We'll go out tomorrow to the next extractor, and hopefully Terry's code solution works there, too."

"What time are we going out tomorrow?" Terry asked.

"We are, you aren't," Doc said. "Only once a week, the doctor and your mom both insisted."

"Oh, that's crap," Terry mumbled.

"That's the rule," Doc insisted.

"You tell 'em, kid," Tina whispered, making Terry grin.

"Don't encourage him," Doc admonished. "You can use the time to figure out the programming and help us figure out where the extractors have been stashing the goodies."

* * *

The minute Terry got back, his friends Colin, Dan, Taiki, and Katrina were waiting to help him give Pōkole his afternoon feeding. The calf was just as attached to them as he was to Terry after months of their feeding him during Terry's coma. He'd still wanted to talk to them about having heard the voices talking in his mind. However, as time went by, he'd decided he'd probably just imagined it. Comas were weird, apparently.

"How'd the diving go?" Colin asked as they were getting out of their gear.

"Good," Terry said and told them about the extractor and figuring out the code.

"Cool!" Katrina said. "You figured it out all by yourself." She punctuated her comment with a wink. Terry felt a shiver go up his spine, but not in a bad way.

"Thanks," he said, managing not to stammer.

Katrina walked with him back to his quarters, which were only a short distance from her own family's. She hung on his every word, excited by the talk of being outside again.

"I can't believe you went out there," she said, glancing down at his leg. "I'd have been terrified." He just shrugged, not knowing what to say. "Did it hurt? The leg, I mean?"

"I wasn't awake when they took it off," he said. "The hip hurt worse, as I remember."

"I didn't know you were hurt there, too."

"Oh, yeah. I have a killer scar." He pulled his shorts down for her to see, and her eyes bugged out at the long line of scar tissue. She reached a hand out and touched the pink scar on his hip, tracing its line inward. He shuddered and stammered, "T-They took this tooth out, too." He pulled it out of his shirt with the other hand.

"I wondered where you got it from," she said.

The door to his quarters opened and his mom stepped halfway out, coming to a sudden stop when she saw the two kids standing there. Her eyes went down and Terry suddenly realized he had his pants half pulled down. Katrina also must have realized the situation because she squeaked and took a step back.

"Well, hello, young man," his mom said, slowly looking Katrina over in a critical manner he'd never seen her use before.

"M-mom!" Terry said, yanking his shorts up. "Uhm, you know Katrina?"

"H-hi, Mrs. Clark," Katrina stammered.

"Ms. Clark," she corrected, "and yes, I know young Miss Long. I know her parents, too." His mom's eyes narrowed. "I'm sure your parents will be wondering where you are."

"Bye!" Katrina said, and skittered off like she was being chased. Terry slipped in past his mom and headed for his room.

"Just a sec," she said behind him.

"I wanted to get a shower before dinner," he said.

"First let's have a talk."

"Oh, Mom," he said and continued.

"No 'oh Mom.' Now."

Terry stopped and turned around, sighing. "Yes?"

"First, how did it go? I already heard from Doc you were a great help."

"It went fine," he said. "I broke the code and got us into the extractor." He took a data chip from his pocket and held it up. "I need to get to work on the programming to help figure out what's going on with the other extractors."

"Good," she said and came closer. "Now, how about the scene I walked in on?"

"I was just showing Katrina my scar," he said.

"It looked like you were showing her a lot more than your scar," she said in a condescending tone.

"It doesn't matter what it looked like," Terry said. "That's what I was doing."

"Terry, your father took himself out of the equation before he had time to give you 'The Talk.'"

"What talk?'

"About boys and girls."

"Mom," he protested, his voice rising in alarm and cracking, furthering his humiliation. "We were just talking!"

"When a girl touches you there…"

"MOM!" he yelled, turned, and ran into the bathroom.

"Terry," she said from the other side of the door. He stood there staring at the toilet, which had been installed while he was out of it. The previous one hadn't been made for Human backsides. "Terry, it's okay to be curious."

Furious, he reached out and yanked the shower curtain aside, popping a couple of the rings in the process, and turned the water on full. He pretended not to hear her.

"Okay," she said eventually. "Later, then."

Terry sighed, stripping and climbing into the shower. As the hot water pelted his skin, he tried to ignore the part of him that had enjoyed Katrina's touch the most, and wished it would go away.

* * * * *

Chapter Eight

Templemer, Planet Hoarfrost, Lupasha System, Coro Region, Tolo Arm

April 24nd, 2038

"Terry?" He turned to see Doc walking into the moon pool. They were the only two currently in the room. Terry was waiting for the machine to make enough milk for Pōkole and for the other seniors to arrive and help.

"What's up, Doc?"

The older man stopped and laughed, making a funny gesture with his hand like he was holding up something in front of his mouth. "Ahhh, what's up, Doc?" Terry's brows knitted in confusion. "Never mind, I need to tell you how I got nicknamed Doc someday. You got a minute?"

"Yeah, the guys won't be here for a few minutes. Junior's starving." He pointed out through the ruby dome to where Pōkole was swimming impatiently in a figure-eight pattern. Moloko was hovering a short distance away.

"Your mom asked me to talk to you."

"Oh, for the love of—"

"Kiddo, it's cool. I don't really care if you play doctor with another kid your age, as long as they're consenting."

"I wasn't…wait, 'playing doctor?'"

"Old saying," Doc said. "Examining each other's bodies?" Terry felt his face turning hot. "Uh huh, that's what I thought. In the hallway?"

"I was showing her my scar," Terry said and pointed at his hip.

"You're off by a few centimeters to the left."

Terry looked down, tracked in the indicated direction, and the hot feeling in his cheeks turned to molten lead. His mouth opened and closed, but only a popping sound came out. It took him a full five seconds to respond coherently. "I was *showing her my scar!*"

"It's cool," Doc said. "I mostly believe you." He shrugged. "Mostly. Now, how do you think it looked to your mom? Her son and a pretty blonde girl out in the hallway, you with your pants half off, and her touching your...scar?"

"I didn't have my pants half off," Terry said, realizing how lame it probably sounded as the words came out of his mouth. Doc put his hands on his hips and cocked his head. Terry looked down. "Well, I didn't."

Doc stared at him with a hard gaze for a long time, then slowly nodded. "But you do like her, don't you?"

"Sure!" he said with a little too much exuberance.

"Okay, well, maybe don't show her any more scars in front of your mom?" Terry laughed and nodded his head. Doc grabbed him around the shoulders and gave him a quick hug. "Good. Now, how's the program coming?"

"I finished compiling it into language I understand; I'm just trying to piece together what it does and why."

"You know how much longer?"

"Maybe a couple days. Hopefully by the time you let me go back out."

"You aren't delaying, are you?"

"No, sir," Terry said seriously.

"Good, I didn't think you would be. Well, we're going to Extractor #4 today to see how much it has on board. The dolphins found it late last night. They're treating it like a game with the orcas, and say they're ahead 1-0."

"Sounds like them, all right," Terry agreed. "Good luck."

Doc left, and Terry pulled out his slate to work on the program while he waited for his friends. A short time later he saw the big submarine and three of the new minisubs pass just within view. A squadron of several orcas and bottlenoses were in closer formation; the cetaceans now all had LED lights mounted on their rebreather harnesses, and they cast beams in the darkness as they swam with the submarines until they were swallowed by the sea.

The machine beeped, notifying him a bottle was full. He switched it for an empty one and went back to work on the slate to forget the fun he was missing out there. He was just changing another bottle five minutes later when Katrina came in.

"Hey," he said.

"Hey," she said back and immediately came over to help him.

The only thing the leg made difficult was carrying heavy things. The full milk bottles weighed in at over 10 kilos. It was a little difficult. She leaned in to help him, and he noted just how blue her eyes were.

"I saw Doc leaving," she said.

"He was in here talking to me before you got here," Terry said.

"Yeah?"

"Yeah, my mom narced on us to him."

Her cheeks grew red, and she stood up, smoothing her shirt back down. He enjoyed the effect. "What did he say?"

"Just that we shouldn't do anything around mom."

"We weren't doing anything," she said.

"I know," he said, "I tried to tell him."

"I mean, I don't even know what you'd want to do."

Terry didn't know what to say in reply. What would he want to do? "What would you want to do?"

"I don't know," she said.

Katrina was so close, just a few centimeters away. She smelled like soap and mystery. "What would we do by ourselves if we wanted to?" It was a stupid question, he realized, when she took a step forward and their lips touched.

Colin, Dan, and Taiki came in talking loudly about a movie they'd watched recently. Terry was helping Katrina lift the last milk jug onto the table. They were both breathing hard and looked a little sweaty.

"You guys alright?" Dan asked.

"Yeah, why?" Terry asked.

"You look worn out," Colin said.

Terry swallowed and began to panic.

"Of course we are," Katrina said and he felt his heart leap into his throat. "You assholes are late and left us to do all the hard work!"

The three guys made rude sounds and waved it off. Terry breathed again and glanced at Katrina, who winked back at him. Terry sat down to let the new arrivals move the jugs onto the edge of the moon pool. It helped him wait until something went away.

The boys went into one of the two small changing rooms, Katrina into the other, and emerged a couple minutes later in drysuits carrying respirators and fins.

"We going swimming later?" Dan asked.

"I need to work on the program," Terry said. He glanced at Katrina, who glanced back at him. Her eyes held something that was better than anything he'd ever experienced. *Oh, boy.*

The moon pool lock opened, and Pōkole raced in. Moloko followed, considerably slower and more careful. The five teenagers slid into the water and spent a few minutes playing with the excited calf as his mother floated around the pool lazily while keeping an eye on her exuberant offspring. They each took a turn being towed by Pōkole, an activity he particularly enjoyed, and then it was lunch time.

As always, Pōkole was voracious. Dr. Jaehnig discussed the option of increasing his feedings to a four-meal schedule instead of the current three. This would necessitate either automating the process, or having some staff handle the middle of the night. Regardless, there was no doubt the calf was thriving; he seemed to grow every day.

The other researchers were against automation, especially Dr. Orsage. Their only biologist specializing in cetacean psychology stated Pōkole got too much from the interaction between Terry and the other teenage volunteers. For the time being, they would continue on as before.

Terry hadn't been lying, he did need to concentrate on the program. Only he'd also promised Katrina she could stay. After the brief and exciting moments of kissing, he'd found it impossible to tell her no. Once the other guys were gone, he and Katrina stayed in an unused room next to the moon pool. Outside, several orcas—including Pōkole and his mother—were chasing a local sea creature.

"It looks like they're torturing it," Katrina said, pointing. The animal was more like an eel than a fish, with a dozen flippers along its length, and a wide mouth meant to eat plant growth from the ocean floor. It was desperately trying to escape its tormentors, but suffering from a major deficiency without vision. The orcas bit at it from all sides, Moloko encouraging her calf to join in.

"They're predators," Terry explained, "called Killer Whales by most people." He glanced at the drama playing out, the calf biting into one of the eel's flippers and tearing a chunk out of it. "It's natural for them."

Katrina looked away as the orcas began to tear the creature to pieces and feast on it. Terry went back to his slate. The Selroth control program was projected via Tri-V in a series of icons, each representing an element of the program. She watched him quietly, perched on the edge of a table. It was really more comfortable than the Selroth-designed chairs anyway, which was why Terry stood.

"You've really gotten used to the leg they made for you," she said.

"Umm hmm," he grunted in agreement.

"It makes you look like a badass."

Terry glanced up at her from the display. She was examining him in detail, her expression indecipherable. He spent a second examining her face, the curve of her chin, the shape of her lips. Her eyes came up and met his. He swallowed and went back to the program. It was just frustrating enough to take his mind away from how it felt to kiss her.

"What is it you're trying to do?" she asked.

"The Selroth wrote a program on their extractors which controlled their actions after they left. Unfortunately, only part of the program was on the extractor. Part is missing."

"So it only works if all the parts are there?" she asked.

"Yeah," he said. "Pretty much."

"It's an algebra problem, then," she said.

"No, programming."

"But I learned programming is like algebra." He looked at her curiously. "You know, based on the programming, only certain codes and processes could exist. Like a jigsaw puzzle."

Terry was shaking his head, then he stopped. "Jigsaw puzzle," he said. She nodded and smiled at him. A short time ago, the smile might have completely thrown him off his line of thought, but her comparison had socked him between the eyes more than her kiss had. "Union standard programming is made up of blocks," he said.

"Right," she agreed, "we learned that in school, but nobody really understands them."

"I do." He grinned. "Well, kinda. The program blocks are like you said, a jigsaw puzzle. Except a woven jigsaw puzzle, where pieces fit together with multiple other blocks as long as you line them up right. The original programmers must have thought in ways we don't understand. It's practically three dimensional. But you're right, I think I can extrapolate the missing pieces."

Katrina was grinning hugely as he set out all the programming blocks from the extractor to create a palette. After just a minute, he was certain he didn't have them all. However, he still had the files from the Tri-V simulation he'd sold to the Maki. He set out that pallet, too, and then compared the two.

"Holy shit, a match!" he said. There were three blocks in the Tri-V sim that hadn't been in the extractor program. There must be hundreds of permutations. He set about figuring out which jigsaw piece set with each hole in the extractor's programming. It took almost an hour for the first match, then 10 minutes for the second. The final piece snapped into place in just seconds to give him a completed program.

"You did it!" Katrina said.

"No, we did," he replied. She was leaning over his shoulder. It was only a slight move to kiss her cheek. She turned her head strategically as he move in, and their lips met instead. His finger absently tapped the *Initiate* icon. He broke the kiss when his slate blanked and a new display came up.

"Oh no, what did I do?" he wondered and frantically tried to stop the process. He knew black programs could wipe out a slate, or even infect an entire network and wreak unbelievable carnage. He needn't have worried. The coding wasn't malicious, it was planning in nature.

The program instructed the extractor to operate until its storage tanks were full, then it would move to a specific location, at which point additional orders would be received. A command subroutine would then delete the parts of the program he'd just replaced, and the extractor would blithely return to its task. He looked at the results again. Coordinates were included.

"I know where the extracted minerals are," he said. "Do you want to go for a swim?"

"Won't we get in trouble?" she asked.

Terry glanced at the time, then shook his head no. "I don't have to meet mom for three hours yet. More than time enough to go out, verify the location, and return." She looked skeptical. "There are two minisubs still; one's mine, and another that Doc's people just finished. It hasn't gone out yet, but I have mine in case anything goes wrong. What do you say?"

"Why not?" she said.

The two young people nearly ran out of the moon pool, heading for the lock where the submarines were kept. Terry had been in such a hurry he hadn't noticed a tiny icon on his slate indicating it had reached out to Templemer's communications array with instructions. He could only think of finding the mineral reserves and being named a hero once again. The slate was in his carrying pouch when it flashed the message *Communication Successfully Sent*, blanked itself, and ended.

* * * * *

Chapter Nine

Volcanic Valley, Planet Hoarfrost, Lupasha System, Coro Region, Tolo Arm

April 24th, 2038

The two minisubs sailed over the ocean mountaintops at a solid 20 knots. They hadn't intended it, but they'd ended up with a massive escort of orcas and bottlenoses. All of them, actually. Doc and his team went in a full-size submarine, and thus didn't need protection from *Oohobo*. The large submarines were tough and armed with lasers. The *Oohobo* likely had past experience with them under Selroth command, and stayed away from them,

It only took Katrina a few minutes to learn the minisub's operation. The controls were simple and intuitive, having been designed for Humans, by Humans. While she didn't have as much dive experience as Terry, she'd gotten more than a little since arriving on Hoarfrost. This was her first time out, though, and Kray had decided they needed a full escort. Not one to be outdone, the bottlenoses had come along.

"We need to get there and back quickly," Terry said over intercom between the two minisubs.

"The adults will be pissed," she reminded him.

"I know, but finding the stash will make it all good. It must have thousands of tons in it!"

The entire purpose of being at Templemer was to operate the mines. If they could generate a massive deposit of minerals for the Izlians in the first year of the contract, Doc had said it would ensure their success. Despite possibly getting in trouble, Katrina seemed excited to break the rules. He'd never had a friend quite like her. A little voice in the back of his mind whispered Yui's name, but the memory of warm, wet kisses made it quiet and distant.

"How much farther?" Katrina asked.

Terry looked at his slate mounted in the minisub's cockpit. The powerful computer was waterproof. The documentation said it would operate in any environment from 5 to 1200 kelvin, and pressure so deep most life couldn't survive, the advantage of no moving parts or internal spaces. It was effectively grown from crystals as a single matrix.

"Looks like 3 kilometers," he said. They were navigating based entirely on the data provided by their reconstructed Selroth program. Since it had provided a destination in the area, he was certain the location must be correct. If it had said the location was on the other side of the planet, he'd have doubted the results.

"Even with the heater, it's cold," she said, a shiver in her voice.

"You kind of get used to it," he replied. The minisubs hummed onward.

Through the glass canopy, he watched Pōkole literally swimming circles around him. Despite not even being a year old yet, he was an incredibly fast, strong swimmer. Adult orca could exceed 25 knots. The calf was having no trouble keeping up with the minisubs' 20 knots.

One of the bottlenoses came racing back from the direction they were heading, suddenly appearing in the dozens of lights from the many cetaceans and orca. It was Wikiwiki, a female known for her swimming speed. She'd often worked as a scout when the Humans had ventured out to explore Hoarfrost's oceans. She'd been clocked at an impressive 33 knots.

For a moment Terry was afraid she would tell them an *Oohobo* was menacingly close, but instead, she had better news. "*Machine near!*" she said excitedly.

"Take us there, please?" he asked. Wikiwiki bobbed her head up and down, the lights on her harness dancing wildly, then she wheeled about and raced back the way she'd come.

"Wow, she's fast," Katrina said.

"*Wikiwiki fastest Swift Brother,*" Kray agreed, his huge bulk accelerating after the bottlenose with powerful strokes of his flukes.

The two minisubs skimmed through the water in the midst of a squadron of orcas and bottlenose dolphins. Terry wondered if this was how a vital ship felt being escorted by warships through enemy territory. He felt incredibly safe.

A minute later, his minisub's sonar showed their destination. Another volcano, this one considerably shorter than the others nearby. Terry watched the depth meter descending and accessed the minisub's built-in dive computer. He and Katrina were already breathing a mixture specially formulated for deeper diving. He entered the numbers and bit his lower lip. It was on the edge of their ability without having to undergo decompression.

"Is it safe to go so far down?" Katrina asked, obviously aware of the issue at hand.

The two minisubs slowed to a stop, and the orca pod circled back to ring them in. Pōkole stopped in front of Terry's minisub, looking through the canopy curiously.

"*What wrong?*" Moloko asked.

"It's very deep," Terry explained. "You know Humans can't dive deep and come up as easily as cetaceans."

"*Want go back?*" Kray asked.

The bottlenose dolphins were clicking and singing ahead, already at their destination, inviting them to come join in the fun.

"No," Terry said. "It'll be okay if we don't have to go any deeper." He moved forward, Katrina fell in alongside, and the retinue of orcas did so, as well.

Terry tried not to watch the depth gauge as they continued downward. Despite his attempt, he ended up fixating on it so much he missed the extractor coming into view. When he looked up, he gasped in surprise.

"What's wrong?" Katrina asked.

"The extractor," he said, glancing over at her and pointing ahead. He could see her inside her own minisub looking in the same direction.

"I know," she said, "it's huge."

"No, you don't understand. It isn't the same as the others. Doc said they were all somewhat different, but..." He shook his head. "It's not even close."

Where the first extractor he'd seen had looked like a motley collection of tanks and equipment mounted on a massive motorized tread-driven base, this one appeared more like a structure built on the surface of the volcano. It was also many times larger than the other extractor. Like five times larger.

"It's like the extractor fell apart," Katrina said.

"Or was rebuilt?" Terry wondered aloud.

They finally levelled out as the minisubs and the flotilla of orcas came even with what used to be an extractor. Now Terry could see his theory appeared to be correct. The extractor no longer possessed any means to move about; instead, it was built into the side of the volcano. Also, unlike the volcano the other extractor was working on, this one showed no signs of life, either fish or underwater plants feeding on mineral-rich ejecta.

"Why did it take itself apart?" he wondered.

"Can a machine take itself apart?" Katrina asked.

"Some can," Terry said. "I think," he corrected. He'd read about nanites in science. The Union had machines great and small. Some were like the *Behemoths*, kilometers across. Others were too small to see, so small they could enter your body and change things. Those were nanites, and Earth scientists had been working toward them for a long time. Naturally the Union was way ahead of them, and had been using them for thousands of years.

It wasn't too much of a stretch to build a machine that could simply take itself apart and rebuild itself to do another job. Maybe lacking the space to store all the harvested material for centuries, they'd taken this extractor apart to create a depot of some kind. Perhaps it had been broken and couldn't move anymore, or its fusion plant had stopped working. It sort of made sense.

He wished the minisub had sensors like a starship so he could scan for a fusion power plant. Unfortunately, he only possessed rudimentary sensors, like a compass, depth gauge, and temperature readouts. The latter showed the water temp down three degrees, further proof the volcano was dormant and extinct. He shivered, and he knew Katrina must be even colder. They needed to get into the base and out of the cold.

"Skritch?" he called over the comms.

"*Terry, Terry!*" the leader of Sunrise Pod replied.

"Can you look for an entrance? A hatch we could use to get inside?"

"*We look,*" Skritch replied instantly.

Terry could see the bottlenoses racing around the tanks and other structures by their headlights. In less than a minute, one of them called. Wikiwiki had found an entrance. Terry let Katrina know, and together they accelerated toward Wikiwiki's sonar beacon.

The inside of the disassembled extractor wasn't like the other one at all. There was barely any area in atmosphere, and what there was seemed almost an afterthought. He knew there were often no spaces in atmosphere in Selroth bases because they were water breathers. Doc had believed the reason that there were extensive breathing spaces on Templemer was the result of the water being unfavorable to the Selroth.

Terry and Katrina spent some time warming up in their drysuits and exploring, but there just wasn't much to see. Eventually he located a data port and used his slate to log into the system. Like the others, its access code was a variation of the correct code, and he was quickly reading through the files.

"This is it," he said excitedly. "There's thousands of tons of sorted minerals here."

"But why is it here?" Katrina asked.

"I have no idea," he said. With full access to the computer, he began copying the entire OS and memory to his slate. With 11 exabytes on his slate, he had plenty of room. He'd only used two exabytes, and the extractor's complete memory was less than 5 petabytes.

He glanced up as the files were copying. Katrina was examining a locker full of rusty gear. He caught himself admiring the way her drysuit clung to her hips and quickly looked away as she turned around. He was certain his cheeks were bright red.

When he looked back at the slate, he saw it had slowed way down. It was struggling with a series of files. *Strange,* he thought, his slate was massively more powerful than the entire processing power of the extractor. No file should be able to tie up his slate, especially one in an industrial machine like the extractor.

Terry waited until the copy was completed, then pulled up the strange file. It was unlike anything he'd seen in the Union to date. At first, he didn't understand how the station's computer could even cope with the thing. Like when he copied it, his slate struggled to load the file.

"This is the strangest thing," he said.

"What?" Katrina asked, coming close.

Terry swallowed when she leaned on his shoulder to look. "It's a file in the computer here. Strangest thing I've ever seen."

She watched the Tri-V display the codes moving in three dimensions. "Weird," she said. She moved around to the side and looked at it from another direction. "It's in three dimensions, layers upon layers."

"I've never seen a program like it." He froze the view and pointed. "Look at those strings. They're almost woven together. How can you even program it? A three dimensional jigsaw puzzle, you'd have to have a strange brain to even understand it."

"Like the code you put together to find this place?"

"A little," he said. "Only a million times more complicated."
Who programs like this? he thought. Even more interesting, why do
computers recognize it?

Terry spent a few minutes examining the other files, then saved
them all and put his slate away. He checked his core temperature,
then his drysuit's power. They'd been gone two hours, and his suit
showed four more hours of power. "How's your power?"

"Three and a half hours left," she said. "Is that enough?"

"Yeah, if we don't spend too much longer."

"We have to go back in the water so soon?" she asked.

"If we don't, we risk running out of power for the drysuits." The
air inside the station was 10 below zero. Their suits could easily handle much lower temperatures out of the water than in it. Even so,
without the hot air blowers, they'd quickly freeze to death. Time to
go.

The return to Templemer took less than an hour. Terry and
Katrina chatted about being out so far and finding the missing extractor. Terry carefully monitored their depth information and ran it
through the dive computer app on his slate twice more to make
100% certain they were safe. As they were approaching the dome
and the lights became visible, his radio came alive.

"Terry, are you out there?" It was Doc's familiar voice.

He cringed. He'd hoped they'd beat the mercs back home.
"Yeah, I'm here."

"Where are you now?" The question was asked in Doc's serious
adult tone.

Crap. "Almost back. We found the missing extractor."

"Come in immediately. Kiddo, you really screwed up."

So much for a celebration, he thought. For the last few minutes of the ride, he ran the chain of events through his head, including how he'd justified their going out alone, despite the little voice in the back of his mind knowing it wouldn't wash with the adults. By the time the cetaceans bid them farewell as he and Katrina sailed in through the lock, he understood that the idea was far from his best one.

Doc and his mother were waiting. Doc looked disappointed; his mother was just pissed. *Yeah, not my best decision*, he thought as he surfaced to face the music.

* * * * *

Chapter Ten

Templemer, Planet Hoarfrost, Lupasha System, Coro Region,
Tolo Arm
May 9th, 2038

Terry held the bottle as Pōkole drained it greedily. He dearly missed his friends' help, but that would still be some weeks coming. Pōkole jerked on the empty bottle, reminding him what he was there for. Terry climbed out of the moon pool and got another, balancing the 10kg container in the water where the calf waited eagerly.

"Here you go," he said and offered it to him. It was taken immediately and hungrily. He used to really enjoy feeding the ravenous little guy. He realized more every day that a large part of the fun had grown to include the companionship of his friends. Not to mention Katrina, of course.

As the calf quickly went through his seventh jug of milk, Terry thought about her. Aside from classes, he hadn't been alone with her since their ill-advised trip to the excavator stash. He'd tried a couple of times, but his mom was always there to stop him with a none-too-gentle reminder that he was grounded—for a month.

She hadn't even wanted to let him continue feeding Pōkole until he played his trump card. "It isn't fair to punish Pōkole for what I did," he'd said. She'd relented only after telling him he had to do it by himself. Feeding the calf a hundred liters a day was no mean feat, especially by himself.

"I miss Katrina," he said to Pōkole.

"*Terr, Terr, more?*"

The young orca's language continued to develop faster than anyone had expected. Dr. Orsage said she hoped they had more calves so she could study whether it was a phenomenon related to the pinplants or not. The bottle was empty, so he went for another. Almost two more weeks before his month of grounding was over. A part of him knew he'd gotten off light. It didn't help when he chafed like he was then. At least she'd also allowed him to continue swimming every day to build up familiarity with the leg. He missed his friends and Katrina then, too. *Crap.*

Finally Pōkole was stuffed, and he swam out the lock to rejoin Moloko and another pair of orcas who were waiting. While the huge predatory cetaceans had no real fear of the *Oohobo*, the calf was at risk. They protected Pōkole with the same vigor they'd protected Terry. He guessed they thought of him as their calf of sorts as well.

His duties to Pōkole discharged, he stopped by the mess hall for dinner. There was a little table reserved just for him, on the far side away from all the others kids his age, or even close to his age. His friends were all there at the table he used to share with then. Dan spotted Terry as he entered and waved. The others looked up and waved. Katrina's eyes lit up when she saw him, and Terry felt his heart flutter.

For a second, he considered sidling over there as if he was going to get something. When he glanced around, he saw Doc with his people nearby, and he was watching Terry closely. He'd hoped the man would at least partly understand and maybe cut him a little slack. Nothing could be further from the truth.

"This is the stupidest thing I've ever seen you do," Doc had said. "Frankly, I expected better of you. But I guess you just had to step over the line in a big way, didn't you?"

Terry hadn't had a response, so he'd kept quiet. Even when the one-month grounding sentence came down, he'd held his peace. What could he offer in his own defense? It *was* a dumbass move. He did his best to hold Katrina harmless, claiming it was all his idea, and it mostly was. Still, she'd caught some blowback. Her own grounding was over after two weeks. He glanced at Doc, then went over to get a drink and returned to his solo table.

Back in his quarters, he was early enough he didn't have to face his mom, which was good. Her reproachful disappointed looks were worse than Doc's by far. She hadn't said anything more about the incident after the first day. "I trusted you," was all she'd said before pronouncing sentence.

He spent two hours doing his homework, and some time studying pinplant technology. Afterward, he went back to his current personal project—the files he'd copied from the strange extractor.

"You want to redeem yourself a little?" Doc had asked. Of course he did. "Figure out what the Selroth were up to from all those files." Offered a chance to get out of the doghouse, he went to it. Only it proved much more exhausting than he'd expected.

Of the thousands of files, most were routine records of one kind or another. The extractor's original OS was still functioning and creating operations logs dutifully, as it had been for more than 300 years. Each subsystem generated a report each hour. There were 122 subsystems. This resulted in a lot of files.

The work was complicated even more because the system didn't seem to follow a normal convention in naming files, or dating them. "It's all designed to stymy investigation," he'd told Doc after two days of work.

"Sounds like a good job to keep you out of mischief," he'd replied. Despite being frustrated, Terry went back to the task.

Now 15 days into his analysis of the files, he finally felt he was making some progress. The biggest part was deciphering the file naming convention. It had taken him two weeks just to realize that each name was linked with the date in a rotating series of identifiers, and those were in Selroth. He got his slate to translate, and things made a lot more sense. For the first time, he eliminated 90% of the files by identifying their timing to coincide with routine equipment log files. Score.

With only a fraction of the files left, he was able to move through them much faster. He hadn't gone back to the weird 3D file yet. He didn't know where to start with it. After the drama about his punishment, he'd checked with the GalNet, but found no help there with the unusual programming methods. So he stuck to what he could work with.

Huge groups of files were put aside using his understanding of naming conventions. The further along he got, the better his understanding grew. He intermittently opened files to look for anything interesting. It was close to bedtime when he came across the first files matching the criteria of the program he'd first cracked.

"Locate and secure," he read from his slate, translated off the program commands. *What does that mean*, he wondered, and dug further into the file. There was some indexed information, but nothing understandable would translate.

Terry ran searches for related terminology in the files and got several hits. Amazingly, most of those were in the discarded data logs. He recalled the files to view and went over them.

"Still working on homework?"

Terry turned at his mom's words, surprised to see her there. "No, I was working on the files…files for Doc."

Her eyes narrowed in suspicion. Nothing had been said in his punishment about working on the files retrieved from his misadventure. "It's late," she said after a few seconds. "You need to go to bed soon."

"Yes, Mom," he said. She watched him a little longer, then went into her room.

Terry waited for a moment, then went into the little kitchenette and grabbed a meal pack from the cooler. He collected his slate and retreated to his room, closed the door, and set up on his little desk.

The meal pack was self-contained and made by their autochef. He squeezed the tab and it chemically heated itself as he went back to his research. The meal was almost cold again before he remembered it was there. He begrudgingly shoveled the fish and noodles into his mouth—feeding the machine, as Doc called it, all the while displaying files on his slate's Tri-V.

He had the machine's Tri-V range maxed out, with nine square meters of space in his tiny room full of file elements and floating descriptions he'd added to them. As he worked, he thought the strange 3D file that had made no sense might be onto something. If you could operate in 3D, you could process and collate an order of magnitude more data.

He caught himself yawning and glanced at the simple chronometer in the corner of his Tri-V display. It was past midnight already.

He needed to get to sleep or he'd be useless in classes tomorrow, which would get back to his mom.

Terry spent another half hour going over the log files, trying to understand what they meant, and what the Selroth were doing with them. However, eventually he gave in to fatigue and crawled into his bed. Shutting off the lights, he drifted off with files and content buzzing ceaselessly through his mind.

* * * * *

Chapter Eleven

Templemer, Planet Hoarfrost, Lupasha System, Coro Region, Tolo Arm

May 10th, 2038

Terry barely got to his class on time. Dr. Patel taught biology and life sciences, but hadn't arrived yet when Terry entered. In these classes, they shared time with the middle school-aged kids, so in addition to the four other high schoolers there were five younger kids. They all looked up when he came in.

He immediately caught Katrina's eye and smiled. She half-smiled back, which caused him to pause. He glanced out the door and saw no sign of Dr. Patel, so he went over to Katrina and his friends. "What's up?"

"You didn't notice all the doctors weren't around at breakfast?" she asked.

"No," he admitted. "I was working late, so I skipped breakfast. What do you think is going on?"

"No clue," Dan said. Taiki shook his head to show he didn't know either, while Colin just shrugged. The middle school students at their own table glanced at the older students nervously. The adults had been scrupulous since arriving on Hoarfrost at maintaining a daily schedule in order to give the children a grounding in routine.

Some of the much younger kids were having regular counseling sessions to help them deal with their new environment.

He sat with his friends and listened while they gossiped about what might be happening. To fill the time, Terry went back to his slate and the files he'd been working on when he'd given in to sleep the previous night.

As soon as he looked for them, he had an epiphany. The Selroth program had set aside one of the extractors to create a storage depot! Which meant they'd always intended to hide all the resources, maybe even for hundreds of years. Which led him to the communications protocol of the original program, and his own slate's communications log.

Betrayed by his own beloved slate. It had used Templemer's own communications system to quietly send a signal to the surface station, which in turn...

"Oh, shit," he cursed.

"Terry!" Katrina chastised him.

"I gotta go," he said, snatching up his slate and running for the door.

"What's going on?" Katrina yelled after him, but he was already out the door and running out of the building. Simulated sunlight shone from the dome above as he ran across the open space, past the swimming pool, to the central building tower that contained Templemer's command center. He saw only a few people between the school and the command center.

Inside he went immediately to the second floor, where the ops room was. As soon as he reached the 2nd floor, he found all the ranking staff of the colony, former directors of the institute.

"We're in trouble!" he blurted.

"Terry," Doc said from where he stood by a Tri-V display. "What—"

"You have to listen to me," he said, and held up his slate. "The Selroth are coming back."

"Son," his mom said, "how did you find out?"

"It was in the program…wait, you know?"

"Yes," she said. "We haven't made any announcements yet. So how did *you* know?"

"It was in the program," he said, then quickly explained how the operating system from the extractors, once reassembled, contained a hidden trigger that sent a signal off planet. "I could have locked down my slate, but I didn't know there was a reason to," he said with a shake of his head. "I messed up again."

"No," Tina said, standing next to Doc. "If you hadn't done it, one of us would have eventually. It's not your fault."

"But how do you know? Did someone else activate the signal?"

"No," Doc said. "The Selroth are landing at the power station up on the surface." He pointed to the ops room Tri-V. On it was the surface fusion plant floating in the melted ice. On the landing pads squatted multiple ships. They didn't look like commercial vessels. Each one had stubby swept wings and a turret on its back. He'd learned about those kinds of craft in MST—dropships.

Designed to transport mercs from space to a planet's surface, dropships were balanced between combat capabilities, cargo capacity, and the ability to quickly drop from orbit to a planet's surface. It was a capability Human mercs greatly coveted.

"What are we going to do?" he asked.

"The Selroth don't negotiate well," Doc said and put a hand on his shoulder. "My team can fight, but we're pretty badly outnumbered." On the viewer, one of the transports' doors were open and huge crabs were skittering out.

"Great, we've got crabs," Piano said. Tina elbowed him hard in the ribs.

"There are at least three platoons," Tina said, examining the images. "Assuming they don't have even more in orbit, of course."

"They're tough bastards, too. The Selroth came loaded for Oogar," Doc quipped.

Terry gave a half chuckle at the pun.

"First thing they did was shut down our link to the satellites in orbit," Tina said. "They've got backdoor codes to everything."

"Did the Izlians set us up?" his mom asked Doc.

"I doubt it," he said. "They weren't happy with the Selroth when they up and ditched the project. I think the Selroth left because they saw potential here. A lot of potential. So they hatched a plot to convince the Izlians there wasn't much here, while the truth was the vents are a rich score. They set the extractors to automatic and left. They were probably planning to come back eventually, but the program was a safety switch in case their plot was discovered."

"And I triggered it," Terry said.

"We triggered it," Doc corrected. "Did you find anything else in the files from the extractor? Something that could help us?"

"They sent it there on purpose to set up a depot to store the other extractors' haul," Terry said. "It looks like there's a facility under the extractor; I don't know what kind, but I know it's suitable for air-breathing life."

"Did the Selroth make it?" Doc asked. "What's it for?"

"I don't know either of those things," Terry said. "I only just figured some of it out."

Doc nodded in understanding and turned to Terry's mom. "We have to get the kids out of here."

"What?!" she said. "Where do we take them? The surface is our only way to get off, and without a way to call for help, we're trapped."

"To the place Terry found," Doc said. She shook her head and he help up a hand. "No, listen. As long as the children are here, we have no ability to fight or negotiate. The Selroth will all be mercs. They don't care about civilians; to them they're just a liability for our side."

"No," she said. "It's too dangerous."

"It's more dangerous to stay here." Doc's mercs nodded in agreement.

"He's making sense, Dr. Clark," Dr. Jaehnig said. The others were reluctantly nodding as well.

"The orcas can help protect us," Terry said.

"Send some of the staff with them, then," she said.

"In all frankness, Madison, I'll probably need them to help fight. The Selroth might be coming to kill us and take the resources, and the presence of Xiq'tal troopers adds weight to the theory."

"It's what I would do," Toothpick said.

On the display, Selroth in heated suits were supervising Xiq'tal unloading submersible craft into the water, one per dropship. Doc pointed. "We don't have a lot of time." Some of the big crabs were slipping into the water.

"This plan is crazy," she said, shaking her head.

"No, just desperate," Doc replied. He turned to Terry. "You can operate the submersible?"

"It's a lot like the minisub?"

"Quite a bit, yeah," Honcho said and nodded. "I can get you up to speed in just a few minutes."

"A few minutes might be all the time we have," Doc said. "Madison, you're in charge. Make the call. Get the kids out of here, or give the oldest ones guns." He looked right at Terry when he said the last. It was exactly the push she needed.

"Get ready to evacuate the kids," she said, then grabbed Terry in a fierce hug. She kissed him on the forehead and turned his face up to hers. "You stay out of this, you hear?"

"Yes, Mom."

"I'm serious. No matter what you hear. Do not come back until at least two of us tell you it's safe. Do you understand?" He nodded, eyes big. "I'm going to tell the cetaceans what's happening and have them go with you."

Doc scribbled on a piece of note paper and handed it to him. "This is the only frequency we'll transmit on. Ignore everything else. Like your mother says, only come back if at least two of us," he gestured around the room, "tell you to."

"I will."

"Honcho, activate the sub and get him up to speed on the controls." He moved next to the cowboy hat-wearing merc, said something in his ear Terry didn't hear, and passed the man something. "Terry, get your dive gear and head for the sub dock. The rest of you, let's round up all the kids, some supplies, and haul ass!" On the display a crowd of Selroth were trotting out of the dropship and into the submersible. A group of Xiq'tal submerged. "Times a-wasting."

* * *

Terry ran all the way to the moon pool to collect his dive gear. He had it all stuffed into a duffel, including extra rebreathers and batteries, when he saw the feeding cart and its milk synthesizer. "Damn it," he said, and rushed into the equipment room. He unloaded the biggest cart he could find, shoved his duffel onto the bottom shelf, and rolled it out into the main room.

Honcho was standing impatiently next to the submarine when Terry came huffing and puffing through the submarine lock door, pushing the equipment cart laden with a massive pile of equipment.

"Kid, what the hell?" he asked when he saw.

"Pōkole will starve without food," Terry explained. "He's not old enough for fish alone."

He'd just gotten the cart up to the sub when the door opened again. Tina, Toothpick, Piano, Hutch, and Peyto were escorting in all the other children. The youngest, a 5-year-old girl, was being helped along by her older brother. A few adults were there carrying babies, and a couple looked pregnant. He'd known there were pregnancies among the colonists, though not how many.

Terry's friends Dan, Colin, Taiki, and of course Katrina, were helping. Each of the children had a bag with them, some several. He was surprised to see the mercs wore body armor and carried various weapons. *When did they have time to gear up?* he wondered and lugged a crate onto the sub.

"Forget that shit," Honcho urged.

"I can't leave it," Terry insisted.

Honcho snarled another curse, then gave a sharp whistle. The mercs looked up. He pointed to the cart, made a whirling gesture over his head, and pointed to the sub. Piano gave a thumbs-up. "It'll get done, now come on, damn it." Terry followed him into the submarine.

He took him into the craft and forward to the cockpit. The controls resembled a minisub in the same way a turkey sandwich resembled a living turkey. "Oh, wow," he said at the dizzying array of gauges, controls, computer screens, and instruments.

"Don't worry about it," Honcho said, squeezing down to fit through the driver's hatch next to Terry. He had to remove his cowboy hat, something which seemed to annoy him. "Hop into the driver's seat, and I'll give you a crash course."

"Can you not say crash?" Terry asked.

Honcho laughed and mussed his hair. "Compared to stabbing a dinosaur in the eye while it's trying to eat you, this ain't nothin."

"I was scared to death, Honcho," Terry admitted. "I didn't know what I was doing."

"Being brave doesn't mean you can't be scared, kid. It just means you can act when most people wouldn't. You've got the knife Toothpick gave you?"

"Sure," Terry said, and looked down. He'd strapped his dive belt on before taking the rest of the gear. The knife rested there in its sheath.

"Good, Doc said to give you this." He held out a holster. Inside was one of the mercs' custom-printed laser pistols.

"Oh, holy cow," Terry said, staring at the weapon.

"Don't go all soft on me now, kid," Honcho said and shoved it at him. Terry took it and Honcho drew his own. "Never put your finger on the trigger until you're ready to fire," he said, and Terry noted how the man held it with his finger along the side of the trigger but-

ton. "Safety here, magazine release here. You got 12 shots, then re-
load. One extra magazine in the holster. Got it?"

"Yeah," Terry said, "but I've never shot a gun before."

"We all start sometime. If you need it, shit's gone sideways.
Selroth are tough, but not too tough. Aim center mass." He patted
his chest, then stomach. "Two shots each. Remember, under water
it's only good for a couple meters. Got it?"

"S-sure," Terry said and put the gun in his lap.

"You'll do fine. Now, here's how you run this beast."

* * *

Halfway through Honcho's crash course, Terry
grabbed his slate from the carry bag and began recording and making notes. The older man was right;
the necessary controls to operate the submarine weren't overly complicated. However, there were hundreds of additional controls that
were complicated. Messing with many of them could cause major
problems. He also needed to keep an eye on a whole series of moni-
tors to avoid needing some of the controls he wasn't learning how to
use.

"That's about it. Got it, kid?"

"I'll manage," Terry said and showed Honcho the notes and recordings. In the 10 minutes it had taken Honcho to explain, Terry
had taken full panoramic images of the control systems and had furiously noted everything Honcho had mentioned.

"Damn, that's pretty good." He pointed to a note. "Put a note on
this one," he said and pointed to another. "If you try to use the
dump ballast control to equalize buoyancy, you'll be on an express
trip to the surface."

"Oh, crap," Terry said and changed the notes. "Anything else?"

Honcho finished scanning and shook his head no. "All good." He glanced at his watch. "You still have thirty minutes."

"Honcho?" Terry heard Doc's voice over the man's miniature earpiece/radio.

He reached up and tapped the radio. "Go, boss."

"Fishes in the water, get the kid wet inside of ten minutes."

"Roger that," Honcho said and turned to Terry. "You hear? Okay, I'm going topside to make sure the sub's 100%. I'll be back in five." Then he was gone, leaving Terry alone and scared. He spent a minute going through the various checklists of function; fusion reactor power output, hydrogen storage, oxygen generator, main pressure pumps, backup pumps, and on, and on.

"You okay?"

He turned his head and saw Katrina crouching in the hatchway of the small cockpit.

"Oh, hey, yeah…kind of," he said, not realizing he was shaking his head.

"Do you need help?"

"Yes." He was about to say he didn't know where she would fit when she slid in and made a seat appear out of nowhere. It flipped down from under a console. He hadn't known it was there, but she'd apparently noticed it.

"What can I do?"

Terry put his slate where she could see it and quickly showed her the various systems, paying particular attention to things he'd been told to avoid upsetting. At first he was unsure whether Katrina would be of any real help, but after less than a minute, his concern was gone. He'd known since they met how intelligent she was, and he should have remembered. She jumped in immediately, taking over some functions from him.

Honcho returned and stopped in the hatch when he found the two kids busily working together, talking through the various functions and how they were delegating them. Terry didn't notice him for several seconds.

"You kids got this?"

"Yeah," Terry said, a little surprised.

"Okay," he said and left them in charge.

They both settled headsets in place, checking comms functions, and got ready.

"Terry, you there?" Doc called over the headset.

"Yes sir, all set," he replied.

"I hear you got Katrina up there helping you?"

Terry glanced over at her, and she winked, making him smile as Doc replied, "Honcho said you got it squared away, so I'm only going to tell you to keep your eye on the objective—keep those kids safe. A lot of the parents are freaking out about this, but despite your screw up, I have faith you can do this."

"Thanks, we won't let you down."

"You have 29 kids on board, and six adult women. All are either parents of babies, or pregnant women.

"We'll try to send the other sub if we have time, but nobody else has experience operating them, and we're going to try and put up as much of a fight as possible. Don't forget, you don't come back unless two of us call. There's enough supplies on there for two weeks, maybe three if you push it."

"Got it," Terry said, shaking slightly with pent-up nerves.

"Help him out, young lady," Doc added.

"Yes sir, I will."

"No time for romance." Terry felt his cheeks burning at his words. "Opening the lock, you are clear to dive."

"Roger that," Terry said, swallowed hard, and used the lateral thrusters to push them slightly away from the dock. "Dive 5 meters," he said.

"Five meters," Katrina repeated, the sound of whooshing air through the hull echoed as the sub's ballast tanks took on water, and they slipped below the surface.

Through the ball-shaped cockpit glass, he had a wonderfully panoramic view underwater of the submarine pen as he oriented himself on the slowly opening iris valve lock.

"We're really leaving them?" Katrina asked. "My mom and dad, your mom, everyone?"

"Just for now," Terry said. He'd promised Doc he wouldn't come back until two of the leaders contacted him, no matter what. The truth was, he'd come back as soon as all the children were safe, and his friends had them under protection.

Honcho had skipped over the vessel's defensive systems during his instructions. Terry clearly saw them, though. The submarine was armed with both close-in defense lasers and torpedoes. It could make a significant difference in the defense of Templemer. He fully intended to return and help in the fight. Just about everyone he knew was in the big ruby dome. He wouldn't abandon them.

Carefully managing the sub's engines, he moved them forward and through the lock as soon as it was open. "Godspeed," Doc called over the radio. "Everyone sends their love. No more transmissions until we call you."

"Good luck," Terry replied, and Katrina turned off the transmitter, then Terry turned on the rear passenger area PA. "We're away," he said. "Everyone sent their love to us. We'll be fine." Despite his words and the sound of the sub's various systems, he could hear crying from the rear. He swallowed back his own fear for his mother, Doc, and everyone else.

Outside a pair of bottlenoses shot into view and circled the submarine, while a single orca appeared; the big male named Byk.

"*Who in tin fish?*" Byk asked over the hydrophone.

"Terry," he replied. "Did my mom tell you what's happening?"

"*Yes, she tell,*" he replied. "*Pod going to machine. We meet. Lead you.*"

"Thanks," he said. Outside, the big orca took up a position in front of them as he matched course and speed. The two bottlenoses raced ahead to scout.

They sailed on, and Templemer's lights were quickly swallowed by the dark ocean depths. The sub continued on, slowly descending toward the extinct volcano where they'd found the excavator. Terry took out the slip of paper with the frequency Doc had given him and typed it into the radio. The frequency was active, and multiplexed with a video feed as well. A screen came alive with an image inside the dome.

"Maybe we should go back?" Katrina said.

Terry was thinking about what to say when he saw movement— Xiq'tal shapes were on the outside of the dome, although the distance made them appear tiny. There was a flash, and the dome he'd thought of as invulnerable cracked. A huge chunk exploded inward, leading a tidal wave of water. In an instant, the camera was hit and knocked out. Templemer was destroyed.

* * * * *

Chapter Twelve

Volcanic Valley, Planet Hoarfrost, Lupasha System, Coro Region, Tolo Arm

May 11th, 2038

The conditions inside the modified extractor were unchanged since Terry and Katrina had last visited it. Doc and his team had explored it afterward, but nothing more had been done. Terry numbly piloted the submarine to the site then docked at the same lock he'd come through before. He sat in his seat for long minutes, trying to decide how to explain what he'd seen to his passengers, only to find out they already knew. The monitor in the cargo area had faithfully shown the same images.

Eventually one of the adults came forward and asked if it was okay to open the lock. Terry forced himself to concentrate on the responsibility he'd taken on, and went aft to verify it was safe. It was, and he equalized the sub's pressure with the extractor's before opening the heavy submarine door.

First, heaters were moved in to warm the frigid interior. Then portable cots were moved into the larger interior spaces of the extractor, and living spaces were set up. The adults took charge of the kids, leaving Terry to battle his own personal demons.

Doc was dead, his mom was dead, all the doctors and researchers of the institute were dead. He was alone with the younger children and a handful of adults who weren't part of the institute's personnel. There was nowhere to go, and no chance of rescue. In short, they were dead once the food ran out.

The submarine would provide air and water for months, thanks to its small fusion reactor. It took Katrina's level-headedness to remind him they were in an ocean full of fish, and the cetaceans could provide them all they needed, so they could survive for quite some time. He was embarrassed that Katrina seemed to be dealing with it better than he did, so he'd asked her how she was doing so well.

"I'm just not thinking about it right now," she'd admitted. "Survive first, think later." That was the right way to think, so he did his best to emulate her.

Somehow he managed to get to sleep. When morning came, he felt no less heartbroken, but he had more resolve. Survive first, think later.

"Kray, are you out there?" he called to the orca.

"*Kray here. Pod here.*"

"We think the habitat was destroyed," he told the orca leader.

"*We know,*" he replied.

"How?"

"*We hear long way,*" the orca explained.

Terry nodded. The cetaceans had sonar sending and hearing; the dome's implosion had probably been detectable for a hundred kilometers. "Can you have the bottlenoses scout?"

"*Already look. Full water. Big crabs. Strange things there.*"

Terry sighed. Katrina was sitting next to him, back in the sub, so they could talk with the orcas. Kray swam into view, looking at him with a big eye. "What kind of strange things?" he asked the orca leader.

"*Like Wardens. Bigger. Breathe water.*"

"Selroth," Terry said.

"*They bad?*" Kray asked.

"They and the crabs killed all our people," Terry said bitterly.

"*Then we kill,*" Kray said.

"No!" Terry said.

"*Selroth kill Wardens. Crabs kill Wardens. Pod kill them.*"

"I wish you could," Terry said. "We all do. But Selroth and crabs have weapons that can kill you."

"*Some. We kill more them.*"

"How do I explain this so they don't get themselves killed?" he asked Katrina.

"We need you," Katrina said. "We need you to get food and protect us."

"*Young Wardens need stay safe?*"

"Yes," Terry said, pouncing on Katrina's brilliant idea. "If you go to fight, the Selroth or crabs may find us and kill us, too."

"*We protect now, kill later.*"

"Thank you," Terry said.

"*Need fish?*"

"We have enough food now. Please ask Sunrise Pod to watch for enemies nearby."

"*Kill them?*"

"If they come near here, yes."

"Terry!" Katrina said. "Without a chance to talk?"

"They killed everyone, and didn't give *us* a chance to talk," Terry said sternly. "Your mom and dad are dead. My mom is dead. Everyone is *dead*." She looked away. He felt a little bad for being so rough on her, but his feelings of loss were slowly changing to anger. The idea of taking the sub with the orcas and killing every single alien sounded pretty damned good. But what about everyone else? They had the one sub. Either the Selroth or Xiq'tal would find them and kill them, too, or they'd slowly starve.

No, he had to stay and help take care of them. Doc had said something once. "As long as you're alive, there are always options." Maybe he'd come across a way to even the score. Later.

"*We watch. Selroth, crab come, we kill.*"

"Thank you, Kray."

The big orca swam away to tell the others, and left Terry to decide what to do next.

His other friends and the adults organized and began to bring order to their meager living space. While the inside of the extractor was larger than the sub, it wasn't spacious. As kids do, the younger ones began to explore and found a pair of bathrooms. They were the Selroth style, the same ones they'd found when first occupying Templemer, but they were usable. Sanitation would have been a problem if they only had the one tiny toilet in the sub. It was one more thing off their plate.

The adult women with them took the kids under their care, freeing Terry and his friends to work on other problems as best they could. Many of the children were despondent, especially the ones old enough to fully understand what had happened. The ones older than five and younger than ten were the ones who didn't fully grasp their parents were dead, and thus running around exploring.

It was late in the afternoon when one of them came back, reporting they'd found a door that wouldn't open. Terry hadn't asked them not to explore; they needed something to keep their minds off what had happened at Templemer. However, he had told them, under no circumstance, should they open a locked door.

"Show me where it is?" he asked the young boy, who nodded. "I'll be right back," Terry told Katrina, who'd become his co-leader for the group of survivors. She nodded, and he followed the eager young boy.

He'd found an access everyone else had missed; a door that appeared to be a panel cover. When pulled, it opened like a door to reveal a ladderway. "Wow," he said, "good job!"

"Thanks," the boy said and set off down the ladder. Terry fell in close behind.

They traveled downward further than Terry had expected. After a minute be began to wonder how far they were going, and if the boy was playing a prank on him. Then they reached the bottom.

The ladder emerged into a circular chamber that looked like it had once contained piping or hydraulic equipment; he couldn't be sure which. A single door was set into the floor, a pressure-type with a circular handle and glass gauge. Terry knelt next to the door and examined the gauge. It showed more pressure on the other side than in the chamber.

It was a damned good thing the boy hadn't tried to work the lock himself, as it swung inward. He couldn't tell the pressure difference, but even a few PSI would be enough to explosively launch the boy across the chamber, and flood it in seconds, perhaps endangering everyone above them, as well.

"Good job," he told him. "Try to find something to put a warning on the door above us, okay?"

"You bet, Terry!" the boy said and set off back up the ladder.

Terry spent a few more minutes examining the chamber, wondering what it might be for, and what it used to do. Looking closer at the door, he noticed electronic connections, so he took out his slate and checked for wireless connectivity. He found it.

"Well, okay," he said. "Let's see what we can see."

He allowed the slate to link and opened protocol to receive data, and instantly a huge file began loading. A *really* huge file. "Woah," Terry said, and activated the slate's protective program. A second later he recognized the type of file; the same strange 3D structure he'd downloaded before from an extractor.

He quarantined it and allowed the file to complete downloading, then began examining the communication protocol attached to the connection. It was all inbound to the extractor's computer link; nothing was outbound. To top it off, his slate tagged the new program as hostile. Whatever was on the other side of the pressure door had just tried to take over his slate.

Terry rejoined Katrina and the others in the overcrowded living area they'd made. He quickly confirmed all the kids were back, and none of the others had found anything like the area he'd been investigating. Next he explained what he'd found to Katrina.

"Do you think it's a Selroth thing?" she wondered.

"No," he said. "The Selroth program was supposed to make this extractor set up a storage location for them to get the minerals later.

This is different." He scratched his chin and shook his head. "It's almost as if something else has taken control of it."

He took his slate out again and linked with the extractor's computer. He had to be careful now, knowing hostile programs were buzzing around. At least the dangerous ones were all extremely large, so he set his slate's buffers to the slowest setting. That should keep an attack from easily succeeding.

Working for a minute, he found the extractor's subprogram which controlled storage. It showed a small amount of minerals. There should have been hundreds of tons. Had someone else found the cache and taken it out from under the Selroth's noses? It didn't seem likely. Then what was happening?

"Terry?"

"Yeah, Katrina?" he replied on the headset radio.

"Trouble. You better come."

* * *

Terry arrived back at the living area less than a minute after her call. She had a little slate from the submarine and was huddled with the other seniors. It's Tri-V was showing camera views from the submarine, part of the sub's hull and dark water.

"What's going on?" he asked.

"Watch," Dan said.

A second later there was a bright strobe-like flash, then another. Suddenly a bottlenose came racing toward the camera at breakneck speed. It was Wikiwiki. In moments she was within hydrophone range.

"Terry, Terry! Crabs!"

"Calm down, Wikiwiki," he said. "Tell me what happened?"

"Chaw spot crabs. We watch, like you say. Then looking. One come this way. Chaw kill. CRUNCH! Taste funny."

"Jesus, did they eat the alien?" Taiki asked.

Terry shrugged. "Maybe. What are those flashes?"

"More crab. Look."

To Terry's astonishment, the slate began to receive an image file. There was little doubt he was seeing the POV of a bottlenose dolphin swimming at incredible speed through the water. Suddenly it turned and crashed into a Xiq'tal. The crab's carapace shattered, and a cloud of blue blood flowed out into the dolphin's headlamps. It looked to the side, and another dolphin was trying to evade a second crab. The alien had a harness welded to its back with weapons and propulsion. A bright beam of light lanced out and pierced the dolphin, who jerked and stopped swimming.

"How are you showing me this?" he asked. The bottlenoses' harnesses only had rebreathers and lights. There were no cameras.

"*Think save,*" Wikiwiki said.

"Who was hit?" Katrina asked.

"*Chaw,*" she replied. "*Chaw dead.*"

"*Terry.*" The hydrophone relayed the sound of Kray's distinct voice. "*We drop rocks. We shoot sonar. Not get close, or light burn.*"

"It's called a laser," Terry explained. "Stay out of range. Be careful, they probably have other weapons that can hurt from a distance."

"Shot metal fish at me," Wikiwiki said.

"Torpedo," Colin suggested.

Terry nodded, then pressed the mute. "I don't know what to tell them to do," he admitted.

"They want to fight," Taiki said. "Let them."

"It wouldn't be fair," Katrina said, shaking her head. "They don't know how weapons work. They'll get killed."

"She's right," Dan agreed. "You remember the video Doc showed us in MST? The aliens have been doing this a *very* long time. They're good at it."

"I'm also more than a little worried about the feed Wikiwiki sent," Terry said.

"Why?" Katrina asked.

"It was a pinplant recording. They've never done that before, and we had no idea they'd figured it out."

"That's good, right?" Katrina asked. "I mean, they're understanding how they work."

"But why haven't they been telling us about it? Dr. Orsage has been carefully keeping tabs on them and their pinplants. He does routine downloads all the time, to make sure they're not having problems." *Though he said he's mostly watching the orcas because the bottlenose weren't showing any unusual traits like the orcas had,* he thought. *Now I can't ask him what this means, because he's dead.*

Terry shook his head. Too many things going on all at once. He was only 13 years old, he couldn't be responsible for all of this. He gave a little sigh. *I miss mom.*

"*Terry want us kill?*" Kray asked.

On the screen an orca swam into view. It was Ki'i, the former leader of the Wandering Pod before the two pods merged. The big male orca had half a dismembered Xiq'tal in his mouth and was flipping it around as he swam, casually crushing the alien's armored shell. *Damn*, he thought, *they don't care that this is life or death*.

Doc had said, "I've found when it comes to life, you either stand, or you fall." He didn't have the luxury to fall. Too many were depending on him. "They're coming here," Terry said. "They must be. They might not know the exact location, but they know the area."

"What do we do?" Katrina asked.

"We need to go somewhere they can't find us."

"Where?" Dan asked.

"Yeah, where can we go that they can't find us?" Colin asked.

Terry unmuted the hydrophone. "Kray?"

"*What Terry want?*"

"Can you lead the crabs away? Lure them?"

"*Not kill?*"

"No," he repeated. "Just give us time."

"*We do. We do.*"

"Okay," he said to his friends. "We'd better hurry. Get your drysuits from the sub; I need some other stuff, too." The others looked at each other, then got up to follow him. "I think we might have an option."

* * *

"Where does this go?" Katrina asked, examining the hatch.

"I have no clue," Terry said above. He was busy setting the emergency pressure door into the ladderway above the hatch, part of the equipment in the submarine Honcho had mentioned off hand during his quick lesson.

Basically an inflatable ring with powerful adhesives and a double zipper similar to a spacesuit, it was meant to create an airlock to facilitate evacuation or boarding of a damaged submarine. Honcho had said he wouldn't need it, but it had turned out he was wrong.

It took Terry a few minutes to figure it out; luckily, there were instructions in the duffel holding it, and he also found a demonstration video on his slate. Once he understood the principle, the rest was easy.

"Have you got the relief valve in yet?" he asked them.

"Almost," Colin said. He and Dan were both holding the drill, while Taiki made sure it stayed on point. Part of the emergency pressure door, it was a drill with a pressure-relieving valve and pump attached. Once the hatch was in place, you'd drill the valve into an existing door to equalize pressure.

Terry was gambling that the higher pressure on the other side didn't mean it was underwater. He was hoping it led to a lower area of the extractor, somewhere the alien mercs couldn't easily follow them. Naturally a lower area would be under higher pressure. The strange computer files seemed to originate down there, too, so his escape plan could also possibly provide some answers.

There was a pinging sound from the drill, and it suddenly stopped. They all looked at the mechanism in alarm until Colin examined its simple controls.

"We're good," he said. "It's installed." He attached the little manifold that came in the kit, and they finally got a look at the pressure differential between their side and the other. "Difference is only 44 KPa, and no water."

"Rebreathers," Terry said, and they pulled their drysuit hoods on and activated rebreathers. "Let's equalize and see what's on the other side."

Because the tap Colin installed was small, it took several minutes to equalize their side's pressure with the other. Finally the pressure glass showed green, so it was safe to open the pressure door.

"You sure about this?" Katrina asked.

"No," Terry admitted and spun the wheel on the door. It gave a clank, and he heaved it up and open. The hatch contained springs, so the weight wasn't as much as he expected.

As soon as it was open, he stepped back and stuck a hand into the bag he'd slung over his drysuit-covered shoulder. The grip of the laser pistol Honcho had given him felt reassuring, though nothing came out of the hatch after them. He'd already decided to go down, regardless of what came out. He removed the holstered pistol and clipped it onto his belt.

"A laser pistol!" Dan said.

"Perceptive," Terry said.

"Where did you get it?" Katrina asked.

"Doc gave it to me just before we left Templemer."

"Why?" Taiki asked.

Terry made an expansive gesture. "Are you serious?" He leaned over the open hatch, shining his helmet light down inside. A seamless tunnel went down for a meter, then gave way to rough-hewn stone. The extractor was connected to the extinct volcano, however there was no way to get down.

"No ladder," Katrina said, echoing his thoughts.

"How much rope do we have?" he asked them. Between the five of them, they had a total of 30 meters. It was quickly tied together and secured. "I'm going down," he said and cinched the bag tighter.

"But you don't know what's down there," Katrina said, her eyes wide behind her mask.

"I know what's outside waiting for us," he said. He didn't want to come out and say he was desperate, but he was. Even if they all climbed back into the sub and headed out, the Selroth and Xiq'tal had the advantage; they were armed and in their element. Whatever was below might at least provide a place to hide for a while. Time gave them options.

Terry had gone mountain climbing a few times on Molokai, so he knew how to rappel, but now he didn't have the proper climbing gear. He was forced to improvise, wrapping the line around an arm and his cybernetic leg, then using his real leg to control the descent. After the first five meters, he was glad Hoarfrost's gravity was less than Earth's.

The tunnel only went another meter before he reached the bottom. He was glad, too. All the swimming he'd been doing to get back in shape after months in a coma was paying off, but his arms were still getting tired.

Setting foot on the ground, he panned the helmet lamps around. The space looked like a partially-collapsed lava tube. He'd seen plenty of those in Hawaii, as well. He also noted in his heads-up display that the air temperate was up 13 degrees. Still below freezing, but a noticeable increase. *Looks like this volcano isn't extinct after all,* he thought.

Terry played the rope out and continued to examine the space. One direction went only a couple meters and ended in crumbled rock. The other direction angled downward and continued. He looked up and examined the tunnel he'd come down. It was rough, yet still looked purposeful.

"There's a tunnel down here," he said over the radio. "I'm going to follow it and see where it goes."

"You're breaking up a bit," Colin said. "I got you, be careful."

"Roger that," he said and set out.

He detached one of the lamps from his helmet so he could use it separately. There was a lot of crumbled rock on the ground, and the floor itself was cracked in places, making for treacherous footing. His cybernetic leg made things a little more challenging, too.

The tunnel went for 20 or 30 meters, then it suddenly opened up into a wide low-ceilinged chamber that his lights couldn't illuminate the far side of. It had the look of a volcanic lava-formed cave, like many in Hawaii. He also smelled seawater.

Terry spent a few minutes playing his lights around, examining the cave. It was fairly featureless, with a sandy floor and a few scattered rocks, the biggest the size of a trashcan. After a few minutes he found the source of the seawater odor, a large pool that took up half the cave. He moved closer and investigated the pool. It was deep enough to swallow his light.

He stood and looked around. The chamber ended at the other side of the pool, the roof slanting down until it met the floor. End of the road. However, as he walked back around the pool, he realized there was ample space in the room. He used the flashlight again in the water and saw movement. Checking his watch, he saw he'd only been gone a few minutes. "Might as well check it out," he said.

Since he was already wearing his drysuit to stay warm in the cavern, all he needed to do was properly seal the helmet and verify the gloves and boots were also sealed. Flipping the rebreather on, he set his bag aside, sat on the edge of the pool, and slid in.

He felt the cold through the neoprene material of the suit stinging his skin. Instantly, the drysuit's heater kicked into high gear, the extra hot air flow making the suit billow out from his skin slightly and alleviating the cold's bite to some degree. He waited while the heater caught up, then submerged.

He kept one of the lamps in his hand as he dove down and examined underwater. He set his suit's buoyancy for a slight negative and slowly sank into the dark water. After only a few meters, he realized the pool was actually an extension of the lava tube he'd been in all along. Small native fish swam around him, their feelers occasionally contacting his suit, causing them to race away from the strange contact.

If there's fish, there must be an exit, he thought. Or was it a huge independent ecosystem? It seemed an unlikely probability, but it was an alien world, so who knew? It widened out the deeper he went, and soon he couldn't see the sides any more. The suit's heads-up display said the temperature was dropping. Another few meters, and he felt a slight current tug at his feet.

He set his buoyancy to neutral and swam around. A larger fish raced past from side to side, confirming what he'd thought. *I'm outside.* The pool above was a moon pool like the one in Templemer, which explained the higher pressure; it was holding the water back from flooding the chamber. He reached a hand up and activated the suit's hydrophone.

"This is Terry, can any orca or bottlenose hear me?" He added a couple of low-frequency calls, knowing the sound range carried better in water. He didn't know whether the Selroth or Xiq'tal communicated with ultrasonic underwater clicks. With his reception volume all the way up, he waited.

He heard a series of clicks on his hydrophone, then several more. He repeated his call until he heard a reply.

"*Terry, Terry,*" came the bottlenose's voice over the hydrophone. "*Where you?*"

"Can you follow my voice?"

"*Keep talk, try find.*"

Terry did as he was asked, and kept up a monologue. A minute later a bottlenose shot into view, arced around him, and came to a stop. He reached out and stroked the dolphin's side. "Hi, Wikiwiki. Are you okay?"

"*Wikiwiki good. Fun mess with crabs!*"

"Has anyone else been hurt?"

"*No more hurt. You say we tease, we tease.*"

"Good." He pointed up into the lava tube. "We're going to move everyone up there. If you follow the tube up, you'll find a big pool and a cave. It'll be safe for a while when they find our submarine. Understand?" Wikiwiki's head bobbed up and down. "Good, go tell your pod and the orcas."

"*Wikiwiki tell pod and Dark Killers,*" she said. "*Bye!*" She shot off into the darkness and was gone. It was a little disconcerting how they often didn't bother with their harness lights. He guessed they weren't important when you had built-in sonar. With confidence Wikiwiki would lead the others back, Terry headed back to the lava tube, and ultimately to the others.

* * * * *

Chapter Thirteen

Volcanic Lava Tubes, Planet Hoarfrost, Lupasha System, Coro Region, Tolo Arm
May 13th, 2038

It took six hours of hard work to move everyone and all the equipment down the tunnel and into the pool cavern. Colin and Dan ended up using tools from the sub to fix metal pipes into the tunnel wall, allowing everyone to move up and down much quicker. Still, it was a slow process.

Terry had expected difficulty convincing the adults to come down. He needn't have worried. They were too despondent to disagree, merely concerned their children were as safe as possible. They couldn't argue with Terry and his friends, anyway; the caverns down the lava tubes would be safer.

Halfway through the move, the first orcas showed up in the pool and examined the new location. They used their sonar and harness lights to look around, then left to give others a turn. The pool was large enough for several orcas at a time to float there, or most of the bottlenoses.

Having the dolphins hanging out in the pool helped the younger children feel better, and when lights were brought down and turned on, the bright colors and intricate stalagmite formations helped more. Then they got to watch Terry and his friends feed an extremely hungry Pōkole. All in all, with temporary cots and the lights, the entire situation took on the feel of a camping trip to the kids.

"So now what?" Katrina asked after they'd fed Pōkole, while Terry checked the tiny autochef they used to make their own food and the milk for the calf.

"We wait and see what develops," Terry said. "We have about five days of food, then we're limited to what the cetaceans can bring us."

"The power won't last much longer," Dan pointed out, "unless we run a line from the sub's fusion plant."

"No," Terry said. "We stay isolated to be safe."

Before they'd closed and locked the hatch into the tubes, they'd set a simple radio tripwire in the sub. If it went offline or someone broke in or destroyed the sub, the vehicle's computer would send a radio pulse letting them know. Terry decided in five days' time, they'd consider going back out for a look.

"I'm out of my element," he admitted to the other seniors.

"We all are," Taiki said. The others nodded in agreement.

"All we can do is our best," Katrina said.

"Thanks to you, we're still alive," Dan said.

So, they waited.

They kept their normal day/night cycle. Keeping things normal helped everyone, and turning off most of the lights conserved energy. The cavern didn't take much to keep it warm, as the geothermal heat radiating from the floor helped.

When Terry woke the second morning, he found Skritch and Wikiwiki in the pool talking to a solitary orca. He climbed out of his bedroll and stretched. Nobody else was awake yet. He checked his watch and decided it was close enough to morning, so he quietly walked over to the pool.

"What's going on?" he asked. The orca was Maka, a female from the former Wandering Pod. Next to Pōkole, she was the smallest of the orcas, and their equivalent of a late teenager. Even so, she was huge next to the bottlenoses.

"Maka think Wardens move now," the orca said.

"You think we should move? Why, are the aliens near?"

"No crabs, no funny things," Skritch assured him.

"Then why should we move?"

"More space, good heat," Maka said.

Terry scratched his head as he tried to understand. The orcas understood that Humans needed warmth to survive. It was a little difficult for them to grasp *why* cold was a problem, as they had evolved to live in arctic cold with ease.

"No, no," Wikiwiki said. *"Too far."*

"Maka, did you find another cave?"

"Not like here," Maka said, rolling on her side and looking at the cavern. *"Like other place."*

"Like Templemer?"

"Not like, some different," Skritch said.

"When did you find this?"

"After you show us here," Wikiwiki said.

Damn it, Terry thought. They're naturals at keeping things to themselves. "Where is this? How far away?"

"Short swim us," Maka said. *"Long swim you."*

Terry looked back at the others. Nobody was awake yet. He decided. "Take me there."

He was forced to mostly swim after he'd donned his drysuit and slipped into the water. The bottlenoses weren't strong enough to tow a Human far, and Maka was unfamiliar with the process. The researchers always cautioned him about being towed by an orca unaccustomed to the process, as it was extremely easy for them to injure him.

After a few minutes of swimming, he began to wish he had his minisub again. With it he could keep up with the orcas, if not the bottlenoses. Then Moloko and Pōkole appeared out of the dark.

"*Terr!*" Pōkole said and nuzzled his head against Terry.

"Hi Pōkole, hi Moloko."

"*What Terry do?*" Moloko asked.

He explained what Maka and the two bottlenoses had said.

"*Yes, strange place.*"

"From now on, when you find something, tell me?"

"*We would,*" Moloko said. "*Kray now look.*"

Terry decided not to push the issue. Explaining what was likely a minor point of timing to beings who didn't understand time was inherently difficult. "Can Pōkole tow me?" he asked the calf.

"*Yes, yes!*" Pōkole said excitedly and rolled to offer Terry his dorsal fin. He gratefully grabbed on and was instantly racing through the water, being escorted by orcas and dolphins.

They took him down the lava tube toward the outside, then turned. He expected the wall to appear at any second. It didn't. Instead they angled upward again. The dark water and strange turns had him disoriented, but he was pretty sure they were moving higher than the pool he'd just left behind. He was so busy thinking about such things that he didn't immediately see the light.

"What?" he said, looking up at the growing light. For a second, he panicked, afraid they were taking him to the surface. If they did so, he'd die a horrible death, the compressed nitrogen in his bloodstream forming fatal bubbles and causing strokes. But there was no way they could have traveled the two kilometers to the surface, the light was the wrong color, too.

Then suddenly he was on the surface, Pōkole stopping next to him. Terry gawked. He was inside a geodesic dome carved from volcanic rock. He bobbed for at least a minute, his head turning every which way as he took in the surroundings. Intermittent glowing light fixtures provided dim if sufficient illumination. The color spectrum was bluish.

The pool he floated in was huge—at least a hundred meters across—and roughly circular. The floor of the dome was paved in a similar manner to the geometric shapes above in the dome. In addition, several small domed structures were scattered seemingly at random around the space. There was no doubt, this was a purposeful structure. It was also obviously not Human, and quite warm outside the water.

"*See, see?*" Maka said, her dorsal fin skimming past a few meters away. Pōkole was enjoying himself by performing jumps out of the water, making massive splashes. Clearly he was enjoying the surface of a larger body of water. Having been born on a spaceship, this was a new experience for him.

Terry swam over to the nearest edge and found the floor of the pool gently rising up to meet him several meters from the edge. He swam until he was only waist deep, then stood to walk out of the water. His suit began to quickly decrease heat output, and the heads-up said the temperature was 19 degrees; comfortable. Standing on dry land, he removed his helmet and gloves. The air felt nice. Even a slight breeze brushed his cheek.

"There's power," he realized, looking up again at the lights, then at the domes/buildings, which all sported a light or two as well. "Where's the power coming from?" he wondered.

Terry checked his laser pistol to be sure it still worked after being submerged. Doc had said the weapons would work in any environment, but he still checked that the power indicator was green, then reholstered the weapon. Nothing about the dome suggested anyone lived in it. Regardless, the hair on the back of his neck kept wanting to stand up.

He walked around the perimeter of the moon pool and found himself examining the roof again. What he'd thought were geometric cuts in the rock structure now looked more like steel panels. Some had lights, some didn't. The ones without lights reminded him of something. The memory was tantalizingly just beyond his reach. He walked toward the closest building.

"*What us do?*" Maka asked. Pōkole pulled off a full 360 degree backflip in the center of the pool, bouncing off Maka's peduncle. Maka pushed him aside gently with her much bigger fluke.

"Can you wait here, please?" Terry asked.

"*We wait Terry*," Maka agreed.

"*Wait, wait!*" Pōkole called and dove deep to jump again.

"Thanks," Terry said and continued on.

The first building he came to was one of the smallest, maybe five meters tall and about ten across. It was also the closest to the moon pool. It reminded him of a doghouse style common back on Earth—an igloo for a dog. After he'd walked all the way around, he realized there was no door. He skirted the outside a second time, just to be sure he hadn't missed it.

"Well, that's strange," he said. His voice echoed slightly until Pōkole crashed back into the moon pool. He glanced back toward them to be sure everything was okay, then reached out and touched the building. It felt cool to the touch, maybe five degrees lower than the air temperature. He couldn't decide if it was stone or metal; the finish was strange. Slightly discouraged, he moved on to the next building.

After a while, he took out his slate and began making notes on the buildings and dome layout. He circled two more buildings and found no entrances to them, either. Not even a window or a pipe. He wondered what they were. Certainly not buildings, if they didn't have any way to get in or out.

He leaned his slate against a triangular section of the geodesic dome, only to have it and several more slide away and send his slate tumbling inside.

"Holy crap!" be barked, and backpedaled, tripping over his own feet and landing hard on his butt. "Oof!" He sat and gawked, his weapon completely forgotten. As he watched, the interior of the dome lit up.

Slowly he got to his feet and cautiously stuck his head inside. He found a series of large machines clustered around the room's center. They were of various heights, with one attached to the roof. Low intensity lights were fixed around the highest part of the room. He bent and retrieved his slate before walking up to the closest machine. As he came close, a screen came alive on its side, slightly lower than he would find easy to read.

Bending over, he examined the display. It was immediately recognizable to him as a power system. He'd seen them on the *Teddy Roosevelt* during visits to her engine room. He was standing next to a fusion reactor and its associated power generation/distribution systems. However, he couldn't read the language.

Terry moved his slate so its pickups could see the display. Centering it, he activated the machine translation feature. For such a powerful computer, it took an inordinate amount of time to find a translation matrix. As it began to display in English, he saw untranslated segments. He'd never seen a result of the sort before. A translation either worked, or it didn't. This was especially true with mechanical and technological devices.

After examining the various readings for a moment, he went into the slate's translation program and inquired what language the machines were using. "*Kahraman*" was the answer.

"Never heard of them," he said and shrugged. He'd read up on them later, and maybe find out why there was an incomplete translation matrix. He could see the power generator was operating on minimum, though he couldn't see how much fuel it had, or its F11 condition. It could be there, but he didn't know how to find it. One of the displays read "Thermal Tap." He wondered if that was like geothermal power? Maybe the base was running off lava under the core.

"Is this what the Selroth are looking for?" he wondered. It was clearly an old base built into a volcano. Even rich and powerful alien races wouldn't go to these sorts of extremes, building a base kilometers under the ice on a remote moon, unless they had a plan. From what he knew about the Izlians, it didn't look like something they'd build, either.

Terry went around looking at the various machines, mostly guessing at their functions, before walking back out the entrance. The triangular sections of the dome's wall that had moved to make a door returned silently to their original position, creating a seamless wall once more. He leaned in closely to examine the sections that made up the doorway and eventually found what distinguished them from all the other sections. One triangular section had a nearly invisible green outline, and it was the one he'd leaned his slate against.

He touched the section, and the door instantly opened again. Out of curiosity, he went inside the dome and found where it folded against the inside. He touched it, and the door closed. "Yes," he said. Another touch of the trigger from the inside, and the door quickly folded open.

Armed with the knowledge, he returned to the first dome and searched for a green outlined section. When he found it, he opened the door and looked inside. It looked like a series of water or air pumps and other such equipment. Since his suit said the pressure was higher in the dome, that only made sense.

He went to the other buildings, looking inside and making notes in his slate. The more he scrutinized, the surer he was that the dome was a serious installation, and it had been empty for an extremely long time. Then he opened a building and stood in shock.

"Those have to be weapons," Terry said. The dome was lower and squatter than all the others, shaped more like a hotdog bun than a regular dome. Inside was a large machine, and racks upon racks of weapons. After seeing pictures of various guns during MST back on Molokai, he was certain. In addition, they were like the guns Doc had talked about. They were unconfigured.

He examined the machine in the center, which, like the power-plant, came alive as soon as he walked up to it. Since his slate was already configured for the strange Kahraman language, he held up the computer and examined the display. "Manufactory Ready."

"Holy shit," he said, walking along the racks of weapons. They were stored in groupings by type, though he couldn't tell what type many of them were. Another rack had stacks of plates. He picked one up and examined it. The material was semi rigid and as light as plastic. The only markings were the Union common numbers in what he guessed was a part or serial number. He had no idea what they might be for.

The door closed behind him as he left and moved to another building. Once inside, he found six blocky structures mounted to the floor, and one hanging from the ceiling, which ended at the height of all the screens on other machines he'd seen. Like the other machines, it came alive as soon as he walked up to it. He used his slate to translate. "Computing and Communications."

"Now we're talking," he said and linked his slate with the controller. Immediately a data packet began to flood in, and it was the strange 3D data. He let out an awkward squeak and quickly made sure it wasn't going straight into open memory. It wasn't, thankfully. He knew from experience that it was too complicated to do anything with, so he ignored it and tried to examine the systems. They were far more complicated than anything he'd ever seen before.

"Whoever created the 3D programming obviously wrote this OS, too," he said after a few minutes. He couldn't get past the operating system to the core controls of the computer, so he settled for seeing what kind of systems the computer was overseeing. It only took a minute to realize the big blocky machines were core memory modules. Unbelievable *huge* ones.

"What could possibly need this much space?" he wondered. Then he remembered how massive the 3D data packets were. If the entire system had been written with it, they must consume hundreds of exabytes. Maybe thousands of exabytes, which would be zettabytes.

The idea of the system needing zettabytes of space to store the strange data went out the window. There was simply no way. As he understood, the entire GalNet was only one or two zettabytes. Maybe if you added all the associated data, you'd maybe double the total. Maybe. Then he found out how to access the communications system. He used it to access the frequencies he and his friends had been using.

"Anyone out there?"

"Terry?" Katrina answered immediately. "Where are you? When we woke up, you were gone!" She sounded almost frantic.

"I'm fine," he explained. "The cetaceans found another cavern. It's artificial, a base of some kind. I'll send Wikiwiki to come get you, and you can see for yourself."

* * * * *

Chapter Fourteen

Kahraman Base, Planet Hoarfrost, Lupasha System, Coro Region, Tolo Arm

May 14th, 2038

Terry woke up and yawned. The ever-present low-level of illumination in the Kahraman base wasn't enough to make sleeping difficult. There'd always been more light on the *Teddy Roosevelt* than he had to deal with now.

When his friends arrived, they'd spent a couple of hours walking around and gawking at the structures. Everyone had been amazed that Terry had figured out how to get into the buildings, then he'd explained he'd done so by accident, and they'd enjoyed a good laugh.

"Do you think this is what the Selroth are looking for?" Taiki asked.

"I was thinking the same thing," Terry said. "The answer is, I don't know."

They still hadn't explored all the buildings when they needed to go back and check on the kids and adults. It was a good thing they had, because when they got there, some of the middle school-aged kids were arguing with the adult women about going back up the hatch and to the submarine. They thought maybe Templemer was still there. Of course, it wasn't.

Terry and his friends calmed the situation down, explaining that they'd found a better place to stay and they'd work out how to get everyone there. Of course, getting them there was the problem. One of the adults had been so shaken by the argument, she was afraid she'd gone into labor, which nearly caused Terry to panic.

Luckily Katrina knew more about such things. She verified in short order that it wasn't actual labor. The woman wasn't due for another two months. Then, while the labor drama was going on, several of the younger kids decided to go exploring. Dan and Colin went to go bring them back. By this time, Terry decided he couldn't leave the rest of them alone, and it was late.

The adults were in no condition to take charge (which was obviously why Doc had put him in charge in the first place.) Two of the women just sat and stared at the walls in shock. They could barely care for own their children, to the point that two of the other mothers did so for them. The last two were quite pregnant and needed to rest. Added to this, the kids were becoming unruly.

Terry left Taiki in charge while Katrina, Dan, Colin, and he returned to the Kahraman base to explore, then spend the night. Taiki wasn't happy, but Terry didn't care. Back at the base, he had the bottlenoses do a check outside. They came back an hour later confirming the Xiq'tal were still searching the area, though it didn't appear they'd found the sub.

They'd bedded down in the open, not far from the armory he'd found. He didn't want to sleep in the buildings yet. Simply put, he didn't trust them. Better to be able to make a run for the moon pool if something weird happened while they slept. He got out of the simple sleeping roll he'd brought and checked on the others. Colin and Dan were still asleep, but Katrina was standing near a building looking at its wall.

"What's going on?" he asked.

She looked up and grinned when she saw him, giving him a patented wink. "Come over here; you might be interested in this."

"What?" he asked as he walked over. He couldn't see anything other than a wall.

"Just watch," she said and slipped her hand into his. She was warm and felt good.

He smiled from ear to ear. Then one of the triangular panels suddenly swung up, and a little animal skittered out. "Wow!" he said and jumped back. She hung on and kept him from retreating further.

"It's okay, take a closer look."

He'd thought it was a spider, but it wasn't alive. He could see mechanical components, and it had a pair of large multifaceted eyes, along with a single antenna. "What is it?"

"It's a robot," she said. "A lot more advanced than any I've ever seen before, even in the Union."

The machine skittered right toward them. Terry was about to move when it changed course, skirted around the two young people, then resumed its course. He took out his slate and snapped a digital image. With the picture, he ran a comparison in the GalNet.

"Multi-Environment Type 92 Service Bot," the slate informed him. "No longer in service. Last used during the Great Galactic War." The robot skittered out of view. Instead of following, he clicked to find out more about the war.

"The Great Galactic War between the Dusman and the coalition led by the Kahraman occurred more than 20,000 standard years ago. Involving all the major member races of the First Republic, the war lasted 322 years, and cost many trillions of sentient lives. After the mutual destruction of the Dusman and the Kahraman, the Peacemakers brought the remaining hostilities to an end and were instrumental in the formation of the Galactic Union, a government designed to make large-scale warfare impractical."

"Wow," Katrina said as she read over his shoulder. "Did you know about this?"

"No," he admitted. "I wonder if Doc was going to teach about it in MST later?" She shrugged. "Where'd the robot go?"

"Don't know," she said. "Another will be along. I've seen three so far."

"You know, this explains why everything's so clean."

"Yeah," she agreed. "I guess these Kahraman left the base, and the robots keep it running."

"The power system said it had something called a thermal tap. I think it gets power from the planet, and there's a fusion powerplant, too. This whole place is weird. Here, come into this room." Terry took her to the armory and watched her eyes bug out at all the guns and stuff. "And this is a manufactory."

"Woah," she said, running a hand along it. "It's a tiny one."

"Well, autochefs are a kind of manufactory. Since this one is here, it's probably designed to make weapons and stuff."

"So maybe this is an abandoned military base," she suggested.

"You know, that makes sense." He suddenly felt like someone was watching him. Maybe there were Kahraman around? He used his slate to find out what they looked like.

"No Data," it told him. Maybe it was data he'd never loaded. Also, the Kahraman were all gone, according to the GalNet. The Dusman and the Kahraman had exterminated each other. There were no pictures or details on the Dusman, either. All he cared was, they were gone, and that meant the base was theirs for the taking.

Colin and Dan were awake when they came out. Katrina explained about finding the little robots. One obliged by skittering by just as she'd finished her story. This time they followed it. The machine led them to a building near the center of the dome, where it went in though a tiny door. Terry walked around until he found a full-sized door and touched it. Nothing happened.

"This is the first time I couldn't get into one," he said and tried again. Nothing. All three of the others tried as well, with no luck.

"Maybe we can sneak through when the robot comes back out," Dan suggested.

"Pretty small hole," Colin said. "Taiki would fit."

"Dan, go back and relieve him, okay?" Dan frowned. "See if you can organize everyone to move. The bottlenoses said the aliens haven't found the sub yet, so go up and get all the drysuits and survival bubbles you can so we can prepare to move everyone here. Don't take long at the sub. We'll be back this afternoon to help."

"Okay," he said, though Terry could see he still wasn't happy about it.

"We might as well keep looking around while we wait for Taiki," Katrina suggested.

Consulting the map on his slate, Terry could see five buildings he hadn't investigated yet. One was the biggest by far, and he headed for it. "Keep an eye out for more robots," he told the others. "I don't exactly trust them."

"They're just robots," Katrina said.

Just robots, Terry thought. That didn't comfort him at all.

They reached the big building. Terry didn't have to look far for a door; one was already open. Like the portal that hadn't responded to him, this was another first. For some reason, he had a strange feeling, and he drew his laser pistol and peered carefully around the corner.

"You see something?" Colin whispered.

"No," he admitted. *I'm getting jumpy*, he thought and holstered the gun.

This was the first building he'd found that wasn't a big open structure. The door opened into a short hallway, and he could see doors on either side, and one at the end. All of them were also open, but no lights were on inside. The lights in the hall matched the same pattern as every other building, scattered and rather dim.

They walked into the building and slowly down the hall. They still had their drysuits on, so each took one of the flashlights from their helmets to see better. Katrina pointed hers at the ground.

"Look," she said. "Dust. The robots don't come in here."

"I wonder why?" Colin asked.

"They're afraid of the vampires," Terry said. Both looked at him, agog. "I was trying to be funny."

"Stop trying," Colin said.

"Yeah," Katrina agreed.

"Sorry."

Katrina narrowed her eyes at him, and he shrugged. She sighed and put her hand on the green spot, and the door opened for her. When the light from her flashlight fell inside and she saw what was there, she screamed.

Terry jerked the laser pistol from its holster and tried to move around Katrina. She was frozen in the middle of the doorway, gasping for breath. He managed to pull her sideways to reveal the threat. Skeletons.

"They're not Human," he said.

"I know," she said, turning and grabbing him around the neck. Hot tears fell on his face. "It's just, all this going on."

"It would have freaked me out too," he said, holstering the weapon. "If I'd opened the door, I probably would have shot the shit out of everything." She gave a coughing laugh.

"If you two are done smooching?" Colin asked.

"We're not smooching," Terry complained.

"Yes we are," Katrina said and kissed him. Colin groaned and rolled his eyes. "You came to my rescue!" she exclaimed. He shrugged. "That almost makes up for the vampire bit."

"Not in my book," Colin said.

"You want a kiss, too?" Terry asked.

Colin flipped him a rude gesture. "Can we see what's inside now?"

The room was maybe eight meters on a side, and a dozen or more skeletons were scattered about. There were six low pallets, which reminded Terry of Japanese-style beds. Two of the skeletons were lying on them, adding validity to the concept. He knew they weren't Human, because they possessed long necks, and almost alligator-type jaws, which came to a point and were full of sharp teeth.

"They weren't very big," Katrina noted, kneeling next to one on a pallet.

She was right; in life it had probably been no bigger than a large dog. Despite its size, its rear legs were longer, so it might have stood upright like Humans, and it was about a meter and a half tall. With so many teeth, he didn't think he'd want to meet a living one.

"I wonder if these were Kahraman," he said aloud. He took some pictures with his slate. It couldn't hurt.

"Why didn't the robots take the bodies away?" Colin asked. "They just left them here to rot."

"Gross," Katrina said.

The three moved around the room that Terry was thinking of as a bunkroom, examining the skeletons. He knelt down next to one that was lying over a pallet and saw a tiny angular hole in its head. He carefully moved the skull, which detached from the long neck, causing a few vertebrae to fall away and rattle to the floor. He found another hole roughly on the opposite side of the head.

"I think this one was shot in the head," Terry said.

"This one, too," Colin said across the room.

"Same here," Katrina noted.

They spent a minute going from skeleton to skeleton, verifying; they had all been shot in the head in an obvious scene of mass execution. In total, there were 14 skeletons. Other than the bones, the room was only rusty with some discolorations on the floor or pallets around the bodies. Terry guessed if they were Kahraman, they might have been killed 20,000 years ago. He wondered if the people who'd first gone into the Egyptian pyramids felt like he did.

"Let's see what's in the other rooms," Terry said.

They exited the bunkroom and crossed the narrow hall. Katrina touched the green space, and the door opened. Terry had a hand on his laser pistol, just in case. The room was the same size as the other, with three long tables less than a meter high. A machine took up half the length of one wall. Terry went over to the machine, and a display came alive on it. He used his slate to translate.

"Autochef Online—Nutrient Reserve Status—Low."

"Food, heat, safety," Terry said.

"Looks pretty good to me," Katrina agreed.

"Going to be tough getting the little kids down here," Colin said.

"Harder for the moms with little babies," Terry agreed. "As soon as Taiki gets back, we'll see if this will work."

"What about the last room?" Katrina asked, pointing back out to the hallway.

"Yeah, let's check it out," Colin agreed.

Terry shrugged and they approached the last door. He was mentally comparing the spaces they'd discovered so far in the building against its exterior size and guessed more than half was left. Katrina opened the door and verified his estimate. After finding a lunch room and a bunkhouse full of skeletons, he guessed he couldn't be surprised. He was wrong.

"What the hell?" Katrina said.

All three entered and looked at what they could see. Three cubical-style workstations were in front of them, and a line of clear tubes to either side. The tubes were full of water, and a creature was suspended in each one. Terry walked over to the nearest workstation, while his friends wandered over to look at the tubes.

Like every other machine he'd encountered so far, the workstation came alive. This one had a complicated wraparound Tri-V instead of a flat display, which made it much harder to translate through his slate. He had to hold the slate at just the right angle and distance, which took several tries.

"Codex Status—Standing By."

"Codex," he said aloud. "What does that mean?"

The submenus were no help either. "Codex correlation," "Biome Codex Indexing." "Task Codex Assimilation," and many more options like them. The words had meaning, but didn't help him understand what they meant in the current context. A few of the menu selections were like the big computer, not translated at all.

After a few minutes, he realized his friends were gone. Since he wasn't learning anything, he got up to see where they were. The workstation shut down as soon as he was a meter away from it.

It turned out there were six small corridors running off from the entry area. They were both halfway down one of them looking at more tubes. As they entered one of the corridors, more subdued lights came on. "What did you find?" he asked.

Katrina pointed to the line of tubes in the corridor. "Look at these," she said.

"Bunch of different fish," he said. He leaned in closer to examine the one next to him. It was a little like a lobster, only much larger. Probably a meter long, it also had a tail that split at the end, and no obvious eyes. It looked like it could be alive; there was no sign of decay.

"Not different," Colin said and pointed to the one next to it.

Terry moved over and examined it. Colin was confused, it was clearly a different species. Then he spotted all the similarities. The only thing different was that the 'head' now had eyestalks, and the second set of legs had tiny pincers. "Evolutionary samples?"

"Keep looking," Katrina said, so he moved to the next one.

Two sets of the front legs now had pincers, and the pincers were segmented to provide articulation. The first set also had a fixed 'thumb.' The eyes were now mobile and compound, and the tail was smaller, tougher, and appeared to be able to curl up under the body. There was another down the line, and the theme continued, with both front sets of limbs showing thumbs and more detailed articulation. The progression was obvious.

"Were they purposely modifying these lobster things?" he asked.

"We think so," Colin said. "It starts down there with a lobster creature half the size of the one you're looking at, and ends over there."

Terry looked at the one Colin had indicated. It was again a little smaller than the largest, and its pincers were basically small three-fingered hands. He also saw unmistakable pinplants on the side of its head. "Hey, how are these here? Aren't they 20,000 years old?"

Katrina moved her foot through the millimeters-thick dust on the floor, just like the rest of the building. "Hard to say how old, but nobody's been in here for a long time."

Terry looked for a display on the cylinders. There wasn't one. There were nine tubes in the corridor, taking the lobster from a simple creature to one that would have been at home wandering through Karma. "Wait," he said, "there's a term for this." He went into the personal files on his slate. He'd downloaded a ton of books and videos while aboard *Teddy Roosevelt*. He typed in a few search words, and up came a term.

"Uplifting," he said. "They call this uplifting. Taking a species from basically an animal all the way to full sentient beings. Doc talked about how they thought some races looked, well, designed." He pointed at the final stage of the lobster-thing. "What are the others like?"

They went to the next corridor. This creature looked like a sea snake he'd seen in an aquarium on Honolulu. Over the next five cylinders it became bigger, its eyes more forward focused, and it grew tentacles on either side of the head, which must be manipulative limbs. Unlike the lobster, it didn't have a pinplant, and seemed to suddenly stop in mid-uplift. *Failed project?* he wondered.

Three of the remaining corridors had progressive examples of different creatures. One reminded him of a sea urchin. There were only four examples; apparently it hadn't worked out early on. The next was a sort of shark with armored plates on its body. This one had seven examples, the most of any, and ended with pinplants and six crab-like limbs—two with vicious pincers, the rest more like hands.

The last was a dead ringer for a cuttlefish. Like the lobster, it hadn't started out with eyes, but they'd quickly added them in. It had only made it to the fifth iteration, where it ended without pinplants.

"I think the pinplants signify that they graduated," Terry said.

"God, I hope not," Katrina said.

"Why?" Colin wondered.

"Because that means there are giant armored sharks out in the galaxy!"

"At least they don't have laser beams on their heads," Terry said. She giggled. They'd both watched those movies a week earlier. It seemed like a million years now, as he remembered everyone was dead. He put it out of his mind.

The last of the six corridors wasn't a gallery of uplifted alien sea life. Instead, it led to another doorway. Terry opened this one himself. He wasn't bothering with the gun anymore. It seemed there was nothing more dangerous here than long-dead alien science experiments and dust.

This room seemed to be the remainder of the large dome, or about a quarter of the space along the back wall. It looked rather boring compared to the dozens of cylinders full of half-uplifted alien creatures.

There were a pair of workstations like the ones in the entry area, one to either side of the door. Further back toward the wall sat a series of a dozen blocky structures set into the floor. The curve of the back wall was interrupted halfway down from the curved ceiling, and came straight down, suggesting there was something behind it out of view.

The only thing that seemed out of place was an empty cylindrical clear tank mounted on treads with several manipulator arms attached. Terry moved closer to examine it, and found the glass covered in a light residue, as if whatever liquid had once been in it had evaporated, leaving a dried scum on the sides. In the bottom were a couple of inlets and outlets that had probably purified the water, a couple of pieces of corroded electronics that might have been pinplants, and what looked to him like a bird's beak.

"What is this place?" Katrina asked aloud. She was looking at one of the blocky structures, which showed no response to her presence.

"Maybe a lab?" Colin suggested. He looked at the tracked tube Terry was examining. "This was an experiment when they all started shooting each other?"

Terry went to a workstation and used his slate again once it came alive, like the others in the entry area.

"Project Suspended—Standing By"

"Analysis Available."

He stared at the options for a moment. Other items in the display noted available quantities on hand of things called biofilm, gene silencers, mutagens, and phages. None of the terms made sense to him, though his translator recognized them. At least as many others were untranslated. 'Analysis Available' was highlighted, so he reached into the Tri-V and touched it. The entire display flashed blue, and another much larger Tri-V came alive.

"What did you just do?" Katrina asked, accusation in her voice.

"It's just a lab," he replied and shrugged. "What can it do?" She opened her mouth to tell him when the new display resolved into an obvious representation of the structures within the dome. He held up his slate, which translated more of the buildings. Habitation, Life Support, Thermal Tap, Backup Fusion Power, Stores 1, Stores 2, Armory, Labs, and Pool. Then a series of white spots appeared. A dozen or so in the pool, and three in the lab.

"That's us," Colin pointed at the lab.

"Which means those are the cetaceans," Terry said and pointed at the pool. As they watched, the simple spots of white grew into perfectly rendered Tri-V dolphins and orcas. Curious and emboldened by his success at bringing the view up, he reached out and touched the pool area. It expanded to take up the entire viewing area.

Like any alien-made Tri-V, the image was true-to-life in full detail. He recognized Moloko with her calf Pōkole, Maka, Kray, and the other orcas, along with numerous bottlenoses. One by one, the representations of each cetacean was taken apart layer by layer, completely deconstructed down to their skeleton, and then popping back into existence.

"Woah," Katrina said, "that's freaky. What's it doing?"

"Scanning them," Terry said. He touched the display and moved his hand sideways until the lab and their three shapes were visible. It was more than a little disconcerting to watch themselves live from above, all their actions perfectly copied. Colin looked up at the ceiling, and his miniature did the same thing.

"That's even more freaky," Katrina said. Then the miniature Katrina's clothes disappeared. She squealed and her hands went to her privates. Her skin was gone, then muscles, and so on.

Terry had been momentarily titillated, then blanched as she was stripped to the bones, just like the cetaceans, only to pop back to normal. He was next, and it all happened too fast for his belated attempt at modesty to work any better than Katrina's had. Colin looked from them to the display just in time to be looking at his own naked miniature.

"What the heck?" he barked as his skin disappeared. He glared at Terry.

"Not like I can control it," Terry said. Katrina looked at them both peevishly, her cheeks flushed bright red.

Terry turned to look at the workstation display. "All Analysis Complete," was displayed.

"Marine Mammal—Fully Actionable / Non-Resident—Analysis Results: Size Class 6 / Biome Type 3 / Tech Index 1 / Combat Index 9—Sapient Stage 5—Candidate Stage 8"

"Marine Mammal—Fully Actionable / Non-Resident—Analysis Results: Size Class 3 / Biome Type 3 / Tech Index 9 / Combat Index 3—Sapient Stage 6—Candidate Stage 10—Special Alert—Multi-Level Nav Candidate"

"Land Mammal—Partly Actionable / Non-Resident—Analysis Results: Size Class 2 / Biome type 2/4—Potential 3/5/6 / Tech Index 7 / Combat Index 10—Sapient Stage 9—Candidate Stage 10"

"Is the last one us?" Katrina asked.

"I think it is," Terry said. "The first must be the orcas, the second the bottlenoses. It looks like the system's evaluated them for uplifting."

"And us, too," Colin pointed out. "Sapient stage 9? I guess it thinks we aren't quite as far from monkeys as we think we are." They all laughed. Katrina made a chimpanzee sound, and they laughed again.

"How's it getting all this?" she asked. "The best scanners we have on Earth are huge and take minutes to get even a fraction of the kind of data they've gotten in seconds. It must have scanned our DNA."

"Those panels," Terry said, snapping his fingers. "They reminded me of something. The walls of the Tri-V theater on the *Behemoth* have similar panels. They're sensors, really, really good ones."

"I guess," Katrina said. "Did you see…"

"Nope," Terry said, hoping he wasn't blushing. He moved the big Tri-V display to the armory building and touched it. Once again it zoomed in, and data began to scroll.

"Manufactory Standing By—Available; 500 Class 1 Type 2/3/4 Configurable Beam Weapons. Available, 100 Class 2 Type 2/3/4 Configurable Projectile Weapons. Available, 400 Units Configurable Armor." It continued to list more items but didn't translate them. He was pretty sure he understood some of it, which made sense from what they'd seen in the armory; there were a lot of guns.

He tapped at the displays of weapons, but it just flashed at him. After the third time, a line of text appeared. "Configure To Match Candidate"

"You better stop before you break something," Colin said.

"This thing is 20,000 years old," Terry scoffed. He glanced at his watch and saw that Dan had been gone over three hours. He was about to use the radio relay through the base comms when Dan's voice came over loud and full of panic.

"They're here!" he yelled. "The crabs snuck into the sub! They're coming in—" The transmission cut off suddenly.

"Dan?" Terry said into the radio. "Get out of there, go, leave! Get everyone through to here!" No response came back. The three friends stood in shock, staring at each other, none of them knowing what to say or do.

* * * * *

Chapter Fifteen

Kahraman Base, Planet Hoarfrost, Lupasha System, Coro Region, Tolo Arm

May 14th, 2038

"What do we do?" Katrina asked.

"We have to do something," Colin agreed.

Terry stared at the armory display. Hundreds of guns, they just needed to be made usable. Could he and his two friends take on all the alien mercs? The answer was almost certainly no. With advanced weaponry, maybe they could kill a whole bunch of them. Everyone else was probably dead. They were it.

He glanced at his two friends, who were having an animated argument about what to do, momentarily forgetting Terry was there as well. He leaned over and tapped the armory display. It pulsed blue.

"Configure To Match Candidate"

He touched the beam weapons, then reached over and touched land mammals. Both pulsed yellow.

"Define Combat Environment—2 | **3** | 4 | **5** | **6** "

He stared at the highlighted 3, 5 and 6. It had said the land mammals, he and his friends, were potentially for those biomes. He knew biome likely meant environment, and as the cetaceans were biome 3, that must be water. Humans were already good for 2 and 4.

What did those mean? Air and...something else. He needed guns that worked underwater, or anywhere else. He clicked 2, 3 and 4.

"Candidate Biome Adaptation Required—Proceed | Artificial Adaptation"

Biome adaptation made him nervous. However, artificial didn't sound bad. He clicked it.

"Candidate Interface Necessary—Proceed"

There wasn't a second option on this one, so he clicked.

"Initiate | Additional Action."

His eyes moved to the cetaceans. Without thinking it through, he clicked additional action, then all three categories, and clicked on the cetaceans. The options were more varied there. He took all the highest actions he could and accepted as fast as possible.

"What are you doing?" Katrina asked, finally realizing Terry was doing something.

"Getting even," he said.

"No," she said, "you don't..."

"Initiate | Additional Action"

"Terry!" Colin yelled. Terry pushed initiate.

Immediately the back wall of the building began to come alive. Hidden panels opened and began to configure into all manner of tables and supports. The blocky structures he'd thought were fixed to the floor fairly exploded into mobile machines sporting all manner of arms. One grabbed Katrina, who screamed in alarm.

"Hey," Terry said, fear making him jump away from the workstation and back away.

Katrina struggled and got an arm free. Instantly a robotic tentacle shot in and jabbed her in the arm. She screamed and began to go limp.

"Stop it," Terry said and drew his laser pistol. "I just said give us guns!" But another robot had grabbed him, and several arms secured his arms and legs, while another snatched the pistol away. "Colin, run!" But his friend stood in stunned surprise as he, too, was snatched by still another robot. Suddenly half the wall split open, and several of the columns/robots came out of the opening, which, Terry realized, was only a few meters from the water.

Spider robots were everywhere, climbing up his legs and swarming into the building. Outside, still more were skittering toward the water. He could see one of the bottlenoses standing on its tail, looking in his direction. He opened his mouth to scream a warning and felt an icy sting in his arm.

Terry, to his horror, never lost consciousness. Not even when he was placed on a table, and he felt a machine begin to drill into his skull. He could only think of the dead creatures in the dormitory and silently scream in pain. There were no words for the feeling, as something entered his skull.

What followed was a short eternity of unintelligible feelings, emotions, and sensations as the alien machines inserted probes into his cerebellum. For a moment, he was sure he had an extra arm, then he could smell colors, and then taste numerical formula. He wanted to scream but was beyond the ability to use his own body in the way he wanted to.

Eventually he was carried by a big, blocky robot and stood against a wall facing the open side of the room. He expected to simply fall over and smash his face on the floor, but instead found himself standing perfectly still and balanced. He couldn't even move his eyes.

An army of spider robots arrived carrying first one, then more bottlenoses. He couldn't control his body, yet tears rolled down his cheeks as he watched the robots place them in shallow pools that hadn't been there before, and the blocky robots began to insert needles into the dolphins' bodies. Like him, they were still awake, their eyes open as probes were inserted into their skulls.

Other robots removed the helmets that held the rebreathers that allowed them to stay underwater for weeks at a time. The equipment was discarded in a pile, like so much junk. Then incisions were made in their sides, and pieces of technology were inserted. Terry couldn't see what, only that the incisions didn't seem to bleed.

The bottlenoses were moved through quickly, operated on, then taken away several at a time. Eventually, as far as Terry could tell, all of them were moved through. Then the first orca was moved in. Despite the despair he was feeling, he was also amazed that the alien robots had created carefully constructed harnesses to avoid injuring the huge cetaceans, who had never been meant to be unsupported on land, even in Hoarfrost's lower gravity.

Where the bottlenoses were worked on three at a time, the orcas were individual jobs, requiring a vast number of spider robots, as well as all of the big blocky robots. Terry tried to close his eyes, but he couldn't. Like the bottlenoses, their rebreather helmets were removed, and bloodless surgery used to insert equipment into their bodies. He was forced to watch as each of the nine adult orcas were brought in for surgery, then removed back to the moon pool. At last, Pōkole was brought in.

Please no, he mentally screamed, but to no avail. The orca calf was subjected to the same procedure as the adults, though he needed much less of the robot's assistance or time. Then it was all over. The pools and equipment used to support the cetaceans were reabsorbed by the building, the wall went away, and the blocky robots went back to being columns attached to the floor. Not a single drop of blood remained. It was as if nothing had happened.

* * *

Terry must have slept, though he had no memory of it. He went from having no control of his body, standing in the corner of the operating room of horrors, watching the robots cutting up his friends, to lying on the floor and blinking up at the dim lighting.

"Terry, are you awake?"

"Yeah," he said and slowly sat up. Everything looked…*different.* He could hear the quiet hum of fans or pumps, see the low lighting and shapes of inactive blocky robots, smell a slight ozone odor, feel the cool floor under him, taste an acid flavor of some kind, and sense available connections.

Wait, *sense connections?* He concentrated, and the familiar ID of his slate seemed to appear in his mind's eye. He *touched* the connection, and the home menus of his slate appeared. In his mind. Another connection was "Operations Control." He touched that one, and it was the same one he'd used his slate to access in the medical theater prior to approving the horror.

"Why can I see computers in my head?!" Colin asked.

"We all have pinplants," Terry said.

"Why did you do this?" Katrina asked.

"Because the aliens are going to find this place and kill all of us anyway," he admitted. "Do you want to let that happen and do nothing?"

"No," she admitted. "I wanted to know what was about to happen, though."

"I wasn't sure myself until I did it," he said.

Terry got to his feet. It was surprisingly easy. He didn't feel any pain, discomfort, or disorientation. Considering that he'd just had a hole drilled into his brain, he found the lack of aftereffects more than a little disconcerting.

"Did they really drill holes in our heads?" Colin asked, echoing his thoughts.

"Didn't you feel it?" Katrina asked.

"Sort of," Colin said. "You'd think it would hurt more to have a hole drilled in your head."

"I'll never forget what red tastes like," Katrina said and shuddered.

As he walked around, Terry remembered all his studies on pinplants as he'd researched the cetaceans' models. There was a section on calibration, where the recipient was fed specific impulses and their responses monitored to be sure the nanoprobes were in the correct parts of the recipient's brains. At the thought, complete 3D renderings of his brain appeared in his mind, including the thousands of microscopic filaments now woven throughout it. *If this machine did it so easily, why aren't they available on Earth yet?* he wondered.

Remembering the cetaceans' implants, he reached up to the side of his head and felt a tiny connection point behind his right ear, and another behind his left. They were much smaller than he expected, and he wondered why.

Combat Qualified Implant Includes Wireless Synaptic Terahertz Frequency Modulated Interface.

He blinked as he digested the statement. A complete user manual appeared in his mind to go with it. He absorbed the entire manual in less than a second.

"Holy crap," he said.

"What?" Katrina asked.

"I just read a 2,000-page manual in a second." He thought about how to interface his pinplants with a strange computer, and instantly knew how, where in the manual it was located, and word for word cross-indexed uses. "And I remember all of it."

"Do the orcas have the ability, too?" she asked.

"They must," he said, "though they don't have these models." The details on the orcas' implants were shown to him, including updates the Caretaker had performed. The implants, while simple, were sufficient, so they weren't replaced, merely augmented.

"How do you read manuals?" Colin asked.

Terry found his connection, linked their minds, and sent him the manual. "Just *read* it," he said.

Colin was on his feet, standing a short distance away. He closed his eyes and his eyebrows wrinkled in concentration. Suddenly his eyes shot open and he blinked. "Oh, wow!"

"I know, right?" Terry said.

"I see," Katrina said. "Found it and read it. This is a little like VR, except without stupid goggles."

"Yeah, kinda," Terry agreed. "It's 3D." *Like the weird programming*, he thought. Like so many other things with the pinplants, one of those 3D programs appeared. *Kut-Akee* was the programming language. It didn't translate, not even in the deeper understanding granted by the pinplants. He looked at the strange 3D program, and a *tiny* bit seemed to make sense.

"What do we do now?" Katrina asked, snapping him back to reality.

"The Caretaker says we're free to act," Colin said.

"Wait, Caretaker?"

"That's the computer of this base," Katrina said and made an expansive gesture around her.

Terry found the main connection again and linked with it. *"Caretaker?"*

<What do you require?>

"It talks!" Terry blurted.

"You just realized?" Katrina asked.

He was glad she didn't hate him as much as he hated himself.

"Did you notice your leg?" Colin said and pointed.

Terry looked down at his left leg and gawked. Gone was the mechanical-looking prosthetic made by Doc's people. It still wasn't *his* leg, but it looked just like it. Perfectly molded, he suspected, from his right leg, it worked perfectly, and looked perfect except that it was a metallic tint of blue. He reached down and touched it. The skin felt like the same material as the dome. His drysuit had been cut and molded to seal where the artificial leg met his stump. *They're very efficient*, he thought.

<*I am waiting,*> the Caretaker said in his mind.

"Will you do whatever I ask?" he said.

<Within programmed parameters, absent command override.>

"Who gives command override?" Katrina asked. Terry hadn't been aware that she was there in his mind with him. He thought about it and understood that she wasn't, they were just on the same channel communicating with the Caretaker.

<Information beyond your authority.>

"*This is frustrating,*" Colin said, also on the channel.

<Irrelevant. What do you require?>

"What did you do to the orcas?" Terry asked.

<Candidate species orca, now designated candidate KilSha upon consulting with candidate, as per protocol. Actions per operator Terry include as follows:>

All three of them saw 3D images of the surgeries performed on the orcas, now KilSha, as well as alterations to their DNA! The Caretaker stated the KilSha were now Sapient Stage 6, which was the best alteration possible within the current generation.

"You uplifted them?" he asked.

<Indexing operator language…term 'Uplift' acceptable analogy and is indexed within database. KilSha partially uplifted and adapted as requested.>

"God, Terry," Colin hissed aloud.

"I didn't think it would *change* them," he pleaded. "I thought it would *arm* them."

"You just didn't think," Katrina said.

Terry sighed and nodded. "Are the orcas…the KilSha, okay?"

The back wall of the room split open again. All three stepped back, the memory of the flood of robots too fresh in their minds. There were no robots, just the moon pool a short distance away. It was crowded, with all the cetaceans sitting calmly on the surface. None of them were wearing their rebreathers, and when he looked, there was no sign of them either. The three walked outside, and the wall closed behind them.

"Are they alive?" Colin asked. A plume of water vapor and a *Whoosh!* from one of the orcas answered the question.

"Hello?" Terry called as they reached the edge of the water.

"Hello, Terry," the closest KilSha answered. The English was perfect, and it brought goosebumps to his skin. English, without him needing a translator. For that matter, his translator was gone. "How are you?"

"We're fine," he said. "Moloko? How are you?"

"Yes, I am Moloko, and I am very fine!"

"I'm sorry they hurt you," he said, stepping into the water enough to touch her side.

"Do not be sorry," Kray said, gently pushing Moloko aside to come closer. "This is a great gift!"

"They cut on you and changed you in ways you don't understand," he said.

"You do not understand. We asked them to do this when the Caretaker's machines came for us. It needed to happen, and is why *Shool* brought us here. We understand," he said, "we have the files in our pinplants. We can talk perfectly now! It was so hard for us to talk before, to make Humans understand us. Our language is much more different than you understand."

Terry shook his head. It was disconcerting to have an orca talk to him like an adult Human. Gone was the stilted speech that had been more like talking to a child, or someone with a mental disability.

"We are happy to be KilSha!" All the newly-made KilSha bobbed their heads, and some blew misty plumes as if they were exclamation points. "You do not have to be Wardens anymore, now we can work with you as allies, friends."

"Sounds wonderful," Terry said. He glanced at Katrina, who was frowning; Colin was just slowly shaking his head. "I'm still sorry. I should have asked you."

"We would have said yes," Kray repeated.

"Like new brain, Terry!" Pōkole popped his head out and nipped at Terry's hand. Terry stroked his side, and he felt a pinplant link from the baby orca with, he would swear, a hug emoticon?

"Hey, little guy," Terry said.

"Pōkole like Terry! You make Pōkole have big smarts!"

The calf still sounded like a kid, but maybe a three- or four-year-old, not a one-year-old. The changes to the youngest member of the pod were the most profound and hinted at what was to come.

"'Sup, Terry?"

A bottlenose rocketed out of the water between Kray and Moloko, did a triple flip, and hit the water on the other side perfectly, not even touching either of the KilSha, who both looked back and gently shook their heads.

"We're BotSha now!" All 18 of the former bottlenose dolphins stuck their heads out and jabbered about how awesome it was to be a BotSha. It was like being in the middle of a crazy internet chatroom full of gamers.

Terry sighed and sat down at the edge of the water. *Doc's going to kill me*, he thought, then winced when he remembered they were all dead. The thought brought him to the present, and why he'd done what he did.

"You know all the wardens, I mean all the other Humans on Templemer are dead?" he asked the KilSha.

"We know," Kray responded.

"Do you want to help me get even?"

"Terry," Katrina hissed, "what are you suggesting?"

"I'm suggesting we kill the alien bastards."

Collin set his jaw and nodded. Katrina frowned more, but slowly nodded, too.

The KilSha rolled partially onto his side and opened his mouth to show teeth no longer blunt white, but sharply pointed and glinting with a silvery alloy. "We want to help kill them."

"Caretaker?"

<*Still waiting.*> It somehow managed to sound impatient.

"Is the equipment I requested ready?"

<Manufactory is 89% completed on weapons, standing by to begin armor fabrication.>

"Then let's get to work."

* * * * *

Chapter Sixteen

Under Extractor, Planet Hoarfrost, Lupasha System, Coro Region, Tolo Arm

May 15th, 2038

Selroth unit commander Gloot was running out of patience. The operation was taking much longer than anticipated, and his company commander was threating repercussions.

"Find the cache and get it back here," the company commander yelled over the commlink. "The Izlian representative could be here anytime, and we need to exit this entropy-cursed system before they arrive."

Like everyone else in his company, Gloot hadn't yet been born when some high-ranking Selroth leader had hatched the plan to falsify mineral yields on the planet's extractors. It was an intriguing deception, one that had apparently worked on the gas bag Izlians. Though the water burned their skin, its volcanos belched vast quantities of valuable minerals and rare earths into the ocean.

The problem was, the original plotters hadn't counted on it taking three *centuries* to yield results. That was so long nobody had remembered the plan even existed until some intelligence expert on their home world had received a cursory notification from the Izlians that they'd granted a lease to a race known as Humans to operate the abandoned mining colony. However, the notification triggered an old, highly-classified file.

Months had passed before the right people in the Selroth leadership were made aware of the situation. Panic ensued. Regardless of how long ago it was, should the Izlians discover the Selroth's duplicitous dealings, the repercussions would be dire.

Gloot's company was hastily moved to Karma, the next closest location an unattached merc company could go to without drawing attention. No sooner had they arrived than a coded signal came through on a courier from Lupasha. The dormant program running the extractor scheme had been triggered; the Humans had found the hidden stash.

The Humans were the newest mercenary race in the galaxy, which concerned the commander. With only two platoons of Selroth mercs, Gloot's commander had decided additional firepower was warranted. The problem was, they needed mercs who were able to operate deep underwater, were good fighters, and could keep their mouths shut. The Xiq'tal fit the bill. Thus reinforced, they raced to Lupasha, and landed on the moon now named, for some strange reason, Hoarfrost.

"What is a hoarfrost?" the company commander had demanded.

"How am I to know?" Gloot had retorted. He'd never even seen a Human.

The Humans might be a merc race, but they weren't terribly knowledgeable about war. With the Selroth forces restricted to firing on the planet below 10 miles by Union law, it could have been a tough landing, but since there weren't any surface defenses, the Selroth landed, unloaded their submarines, and descended into the water.

The Xiq'tal had many advantages when operating in deep ocean environments. One of them was that they could equalize their internal pressure and dive *very* fast. They'd arrived at the habitat dome long before the Selroth's submersibles could. One advantage the crustacea *didn't* have was good tactical doctrine. They simply blew a hole in the dome and killed everyone inside.

Without the Humans, the Selroth didn't know where the stash was, because the dome computers were wrecked. Even fixing and repressurizing the dome didn't help. However, once inside, they found a distinct lack of bodies, and a missing submarine. Thus Gloot had spent the last several days in the miserable skin-itching water looking for the submarine and the Humans.

It turned out the Humans hadn't been alone. They'd managed to domesticate some extremely large predatory marine mammals. They were formidable, but luckily possessed no arms or armor. Despite this, the Xiq'tal had only killed one of the smaller subspecies' members while losing an entire platoon of their numbers. Gloot didn't care about the losses; let the stupid crustacea absorb them.

They'd found the submarine and what was left of the extractor stash a few hours ago, along with a bunch of unarmed Humans. The pathetic bunch were huddled in the center of a cavern under the submarine, mewling piteously. Apparently several others were missing, having located another cavern. Gloot had scouts searching for them.

The Humans watched the small circle of Xiq'tal troopers who surrounded them. Their soft fleshy faces were covered in liquid leaking from their undersized eyes in some strange display. How these helpless creatures could live so far under the ice was a complete mystery. The waters at this depth felt cool to Gloot; they must be freezing to these beings. They were mostly hatchlings and pregnant females. Maybe only the males were mercs?

The only Human who seemed knowledgeable about the missing ones was an immature male. Two Xiq'tal were trying to interrogate him. They were taking turns asking questions and using their claws to nip off bits here and there. The pathetic thing kept losing consciousness, slowing the process. He was about to just tell the Xiq'tal to kill the Human when his radio came alive.

"Search team, contact!"

"Report," Gloot said.

"Humans in a lower tunnel. They're armed—" The transmission cut off suddenly, and an explosion reverberated through the cavern seconds later.

"I guess the Humans have a few mercs after all," Gloot said. "Prepare for battle."

The two Xiq'tal tossed the mutilated Human aside and scooped up lasers designed for their kind. These troopers didn't have weapons welded to their carapaces, like the heavy combat Xiq'tal or the huge King Crabs. Those were more like tanks than living beings. Gloot's team armed weapons and he readied the laser carbine he carried.

Something raised out of the pool slightly, and a flurry of fire from the mercs met it. It dropped below the waves with deceptive speed. There was nothing for a long moment, then a huge metallic and glass shape rose out of the water.

Gloot had half a second to recognize one of the huge black and white marine mammals before he realized it was clad in combat armor. "Impossible," he said. Robotically-controlled weapons on the armor moved, and Gloot dove for cover.

Powerful lasers raked the assembled mercs. Selroth troopers sought cover, while the Xiq'tal did what they always do; they charged. They charged right into death. Gloot only got a few momentary images of the marine mammal in its incredible powered armor, using precise fire from a pair of turret-mounted lasers to carve the Xiq'tal, and several of his own troopers, into bloody pieces, while avoiding the screaming Humans, sometimes by mere millimeters.

"Withdraw!" he yelled. "Whoever is alive, get out!" The damnable marine mammals didn't have legs, at least. So he ran for his life.

He reached his submarine, which was docked to one of the extractor's ports with the remainder of his command—nine troopers. He'd arrived with 25 and a squad of 10 Xiq'tal. Entropy, what had he stumbled into? The last man in closed the hatch and flooded the lock with sweet water, chemically balanced the way the Selroth liked it.

"Get us out of here!" he screamed at the pilot, who nodded his head, bubbles popping from his mouth to show the fear in his face.

"What happened?" he asked as he undocked and spun the submarine away from the extractor.

"The big marine mammals have powered armor and modern weapons!"

"Impossible," the pilot insisted. "They would have used them already!"

"You would think," Gloot mumbled. "However, my dead troopers would contest your statement."

"What about the rest of the Xiq'tal?" his second in command, Yoold, asked.

"To entropy with them."

The sub's water turbine spun up to a scream as the submarine accelerated away from the extractor. Gloot could see through the front cockpit bubble as all three of the single-man attack subs fell in with them. He activated the radio.

"Be alert," he warned. "The big marine mammals have modern weapons and armor. Only lasers, though. Engage with torpedoes on first sight!"

"Acknowledged," the attack subs replied.

With their escort, they raced away at better than 30 knots. There was no way the massive mammals could match their speed. Sonar bleated an alarm. Four small returns raced past them at better than *50 knots!*

The returns were too small to be the big predators, and he thought at first that they were poorly fired torpedoes, until they slowed and turned around to face them. It was then that he remembered the smaller subspecies of marine mammals.

"Engage them!" he ordered the attack subs. Instantly, the three accelerated ahead of the transport, and Gloot saw a torpedo launch from each one.

The sonar was a good model and provided highly detailed 3D imagery. It zoomed in on the four creatures facing them, and now he could make out the sleek, long forms with powerful flippers. They had proven fast and maneuverable, but against high-tech seeker torpedoes, they would be no match.

The torpedoes streaked toward them at 100 knots. Gloot nodded as the torpedoes unerringly sought their targets. Then, when the torpedoes were less than 100 meters away, there was a flash that made the screen white out. When it cleared, the torpedoes were gone, and the marine mammals were accelerating toward them.

"What happened?" Gloot demanded.

"A sonar burst," the pilot said. "It was extremely powerful. It overwhelmed our receivers, even a kilometer away."

Resolution began to return as the sub's sonar recovered from the burst, and Gloot saw the torpedoes. Three marine mammals had the torpedoes in their mouths like fish.

"The sonar must have functioned as a weapon and disabled the torpedoes," the pilot said needlessly. "They'll be in laser range in five seconds."

"Engage with lasers at close range," Gloot ordered the attack subs, which acknowledged the order. The mammals raced toward them at an amazing speed. The seconds ticked down with the range, and Gloot tensed in anticipation of watching the annoying creatures cut into bloody chunks. Then the images became fuzzy.

"They're employing sonar again," the pilot said, manipulating his controls. "The signal is incredibly complicated, and the frequencies are slightly different from each creature."

"Are you saying the sonar is a biological feature of the animals?"

Before the pilot could answer, the attack subs fired their lasers, to absolutely no effect. The beams hit the sonar distortion and attenuated in less than a meter. Lasers only worked at short range underwater, and even then, they were less reliable. The sonar distortion was acting almost like a laser shield. *How can they know how to do this?* Gloot thought.

The attack subs maneuvered out of the way of the streaking alien mammals, firing their lasers without effect until the quarry was no longer in line with the bow-mounted weapon. As the aliens passed the attack subs, two of them maneuvered so they could face the subs. Another burst of sonar static came from the two creatures, and the attack subs spun out of control.

"What happened to them?" Gloot demanded.

"They don't respond," the pilot said.

"It was some kind of attack," the remaining attack sub pilot yelled over the sound of his craft's straining engine. "They're not responding." A Tri-V came alive, showing the attack sub pilot inside his wet cockpit.

"Get away from them," Gloot ordered the attack sub pilot, then addressed his pilot, "Emergency speed, head for the dome."

"I'm trying," the attack sub pilot yelled, "the aliens are too maneuverable!"

On the display showing the attack sub and the aliens, two others swept around and aimed their heads at it. The distortion returned. The attack sub pilot screamed, and the screen showed an all-too detailed view as the pilot was hit by a concussive wave of force transmitted through his craft's wall, and by the water he used to breathe, pulping his flesh. The exploding cloud of blood and tissue almost managed to obscure the view of his gaping skull.

"Entropy!" his pilot gasped.

"Get us out of here!"

* * *

"Wikiwiki reports the small subs are destroyed," Ki'i told Terry, who was riding on his back.

"What about the big sub?" he asked the KilSha.

"They let it go as you instructed. It is fleeing at high speed back to Templemer."

"Excellent," Terry said.

"Why bother letting them get back?" Katrina asked. A dozen meters away, she was astride the female Uila. Colin rode on Maka just behind them. All the members of the former Wandering Pod were in the second group. Kray and those from the Shore Pod were the lead element, with the exception of Moloko and Pōkole, who remained back at the Kahraman base, protecting the children and mothers. The little calf was quite upset at being left out of, as he called it, the coming fun.

"Because I want them to get back and either evacuate toward the surface, or even better, come out and try to fight."

"Then we kill them," Ki'i said.

"Absolutely. Skritch, are your scouts there yet?"

"Yeah, yeah, they're checking it out now, man!"

Terry shook his head; the mannerisms and turns of phrase of the new BotSha had him bemused. They were like some of the surfer dudes back on Hawaii. It had to be on purpose; they were all talking the same way.

The BotSha leader came back on the radio a minute later. "Wikiwiki says the dome is fixed and full of air, dude!"

"How did you know they'd fix the dome?" Katrina asked.

"The Selroth made the dome," Terry said. "They don't like this water."

"The water is awesome, dude," Skritch said.

"For you and the orc—the KilSha, sure. Not for the Selroth. I don't know if the Xiq'tal like it."

"No matter," Kray said from further ahead. "They will die in it."

"We'll need the dome," Terry reminded everyone. "Be careful."

"There're a bunch of crabs coming out of the dome," Wikiwiki called on the radio. "There're crabs everywhere, dude!"

They're coming out to fight, Terry thought. *Doc's right, aliens are predictable.* "Kray, go ahead and attack their front ranks, we'll begin our flanking maneuver."

"Yes, General!" Kray replied, a hint of humor in his voice.

"Don't call him General," Colin said. "His head will get too big for his helmet." Terry could hear Katrina chuckling over the radio.

"Remember what they did to Don," Terry said, and the other two went silent. Their friend was alive, but horribly mutilated. The crabs had cut off both his feet and his right hand.

"And remember our families," Katrina added. It was the fact that the aliens had murdered everyone that sold her on this plan. Payback was a powerful motivator. The KilSha just wanted to kill the aliens.

Now that they were close, the KilSha began sharing live feeds from their pinplants, constructing 3D maps in his head that the pinplants labeled a 'battlespace.' It seemed like it would be hard to separate things, but the implants made it easier than a computer game back home. The enemy units were highlighted in blue as they were identified, friendly in red. The colors felt strange, so he thought about it, and it reversed.

As the four KilSha in Kray's group swept in on the Xiq'tal, Terry took Ki'i and the other four in his group and angled sideways, then toward Templemer. The lights of the dome slowly became visible out of the gloom. Where they'd tried to make a home. Where Doc and his mom had died. He gritted his teeth and urged Ki'i to speed up.

A pair of BotSha came in from either side, matching their course and speed. "Crabs ahead, dude," Wikiwiki said.

"'Sup dude," Toba added from the other side.

"I thought you were supposed to be helping Kray's group," Terry said.

"Naw, he's got that, I wanna hang out with you!"

"More fun here," Toba agreed.

A laser beam from below hit Niho just to Terry's right. A Xiq'tal's red icon appeared in Terry's head below them. The male KilSha yawed over hard, and Terry could see the glowing line on his armor. As Niho rolled, one of the two laser turrets mounted on his armor's side, just behind the head, rotated and pulsed laser fire. A hundred meters below them, the Xiq'tal who'd fired from ambush was scored several times, and the red icon disappeared.

"Below us," Terry said to Wikiwiki.

"On it, bro!" The two BotSha rocketed downward as the KilSha began to evade more shots coming up from below.

"There's a bunch of them, let's go," Colin said.

They didn't want to leave Wikiwiki and Toba to deal with the crabs themselves, so Terry agreed, and all five KilSha dove as well.

The Xiq'tal had a squad of their troopers hidden on the rocky side of the volcano Templemer had been built on. Terry didn't think they'd planned to attack when it had happened—maybe one of the crabs jumped the gun? Either way, the KilSha and BotSha were among them too quickly, and they were caught trying to hide from an expected attack.

This was the first time Terry had been directly involved in a fight, and his heart was racing. He could feel sweat on his skin, despite the armor. The Caretaker had called his armor a 'Konar,' and it had been custom-built in the manufactory in only minutes. The armor the Kil-Sha and BotSha wore was unique and required slightly more time. With segmented armor from just behind their pectoral fins all the way back to their flukes, Terry was amazed at the final product. The way it articulated to open and allow the operating cetaceans to simply swim into it was even more amazing. He, Katrina, and Colin had just put theirs on by climbing into it from behind, and the armor had closed over them.

Doc would have loved these things, Terry thought as he watched them dive toward the enemy through his pinplants. It really was just like a video game. Each of the KilSha's armor had an indentation just behind the dorsal fin where a Human could sit. Both armors then linked systems, almost like a spaceship docking. It had once felt incredible to be towed through the water by the powerful strokes of a bottlenose. Riding on the back of a battle armor-wearing KilSha made him feel like a *god!* The god of war, to be precise.

Mated to Ki'i's back, Terry gained access to the KilSha's own weapon system, effectively becoming like a rear gunner in a fighter. The Xiq'tal, realizing they couldn't escape, began firing at the diving cetaceans and their Human riders. Terry saw Uila and Katrina take out a torpedo with a directed sonar blast and kill the Xiq'tal with their own torpedo.

"How do I know how to use this stuff?" Katrina wondered.

"The pinplants are doing the heavy lifting," Terry said.

"Like looking up a file," Colin agreed. "Point and click."

"Point and kill is more like it," Katrina lamented.

"It is glorious," Kray said, either not catching her sentiment or simply not caring.

Another Xiq'tal was dispatched by Colin and Maka, leaving two who were trying to race away with a sort of underwater jetpack the aliens had mounted on their shells. Terry used one of Ki'i's lasers and hit a fleeing crab, disabling the jetpack. Ki'i raced in and seized the alien in his jaws. The being made a hideous screeching sound as Ki'i's reinforced metal teeth crushed the life out of it with an explosion of blueish blood and insides. Terry tried not to think about the fact that they'd just killed an intelligent being, focusing instead on what those beings had done to his friends and family.

Further ahead, Wikiwiki and Toba used the lasers on their own powered armor to disable the last Xiq'tal's jetpack and weapons. Then they moved in and tore it limb from limb with their own reinforced teeth.

"Wimpy crabs," Toba said when the Xiq'tal only had one pathetic limb left. The Xiq'tal was trying to crawl under a rock outcropping as blue blood pumped from its many severed limbs. The two BotSha harassed and snapped at it until Katrina dispatched it with a laser.

"Spoilsport!" Wikiwiki cried.

"That wasn't sport," Katrina said. "It was torture."

The two BotSha left without comment, obviously disappointed that she'd ruined their fun. Terry observed the battlespace and saw that Kray's forces had neutralized all the Xiq'tal, with only one minor injury; Byk had a pectoral fin pierced by a laser and a torpedo had exploded against his side. The injury was minor, and his armor was still functional. *They* are *like warships,* Terry thought.

"The Selroth are retreating into Templemer," Kray reported.

"Time to finish this," Terry said.

* * *

Gloot ran across the open area of the dome as fast as he could, his big, webbed feet making wet slapping sounds on the carved rock as he ran. One of the ridiculous paintings the Humans had executed on a building was visible as he went, the image partially degraded from being flooded. This particular painting looked like the dome he was running in with the cursed marine mammals swimming around it, though without the powered armor they now wore.

"How did these Humans and their pets get such advanced technology?" he yelled in rage as he ran. Nobody was nearby to answer him. His company commander had been outside leading the Xiq'tal against the same marine mammals. The initial wave of attacks had been swift and devastating. His commander had died in seconds.

"What's happening, Unit Commander?" asked a technician moving a loader full of equipment.

"We're losing," Gloot said as he ran by.

"What should I do?"

"Run for your life, you fool!" Gloot yelled over his shoulder. Thanks to Gloot's widely-set eyes, he had a good look at the technician staring after him as he ran.

The three heavy submarines were docked in the bay. He'd sent the general evacuation order the minute his commander was slaughtered. To entropy with the high command, the Izlians, and in particular the cursed Humans and their murderous pets. If they could control the aquatic death machines, they would soon depose the Veetanho from the Mercenary Guild and be running everything. If the galaxy was smart, they'd destroy the entire race now, while they still could.

Gloot was emboldened to see an entire squad of his troopers waiting at the entrance to the main lock. All were in full combat armor with laser weapons, and one had a rocket launcher.

"Where are the rest of the Xiq'tal?" a trooper asked.

"Dead, maybe," he said. "Do you want to wait for them?" They shook their heads. "That's what I thought. Let's get out of this entropy-cursed place."

They entered the airlock and passed through into the docking bay. Their submarines were sitting there with support crews rushing to load anything of value. "Get in the subs, you fools!" he yelled at them. Being non-combat personnel, they were responsible for the gear; they looked confused to be told to leave it behind. He turned toward the submarine and saw one of the armored marine mammals surface just behind it.

"Contact!" he yelled and raised his laser, but the mammal disappeared below the water the second it was spotted. Regardless, several of his troopers snapped shots after it. "Don't waste ammo," he said. Then the meaning of the creature dawned on him.

"Why is the outside lock open?"

"We opened it in preparation for departure," a technician said.

He pointed at the water, where another of the smaller marine mammals was skimming the surface, apparently to get a sight picture of what was going on. "You didn't consider hostile action first?"

The technician looked from Gloot to the water, not understanding. Then the marine mammal surfaced and shot the technician with a laser, killing him instantly.

"Take cover!" he ordered the squad, and they piled behind a concrete barrier.

Lasers began snapping regularly, picking off the feckless technicians with precision fire. Half of them were gone before the rest realized they were targets. Non-combatants weren't often singled out during merc battles; there wasn't any profit in it. Finally understanding what was happening, their response was to run in circles screaming.

"Suppression fire," Gloot ordered. His troopers tried to help the technicians, but their panicky behavior worked against them. His own people killed two of them as they ran into friendly fire. Only one managed to get behind cover, leaving the dock next to the subs littered with dead and dying technicians.

"What do we do?" a trooper asked him. "We can't reach the submarines while those creatures are in the water."

"We wait," he said. "If they want to attack us, they must rise up higher in the water, then we can engage them from cover. Once we kill a few, they'll tire of this."

But the small marine mammals didn't expose themselves. They stopped attacking, and the docking bay fell silent. He began to consider a rush for the submarines, since they had heavier weapons, when something large began to surface. He stared in horror as one of the huge marine mammals broached the surface, its laser turrets seeking targets.

"Fire!" he yelled.

The squad rose as one and targeted the creature. The segmented armor plates covering its body seemed to move, and its head dipped downward. The laser fire hit the armor and was reflected. The armor was mirror shiny and somehow articulated. The tiny plates both deflected and broke up the beams in a way Gloot had never seen.

"Try to concentrate on one spot," he said, but a rocket shot by him and detonated, killing two of his troopers. Not only had another huge marine mammal surfaced, it was walking up the landing on massive mechanical legs! "They can come on land!" he said in shock.

The armored monster snapped its jaws, revealing rows of silver daggers. A pair of articulated arms tipped with razor-sharp claws gestured at them, seemingly saying, "Come to me." His men threw their weapons over the barrier and raised their hands. The beast looked disappointed.

* * *

Terry walked out of the water in the submarine dock, the last place he'd been in Templemer as they'd fled five days prior. Bodies of dead Selroth littered the deck. A couple still twitched. He carried his laser weapon in both hands as his armor-clad feet clanked against the carved stone decking. Katrina and Colin were right behind him.

Kray and his mate Ulybka stood next to a group of Selroth prisoners. The KilSha's powered armor moved them on powerful robot legs, which served double duty as manipulators if necessary. Terry suspected the aliens had been more than shocked when five tons of cetacean had walked out of the water in gleaming armor. Ulybka's armor was discolored in places from laser hits, though none of them had penetrated the armor.

"They surrendered," Kray told him as he approached.

The Selroth looked at the KilSha in shock.

"They speak?" the alien said, his bubbling/gulping language instantly translated by Terry's pinplants.

"Yes, of course," he said. "Meet the KilSha, our friends and allies."

"There is no race called KilSha," the Selroth said.

Wikiwiki and Toba walked out of the water, their own armor performing the same feat as the KilSha's to let them move on land. "Those are BotSha," he told the Selroth.

"Did you, did you *uplift* those creatures?" the alien stammered. Terry just stared at him through the armored glass of his Konar. "That's illegal!"

"What are you talking about?" Katrina asked him.

"Uplifting lower races is *illegal* by Union law, you stupid Human."

"Do not speak to them like that," Kray snarled, his voice amplified by his sonar with enough intensity to knock the five surviving Selroth backward. They crawled backward until the wall stopped them.

"What are we going to do with them?" Colin asked.

"Kill them," Wikiwiki said. "Just like they killed all your dudes."

"No," Terry said. "Not yet, anyway." He looked at the first Selroth who'd spoken. "You the leader?"

"My commander is dead, so I'm in charge."

"You have a ship in orbit?" The alien didn't respond. "Kray, convince him to talk."

Kray directed a sonar beam at the Selroth, who jerked in surprise. The attack pulsed over and over, slowly increased in intensity. The Selroth jerked as its armor began to vibrate, then crack. Terry held up a hand, and the attack stopped.

"Feel like talking?"

"Yes," the alien said. "We have a merc cruiser in orbit."

Terry nodded. "Thank you. I'll have more questions for you. For now, stay here and don't cause any trouble." The alien looked at the two KilSha in powered armor and slowly nodded. "Good boy, or whatever you are." He turned and walked back toward the dock. Their submarine was surfacing. Onboard would be all the children, what was left of Dan, and Taiki's body. His teeth ground together as he considered killing the Selroth.

"You wouldn't have let Kray kill it, would you?" Katrina asked.

"Why not?" Colin asked and looked at the sub. "I don't think Taiki would have a problem with it."

"I don't know," Terry said and shrugged, his armor perfectly duplicating the movements. "The other BotSha are sweeping the facility looking for any surviving crabs or Selroth?" He'd been too busy with Kray and the Selroth to keep in touch directly.

"Yeah," Katrina said. "They found a couple, but they were confused. The huge crab Kray killed outside was their boss; now the others don't know what to do."

He nodded. The file he had on the Xiq'tal confirmed the information. Leaderless, the crabs were clueless. They could also be unpredictable. "Are they killing them?"

"Yes," Katrina said in an emotionless voice. "Needed to be done."

They walked out of the docking bay, through the airlock, and into the dome. Everything looked so familiar. Had it really been just five days? It was disconcerting. A pair of armored BotSha walked by on their robotic limbs. They were chatting like a pair of guys heading out to surf, but they were talking about how fun it was to kill the Xiq'tal, and hoping there were more. Behind them was the mural Terry had helped paint of a shining dome under the water where orcas and dolphins played.

A tear rolled down his cheek, and he shook his head angrily. There was no place for regret in his world. Not anymore.

"Are you okay?" Katrina asked.

"Yeah, I suppose," Terry said. She stepped next to him and slipped her armored hand into his.

"We'll get through this," she said. "Somehow."

Colin put his hand on Terry's shoulder. "We saved the kids," he said.

Terry pointed at the BotSha walking into a building, lasers at the ready. "At what cost?"

"Terry, dude!"

"What's going on, Ihu?" Terry asked, responding to the call sent through their linked pinplants.

"Come to the moon pool, man, right away!"

All three of them ran on their power-assisted legs, far faster than they would have been able to without, reaching the door to the moon pool in just seconds. They had to wait for a second as the lock cycled before they could go inside. He was expecting to find a bunch of dead Xiq'tal, or maybe a holdout group of Selroth. The inside door opened, and they moved in, weapons at the ready, to find a crowd of people.

"What?" he said, stopping and lowering his weapon.

"Terry?"

His armored head turned at the sound, and he saw his mom moving to the front of the group. "God, Terry, is that you?"

"Mom?" At a mental command, his helmet split open and pivoted up. "How?"

Doc appeared and shook his head. "Jesus Christ, kid," he gestured at the three armored teenagers. "How? What?"

The armor opened, and he climbed out the egress point in the rear. Coming around the armor, he grabbed his mom and hugged her as hard as he could. She cried on his shoulder, and he did the same in her hair. "You're alive," he said over and over. Katrina was with her mom and dad, and so was Colin, though they were still in their armor for some reason. Everyone was there, the entire colony. They'd all survived.

"Bodacious," Ihu said, and used his robotic manipulator to flip Terry a recognizable shaka.

"How are you all alive?" he asked Doc, who nodded in approval. His mercs were examining the empty armor, and in particular, the laser carbine it still held.

"Backup power room under the moon pool," Doc said. "We only found it the day of the attack." He shrugged. "It wasn't even on the maps. We were rushing everyone who couldn't fight down here when they blew the dome. Barely got the door closed in time. Me and the guys were just trying to figure out how to make a break out when the shooting started."

Terry nodded. "I can't believe you're alive. I have so much to tell you!"

"I bet," Tina said from next to Terry's empty Konar. "But maybe you should put some pants on before we talk about this?" It was only then that Terry remembered they had to be naked in the armor for them to work properly. Tina raised an eyebrow and nodded in appreciation. "Not bad, kid. Not bad at all."

* * * * *

Epilogue

Templemer, Planet Hoarfrost, Lupasha System, Coro Region,
Tolo Arm
December 25th, 2038

Terry watched the younger children singing a Christmas carol on the stage with a small smile on his face. Dr. Orsage was still working with them on therapy sessions. Despite none of their parents actually dying, the battles and watching Dan being tortured had left scars that had yet to heal. They might never completely heal, Orsage said. Time would tell.

Katrina squeezed his hand, and Terry smiled at her. He'd been careful with her after the events back in May. Part of him wanted to do things with her, but part of him wasn't ready for those things. He'd turned 14 back in October. He felt like he was 40. His mom and Doc, on the other side of Katrina, watched the kids' performance and clapped at the end.

The children began another song. Terry's smile faded as he looked up and saw the KilSha watching from outside the dome. Some of the BotSha were there, too, but most of them were still off on their last mission. The ones who remained were pregnant and getting ready to have their own families. The anti-fertility drugs had been stopped right after the battle, at their insistence. Breeding had commenced in the pod with embarrassing regularity.

The mission was with the KilSha on their seemingly never-ending search for *Shool*. Terry had thought that, after they'd been uplifted, the KilSha would give up their quest to meet god in the cold depths of Hoarfrost. Nothing could be further from the truth. Along with the other modifications to the former orcas and bottlenoses, they now could dive deeper and return quickly, without ill effects.

The KilSha watched the performance silently, without moving so much as a centimeter. They seemed to be completely engrossed in the proceedings. They wore their Konar, as they usually did. The armor was quite comfortable, and Terry wore his whenever he went out, as well. The BotSha mostly weren't wearing theirs, as they said the armor was uncomfortable when they were pregnant.

"Do you want to listen, too?" He sent the question through his pinplants to the KilSha and BotSha in general.

"Yes!" Pōkole replied right away. "Yes, yes, please!"

"That would be rad, dude," Wikiwiki replied. Terry had been surprised to find out she was pregnant at the time of the fight and had never considered whether to participate.

Terry set his pinplants to record and relay, and the cetaceans listened to a bunch of children singing Jingle Bells. He looked up and saw the half dozen BotSha bobbing their heads in time with the song, and chuckled.

"What?" Katrina asked. Terry tilted his head up. She followed his gaze and chuckled. The BotSha were singing along, and Terry added her to the channel.

"What are you two laughing about?" Doc asked, leaning over Terry's mom to stage-whisper at him.

"The BotSha are singing Jingle Bells," Terry said and pointed at the cetacean audience.

"How do you know they're singing?" his mom asked.

Terry reached up and touched the external connection on his pinplants. She blanched and looked away. Like the little kids, his mom hadn't quite come to grips with the events of the Selroth invasion.

He recognized Kray in the group of KilSha; he was noticeably bigger, and his dorsal fin had a particular curl to it. Shortly after the battle, he'd asked Kray about the name KilSha. The Caretaker had said that an uplifted race's name came from their species name with "Sha" added to the end, by some tradition.

"You should have been OrcSha," he told Kray.

"We know, but we chose to use Killer Whale instead. KilSha."

"Why?"

"Because we like to kill." He'd have sworn the whale was smiling when he said it.

At the back of the audience, the 11 surviving Selroth were sitting uncomfortably on chairs, pointedly ignoring the goings on. They were basically permanent prisoners. After Terry had explained about the law against uplifting, and Doc had verified it through the GalNet, it had been agreed that the Selroth couldn't go home, and the grownups couldn't bring themselves to kill them outright. They were also a little horrified that the BotSha really, really, wanted to kill the aliens.

The Selroth were being cooperative in getting the habitat fully operational. In exchange for their cooperation, they were given a large amount of freedom and good treatment. They refused to go anywhere near the cetaceans, in a mixture of fear and revulsion.

Terry, Colin, and Katrina, along with Doc and his crew, rode the shuttle up to the Selroth's ship in orbit and took it from them. Terry and his people did most of the work. Their Konar easily handled the pressure differential they needed to maintain to avoid ill effects. The mercs had to wear clunky pressure suits, and ended up being little more than observers. Four of the 11 Selroth were the surviving crew. Terry's mother had nearly freaked out when he got back in his Konar armor and went with Doc. They'd taken two of the BotSha, because the former bottlenose dolphins had insisted.

There really wasn't a fight; the Selroth hadn't been expecting an attack from their own shuttle. Afterward, Doc's people treated Terry, Collin, and Katrina differently. They'd exchange a nod with him when they walked by. Sometimes at meal time, they'd lift a glass in his or his friends' direction. He'd asked Doc about it once.

"We're part of the same club," he'd said. "You're too damned young, but you're one of us now."

They'd flown the ship to the Lupasha Independent Trading Station, where Doc registered the Selroth's ship as a war prize, so it now belonged to them. They returned afterward and parked the ship in orbit. The BotSha spent the whole time with Tina, examining the ship's nav computer and talking among themselves. When asked what the BotSha were up to, they weren't interested in sharing. However, they'd been excited at whatever they'd found.

After the concert, the Selroth returned to their quarters, while the Humans went to the mess hall for cake and ice cream. Terry enjoyed seeing everyone so happy. Dan was moving around like nothing had happened with his metallic blue artificial feet and hands. The Caretaker had fixed him up and given him pinplants, as well.

The Caretaker had said it would give pinplants to anyone who wanted them. Doc and his people were planning on it before they went out on contract in March. Terry thought they were probably working up the nerve to undergo the procedure. Regardless of what they'd said, it was obvious the mercs didn't trust the Caretaker. Despite that mistrust, they'd discussed Konar for them, and discarded the idea.

"What do you think would be the reaction if we went out on contract wearing those technological marvels?"

"I don't know," Terry said.

"Sure you do. They'd want to know where we got them. They'd *really* want to know."

That made sense, of course. Technology was power, and nothing like the Konar existed in the galaxy. Nothing the Humans had encountered in the current era, anyway. Everywhere he looked, the people of Templemer were happy, or at least content. Maybe it was enough.

"We going to the Caretaker as planned?" Doc asked him over vanilla ice cream.

"You bet," Terry replied. He knew Doc wanted to try to get the Caretaker to follow his orders again. It hadn't worked yet, and wouldn't work ever. For whatever reason, it only listened to Terry, Colin, or Katrina. Terry seemed to be the one it listened to first, as well. The leader. "You know it wants to see the newborn BotSha, right?"

"Yeah," Doc said. "The moms are fine with it."

Terry nodded. He'd seen the ultrasound of Wikiwiki's baby, done by Dr. Jaehnig. The baby's pectoral fins had *fingers*. The Caretaker had altered the bottlenoses' DNA. Hula was only four months pregnant, too soon for a good ultrasound on a KilSha. Terry knew what it would show; the same as the BotSha, maybe even more advanced.

As the Christmas celebration was breaking up, Terry found a minute alone with just his mom and Doc. "I wanted to tell you something," he said to his mother. She looked at him expectantly. "I'm going with Doc and Last Call on contract." Her mouth dropped open. "Colin and Katrina are going too. They're telling their parents right now."

"You can't!" she said, looking at Doc for support and, to her horror, finding none. "You're only 14 years old."

"And I was 13 when I led the assault that killed the Xiq'tal and Selroth."

She teared up and looked away.

"It's a different world," Doc said.

"I don't like this world," she said and looked at her son. "Things are too black and white for my liking."

They left the mess hall for the walk back to their apartment, the one Doc now shared after he and Terry's mom were married a month ago. It was a quiet walk, each of them lost in their own thoughts. Terry's thoughts were closer to his own person. Because, if the Caretaker had altered the orcas to KilSha, and the bottlenose dolphins to BotSha, what had they done to him and his friends? Maybe he'd ask the machine. Maybe it might answer.

# # # # #

ABOUT THE AUTHOR

Located in rural Tennessee, Mark Wandrey has been creating new worlds since he was old enough to write. After penning countless short stories, he realized novels were his real calling and hasn't looked back since. A lifetime of diverse jobs, extensive travels, and living in most areas of the country have uniquely equipped him with experiences to color his stories in ways many find engaging and thought provoking.

Sign up on his mailing list and get free stuff and updates!
http://www.worldmaker.us/news-flash-sign-up-page/

Caution – Worlds Under Construction

Titles by Mark Wandrey

* * * * *

The following is an

Excerpt from Book One of the Earth Song Cycle:

Overture

Mark Wandrey

Now Available from Theogony Books

eBook and Paperback

Excerpt from "Overture:"

Dawn was still an hour away as Mindy Channely opened the roof access and stared in surprise at the crowd already assembled there. "Authorized Personnel Only" was printed in bold red letters on the door through which she and her husband, Jake, slipped onto the wide roof.

A few people standing nearby took notice of their arrival. Most had no reaction, a few nodded, and a couple waved tentatively. Mindy looked over the skyline of Portland and instinctively oriented herself before glancing to the east. The sky had an unnatural glow that had been growing steadily for hours, and as they watched, scintillating streamers of blue, white, and green radiated over the mountains like a strange, concentrated aurora borealis.

"You almost missed it," one man said. She let the door close, but saw someone had left a brick to keep it from closing completely. Mindy turned and saw the man who had spoken wore a security guard uniform. The easy access to the building made more sense.

"Ain't no one missin' this!" a drunk man slurred.

"We figured most people fled to the hills over the past week," Jake replied.

"I guess we were wrong," Mindy said.

"Might as well enjoy the show," the guard said and offered them a huge, hand-rolled cigarette that didn't smell like tobacco. She waved it off, and the two men shrugged before taking a puff.

"Here it comes!" someone yelled. Mindy looked to the east. There was a bright light coming over the Cascade Mountains, so intense it was like looking at a welder's torch. Asteroid LM-245 hit the atmosphere at over 300 miles per second. It seemed to move faster and faster, from east to west, and the people lifted their hands to shield their eyes from the blinding light. It looked like a blazing comet or a science fiction laser blast.

"Maybe it will just pass over," someone said in a voice full of hope.

Mindy shook her head. She'd studied the asteroid's track many times.

In a matter of a few seconds, it shot by and fell toward the western horizon, disappearing below the mountains between Portland and the ocean. Out of view of the city, it slammed into the ocean.

The impact was unimaginable. The air around the hypersonic projectile turned to superheated plasma, creating a shockwave that generated 10 times the energy of the largest nuclear weapon ever detonated as it hit the ocean's surface.

The kinetic energy was more than 1,000 megatons; however, the object didn't slow as it flashed through a half mile of ocean and into the sea bed, then into the mantel, and beyond.

On the surface, the blast effect appeared as a thermal flash brighter than the sun. Everyone on the rooftop watched with wide-eyed terror as the Tualatin Mountains between Portland and the Pacific Ocean were outlined in blinding light. As the light began to dissipate, the outline of the mountains blurred as a dense bank of smoke climbed from the western range.

The flash had incinerated everything on the other side.

The physical blast, travelling much faster than any normal atmospheric shockwave, hit the mountains and tore them from the bedrock, adding them to the rolling wave of destruction traveling east at several thousand miles per hour. The people on the rooftops of Portland only had two seconds before the entire city was wiped away.

Ten seconds later, the asteroid reached the core of the planet, and another dozen seconds after that, the Earth's fate was sealed.

* * * * *

Get "Overture" now at:
https://www.amazon.com/dp/B077YMLRHM/

Find out more about Mark Wandrey and the Earth Song Cycle at:
https://chriskennedypublishing.com/

* * * * *

The following is an
Excerpt from Book One of the Salvage Title Trilogy:

Salvage Title

Kevin Steverson

Available Now from Theogony Books

eBook, Paperback, and Audio

Excerpt from "Salvage Title:"

A steady beeping brought Harmon back to the present. Clip's program had succeeded in unlocking the container. "Right on!" Clip exclaimed. He was always using expressions hundreds or more years out of style. "Let's see what we have; I hope this one isn't empty, too." Last month they'd come across a smaller vault, but it had been empty.

Harmon stepped up and wedged his hands into the small opening the door had made when it disengaged the locks. There wasn't enough power in the small cells Clip used to open it any further. He put his weight into it, and the door opened enough for them to get inside. Before they went in, Harmon placed a piece of pipe in the doorway so it couldn't close and lock on them, baking them alive before anyone realized they were missing.

Daylight shone in through the doorway, and they both froze in place; the weapons vault was full. In it were two racks of rifles, stacked on top of each other. One held twenty magnetic kinetic rifles, and the other held some type of laser rifle. There was a rack of pistols of various types. There were three cases of flechette grenades and one of thermite. There were cases of ammunition and power clips for the rifles and pistols, and all the weapons looked to be in good shape, even if they were of a strange design and clearly not made in this system. Harmon couldn't tell what system they had been made in, but he could tell what they were.

There were three upright containers on one side and three more against the back wall that looked like lockers. Five of the containers were not locked, so Clip opened them. The first three each held two sets of light battle armor that looked like it was designed for a humanoid race with four arms. The helmets looked like the ones Harmon had worn at the academy, but they were a little long in the face.

The next container held a heavy battle suit—one that could be sealed against vacuum. It was also designed for a being with four arms. All the armor showed signs of wear, with scuffed helmets. The fifth container held shelves with three sizes of power cells on them. The largest power cells—four of them—were big enough to run a mech.

Harmon tried to force the handle open on the last container, thinking it may have gotten stuck over time, but it was locked and all he did was hurt his hand. The vault seemed like it had been closed for years.

Clip laughed and said, "That won't work. It's not age or metal fatigue keeping the door closed. Look at this stuff. It may be old, but it has been sealed in for years. It's all in great shape."

"Well, work some of your tech magic then, 'Puter Boy," Harmon said, shaking out his hand.

Clip pulled out a small laser pen and went to work on the container. It took another ten minutes, but finally he was through to the locking mechanism. It didn't take long after that to get it open.

Inside, there were two items—an eight-inch cube on a shelf that looked like a hard drive or a computer and the large power cell it was connected to. Harmon reached for it, but Clip grabbed his arm.

"Don't! Let me check it before you move it. It's hooked up to that power cell for a reason. I want to know why."

Harmon shrugged. "Okay, but I don't see any lights; it has probably been dead for years."

Clip took a sensor reader out of his kit, one of the many tools he had improved. He checked the cell and the device. There was a faint amount of power running to it that barely registered on his screen. There were several ports on the back along with the slot where the power cell was hooked in. He checked to make sure the connections were tight, he then carried the two devices to the hovercraft.

Clip then called Rinto's personal comm from the communicator in the hovercraft. When Rinto answered, Clip looked at Harmon and winked. "Hey boss, we found some stuff worth a hovercraft full of credit…probably two. Can we have it?" he asked.

* * * * *

Get "Salvage Title" now at:
https://www.amazon.com/dp/B07H8Q3HBV.

Find out more about Kevin Steverson and "Salvage Title" at:
https://chriskennedypublishing.com/imprints-authors/kevin-steverson/.

* * * * *

Made in the USA
Middletown, DE
19 February 2022

61546319R00285